AMERICANO

Deadly Dreams

1896 – The Beginning

Book 1

Phil Cuda

Copyright © 2020 Phil Cuda

All rights reserved. No part of this book may be used or reproduced by any means, graphic, electronic, or mechanical, including photocopying, recording, taping or by any information storage retrieval system without the written permission of the author except in the case of brief quotations embodied in critical articles and reviews.

Proisle Publishing Service
1177 Avenue of the Americas, 5th Floor, New York, NY 10036, USA
info@proislepublishing.com

Because of the dynamic nature of the Internet, any web addresses or links contained in this book may have changed since publication and may no longer be valid. The views expressed in this work are solely those of the author and do not necessarily reflect the views of the publisher, and the publisher hereby disclaims any responsibility for them.

ISBN: 978-1-7362280-1-2 (sc)

PROISLE PUBLISHING
SERVICES LLC

This book is dedicated to the memory of my grandfather and his six brothers and to my grandmother, a beautiful, gentle, yet strong woman.

OTHER BOOKS by Phil Cuda

AMERICAN CALABRESE SERIES

Book 2 Americano	- 1902 Shattered Dreams.
Book 3 Americano	- 1904 Kill or be Killed
Book 4 Americano	- 1910 Pittsburgh at War
Book 5 Americano	- 1913 Forever Dead
Book 6 Americano	- 1914 Time to Die

BURNING BORDERS SERIES

4 Books in series

BURNING BORDERS: DIAMONDS FOR DRUGS
BURNING BORDERS: MONEY TO KILL FOR
BURNING BORDERS: KILLERS CHOICE
BURNING BORDERS: MISSION TO KILL

Prologue

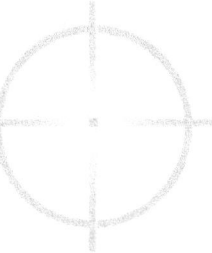

Filippo Cudoni and his six brothers and sister and parents lived in poverty in a dangerous part of Calabria, Italy but they all had dreams and ambition. The three eldest brothers left Calabria, including the Mafia there, in 1898 to travel to the United States of America to seek that fortune.

In Pittsburgh, they found the deadly Sicilian Cosa Nostra far worse than the Mafia in Calabria.

They remembered the history and deeds of their brigante warrior grandfather and chose to fight.

Their dreams were high, and the risks were deadly.

The characters and some events are based on real people who lived at the time.

The Cudoni clan had a creed: No man who kills a Cudoni dies of old age.

Chapter 1

June 16, 1896

The booming sound of a shotgun blast totally overshadowed the strangled bleating of a small lamb on the mountainside. The bleating had momentarily broken the stillness and silence of the warm midday Sunday siesta. The piercing sound of the bleating lamb had given a clear warning of impending danger to the two young men on the mountainside.

"There—there he is. The fire of hell be on the rotten devil: He's just stolen another one—and in the middle of the day as well," a tall, lean young man had angrily and excitedly exclaimed to his older brother as he pointed from where he stood on the small hillock on the mountain.

The older brother had already jumped to his feet, grabbed the new shotgun he had left leaning against a large rock and after planting one foot firmly on the rock in front of him, he taken quick but careful aim. A look of anger and determination had come across his face. *You're going to die this time, you rotten thief*, he thought as he pulled the trigger on the shotgun his father had given him a few weeks earlier. The recoil of the gun as it blasted out its deadly missile vibrated against the young man's strong shoulder. A puff of smoke followed the bullet out of the barrel, and the bullet found its mark with fatal accuracy. It ripped into the thief's upper ribs and shattered his spine on its way out. The would-be thief hurtled into an outcrop of rocks and slumped lifeless to the dusty ground. His mouth opened and the lamb, still alive tried to run to its mother.

With the sound of the blast still echoing across the mountain-side, the young man put the gun back against the rock. "He's dead for sure this time, little brother," the older brother remarked with a smirk on his face.

The younger brother had started whistling a local tune to the sheep and goats as soon as his brother had fired. The startled sheep and goats had jumped with fright at the blast of the gun and collected a short distance away from the two young men. The whistling had a soothing effect on them as they peered cautiously towards the dead wolf.

"I'll make sure," the other retorted with a lusty "ha." He nimbly raced barefoot over rocks and parched earth to where the huge grey wolf lay dead on the dirt.

The young man looked at the grey wolf's still-open eyes for a moment. He slowly reached down to his wide trouser belt with his right hand and pulled out a shiny wedge-shaped solid axe held within it and waved it over the wolf's head for a few seconds. Suddenly he smashed the back of the axe brutally into the back of the wolf's head. For a moment, the wolf's convulsions stopped.

A few minutes later, he returned to where his brother stood, a satisfied smirk across his face. "He's dead. Pa will sure be glad to hear the old grey devil is dead."

From a ridge some six hundred meters away, they heard a floating, echoing call: "Don Filippo, Lai sparato il diavolo?" (Have you shot the devil, yes or no?)

Both young men looked out towards the next ridge, where a middle-aged shepherd was frantically waving to them. Signore Salvatore Ferarro did not have the best eyesight, but he had a hunch about what had happened. The old man had heard the shotgun blast, and he knew that the boys would not be shooting just to scare the goats and sheep away.

Filippo picked up the gun and waved it over his head. "Si, si questa volta la Volpe e morto" (The wolf is dead), he yelled back over the small valley between them.

Ferraro waved back, nodding happily to himself. He too had lost many small lambs to the old grey wolf, but his thoughts turned to the young Filippo who had shot the wolf.

"If only that young man would look at my little Concetta one day," he mumbled to himself.

The two young men turned their attention back to staring out across the Mediterranean Sea as the dry hot early summer wind blew gently over the mountainsides. The two young men, now seemingly unconcerned about what had just happened, looked out over the blue waters of the sea.

The land around the mountain ridges where they stood was dry, and the vegetation and grass were brown. Only the odd patches of fruit trees in the low-lying distance were showing some green leaves, but they too needed rain. Somehow only the countryside down on the coast and alongside the small river appeared through the after- noon haze to be much greener.

On a clear day, the top peaks of the mountain range across the south-west side of the land jutting out into the Gulf of Sant'Eufemia could be seen as they rose over the south-west horizon, and at night when the volcano was erupting, the fiery haze from the volcano on Mount Etna in Sicily was faintly visible in the dark. From this vantage point on a small mountain range in Southern Italy, one could see the dull glow in the sky that permeated from the volcano, particularly in the darker night sky. When the volcano erupted, the glow turned into fiery red balls of flashing and shooting lights, which brightly lit the night sky. These would then fall back to the mountain and roll down its sides, and the bright lights would fade and disappear, only to be observed seconds later by fiery new ones.

The two young brothers standing under the huge olive tree on top of the knoll knew these lights for they had seen them several years ago at the time of the big eruption. However, it was not only the lights that fascinated them but also the call of the ocean, which seemed to constantly beckon them to it—away from the smell of the goats and the sheep they tended, away from the mundane life of a goat herder. To the two young men on the mountain, financial and social progress seemed to be somewhere else, not here. Maybe in Rome, they thought life could be and would be better and have some real meaning or sense of progression; maybe they could find more such success much more success far, far away on the other side of the sea—in a new land, a new world for them.

"One day, Gennaro, I'm going to sail over the sea to America and make some money," the older brother casually remarked. "It's either that or travel by train to Rome and see the rest of the world from there."

"Me too," Gennaro replied, just as matter-of-factly. "I'm going to get rich too one day, you know."

Filippo laughed. "You always want to get rich, don't you? I want to make plenty and see the world, but you—you want to get rich." He thought for a moment and then, on a more serious note, warned his brother, "Whatever you do, I don't want you ever to join the rotten Mafia crowd. You'll just end up shot dead, little brother."

Gennaro did not reply, his mind going back to the letter from his American relations. Slowly he scratched the side of his head with his right hand, his left hand resting casually on his sharp axe.

The two minding the sheep and goats had five younger brothers, and normally one or two of the youngest brothers would be tending the flock; but that day, Papa Francesco Cudoni and Mama Rosaria Cudoni were taking the rest of the family to Sambiase. It would be the biggest day of the year for them. They would eat gelato in the piazza and buy new clothes for the boys to wear and a new dress for their little sister, but first they would attend Mass at the Catholic Church in Sambiase.

The parents were devout Catholics, and Mass on Sunday was not to be missed for any reason. But this day was not just any day. It was the thirteenth day of June 1895—the feast of Santo Antonio. The little town would be bursting at the seams that day.

Thousands of people from the surrounding towns and countryside were coming. Some had come the day before. Friends and enemies alike would all be there.

On their little plateau on the mountain overlooking the sea, Filippo and Gennaro waited impatiently for the sun to approach the western horizon. The two could take the herd of goats and sheep home early that day so that they too could get to the feast in the early afternoon.

As they waited for the sun to move to the west, they talked of all the things they would do, the places they would travel to, and the fortunes they intended to make. The older youth picked up a stone and threw it down the steeper side of the mountain. He watched and listened as it bounced down the mountain.

"Gennaro, I think we can take the herd back and lock them up very soon."

Invariably, the topic returned to travel. "I want to travel, to make money. There is little chance of doing that here, *fratello mio*. They tell me that in America, people are getting rich quick," Filippo solemnly said to the other.

"Me too. I'm going to travel and get rich. We can go to America. We have relations there. Remember Michele, Benaldo, Palmo, and the two little brothers," Gennaro said. "I bet they are rich in Pittzaburgh, and I bet they are not looking after goats and sheep. I'm going to go to Pittzaburgh as soon as I can."

The older brother replied, "I'm going to Pittza-burgh one day too. Did you know that Papa said he had decided to go to America before Zio Nicola went? He actually left Sambiase and went to Paris to get a boat from there to America. It was after Antonio was born. Papa got to Paris, but before he could pay for his passage across, he was mugged and robbed of everything but the suit on his back, and he barely made it back home."

"So why did he not go afterwards?"

"Well, I think he had the other boys and little Theresa to think about and no money."

The two youths discussed how and when they would go to America. They knew that life in Calabria was only good if one had loads of money, and they did not feel a life of peasantry was for them. The idea of hard farm work for little profit did not fulfill the dreams of young Calabrian boys, let alone young men who wanted to see, feel, and experience the world. Not for them the picking olives, making olive oil, maintaining the vineyard, the making of wine, and the planting of the small crops of vegetables that provided the meager family income while needing to be done would not make them rich or fulfill their dreams.

News of the New World had filtered back to them from some of their relations, along with stories of fortunes to be made.

"Well I'm going to go as soon as I can." Gennaro responded.

Filippo laughed again. "Me to: As soon as I get back from the army I will be looking at how I'm going."

It was the land of opportunity, the land of milk and honey, for those who were prepared to work; and they were prepared to work to make money so that they could return and be the big land barons they had, in recent years, dreamed of being. This was the start of a new dream. These two brothers knew that their dreams and futures could only be achieved elsewhere—maybe in America.

Filippo was the eldest of the seven boys. The following week, on the twenty-first day of June 1896, he would reach the ripe age of twenty-one years. He was a few inches over medium height, standing about six feet tall, and he was extremely good-looking, well built, athletic, and strong. His face had a long square shape that culminated in a strong and prominent chin that gave him a look of strong determination and natural leadership. He had long black hair, but unusual for someone with dark hair, he had very light greenish-blue eyes. They were remarkable eyes and were unusual for Calabrian people. When he flashed a smile, with his even teeth and bluish eyes, many a young lass's heart would flutter and melt in his searching, cheerful, and engaging look. His father told everyone that he was a throwback to when the Cudoni's had come from the north.

Gennaro had just turned nineteen, and he had long black hair and dark brown eyes. He was different from his brother in that he was taller and not yet as filled out. He was lean and looked to be still growing, but years of hard work had made him much stronger than he looked.

With the herd locked up, the two brothers quickly washed and were soon ready to leave. They were dressed in dark woolen trousers that reached down almost to their ankles. Gennaro wore a grey colored flannel shirt, while Filippo wore an off-white-colored shirt. The family was very poor, but their mother made sure they were as clean as she could possibly keep them.

Both youths were impulsive by nature, but already the years of hard work and rough times had taught them to be a little cautious. It was easy in Calabria to join the various groups of young men whose sole aim was to get richer by stealing from anyone. One could get into fights and arguments stealing or even be killed by rival groups. In Calabria, the shotgun was mighty, and every young man carried at least a knife.

Both brothers carried knives slung in leather pouches on their belts during the day and at night.

Carrying their home-made shoes in their hands, they set off barefoot towards Sambiase, racing down the winding goat track that served as a road, dressed in their colorful clean clothes— the only going-out clothes they had. The three kilometers to the town seemed like nothing, and soon they were on the outskirts of the town. The town, which had been built at the foot of the mountain range, was on reasonably level ground, so the running from the farmhouse was comfortably downhill.

Chapter 2

The Church of Santo Antonio was on a small rise overlooking the main piazza of Sambiase and was some two hundred meters away from it.

The track the young men followed turned into a narrow road and, where it reached that part of the town where the houses were it was paved with stone. They stopped and put on their hand-made leather shoes. The road took them through the piazza until they reached the church. This street continued past the church and then led to the town cemetery.

When they turned onto the street towards the church, they saw that the main part of the procession that took place after Mass finished had left the church and was heading towards the cemetery. The last people coming out of church were just walking down the steps when Filippo and Gennaro arrived and joined in.

Filippo and Gennaro could see the statue of Santo Antonio in the forefront of the procession and could hear the voices of the men carrying it, asking the people to pray and contribute towards the cost of holding the feast and the upkeep of the church. When the men stopped calling for donations, the women would start the recital of the rosary.

Filippo and Gennaro followed the tail of the procession until they passed a narrow lane to one side of the street when Filippo heard his name called out.

"Filippo, Filippo mio," a soft young female voice called.

He turned and looked towards the lane. "Maria, ma che cosa fai qui?" (What are you doing here?) Filippo demanded as he strode towards her. While surprised to hear Maria call out to him, Filippo never the less flashed Maria a big smile.

Her pretty face lit up as she noticed his charming smile. "Aspeto e te" (Waiting for you), she answered.

Gennaro followed Filippo as he walked towards Maria. Two very pretty young girls wearing colorful blouses and long red skirts with green sashes tied around their waists came out of the shadows of the buildings. The older girl was about nineteen; the other was about seventeen. The older girl, Maria, wearing a big smile, giggled and skipped merrily as she ran towards Filippo. She threw her arms around him, kissing him on the lips.

The other girl was her younger sister, Catarina. Maria was very pretty with a bubbly personality, and she was as happy as a lark, especially now that her handsome, secret, and lovable boyfriend, Filippo, was with her. Catarina was a bit shy and did not seem at all comfortable with her sister and her boyfriend and his brother.

"Filippo, *amore mio*, I have to talk to you," a passionate Maria said after she first gave him a quick kiss on the lips and then took his arm. She turned to her sister. "Catarina, you better go back and join the procession before Papa realizes that we are both missing."

Catarina looked at her. "What will I say to Papa if he asks where you are?" she asked.

"Just say that I am talking to some of my friends on the other side," Maria said as she pulled Filippo by the arm towards the lane where the girls had come from.

Gennaro followed Catarina back to the procession, and soon both disappeared into the crowd. Filippo and the young beautiful Maria headed down the narrow lane. She had her arm tightly around his as she pulled him close to her, and her firm but nicely proportioned breasts rubbed against his arm and sometimes the side of his chest as they walked along. She smiled and sometimes giggled as she skipped happily down the lane with her prize.

Filippo pulled her to him for a moment, and his hungry lips sought hers in a hot but hurried kiss. Maria was a housewife-in-waiting that is she did as all good young women did in Calabria in these times: she dreamed and waited for a handsome young man to woo her.

At the end of the lane was a small pebbled street, and on the other side of the street was an outcrop of rocks surrounded by large oak and willow trees. They ducked under the branches of the trees and were out of sight to any prying eyes, but they knew there was no need to worry as everybody else were either in the procession or watching it move along the main street.

Inside the clump of trees, there was a small clearing, and on the right, coming from under the jumble of rocks, was a spring of clear fresh water. The locals had built a rock pool out of rocks and cement, and coming out of it was a spout that had drinkable fresh water pouring out the end. A pathway led down from the pool and around the trees to the street below.

Filippo had a quick drink and then sat on the edge of the fountain. Maria decided to sit on his lap.

"I haven't seen you for over a week. I miss you so much," Maria said after they sat down. "Filippo, I know you have to leave for army training soon, so when can I see you again?"

Filippo was busy running his lips over her neck and right ear as she spoke. "I might be able to come to town late in the week. Why?"

Maria blushed. "Well, I love being with you and touching you like this."

She held his hand in hers on her lap. She slowly brushed it over her pelvis, stomach, and breasts and then rubbed it against her face and lips as she kissed his hand. She could feel his young manhood growing harder under her soft buttocks. He turned her gently more towards him, put his left arm around her head, and pulled her to him. She looked longingly into his blue-green eyes and saw again his flashing wide smile. Her heart fluttered as she released his hand and put her arms around his neck. Slowly at first, their faces came closer until their lips touched. Then with fiery passion, they kissed.

For a long moment, they kissed, and then Filippo put his right hand firmly over her left breast and pulled her tightly to him with his other hand. They kissed for as long as they could hold their breath, a kiss that both warmed and heightened their desire.

The passion in their young bodies stirred as they kissed again, each tongue searching for the other. Filippo's right hand slipped down from her breast to rest on her thighs; then he slowly reached under her dress and gently rubbed the inside of her thigh, moving his fingers higher and higher until they were warmly rubbing her virginity. She opened her legs so that he could touch her vagina more easily. She moaned with pleasure and ecstasy as she allowed his fingers to gently explore inside the lips of her vagina.

Still in Filippo's embrace, she tried to stand up. He moved up with her, holding her tightly. He placed his leg between hers and his foot on the edge of the pool. She pulled herself closer to him so that his thigh was firmly between her legs. She could feel the huge stiffness of his manhood pressing gently on the inside of her thigh, and this made her desire for him grow. He stopped kissing her lips, and his lips searched for her breast and nipple while his fingers pushed her brest and nipple upward.

The touch of his lips on her nipple sent a hot flush of desire through her young body. With passion welling up inside of her, she moaned softly as he squeezed her nipple with his lips. She changed her stance and placed her leg between his, standing on the toes of

She reached down with one hand and pressed gently but firmly on his penis until she could feel it throb. In her mind, she could feel it as if it were inside of her. It felt so hard, she thought as her heart beat faster. Still a virgin, she wondered how such a large penis could fit inside her small opening. Her fingers tightened around the large erection.

The pain from her fingers around his erection was nothing compared to the desire he felt to have it inside of her. His fingers slipped easily over her moist vaginal opening.

"Amore mio, ti amor," she moaned. "I want you. I want you. I want you inside of me now." She moaned repeatedly as she pulled him tighter against her aching breasts.

Filippo Cudoni suddenly realized that Maria was more than happy to risk getting pregnant. If she did get pregnant, she would be free of her father's control and have her own family after she was married. He knew he was enlisted to join the military; having a child was not what he wanted.

It struck him that if he was the father of this young woman, he would have shot the animal that violated his daughter, or as was the custom in Southern Italy, he would force the man to marry her.

A short time later, the pair left the fountain to return to the crowd celebrating the feast in and around the piazza. Holding hands, they walked back through the narrow side street to rejoin the throng that had by now moved well up the street. Maria, very disappointed, did not seem as happy as when they had walked down to the fountain under the old tree.

"Maria, I will try to see you soon, and we will be together again before I leave. We will get married when I return from the army." Filippo tried to cheer her up as they walked.

They were fifty meters from coming out of the little street when three young men in their early to mid-twenties walked into it from the end towards the piazza. The three had the look of trouble written all over them.

Filippo recognized one of them as the Mafioso Mario Cirillo—an older brother to Bruno Cirillo with whom he had fought and really belted up about a month ago. He had almost belted him into the ground when a group of Cirilo's friends had stopped the fight. Cirillo had vowed to kill him for the thrashing he had received.

Of the other two, he knew one as Pugliese, but he did not know the other. He knew these three would be after him, but he was too close to retreat, and he had Maria with him as well. He did not want to run away in front of his adoring girlfriend—especially not from these three hotheads—but common sense took over, and he thought it was better to avoid a confrontation if possible that day.

Holding Maria by the arm, he steered her to one side and hoped that the three, who had already been drinking large quantities of cheap wine, would not notice them. He was wrong. In her haste, Maria had left the top button on her blouse undone, and an appealing portion of her breast was showing through the opening. Pugliese whistled in appreciation of her breast and then stood in front of her to block her access to the street. The three young men circled the young couple.

The one Filippo knew as Pugliese, recognized Maria and spotted a twig caught inside her blouse, sticking out just above her partially exposed breast.

"Come on, Maria. If you could show it to Cudoni, you can do the same for me. You know I love those big tits of yours, and I cannot wait to give you my *pistola*. Mine is extra-large and at least twice as big as his is. Apart from the fact he doesn't know how to use it," he crudely and arrogantly boasted.

Mario Cirillo was now behind Maria; he wrapped his arms around her and pinned her arms to her sides. Holding her with one hand his fingers from the other hand searched for her breasts. He succeeded in fully exposing one breast.

Pugliese moved towards her as well and, reaching forward with his hand, attempted to slide his hand inside her blouse to fondle her other breast as well. His hand was inside her blouse and around the other breast when he groaned in sheer agony as Filippo's big toe hit him in the testicles and groin. He fell to his knees, clutching at his balls as very severe pain shot through his body. Pugliese pulled Maria's other breast out of her blouse as he fell to the ground.

Cirillo, who was still holding Maria now had his fingers around her exposed breast; suddenly he pushed her out of the way to lunge after Filippo.

"Run, Maria, *scappa*!" Filippo shouted to her as he stepped backwards. "Get out of here—quick."

Maria looked at Filippo with despairing eyes. She knew there would be trouble—serious trouble. She mentally debated whether to run or stand by her man. She knew these young men were part of the Mafia and quite capable of even killing someone. She wanted to beg them to let Filippo and her go, but Filippo screamed at her.

"Vai via adesso!" Filippo shouted to her again. "Go."

This time, she turned and raced to the road; at the same time pulling her blouse up to cover her exposed breasts.. Her prayer was someone was close and would come to help her man.

The third man, who Filippo Cudoni was to later know as Ugo Bartocchi swung a huge roundhouse punch at Filippo's face just as he told Maria to run. With just a spilt second to spare, Filippo ducked his head forward and down, trying to avoid the major part of the punch. The blow missed his nose as Cudoni turned, but it smashed into his upper cheek and left eyebrow.

Cudoni staggered backwards from the blow and nearly fell over Pugliese now lying on the ground. He tried to straighten up, but Cirillo smashed into him, sending him on his back to the paved street.

The third man jumped on top of Cudoni, raining punches to his face and head while Cirillo kicked him hard in the ribs.

Filippo tried to grasp Bartocchi on top of him by the shirt and swing him into Cirillo, but he was too heavy, and Cirillo landed another boot to his side, but the third man's body saved him the major impact of the kick.

"Take that you piece of shit."

Cudoni gasped with pain as the boot hit one of his ribs. Bartocchi hit him with a blow to the side of his head as Cirillo lined up another kick to Cudoni's head this time.

Filippo Cudoni realized instantly a direct kick to the head could and would cause him a load of grief. He twisted his shoulder to wear the impact.

Cirillo shifted his position and drew his foot for another kick.

"Kick him, and I will blow your head off!" a voice boomed down the narrow street.

The sudden threat caused Cirilo to turn; his foot stopped centimeters from Cudoni's face as the man on top of Cudoni tried to stand up. Filippo Cudoni grasped Cirilo's boot and twisted it as hard as he could while he tried to head-butt the man trying to stand up. Cirillo groaned as he fell sideways.

Pugliese, who had been lying on the ground, clutching his bruised, swollen, sore, and tender testicles, slowly tried to stand up.

Filippo had heard the voice of his grandfather, but he doubted he had a gun with him. Now he thought was a good time to stand up and retreat. He stood up and started walking towards his grandfather.

"Come back here, you coward son of a bitch," Cirillo lying on the ground, shouted after him. Then he shouted even louder, "Hit him in the back."

Filippo heard the order and realized instantly that Cirilo's statement was likely a command to hit him in the back with a knife.

The other man had pulled out a flick knife from inside his jacket pocket. He hurled it at Filippo's departing back, and it sailed through the air just as Filippo approached his grandfather. The blade of the knife deflected of a thick leather jacket placed in its way. It cut a small hole into the soft leather jacket and fell onto the lane's paving.

Filippo turned and looked squarely at the man who had thrown the knife. The face of the snarling man whose throw had missed his back by centimeters was etched into his brain for years to remember.

His grandfather, Pietro Antonio Cudoni now in his late sixties was still a big and daunting figure. *The brigante*, as he was sometimes called had watched as the man pulled the knife from inside his belt and quickly pulled his own jacket off. The jacket had saved the life of his grandson.

"I don't have a gun, son, but we can go back and fix those three Mafiosi," he told his grandson as he picked up the knife from on the street floor and started to stride down the lane towards the three.

The three Mafiosi saw them heading back and quickly stepped backwards a few paces, still glaring at them. Even Pugliese had struggled to his feet.

Cudoni and his grandfather had travelled about ten meters towards the three who had not run off when two more men entered into the small laneway.

Mario Cirillio saw his brother and the other man and laughed loudly. "See who wins now you stinking piece of shit."

The Cudonis heard the glee in their voices and turned to look back. What they saw was not looking good. It was Bruno Cirillo and another man Filippo had not seen before. In the far background the sound of the singing and chanting of the Rosary could be heard getting closer.

The other man had a revolver in his hand as he strode towards them. Mario Cirillio and his other friend began walking towards the two Cudonis.

Pietro Antonio turned to face the man with the gun. "You would not dare to use that thing with so many people about."

The man smirked with laughter. "I'm a Carabineiri. You two were attacking these three nice young men. You even pulled out a knife, you fuck arse: So no trouble shooting both of you."

The two walking down the lane had stopped while talking. They started walking closer to the two Cudonis.

Suddenly a flying, lean young man hurtled through the air his feet landing onto the back of the man carrying the gun. The man crashed down, landing on his face on the hard street floor. The gun went flying out of his hand towards Filippo Cudoni but not before discharging a shot first. The bullet ricochets off the paving stone. Filippo Cudoni took one step to race over and grab it. But b efore he could start to run Mario Cirillio slammed into his back knocking him down.

Pietro Cudoni managed to kick it towards Gennaro Cudoni before Bruno Cirillio could get his hands onto it.

Gennaro Cudoni was very athletic and fast. He took hold of the revolver and handed it to his grandfather.

"You were saying you are a carabineiri and it would be no trouble to shoot us." Pietro Antonio walked across to the policeman and held the pistol under his chin. "I say I could easily blow your head off with your own gun. What do you say to that?" He jabbed the pistol under the man's chin, slightly rubbing the sights across the man's neck. "But I'm not going to, but if you ever threaten a Cudoni again you will die. Nobody kills a Cudoni and dies of old age. That is a promise my friend. Your gun will be handed in tomorrow. Now get lost before I change my mind."

The man was looking towards the entry to the laneway. His scowl turned into a jeer. "I don't think so you stupid old man. You're the one going to jail. Give me the gun."

"Two carabineiri with revolvers are coming behind you, Nonno." Filippo Cudoni informed his grandfather.

Pietro Cudoni still had his gun under the carabineiri's chin. He suddenly turned and at the same time wrapped his left hand around the man's neck, pointing the gun at the side of his head.

The two new carabineiri stopped walking towards the group.

"Don't be silly, old man," one of the approaching policemen told him. "You can't fight all the police in Sambiase."

"Don't come any closer or you will be a dead young man, son." Cudoni snorted back. "So will this man."

The policeman who had spoken first asked. "What has happened here? We heard a gunshot."

Before Pietro Cudoni could answer Maria Valenci raced into the laneway. "Those three men tried to take my clothes off and possibly rape me. Filippo tried to fight them off. They are the ones who should be in jail." She yelled at the two carabineiri.

Filippo Cudoni ran towards his girl. "She is right. These three tried to undress her. They ripped her blouse down and that is when I kicked Pugliese. The other two then tried to kill me."

"Let them go." He turned and looked at his grandson's face. It showed the battering he had received," Pietro Antonio told his grandson, "Those mafiosi will not forgive or forget what just happened; they will be out to get you, one way or another. Also remember one thing, my son. Honor and protect the ones you love, but be smart about it."

Chapter 3

The following Saturday morning, Francesco, Filippo, and Gennaro Cudoni, each carrying a shotgun, left early in the morning for a quail and pheasant-shooting expedition in the ranges to the west of Sambiase. The local community authorities set aside the month of June every year as open season for all bird shooters to legally shoot and take home game from the reserve.

Francesco Cudoni's father, Pietro Antonio, had passed this tradition of quail shooting down to him and had taught him to be a great shot with a shotgun. He had taught him to shoot the birds on the fly and in the head. Francesco had taken Filippo and Gennaro to this same reserve the year before, and both boys were familiar with the area and knew what to expect there. Francesco had spent time teaching the boys how to shoot with a shotgun. He had tossed stones into the air for them to shoot at. The accuracy of hitting the birds in the head determined how good the birds would later be for eating.

That particular morning, the three arrived at the bottom of the range just as the sun appeared above the top of the horizon to the east. They knew that areas close to farmland would not have many birds left as those areas were the first places the shooters sought. People living nearby shot the quail and pheasant there whenever they believed they could get away with it.

Francesco pointed to a small peak one kilometer away. "We'll go that way. There are a few grassy valleys over there, in amongst those tall trees. There will be bigger quail and possibly some mountain pigeons, which are better than the quail anyway."

An hour later, they had reached the top of a small ridge not far from a peak with a huge exposed rock near the top of it. It was a distinguishable landmark. It appeared that a small valley ran down the range from the steep base of the rock. The countryside they had travelled through had become dense with giant trees on the slopes and ridges. Gennaro, carrying his single-barrel shotgun and running ahead, led the way. Filippo and Francesco followed behind, walking between large, tall fir trees.

"We'll go down the right side of this ridge, down into that valley, and across to the base," Francesco told the boys.

Gennaro was about to head in the direction his father had indicated when a dozen large pheasants, screeching and flapping their wings, flew out of a tree to his left and landed on another tree about a hundred meters to his left.

"Pa, I'll meet you at the base of the peak," Gennaro called as he raced after them. "I'll be quick." Carrying his shotgun in one hand, he nimbly darted through the trees towards where the pheasant had landed. He followed them to a small valley. The birds took fright once they spotted Gennaro and flew off.

Gennaro realized he had been too hasty trying to get too close to the birds, so he tried to make sure the birds did not spot him from where they had landed. He slowly crept towards them, his gun ready in his right hand. This side of the ridge was more rugged, dotted with large outcroppings of rock. As he stalked closer, he realized he would need to skirt around a small rocky ledge closer to the bottom of the ridge. He followed the pheasant towards the base of another ridge. He made his way down towards the valley floor and was surprised to see a small but long grassy clearing ahead of him in the small valley between the two ridges.

Gennaro picked up a small rock and, carrying it in his left hand, slowly made his way closer to the grassy clearing, keeping inside the shadows of the giant trees that surrounded the clearing. He had not forgotten past experiences, which told him that the grassy patch could have any number of quail feeding in it. He noticed a large rock outcrop protruding out of the ground on the fringe of the trees, and he made his way behind it.

Once behind it, he checked to make sure his gun was ready, and holding the gun in his right hand, he rolled the rock he had picked up into the grass. With a whirring of wings, a brace of quail, led by a large male, flew up out of the grass and towards the upper end of the small valley. Gennaro lined the biggest bird up in the sights of the gun, and as the bird climbed higher in the sky, he gently squeezed the trigger. Almost simultaneously, two shots rang out in the early morning light.

Gennaro, concentrating on his own shot, wondered about the other shot but did not worry about it. He saw the bird swerve one way and then the other and then fall to the ground near a stand of trees. He leaned his gun on the rock and raced out to retrieve the quail. He saw the limp bird on the ground, walked over, and then squatted down to admire it before picking it up.

As he picked up the bird, a leather boot hit him solidly in the side of his torso and knocked him sprawling to the ground. Panting with pain and gasping for air, he rolled over to see a solid young man of about twenty years of age standing over him with a gun in his hand. The stranger took a step closer to Gennaro and raised his foot to kick Gennaro in the head. This time, Gennaro was quick enough to grab the man's boot as it came towards him. Gennaro steered it past his head and upward as he climbed to his feet. The young man's other foot came off the ground as Gennaro pushed his foot up and then let go. The man crashed back onto his head and shoulders as Gennaro released him. Gennaro kicked the man in the solar plexus, just as he had done to Gennaro. A groan of agony escaped from the man's mouth as the blow landed.

"What the hell did I do to him?" Gennaro half muttered to himself as he kicked the dazed man again. He thought of the lessons his grandfather had taught as he raised his foot to kick him once more for good measure when the click of a shotgun hammer close to his ear made him freeze. Suddenly, Gennaro's head jolted backwards as the end of the shotgun barrel hit him in the side of his head. He fell over the man on the ground, blood pouring from the open wound on the side of his head.

It was a small miracle the gun had not discharged and blown his head off in the process.

The man who had hit Gennaro reversed the gun in his hand and, holding the barrel in both hands, lifted it to smash the butt into the back of Gennaro's head. The sound of a shotgun hammer clicking into place and the cold voice of Filippo Cudoni froze the man with the gun held high above his head.

"Hold it. Put it down—very slowly—or you will die now." Filippo Cudoni stood there with a single-barrel shotgun aimed at the man's head.

Slowly, the man straightened up, looked at Filippo Cudoni's gun pointed at his head, and let his gun fall back behind him.

Filippo stepped up, picked up the gun, and hurled it away. He recognized the man as the third of the three who had tried to be fresh with Maria and beat him up—the man who had tried to kill him with the knife. "Now tell me what the fucking hell is going on, you son of a bitch!"

The older man turned. He was obviously an older brother to the younger man on the ground. He looked up and smiled at

Filippo. It was an arrogant, conceited look, which Filippo had come across before. It usually meant big trouble was coming his way, yet he was the one holding the gun.

"Go and get it stuck up your arse, you heap of shit," he growled. As soon as the man finished speaking, it struck Filippo that he must not be in charge here. He knew something was wrong, but it was too late. A double-barrel shotgun w as rammed solidly into the small of his back. The impact made Filippo stumble a pace forward onto his knees, his shotgun falling from his hands. The much older man raised the gun to his shoulder and aimed it at Filippo's head.

Fear and worry would not help. Cudoni instantly realized that his death was very close unless he acted—and fast. He dived forward towards his fallen gun only to hear the sound of a gun blast. With sweat pouring from his body, he rolled onto his back as soon as his hands picked up the gun and aimed at where the man behind him was supposed to be standing.

The gun in the man's hands had exploded as Filippo reached for his shotgun. The pellets from the shotgun flew past Filippo's head and shoulders as he dived forward; a few ripped his shirt near his shoulders and ripped his skin in two places as well, but most hit the ground a few meters past him as he prepared to fire back.

However, there had been two shots—one shot from another gun a split second earlier, which had blasted the man's gun away and shredded the flesh of his left hand. Pellets struck the man's gun barrel, and sparks flashed as the pellets bounced off. The man's bleeding fingers were now hanging in threads from his badly battered left wrist. Francesco Cudoni stepped forward, smoke coming from one barrel of his double-barreled shotgun. "Filippo, pick up the gun," he ordered his son, his voice quivering with anger.

Filippo, still shaking from his near-death experience, painfully struggled to his feet and did as his father told him. He knew his life had come within a mule's whisker of ending when the man's finger had started to squeeze the trigger. Filippo looked at his father; he had never seen his father so enraged.

His father swung back to the three strangers who were obviously a father and two sons. "*Parla, presto*. You are this close to dying, you *assassino maledetto*." He held up his thumb and first finger, opening and closing them. "Why?"

"No man aims a gun at a Bartocchi or his boys and lives to talk about it." The father's pain-wracked voice also filled with rage as he growled back to Francesco. "I'll meet you in hell somewhere, and you will burn for this."

"No man aims a gun and shoots at a Cudoni and lives to tell the tale either," Francesco coldly growled back. He lifted his shotgun and aimed it squarely at the older man's head. "Prepare to die."

Francesco looked coldly at the man he was about to shoot, and as he did so, the older brother stepped between Francesco and his father. "You will have to shoot me in the back as well," he muttered. He had realized and desperately hoped that Francesco was not normally one to shoot unarmed men in the back.

Francesco looked thoughtfully for a moment at the son who had risked his own life to save his hotheaded father. "You have your sons with you, so count yourself lucky that I did not shoot you in the head, you ignorant imbecile. I will give you and your two son's one chance. You can go and pick up your guns and try to finish what you started now, or you can pick up your boys and crawl off. Your choice?"

The man looked at Francesco's cold, solid face. Bartocchi knew that if he made any attempt to pick up a gun, any gun, someone would die—and it would be him or one of his boys. He was no sniffling coward, and he would not hesitate to shoot anyone—even in the back—but he was not a fool, and his hands needed attention. He knew his left hand was probably finished. He took off the red bandana he wore around his neck with his right hand and wrapped it around his left hand; then he reached down with his right hand to help his youngest son to his feet, the older brother helping.

With his arm around his youngest son's chest, he hissed back with deadly venom at Francesco Cudoni, "One day, *caro amico*, we will meet again." The cold, ironic tone of his voice told Francesco Cudoni that the next time they met could mean a bullet in the back from someone who would not give him a second chance. But he was not—and never intended to be—a cold-blooded killer. He would deal with that situation if and when it might arise. Francesco knew the younger Bartocchi had saved him from doing something he really had not wanted to do, but it was something he should have done.

Filippo had not forgotten that the oldest brother had tried to plunge a knife into his back a week earlier. "The next time you try to stick a knife into me, you better do it right, or I will blow your head off, you sick *cornuto*," Filippo told him as he suddenly rammed the shotgun he had picked up into the man's lower ribs. The man slumped to the ground, clutching at his bruised ribs.

The three Cudoni's watched as the Bartocchis helped each other up and then slunk away.

"They are very dangerous people, Pa, and they will not hesitate to shoot any one of us in the back," Filippo told his father.

"I know, son, but I fear this will not end here."

Chapter 4

A few days later, Filippo went to see his grandparents. His grandfather was still very active for his age and was in the garden, tending to his vegetable patch. Filippo walked over to talk to him.

"Caro nipote," his grandfather welcomed him. "Come stai?"

"Bene, bene, grazie, Nonno. Evoi come state?"

"Si, si bene ance me."

Grandfather Pietro Antonio leaned his hoe against a small tree and looked at his eldest grandson. "Filippo, About last Saturday; be careful who you trust and keep your guard around the Cirrillos. Now do you remember the stories I have told you about our family? Where we came from and our traditions and beliefs?"

"Si, I do, Nonno."

"I can see that one day, Filippo, you will be a leader in our family. You will at times have to make very serious and hard decisions. I want you to remember this and pass it on to your brothers and family that if something bad should happen to your father or family, our creed will punish those responsible. It has been our family creed since the days when the three brothers carrying our Cudoni name came from Piedmont, near the French border. No one who kills a Cudoni dies of old age," his grandfather told him seriously.

"I will always remember that, Nonno," Filippo told him, just as seriously.

"My nonno told me, and his nonno told him. Your father and his brothers also know this. That is why the Cudoni's are left in peace by the Mafia most of the time. Everyone here knows that to pick a fight with one Cudoni is to pick a fight with all Cudoni's.

Now, let us go inside and have a nice glass of my favorite red wine."

Filippo followed his nonno inside.

The following week, Filippo and his family were again in Sambiase, but this time it was not a joyous occasion. Filippo had received his military call-up, and his train was departing that morning. About twenty young men from this area had been called up for military training, and the little railway station was full of family and friends saying goodbye to their loved ones.

Filippo and his family had left the farmhouse early that morning. On the way to the station, they had first called in at the house of their grandparents. His father's parents were both still alive. Pietro Antonio, Filippo's grandfather, was now in his early seventies, and his grandmother, Rosa, was four years younger. One look at the grand-father and one could see where Filippo got his sense of humor and his spontaneous good nature and smile. The family—in particular Filippo—said goodbye to them and then proceeded to the little rail station.

Filippo let the family continue on, but he went to Maria's house to see her. To his great disappointment, her mother said she had gone to a cousin's place but that she was going to get to the station before the train left.

Once at the station, his little sister, Theresa, and then his brothers Gennaro, Antonio, Giovanni, Peppino, Carlo, and young Giuseppe wished him the best. Gennaro told him to be careful with the girls from the north. Giuseppe, the youngest of the brothers, cried a little as he watched his favorite big brother prepare to leave. Filippo said goodbye to his family, but his eyes were searching everywhere for Maria, who was nowhere to be seen.

His mind raced like the wind. What could have happened to her? Had she changed her mind about him? Did she still love him? Was she still mad at him for what had happened last week? Time was running out. Was she coming? He prayed she would; he wanted so badly to hold her in his arms before he left, to say he was sorry for what had happened at the fiesta, and to tell her he still loved her.

But time had run out; he had to leave. He had to board the train.

Just as he stepped on board the train, he saw her running down the platform towards him. A huge smile of relief and happiness came over his face. He put down his luggage and raced to meet her. He put his arms around her and lifted her off her feet. "Io ti amo," he mumbled in her ear.

"I love you too. I will wait for you," she passionately promised him. She had overcome her disappointment at not having him the previous week.

"I thought you might not be coming to see me go, and I could not bear the thought of that." Tears of joy poured from his eyes.

"My cousin's watch stopped. That's why I'm late. I ran all the way to the station," she whispered.

The train's whistle blew for the third time, and the train's steam engine was gathering power. The wheels of the little train slowly started to turn.

Still carrying her in his arms, Filippo shuffled towards his luggage. The train gathered speed as he kissed her sweet red lips, let her go, grabbed his luggage, and raced for the door of the train. Every person on the platform clapped as he made it onto the train.

As he turned to wave, he could hear them call out his name: "Filippo e Maria sono innamorati."

The last thing Maria saw was his big, wide smile as he waved from the train in the distance. She stared at the slowly disappearing train and wondered if he would ever return to her and they would marry.

Chapter 5

Filippo Cudoni returned to Sambiase twice during his military training. He missed his hometown and his mother's cooking. The first trip home was for four days in early April 1897. He went to see Maria as soon as he got off the train, only to be advised by her father that she had left for Naples with her mother to see a sick aunt.

As he turned to leave, he almost walked into Catarina, her younger sister, who was returning home. The father had shut the door almost in Filippo's face and did not see his younger daughter returning. She gave Filippo a kiss on the cheek, but as she did so, she stood on her toes, and her lips went to his mouth. Filippo felt the warmth there but pulled away. Catarina then took him by the arm and led him to the side of the house. She told Filippo that Maria was due back in a few days.

The younger sister had since grown out of her shyness and gave Filippo a big smile as she told him. "Maria could be back soon, but I'm here if you need someone to talk to while you're back. I would be very happy to do that."

He failed to notice the true meaning of what she murmured as she winked at him. A few days later, he was to realize what she meant. Filippo dejectedly went to his parents' place. His family was happy to see him, and the older boys in particular wanted to know everything about his life and time in the army.

He called in to the home of the Valencis two days later. Catarina answered the door. "Buon Giorno, Filippo. Vieni dentro."

"I've come to see if Maria is back," he told her.

"Si, si, I know. Come in, and I will tell you," she replied. "I am the only poor girl at home."

Filippo followed her into the house. She offered him a chair around a table. "Can I get you a glass of wine or something to eat?" she asked as he sat down on the chair she had pulled out for him. She put a hand on his shoulder.

"Eh, no, no. I don't want to put you out. I just came to see if Maria is back. I really do want to see her if she is back," he replied.

"Si, I know, but you can have a glass of wine while I tell you," she replied as she took her hand off his shoulder and gently rubbed it once across his lips and cheek before walking to a cabinet. "No, she still has not yet returned from Naples." She walked back with a glass of red wine in her right hand.

She placed the glass on the table in front of him as she placed her left hand on his shoulder. He turned to look at her as she pressed her fingers gently into his shoulder.

She leaned her face close to his. "Drink this. It will make you feel better."

He looked at her and then at the glass of wine. "Catarina, I don't think this is a—"

"Sho, sho," she whispered in his ear. She put her right hand around his wrist and lifted his hand, making sure it rubbed along her pelvis, waist, and breast before resting on the glass. His fingers closed around the glass to avoid spilling it.

Her right hand went up to his face, and again she gently rubbed his lips with her fingers. Passion and desire took hold of her. She pulled his face to her, and her lips searched for his. He lifted his l e f t hand to push her away, but instead it wrapped around her firm breast, her nipple pressing firmly into his palm through her dress. Meanwhile, her lips had found his. He forgot for the moment the reason he had come for as her tongue sought his, and his manhood became erect, but then his sanity returned.

"No, Catarina, we can't do this. It's your sister I love," he told her as he gently pulled his face from hers and pushed her away with his hand still on her breast.

"Don't worry about Maria now. I'm here, and I want you—and I know you want me," she quickly replied. She had felt his rise, and she reached down and took hold of his remaining erection. "See, you do want me."

Sanity had returned to Filippo. "No. You're a beautiful girl, and many men will fight over you, but I want Maria."

"I don't think Maria will want you or wait until you get back," she called out to him as he left.

The words echoed in his brain, but he figured the little sister simply wanted what the older sister had. A few days later, he returned to his base near Bari, on the east coast of Italy.

In the second year, he returned home from military training for three days in late March. There had been a late winter that year, and a frosty wind was still blowing. Touches of snow were visible on the tops of the high mountains.

Filippo went to Maria's place early the next day, only to find out that Maria again was not home. Her father, Ernesto, said that she had gone with her cousin and her family to the Sila area and could not return due to the late snowfall.

Filippo asked her father to tell her that he had called to see her and, if he did not see her, to tell her that he would be back for good in June the following year.

"Si, si, sicuro." Her father promised to tell Maria when she returned that Filippo had come to see her.

Filippo trudged slowly to his parents' place. On the way he met Gennaro, who was returning home from visiting his grandparents and his uncle and aunt who lived farther down the road. Gennaro was glad to see his older brother, but he informed him that their father was a little upset after an incident that had occurred a few weeks before.

"Remember the episode in the forest before you left for the army? You know, when Dad shot the Bartocchi fellow that was taking aim at you to blow your head off and blew his hand into bits instead?" Gennaro explained further. "The man had lain in waiting for our father down in the narrow cutting in the road a kilo- meter away from our house. When Father got close, the man fired at him.

However, because he had lost most of the feeling in his left hand and could not hold the gun steady, the shot had almost completely missed. A few pellets had grazed Dad's left arm, but the majority had missed. The man had a single-shot shotgun, and as he desperately tried to reload it with his good hand, Papa managed to come upon him after scaling the small rise from the road. The man had desperately raised his shotgun to shoot, and Father had no choice but to shoot him with his revolver."

"The bullet from Papa's revolver hit him in the chest but did not kill him instantly," Gennaro continued. "Papa went back to Sambiase and notified the *carabinieri*, who came to see for themselves. When they got there, the man was gone. Pa told us, and we thought that his sons may have taken him home. Now the news is that he died five days ago. We heard about it yesterday."

Filippo chewed over what his brother had just told him. He well knew what the consequences of what Gennaro had just told him could and would be. He knew that the man's sons would be out to avenge the death of their father, and they would not be satisfied with just the death of his father. No, it would be more than his father who would pay the price.

"Gennaro, do you know where the consequences of this may lead to?" Filippo asked his brother, but he already knew that Gennaro was well aware of the ramifications.

Filippo and Gennaro found their father and the next two oldest brothers, Antonio and Giovanni, in the vegetable patch close to the house. Filippo noticed that two shotguns lay on the ground close by. Francesco and the two boys were happy to see Filippo home from his military training. There were many hugs, but Filippo could see his father was upset about something.

"Papa, Gennaro told me what happened—about the shooting."

His father nodded solemnly. "*Le cose non sono tanto bene.* It is not good."

Filippo understood. He could see his father was not shattered about it. Francesco Cudoni was a big man, and he had never had to resort to killing to defend himself. He had killed a man once by sheer misfortune, when a tree he had cut in the woods had accidentally rolled down a steep slope and crushed a man who was asleep lower down the mountain.

"I simply had no choice, son. It was a case of him or me, and the *carabinieri* have accepted that," Francesco, who was relieved t h e police had understood his position, explained to his son. "The Cudoni's do not shoot to kill unless there is no other way. But that is not now the problem, *figlio mio*. The man has three sons. Remember the time in the woods. Those three were mean then. They will not hesitate to shoot me or any of you boys—and, for that matter, your mother and sister as well."

Antonio and Giovanni nodded quietly as their father spoke. Filippo knew that the boys were well aware of what might happen.

Filippo and his father and brothers went to the house to see the rest of the family. His mother and young sister were extremely happy to see him.

For the next three days, the weather remained cold, and snow continued to fall in the high country, leaving no chance of travel to or from the higher country.

Filippo went to see if Maria had returned before he left, only to be told by her father, with a shake of his head, that she had not returned. At the station, his parents noticed his disappointment, and his mother told him, "If it is meant to be, it will be. But if it is not meant to be, well, don't worry too much about it."

"Take extra care, Papa," Filippo told his papa as the train started to chug away, and he waved goodbye to the others.

Not for one moment did Filippo dream that the rest of the Valenci family had ploted against him and Maria to keep them apart.

Chapter 6

One warm June afternoon, the train chugged into the little railway station of Sambiase. The town looked sleepy and peaceful. It was siesta time, and as was the custom in all of Southern Italy, the towns- folk were enjoying a nap. The doors to the shops and stores in the nearby piazza were closed for business, and some of the people could be seen resting in chairs or sleeping under trees in the open areas.

One of the first passengers to jump off the train was a young man dressed in army clothing and carrying a bag. Filippo Cudoni had returned from his military training. He was a man in a hurry; he had not seen his sweetheart for three long years, and he was dying to see her. Every night in the army barracks, he had dreamed of his lovely lady waiting for him, and today was the day he had been waiting for. He had not informed his parents that he was coming, and no one knew to expect him.

With his heart racing as fast as his legs, he skipped down the street, carrying his bag; he ran past the sleepy piazza to the other side of town where Maria lived with her parents. A little out of breath, he knocked on the front door of the house. For a while no one answered, and Filippo started to think that no one was home.

"Un momento," a woman's voice called out from inside the house. A few minutes later, a dark-haired, attractive, mature woman in her mid-forties opened the front door. It was Sarina Valenci, Maria's mother. Her smile of welcome transformed into a frown when she realized that it was Filippo Cudoni.

"*Buon giorno*, Filippo. You better come in," she said with a half-frozen smile. Before he could speak, she beckoned him inside. She pointed to a chair at a table, and he sat down. She sat on a chair opposite him.

"I have come to see Maria," he said.

"I know," she replied. "But I am afraid I do not have good news for you."

"Is Maria sick? Is there a problem? Please tell me," he said quickly. "No, no, it is not like that. But you will not be happy," she replied. "Maria does not live here anymore. She is married to Vincenzo Pasqualle, and she has a beautiful baby girl. Maria was heartbroken when you did not call to see her early last year, so she accepted the offer from Vincenzo when he asked her father for his daughter's hand in marriage. She had not heard from you for two years. She thought that you no longer cared for her, and she was very upset. She was upset and angry that she had missed not seeing you two years ago. Not letting her know that you were home last year and not calling to see her really made her very angry when she found out you had been home," Sarina told him as she ran her fingers through her long black hair.

"But I do not understand. I did call in to see her last year. Your husband told me that she was not home. He said that she had gone to the Sila country with her cousin and that the roads were blocked by snow and that they could not get back," Filippo told her.

"I know that now, but my husband wanted her to marry Vincenzo, and he did not tell her that you did call to see her," she replied. "She is happily married now. Please, you must not see her now. You cannot tell her that her father did not tell her. You will destroy her marriage and her family if you see her now. You must promise me that you will never tell her what happened.

Fury and rage welled up inside Filippo. His first instinct was to confront her father and choke him to death.

"Where is the imbecile now?" he demanded as he thumped his closed fist on the table. "I will kill him. I'll break every bone in his rotten body."

"*Per favore no*," Sarina cried. "He is a sick man, and he is now sorry. He realizes he should have told Maria and that he was wrong in not telling her, but you will ruin her life if you tell her now. It's too late. You must forget her now."

Through the pain and anger coursing through him, Filippo could see that she was right. It was too late. She was married now. She had a daughter.

Ironically, he thought it could have been his daughter if only he had done what she wanted. His mind kept telling him it was not fair. She should have been his wife. Her father had had no right not to tell her. He had been here to see her last year. Her father had promised that he would tell his daughter, and all this time she was married. His mind wandered as he slowly walked up the path that led to his parents' farmhouse.

He dragged his thoughts away from his pain as he approached the house. His little sister, Theresa, was the first to see him walking up the path towards the house.

"Mama, Mama, come and look, quickly! It is Filippo. Filippo has returned from the military!" she called at the top of her voice.

Most of the family heard her calls, and soon they were all there to greet him, except Giuseppe, who was out looking after the flock. There were many kisses and hugs for Filippo on his return from the army.

Gennaro called Filippo the General, as he pranced around in the new beret his brother had just given him.

While his mother prepared a meal, Filippo got a moment to talk to his father. "Papa, I have worried about the Bartocchi family. Has anything happened on that score since I was away?"

Francesco rubbed his hand over his chin, which was now covered with a two-day stubble. "Yes, but not to do with us. It seems the eldest son was arrested a few days after you left for robbing and bashing the town clerk. I understand from my brother that he received a two-year jail sentence with hard labor. He may be out now."

"Pa, they will not forget about how their father died. We will still need to be on guard."

His father nodded in agreement.

For six weeks, Filippo worked on the farmland, and it almost seemed as if he had never been away. He kept away from the town, and he did not see Maria or her family.

One Saturday morning, Gennaro asked him to go to town with him. Filippo knew that he could not stay away from town forever. There were a few things that he needed to buy there and so agreed to go. The army boots he had been wearing required new soles, and he needed to take them to the shoemaker.

It was midmorning when the pair strolled into the piazza at Sambiase. They first went to the shoemaker so that Filippo could have his boots repaired while they went about their other business.

Rosaria had given the boys a list of things to buy for her: some rolls of cotton and five or six sewing needles, five kilos of salt, and five kilos of sugar. Filippo also wanted to buy some writing paper and a pencil. One of the things that he had learned during his time in the army was to write. He had learned enough to read and write a letter. Gennaro walked ahead of him into the small store that sold these things, and Filippo was about to walk in the door when he noticed a good-looking dark-haired woman carrying a small child in her left arm coming out of the bakery across the piazza. He almost froze as he recognized Maria. Maria, the first woman he had believed he had loved—his Maria. The very woman he would have killed for, now with a child.

He stayed inside the doorway and turned to look back. In the shadow of the doorway, he thought she could not see him, but he could see her clearly, almost as if she were within reach of his arms. She seemed more beautiful than she had three years ago. Her long black hair glistened in the morning sunlight, and her lean, young body swayed as she walked along, carrying the baby girl. It hit him like the blow from a big hammer; that baby could have been his if he had given Maria what she had craved.

The baby wriggled in her arm as she walked, so Maria ran her other hand over the baby's head and patted her gently.

She walked across to the other side of the piazza from where he stood, and he watched her until she walked into a doorway, and he could no longer see her. The ache, the pain, and the longing for her all returned in a flash. He knew, however, that even if he still loved her, it was better for him not to see her anymore.

He walked into the shop after his brother. They purchased all the goods that their mother required, along with the pen and paper he sought. Filippo had learned while in the army to smoke a pipe, so some tobacco was added to the list. They put all the items into a soft leather bag that Gennaro had brought with him and walked out.

They returned to the shoemaker and collected the boots.

"There is no rush to get home, and there's a great chick working in this new pizzeria. Do you feel like a cup of coffee and a piece of pizza at the new pizzeria?" Gennaro asked Filippo.

"Si, sure. I am a little hungry, and a cup of good coffee sure sounds like a great idea to me," his brother replied.

The two men walked across the piazza, past the doorway Filippo had seen Maria walk into, to the pizzeria next door.

Unbeknown to Filippo Cudoni, Maria had spotted him walking into the shop. He heart had, for a brief instant of joy, fluttered like a feather in the breeze, but her anger at his callous refusal to see her for all the previous two years quickly put an end to that. She had never really forgiven him for refusing her that time under the tree near the fountain.

The front of the pizzeria had a big awning supported by two big columns, and farther back was a doorway leading into the kitchen. In the shade of the awning, two groups of four men were playing briscola. Some of the men were drinking coffee, but a few were already drinking wine.

Filippo and Gennaro sat at one of the empty tables, and soon a short thickset man of about forty-five came out to serve them.

"*Ragazzi*, what would you like?" he asked.

They each ordered a coffee and pizza and made themselves comfortable as they waited.

A few minutes later, an attractive young waitress carried a dish with a large pizza on it to one of the tables with the card players. The smell of freshly cooked pizza drifted through the air.

"La pizza e bella, ma lei e piu bella," one of the younger men playing cards told the young lass.

She blushed and then smiled ruefully at him, said thank you, and walked back inside.

Five minutes later, she came out again carrying two large mugs of steaming-hot coffee in her hands. She put the mugs down in front of Gennaro and Filippo and told them the pizzas would be another ten minutes. She looked at Gennaro as she spoke, and he gave her a big toothy smile and a slow nod. She gave him a faint smile as she left.

"See what I mean?" Gennaro quipped when she had left.

Filippo was preoccupied with his own thoughts but heard his brother's comments. "*Si, si.* Not bad at all," he replied softly with a grin.

The man who had paid her a compliment earlier gave Gennaro a dirty look, as if to say, "Mind your own damn business." Gennaro gave him a scowl back.

Filippo, who was facing the way they had come, looked down the street. He could still see the bakery. *I wonder what happened to Maria,* he thought. He had not seen her walking back from the bakery.

A short time later, the waitress returned carrying two large dishes, each with a large pizza on it. The pizzas were topped with salami, olives, cheese, tomatoes, and anchovies. They looked and smelled great.

As the waitress left, she brushed against Gennaro. The man who was playing cards gave Gennaro another ugly look. He had noticed the pizzas and the fact that she had rubbed against Gennaro.

They tucked into the delicious food, stopping only occasionally to talk to each other. The waitress came out and topped off their coffee cups with more steaming coffee.

Again the waitress exchanged smiles with Gennaro.

The two men who had been playing cards against the younger man and his partner stood up. "We have to go," one of them said. "*Il lavoro aspetta.*"

The younger man, whose partner had called him Giovanni, looked at Gennaro and Filippo. "Hey. Do you two want to play briscola?" he asked.

Gennaro looked at him. "I don't know how to play cards well. But I wouldn't play with you anyway."

Giovanni stood and walked up to the table where the two brothers sat. "What did you say to me?" He scowled.

Gennaro smirked at him. "I said I wouldn't play cards with a shithead like you anyway."

Giovanni had a fiery temper, and on top of the fact that the girl had paid him no attention, this was more than he could take. He kicked the chair out from under Gennaro, who sprawled flat on his backside on the ground. Giovanni, like all bullies who thought they had just flattened the town weakling, laughed mirthlessly.

Gennaro pulled his feet under him and, in one smooth motion, sprang to his feet. He too was now angry. He banged his open hand into Giovanni's laughing face and pushed him hard, sending him flying backwards. Giovanni crashed into the table where the other four men were playing cards. The table broke under the weight, and all five men ended up on the floor.

Giovanni rolled over sideways onto his haunches and then pulled out a wicked-looking knife from inside his boot; blood was dripping from his busted nose.

Giovanni's partner swung a wild punch at Filippo, who had stood up. Filippo allowed the punch to whistle past his head, grabbed the man's arm as it went harmlessly past, and, as he had done so many times in the military and his grandfather's coaching, turned his back slightly to the man and pulled the man flying over his back. Still holding the man's arm, he slammed the man, back first, hard onto the top of a table. The man slid slowly to the floor, the wind knocked totally from him.

One of the other men who had been playing cards with Giovanni picked up a wooden chair and slammed it onto Filippo's shoulders. From the corner of his eye, Filippo saw it coming, and he moved into the man, reducing the impact, but it still knocked him to the ground.

One of the men on the ground tripped Gennaro as he turned to face Giovanni and his knife, and Gennaro crashed into a chair and onto the ground. Giovanni lunged with the knife, intending to slash Gennaro across the chest. Filippo's boot caught him in the groin, and the knife flew out of his hand towards Gennaro, who casually picked it up by the tip and then hurled it unerringly at a rafter in the ceiling, where it stuck.

The fight was on. Two of the older men stayed out of the fight. The other four men attempted to beat the crap out of the two cocky brothers. However, it soon became obvious that the four townsmen were on the receiving end.

In his rage and pain, Giovanni feebly attempted to pull a revolver out of his pocket, but Filippo's boot in his stomach made him drop it. Filippo picked the gun up and pointed it at the other card players. Filippo's army training and Gennaro's speed and agility had been too much, and the sight of the gun pointing at them made the three men still standing stop in their tracks.

The three helped their three friends on the ground to their feet and limped away.

A small crowd had gathered to see the fight, and some clapped as the six sore losers scurried away. Within a few minutes, they had disappeared.

The waitress—who, in a sense, had started the whole thing—came out with a rag and gave it to Gennaro to clean his face. "Are you all right? You are not hurt?" she asked him.

"You enjoyed that, didn't you?" He grinned at her. "You wanted me to belt that idiot, didn't you?"

She smiled back at him but did not say a word.

Chapter 7

At the back of the crowd, a beautiful dark-haired young woman holding a baby girl had watched Filippo and his brother give the card players a rough hiding. The faint look of concern that had first come over her when she'd recognized that one of the men was Filippo Cudoni was replaced by a look of disdain and bitter resentment as she remembered what had been—or not been—between them.

The bitter look was the look that Filippo first saw as he spotted her at the back of the crowd. The first instinct from his heart was to wave to her. His hand started to move up, but his head killed the instinct as quickly as it had appeared. He stood there for a long moment, looking towards her. The wide charming smile that had come to his face faded, slowly replaced by a more somber look. His heart was pounding, begging him to go to her, to tell her that he still loved her, that he had always loved her, that he had been to see her—that it was her father who had come between them. But his head held firm.

Their eyes met for a brief moment, but to Maria, it felt like forever. Her heart seemed to leap or stop—she wasn't sure which.

How handsome he looked was one thought. That damn charming smile hit her heart like a huge hammer, but then filled her with rage. This was the man who had forgotten her. This was the same man who had not even bothered to see her for two long years, she thought.

Where had he been when she had needed him, when she had needed his protection against the consequences she'd had to endure since? She remembered that she was married and that she had a daughter. *A daughter from those consequences.* She turned her back to him and walked away.

Filippo and Gennaro returned to their table and sat down. The two older men who had been playing cards on the other table, not against Giovanni and his partner, came up to them. "Can we sit with you?" one asked.

"Sure, please do," Filippo said.

"You have gotten yourselves into a lot of trouble," the older man told them.

"How is that?" Filippo asked politely.

"Giovanni is the brother of one of the local *poliziotti* Cirillo," he replied. "You will find that they don't forgive or forget."

"Thanks for the advice. But they got what they deserved," Filippo told him. He wondered if he was related to the Cirillo he had fought with. There did seem to be some resemblance.

"Sure, they did, but you better be very careful. They will get even. By the way, my name is Severio Rocca, and this is Dominico Pasteri." He waved the waitress across. "Two glasses of red wine for me and Dominico. My friends, what would you like?"

"The same for us as well," Filippo replied.

The sun was close to disappearing when the two brothers trudged out of town along the path leading to the farmhouse. They slung the supplies that they had purchased over their backs. They had drunk more than a little wine over the last three hours, and they were in a jovial mood as they walked home.

"Just as well the military people did not see you fighting those clowns back in town," Filippo joked to Gennaro. "Or you would be in the military, training on those feet of yours."

Gennaro laughed loudly. "That medical man in the military—he's a regular saint. There is no hope for me with my flat toes, he reckons. He never saw me with Nonno."

Filippo's mind kept haunting him with the look of contempt that had come over Maria's face. He believed that he had done her no wrong; he knew that if he had done her wrong, then there was nothing he could do about that now. He knew in his heart that he did not want to see that look again. He wondered what had he done wrong to get that look.

"Gennaro, I have been thinking," Filippo said as they walked along.

Before he could say any more, Gennaro butted in. "You do seem to have been doing a bit of that lately."

"No, I am very serious. I have been doing a lot of thinking about going to America," he replied. "Father has some land, but we are seven brothers. We will never get ahead by working on this land. It is not enough for all of us. Sure, we can buy some more, but it will be a struggle for the rest of our lives. I have heard that people in the New World are making plenty of dollars. In a few years, we could make enough money to come back and buy all the land we want. Do you want to come?" He turned to his brother.

Gennaro realized that his older brother was serious. He had been having the same kinds of thoughts. He had not dared to tell his parents because he knew that they would be upset. He also had heard the many stories that had come back to this part of the world from people who had been there. He had heard of the money that could be earned in America, but he had also heard of the hardships and deaths of some of those who would never return.

"I have been thinking of going there myself," Gennaro replied, "but I don't have the money, and I just couldn't ask Papa for it. But I would love to go there, and if I can raise the money, I will go."

"Well, Gennaro, I haven't told you this, but during my years in the military, they paid me a small weekly allowance. It is not a lot of money, but it should be just enough to get us there. I have enough money to pay for all the expenses. You can repay me later if you like," he told his brother.

"I'm ready to leave straight away if you are," Gennaro told his brother. "But you better tell Pa. He will listen to you more than he will to me."

The rest of the way home, they discussed all the details. They had heard that there were only two places to depart from— either from Naples or from Marseille in France.

They could not see any point in going to France overland, so the best idea seemed to be to take the train to Naples and then organize a boat fare from there to New York.

"New Yorka, New Yorka, here we come!" They burst out in song occasionally as they picked up pace for the rest of the walk home.

At breakfast the next morning, Filippo informed his parents of the decision that he and Gennaro had made.

Their mother burst into tears and begged them not to go. "No, no, my sons, it is much too dangerous to go to America. Too many people have died over there. You could be robbed and killed. You cannot go. Papa, tell them that they cannot go."

Papa Francesco was silent. He was a big man—just above aver- age height, but very solid. Even now, in his late forties, he was still a strong man. He too had heard the stories from the New World. He knew that his brother Nicola and his wife, Theresa, and their family were already there, along with some of his other nephews and younger cousins. A few of his family members had returned with plenty of American dollars, but he had also heard how wild it could be there.

His brother had returned eight years ago, collected his whole family, and gone across to live in America. Francesco himself had made plans to go to Pittsburgh eighteen years ago and had gone as far as Paris by train. During the trip, he was befriended by a group of young people talking about a new way of politics and of overthrowing the current governments of most of the countries in Europe. They called themselves new wave communists. Most of their beliefs were not in line with his, and he took no part in their babblings during train stops.

When the train arrived and they disembarked in Paris on a dark, damp night, the group attacked and robbed him of everything he possessed; leaving him with only the suit he had worn for the occasion. During the fight, the local police arrived. Francesco had laid out two of the group before he was knocked unconscious from a blow to the head. The police took the three men and locked them in jail, where the other two accused him of being a communist and trying to rob them.

He spent seven days in jail before he was released, with orders to stay around until his trial. Once out, he decided he could not wait in Paris and returned to Sambiase.

A warrant for Cudoni's arrest was issued by the police in Paris when he failed to appear in court. He was lucky to make it safely back to his family, to a wife and three young sons he had left behind.

His wife was happy to see him back home, and with a warrant for his arrest in France, he did not think of leaving Italy again for some time.

Later in life, because of his large young family, he eventually decided it was best not to go.

He turned to his two eldest sons. "You have heard the stories from the New World, and you still want to go?" he asked them.

Both young men nodded.

Their father nodded, and then he slowly shook his head. For a long moment, he was silent; then he put his arms around his two eldest sons.

"*Figli Miei*, if you really want to go, then it's okay with me, but I must warn you to be very, very careful. I don't want America to have my two oldest boys die there," he told them. "Mama, if they want to go, we must let them go. There is much more future for them in America than there is in Sambiase. My older brother and his five boys and their cousins are there. You can join them. You will need to find out how to go to where they are. I am sure they will help you and look out for you when you get there."

Chapter 8

Several days later, Filippo and Gennaro returned to Sambiase to arrange train fare to Naples. Filippo had sufficient clothing from his army days, but Gennaro needed to buy some shirts, a jacket, and trousers. They knew they could buy better clothing in Naples, but they wanted some right away. The tailor's shop was close to the bakery where Filippo had seen Maria a few days ago.

Filippo kept a wary eye open in the event that he should spot Maria. He was not keen to see her after the scathing look she had given him a few days ago, but he was curious as to whether the baker nearby was the one she had married, and he wondered what he looked like. He imagined her husband was some fat, pot-bellied, middle-aged man with receding black hair streaked with grey.

After making their purchases, Filippo and Gennaro walked out and past the open doorway of the bakery. As Filippo glanced inside, he saw behind a table a dark-haired man in his late thirties talking to a woman who had her back to the door. The man was lean and rather good-looking, with dark, smooth features and a wide mouth.

"I'm going to say *buon giorno* to the lass that got us into trouble the other day. You coming?" Gennaro asked his brother.

Filippo chuckled. "I'd better, or you will be in trouble again."

It was still some time until siesta, and the pizzeria was almost empty. Gennaro spotted the young lass walking to the back of the shop, and while Filippo sat on a large rock in the piazza near the front, he went in to talk to her. She was about to close the back door when Gennaro stopped the door from closing with his hand. Without saying anything, he swept the girl into his arms and started passionately kissing her.

A few minutes later, and with an angry owner telling him to get lost and let his staff work, Gennaro came out. "She is hot, that Francesca. *Mama mia*, she nearly ate me alive," Gennaro boasted as he came closer to where Filippo was sitting on the rock.

With Gennaro still laughing, the two young men set off back to the farm.

Twenty minutes later, they had left town and were walking along the road near a narrow bridge that spanned a small stream, when they heard a groan coming from the bushes and trees a little upstream. Filippo touched Gennaro on the arm to stop him. He too had heard the groan. Then the silence of the still quite afternoon was interrupted by the throttled sound of a woman's scream before a thud cut the sound off.

Filippo motioned for Gennaro to be silent as he carefully crept towards the bushes where the sounds had come from. Gennaro pulled out the revolver their father had given them to take with them. From the top of the stream bank, they saw two men trying to search through the pockets of a man lying on the ground.

A short distance away, an elderly woman was slumped on one knee, begging the men not to kill them. One of the men was jabbing the air with a long knife, telling her they would both be dead if they had no money. The Cudoni brothers recognized them as the two oldest Bartocchi brothers with whom they had fought in the forest three years ago—the sons of the man Francesco Cudoni had shot the year before.

The instant Filippo landed on his feet not far away, the two Bartocchi men recognized him as well.

"Well, well, well, if it's not the Cudoni bastard we were looking for," the oldest growled menacingly as he swung his knife towards Filippo. "Now you have saved us the trouble, shithead."

A cold look came over Filippo Cudoni's face, but he took no notice of the man's words. "Tell your worthless brother to leave that man alone before I break his ugly neck," Filippo told Bartocchi in a cold, hard voice.

The other Bartocchi laughed and pulled out another long knife as he stood up. "It's about fuckin' time we taught you Cudoni bastards the way to die—balls first, eh, Ugo?"

The two men turned to launch themselves at Filippo. They had not seen Gennaro sneaking up at them from behind. Before Gennaro could say anything, the two Bartocchi men rushed Filippo with their knives raised in front of them.

Filippo took a step back to be ready, but as he stepped back, his foot hit a small sapling, and he fell to one side.

The gun in Gennaro's right hand roared as he fired at the closest man to his brother. The bullet hit Ugo Bartocchi in the back of the upper right shoulder, spinning him around and knocking him to the ground.

The knife in Bartocchi's hand sank into the ground close to Filippo's head. The other Bartocchi froze on his feet as he heard the hammer of the gun behind him being re-cocked. He watched his brother hit the dirt, his face inches from the water in the stream. Slowly, he dropped his knife to the ground, his back still to Gennaro. He heard a small mirthless chuckle come from behind him.

"You were the man who was going to shoot me in the back a few years ago, shithead. Remember?"

Filippo had now stood up, and he walked to where Ugo Bartocchi was lying, picking up the knife on the ground on the way. He rolled him over with his foot. "He won't die—yet."

"You better kill me now, you...you filthy swine," Ugo Bartocchi hissed through a bloody mouth as he tried to stand up. Blood from his wound was soaking his shirt and coat.

Filippo Cudoni laughed. "No, not yet, compa. Jail first."

Forty minutes later, with the younger Bartocchi helping his limping brother along, Filippo, Gennaro, and the grateful couple—a distinguished but elderly man and his wife—walked into town. The man explained that his name was Giuseppe Renaldo, and his wife's name was Antonia.

The Bartocchi men screamed curses and retribution at the two Cudoni brothers as they walked at the point of Gennaro's gun.

A small crowd soon built up around them as they walked farther into town. The elderly man explained to the throng what had happened and how these two brave young men had saved his wife and him from possible death at the hands of the *duii maledetti*.

Two carabinieri came to investigate the commotion. As the couple explained to the carabinieri what had occurred, the two brothers soon learned that the elderly couple did have money, and the man was the mayor of Sambiase. The mayor, Signore Don Giuseppe Renaldo, told the carabinieri to take the two Bartocchi brothers with them and lock them up; he would deal with them in the courthouse. "Ragazzi, sono molto contento per tutto." Don Giuseppe started to thank Filippo and his brother when a woman aged about forty-one and a young woman of about twenty came rushing up to them.

"Ma, Papa, are you hurt? Young Augustino just told me you were both nearly killed by some *maladhiti* [bad people]." The older of the two women panted as she reached to hug the elderly woman. The younger woman wrapped her arm around Don Giuseppe.

Don Giuseppe put his arm around the young woman. "*Non ti preccupare, cara mia*. These two brave young men saved us from being killed by the Bartocchi brothers. Your nonna and I are well— and very lucky too."

Don Giuseppe explained to his daughter and granddaughter just what had occurred and how both of them would have been dead if not for the help from the two young men. "Filippo and Gennaro, meet my daughter, Sarina, and granddaughter, Gina."

Sarina looked at the two brothers and, as was the custom in Calabria, gave each a mighty hug and kissed each of them on the cheeks. Young Gina's expression turned to admiration and gratitude as her grandparents explained further. She put her arms around each of the brothers in turn and, pulling them to her, gave each a quick kiss on the lips.

Don Giuseppe and his wife both insisted that the two brothers accompany their family to their home for a glass of wine and some *mangari* (food). The two brothers had no choice but to go to the home of the Renaldos.

Don Giuseppe soon produced his favorite red wine, and the women prepared a platter of home-made salami, cheese, and hard bread while the three men talked about the incident that had occurred. Soon the women joined them, and several hours passed before the Cudoni's left.

After the brothers said their goodbyes to Don Giuseppe and Sarina, Gina walked outside with the brothers. "Sono molto contento di tutto quello ce voi avete fatto per i nonni." (We are very happy with everything you have done for our grandparents). She gave Gennaro a quick kiss on the lips, but she pulled Filippo closer to her and gave him a lingering kiss on the lips. "Please come and see me—eh, us—when you are in town." She smiled sweetly at Filippo. "Si, si," he promised her, still holding her hand and looking into her shining black eyes.

As she smiled back at him, a promise of something flickered through her bright eyes.

"I wonder how long before those two pieces of scum create more trouble," Filippo told Gennaro as they walked home in the early evening darkness.

"I am sure they will," his brother replied.

As they walked, Filippo could still feel the warmth and sweetness of Gina's lips on his and could see her imploring look for him to go see her again. *She really is a sweet girl—and a pretty girl at that*, his mind kept telling him, but he knew he was leaving Italy. To pretend he would be serious about her would be wrong, and her parents and grandparents would think poorly of him if he did.

Then he thought of Maria, how she had looked at him in anger, disgust, and scorn. What could he have done to deserve that scorn? He saw in his mind a picture of the little girl walking along with Maria. He knew he should not to see Gina again. She was young and very pretty, and she would soon find someone else.

Two weeks later, on a trip into Sambiase to buy some things for his mother, as he was buying a bottle of marsala for his father, Gina walked into the shop. Filippo was about to pay for the wine and did not see her come in.

She put her arm around his shoulder, and as Filippo turned to see who it was, she gave him a quick peck on the cheek. "Buon giorno." She smiled at him.

Filippo smiled down at her and then gathered the change from the owner. He put his arm around her shoulder and steered her towards the door. "Gina, come stai?" he asked her as they walked out. "Male, male. Non sei venuto a trovarmi," she reproached him.

She put her arm around his waist as they walked out into the piazza. She turned to face him. "Baci me," she told him as she lifted her face to his. Rather than argue, he quickly and lightly kissed her on the mouth; before he could pull away, she put her other hand around his head and tried to get him to open his mouth and return her passion. He gently pulled away from her, trying not to offend her. She noticed his reluctance and stepped back, looking into his eyes. "What is wrong, Filippo? Are you married? Did I embarrass you? But I did so want to see you."

From across the piazza, in a small lane, another young woman watched in a jealous rage as Filippo seemed to hug and kiss the pretty younger girl. *He should have been mine,* she thought to herself as she gently guided a little girl down the lane. She picked up a small pebble and angrily threw it down the lane.

"No, you did not embarrass me, Gina. No, I am not married, but believe me, it was not easy not to grab you and hug you to death," he told her. "You are such a beautiful and warm girl that I could hardly resist you. However, I could not do that to you. I am going far away very soon, and I will probably never see you again, so I do not want to encourage you to think of me. I am going to America, Gina."

One month later, the Cudoni family was again together at the little train station in Sambiase.

Filippo and Gennaro Cudoni had said their goodbyes to their grandparents the day before.

Before they left, their grandfather, Pietro Antonio, had given them his advice: "*Ragazzi*, you are going to a new country. Be brave, be strong, work hard, and do not forget the country you came from. Remember the Cudoni creed. Now go and make your fortune, and come back even better than you are."

Antonio, the third oldest brother, was the first to say goodbye to his brothers. It was a little unusual, as normally he was the last to say anything, but with the excitement of the moment, it went unnoticed.

The two young men gave hugs and said all their goodbyes to the family and the many friends who had gathered to say farewell.

"Don't forget to bring me a new dress and things from America when you come back," Theresa excitedly reminded her brothers for the tenth time since they had told the family of their plans to go abroad.

"Look after each other over there," Francesco told his two sons. "You know we will be all right over here."

It seemed a little strange to Gennaro that he could not see his younger brother Antonio in the crowd, but the train was ready to leave. With a last hurried hug for each of the family, they boarded the train for the adventure of a lifetime.

They waved from the doorway of the carriage as the train left the station.

They went in and sat on the hard timber seats. The steam engine powering the train built up steam, and as it did so, it picked up speed. It chugged and pulled the wagons along the railway tracks. "I wonder what happened to Antonio when we left. I could not see him anywhere when we got on the train. Did you see him?" Gennaro asked his brother.

"Not at the end, no." Filippo thoughtfully scratched his chin. "But a little earlier, he said that America will be a great place to be." The journey from Sambiase to Naples was over three hundred kilometers. The train was due to stop at most of the stations along the way, and the stationmaster in Sambiase had told them it would be the next morning before they arrived in Naples.

The carriage that the two young men were in had about twenty people in it when it left Sambiase. During the afternoon, most of the people left. By eight that night, only six men and two women remained in the carriage.

An hour later, Filippo and Gennaro were startled to see a man trying to climb into their carriage through the open window. The moon was well up in the night sky and provided sufficient light to see that it was a young man getting in.

"Filippo, Gennaro, is that you in there?" they heard the young man call.

"Antonio, what the hell? Is that you?" Filippo realized it was their younger brother who was climbing in through the window.

They heard the chuckle. "Si, si, sono io," Antonio replied. "It was starting to get cold, and I was getting very hungry in the wagon with the sheep in it."

The two older brothers' first thought was to send him back. However, this was not as easy as it sounded. They would have to go all the way to Naples before he could catch a train returning south.

"There is no point trying to send me back," he told them. "I am not going back. In a month's time, I will be getting a letter from the government, telling me to report for military training. I do not want to go, and there is no way to dodge it. So I'm going to America."

Antonio also informed them that he had told their brother Giovanni, who had helped him by carrying the few belongings he was taking with him to the station for him. Giovanni would tell his parents once the train had left the station. He did not want his parents worrying and searching for him.

Filippo and Gennaro realized that unless they went back with him, there was no way they could force him to go, and besides, if he was going to run away to America, he might as well go with his brothers.

They arrived in Naples early the next morning. The two older brothers stepped down from the train, but because Antonio had no ticket, he climbed out of the rear window. He walked around the train and soon met them at the end of the platform.

The three were imposing figures of young manhood as they strolled towards the wharf. Antonio was not quite as tall as Gennaro, but he was solid and as strong as an ox. He would be twenty-one years of age in a month's time, but he still had a boyish look about him. He had a devil-may-care attitude, but he was no fool. Under that devilish attitude was a clever brain.

Antonio presented a problem they had not expected. He had no clearance and no money. He would not be able to get clearance to depart from Italy as the authorities would want to see his military papers first. This was no problem for Filippo and Gennaro, but Antonio was a huge obstacle to get over.

"There is no way that the authorities will issue clearance papers for Antonio's military training if he has not done it," Filippo told his brothers. "I know how the military and the system work. The only way we can leave together is to get work on a boat and work our way across."

His brothers agreed.

The wharves in Naples were large. The harbor seemed to be full of small boats, most of which were owned by local fishing men. A number of big ships moored out in the middle of the harbor plied their wares from city to city along the shores of the Mediterranean Sea. Men in small rowing boats were moving about between them and the docks.

Although it was still early, the place was bustling with activity. One of the largest vessels was having its cargo unloaded, and crates were stacked everywhere on the wharf.

They approached an older man wearing a captain's hat who was busy castigating a sailor who had dropped a crate from the platform between the boat and the hard timber planking of the wharf.

"You stupid imbecile! Don't you know how valuable those boxes are?" he shouted at him. "If anything is broken, I'll break your stupid neck, and it will come off your pay."

He did not hear the three men approach, and when Filippo tapped him on the shoulder, he roared like an angry lion. "What the hell do you three want? Don't you see that I'm busy?"

"I'm sorry to disturb you, *Capitano*, but we are looking for work on one of the ships going abroad," Filippo replied quietly. "Do you have any work, or could you tell us who might be able to give us a job?"

The man adjusted his captain's hat on his head and took a good look at the three before him. "I can use some men that can work today and tomorrow. All this shit has to be taken off the boat and put into that warehouse." He pointed to a large warehouse about 150 meters away.

"If you are as lazy as that idiot, get lost. If you want to work, you can start now. I want all this stuff into that warehouse now, and I don't want it broken," he told them in a voice that reminded Filippo of his drill sergeant back in the army.

The three looked at each other. Hard work had never frightened them before, and it sure was not going to now. They all nodded.

Filippo spoke for the three brothers. "Sure, we can start now. You got a deal. We are not afraid of a little work."

"By the way, I'm the skipper of that boat there. Call me Benaldo. Who the hell are you three?" he asked gruffly.

Gennaro answered, "This is Filippo, this is Antonio, and I am Gennaro. We are the Cudoni brothers. Filippo is the oldest, and he is the general."

That night, they shared a room at the local tavern a few hundred meters from the wharf. It had been a busy few days, and with not much sleep the night before, the boys decided to have an early night.

The next day, Filippo questioned Benaldo about getting work on a boat to France or Spain.

"The *Portella* will be going to Genoa, Marseille, and Barcelona, but we won't be leaving for another four days. All the freight to bring back has not arrived. If you are still here, come and see me in another three days. I might need a hand stacking it in the boat," he told Filippo.

Four days later, they set sail for Genoa. After two rough weeks at sea, including two days at Genoa, they made it to Marseille in France.

The captain paid the three brothers what he owed them, and they then decided to set out to find something to eat and explore the city. After being on a boat for two weeks, it felt good to be on land again.

Chapter 9

Marseille was a bustling commercial center on the Mediterranean Sea. The wharves and docks were a little bigger and busier than the ones the boys had seen in Naples or Genoa. Many more pleasure boats were here, and out in the bay, a number of large ocean-going steamships remained anchored. Some of these were ships that travelled to all parts of the world, carrying cargo and passengers.

The city was full of people from different countries. The French people felt that sometimes the city streets were full of strangers, and some resented them. Many Italians, Spaniards, Moroccans, and Algerians, along with a few British and Egyptians, frequented the streets of Marseille.

The three brothers followed the bustling crowd, which seemed to be moving up and down a wide and busy street, and soon they were in what appeared to be the busiest part of the city. It was now early November, and the air was cool as they walked. They passed a number of eating places, but a particularly busy cafe, Milano's Pizzeria, took their fancy, and the boys decided to go there to eat.

The owner was an Italian who had married a French woman and had lived in France for the last twenty-five years.

They had a leisurely meal, and while they were having a cup of coffee, the owner came over to talk to them. The waitress had told the owner that some Italians were having a meal there. Milano told them he was Italian and from Torino originally.

He told the brothers many Italians had been coming through in the last ten years, and most were going to America. Most were going to the United States of America, but some were going to Argentina and others to Canada.

The cafe owner asked them, "Where are you going?"

"To New Yorka and then Pittzaburgh," Filippo replied. He explained to the owner the problem they had regarding Antonio's lack of clearance papers.

The Cudoni brothers talked to the cafe owner for some time. His name, he told them, was Luigi Milano. They now understood where the name Milano's Pizzeria came from. The busy lunch period was over, and he had a bit of spare time for a chat.

While the brothers drank a few glasses of wine, Luigi told them that if they stayed in Marseille long enough, he could help them find work there, and it would be possible to make enough money to pay for Antonio's fare and a ticket that would allow him into the United States. He directed them to a boarding house and wrote a note for them to take to the owner of the boarding house.

They thanked him for his courtesy and help and said they would be back for dinner. The brothers arranged a room for the night at the boarding house after deciding that they could well do without another night on the boat.

That night, they returned to Luigi's for something to eat. The restaurant was very busy. The good, rich Italian food that Luigi made had built a reputation that stretched across the city and beyond. The smell of garlic bread, fried onions, and spaghetti sauce hit the noses of people one hundred meters down the street.

At night, Luigi's family—which consisted of his one son, Alberto, his two daughters, and his wife, Josephine—all worked to cater to the customers they had. Luigi and his wife prepared and cooked the meals, the two girls served as waitresses, and Alberto served the wine and drinks and made sure no one created a nuisance.

Luigi's pasta and pizza was just as good as their mother's, and they thoroughly enjoyed the meal. Later in the night, Luigi came over to talk to them.

"Did you have any trouble in getting a room at the boarding house?" he asked Filippo.

"No, no," he replied. "The lady understood enough, and she did have a couple of empty rooms, so we paid for one week's board."

Luigi motioned to two men sitting at another table to come over. The two men obliged.

One of the men was in charge of a warehouse for a large merchant business based in Marseille. He understood some Italian and informed them he was short of good hard-working men, and before he left that night, he promised to see what he could do to get work for the three brothers.

For just over seven months, the Cudoni brothers worked in Marseille. They became good friends with the Milano family. In particular, Filippo and Alberto Milano, the son of Luigi, became good friends, and they even spent some time touring the South of France. The three brothers even learned enough French to converse with the people. Antonio seemed to be the best at it.

Gennaro and Antonio became attracted to the two young girls. Brigitte and Gennaro and then Antonio and Marcella paired up. While they were not serious relationships in the eyes of the two brothers, they spent quite a lot of time together. The two girls spoke fluent Italian and taught both brothers a spattering of French. Marcella in particular became very attracted to Antonio, and the two would sneak out much more often than the other two.

They were out a lot, and Filippo and Gennaro wondered if the two had become lovers. When they questioned Antonio about it, he only laughed and told them to mind their own damn business.

But in the hearts of the three brothers, their dream was still to go to America, and when they eventually had enough money to pay for their tickets across, they purchased them.

June 14, 1899, was another sad departure day; it was time for the three to leave. The three Cudoni brothers had to say goodbye to the Milano family, and Brigitte and Marcella made no secret of the fact they were disappointed with the departure of Gennaro and Antonio. Even Josephine, who was normally a complacent and unemotional soul, had more than a tear in her eye. She too had come to really like the three boys and had quietly hoped that at least one of the girls would end up with one of the boys.

The two girls cried and begged Gennaro and Antonio not to leave.

On the wharf, the good ship *Fiora* waited. After many hugs, kisses, and handshakes, the three young men boarded the steamship, and from the deck, they waved farewell to their new friends. The two heartbroken girls stayed and waved until they could no longer see them on the deck.

The three brothers had made the decision to go to America when they were in Sambiase, and that remained their first priority. Filippo had written to his family and told them that Antonio was with them, that they were in Marseille, and that they would be leaving France as soon as they had enough money for the voyage across.

He also knew that the postmaster would read the letter to his family.

The *Fiora* carried about a hundred passengers and had twenty-five sailors as crew. The ship was dingy, damp, dark, and cramped. The three were all crammed into one small cabin.

After two days on the Atlantic Ocean, the winds picked up, and after a day of strong winds, nearly all the passengers were seasick. Even some of the sea-hardened sailors looked as if they would rather have been somewhere else.

During the day, most of the passengers spent their time on the small deck of the ship. The passengers were from a variety of different countries, but the majority of them were from France and Italy. A few Greeks were also in the crowd.

The Cudoni's soon struck up friendships with some of the other passengers; with nothing else to do other than talk, many a tall tale was often told and retold.

They learned that most of the people from Calabria were going to Pittsburgh in the state of Pennsylvania. This suited the three Cudoni brothers as they knew that their uncle and cousins who had come to America were in Pittsburgh, and that was where they too were going.

Six days out from New York, the small ship encountered fierce winds and heavy rain. Early that morning, they could see the heavy black clouds roll towards them as the wind picked up velocity.

The passengers were restricted to their cabins, except for the crew, who battled to keep the ship on course. This time, all the passengers were sick. Some thought that their time on earth was coming to its end and swore that if they made it to dry land; they would never again set foot on another ship. Some spent time praying to the Lord for forgiveness and preservation.

Disaster almost struck the little ship on the second day of the storm. A young Greek boy whose antics had provided much amusement over the trip decided to sneak out of his cabin during the storm to watch the lightning. He snuck out while his parents were asleep, and his mother screamed when she realized the horror of a missing son sometime later.

The three brothers in the next cabin heard her scream and went out to see what had caused it; they found the parents in the narrow corridor, calling their son. They all raced upstairs to the deck and, to their horror, saw the young boy clinging to a side rail thirty feet away as the wind, rain, and sea spray swept over the deck. The mountainous seas threatened to wash him overboard at any time.

The father, without any thought for his own safety, made a wild dash to help his son. A huge wave broke across the ship and almost washed him overboard as he reached his son. Filippo pushed the others back inside to keep them from being washed out as the wave hit. He grasped a rope hanging on the inside of the door, reopened the door, and looked out to see father and son still clinging to the rail. Slowly, the two were trying to crawl along the rail back towards the group. Filippo tied one end of the rope around his waist and handed the rest to Gennaro, who placed it around a steel fixture near the door. The crashing waves threatened to wash all overboard.

Filippo made his way to the two, and they tied the rope around the boy's waist as well. All three slowly battled their way back as Gennaro and Antonio pulled on the rope. They were almost back to the door when a huge wave broke across the bow and along the ship.

The mother, without holding on to anything, was desperately trying to reach out for her son when it hit.

Antonio, realizing that the mother would be swept overboard by the huge wave, made a desperate grab for her leg with one hand as the wave picked her up, slammed her brutally against the side of the ship, and threatened to carry her overboard. With one hand around her leg and the other holding the rope, Antonio hung on for grim death; then the wave passed, and the woman fell heavily onto the deck.

In desperate haste before the next wave hit, the men picked up the unconscious woman and went back inside, now totally exhausted. The *Fiora* bobbed and bounced on her way slowly towards the East Coast of America. On the third day after the start of the big storm, the wind and rain eased off, and late in the afternoon that day, the coast of Long Island was faintly visible on the north-west horizon. That night was the last time the *Fiora* and her current passengers anchored out at sea.

Early the next morning, the *Fiora* set off for the port off New York.

The Greek woman—who had now considerably recovered from her battering, other than one side of her face, which was still swollen where she had hit the side of the ship and the deck during the storm—came to see the Cudoni brothers before they left the ship. She could not thank them enough for all that they had done for her and her family.

Chapter 10

The next morning was clear, and the sun shone brightly as the *Fiora* slowly sailed along the south coast of Long Island, through the Narrows, and into New York Bay.

Countless hundreds of ships and boats of all sizes were moving about in the bay. Past the towering heights of the impressive Statue of Liberty, the small ship sailed. To the Calabrese, the newly completed statue looked like the seventh wonder of the world. The sheer scale of activity in the bay left them totally astonished.

It seemed to take forever for the small ship to finally berth at a pier in Ellis Island Harbor as the travelers stared in amazement at the towering buildings in Manhattan. To the new arrivals, the magnificent and large buildings were sights to marvel at.

Once the mooring was completed, all the passengers disembarked the ship. The officials there directed them towards the immigration department office for processing, registration, and approval to land and live in the USA.

At three in the afternoon on Monday, July 11, 1899, the small ship docked at the harbor, and the Cudoni's and the rest of the passengers were able to disembark.

The wharves at New York were located on both sides of the Hudson River, and they seemed to go on forever. They were huge and, without a doubt, the busiest they had seen anywhere in the world. The scene was daunting without some knowledge of where to go, and they could see the risk of easily getting lost. There were thousands of people moving back and forth between the wharves and Manhattan, and even the passenger terminal where they landed were extremely busy.

The Calabrese had decided to stick together. One of them, a man in his early thirties called Batiste Raso, had been to New York before. He had returned to Reggio Calabria to bring his wife, Antonia, and their six-year-old son, Mario, to live in the New World. That night, the group of eighteen men and six women and a boy stayed at a boarding house about half a mile from the wharf.

To the Calabrese who had not been to America before, it did indeed look like a new world. Huge, towering buildings lined each side of the streets.

New York was modern; most of the streets were paved with stone, and some were made of concrete to carry the vast numbers of people travelling in all directions.

Batiste knew the Italian family who owned the boarding house, and Filippo could see that these people knew him. The next morning, the group, carrying their luggage, walked part of the way back towards the wharves. A busy side street took them to the front of the railroad station. Batiste had pointed out the previous day where they had to go to catch the train, first to Philadelphia and then to Pittsburgh.

The group stared in utter amazement at the size of the railroad station and the number of trains that came and left the station.

Grand Central Station in New York was massive as well as grand, its size dwarfing the people who walked inside the huge hall. In Calabria, and more precisely in Sambiase, one little line snaked into the tiny station; however, here there were dozens of separate lines and platforms. Batiste led the Calabrians to a station with a sign that said Pennsylvania Railroad. Here they purchased tickets to Philadelphia and then tickets to Pittsburgh.

It was eleven in the morning by the time the sixteen going to Philadelphia and Pittsburgh eventually climbed aboard to leave. Six of the Calabrians were going to Syracuse and Buffalo, and Batiste pointed out the platform to which they needed to go.

The train headed south across the bridge over Newark Bay and past many factories and residential areas. Slowly, the urban areas gave way to tall, timbered land.

The countryside that the train travelled through that afternoon had tall green hardwood trees. They saw flat farmland full of crops, rolling green hills with cattle grazing, small valleys, and, in the distance, low mountain ranges. The train line passed through and stopped at all the many small towns and villages. It also passed through the larger towns of Trenton and Levistown on its way to Philadelphia.

It was five o'clock on a sultry, warm afternoon by the time the train pulled up at the rail station in Philadelphia. The railway station at Philadelphia, although not as large as New York's, was still impressive. The great railroads from the north-west, linking Chicago, Detroit, Cleveland, and Pittsburgh, came through to Philadelphia. It was also a through line for the trains moving north and south along the East Coast of America.

That night, they stayed in Philadelphia. Batiste knew that there were a number of boarding and guest houses not far from the station, and eventually he found accommodations for all the Calabrians.

With the light of dawn, the travelers were up. The train was due to depart the station at seven thirty that morning, but they were there at six. A small canteen at the station had hot food available, and most of the travelers quickly had something to eat and drink.

The train departed the station on schedule at seven thirty. It travelled west from Philadelphia, past Daylesford, and on to Paoli as it headed towards Harrisburg on the banks of the Susquehanna River. The land there opened up with plenty of flat farmland. They saw crops of corn and tobacco and acres of vegetables; most of the vegetables being grown here were for Philadelphia and New York. It was the food bowl for the eastern cities on the coast.

The train made many stops along the way before it arrived in Harrisburg, where it made a forty-minute stopover, and then it travelled north-west to Lewistown and then headed west towards Altoona.

This was high country, and the train travelled along mountain ranges, over running streams and valleys, and through a large tunnel dug through the mountain.

Up in the Appalachian Mountains, the next major stop was Altoona. It was nine that night when the train pulled into Altoona. Here the train stopped for some two and a half hours so the passengers could relax and eat.

Batiste told the Calabrians that a combination restaurant, bakery, and deli shop close to the station sold many different types of hot meals, cheeses, dried meats and salami, coffee, and of course, bread. Some of the Calabrians, including the young Cudoni brothers, went to the shop to eat. It seemed to be a popular place for weary travelers to eat.

The train left the Altoona station at eleven thirty that night, and the weary travelers tried to settle down to get as much sleep as possible. The train travelled over the Allegheny Mountains on the westward trek past Johnstown to Pittsburgh.

Four hours after Johnstown, and with the red glow of the morning sun appearing hazily through the smog on the eastern horizon, the train reached the outskirts of south-east Pittsburgh. Here there were many rail lines, and trains were going and coming all the time.

As they approached, they could see plumes of smoke coming out of chimney stacks from all directions. They were to learn after- wards that about one thousand different types of factories were operating in and around the Pittsburgh area.

Downtown Pittsburgh was located on a triangular tract of land carved out of the confluence of the Allegheny and Monongahela rivers, where they became part of the mighty Ohio River. Pittsburgh served as the center for industrial manufacturing of steel and, with a massive coal deposit and several huge deposits of iron ore nearby, had facilitated the building of large factories. The smoke from the many factories climbed into the heavy air and hung like a huge dirty blanket over the city.

From inside the slow-moving train, the Cudoni brothers could see the steep other side of the river, including Mount Washington and what appeared to be rail tracks leading up the side of the mountain.

Batiste told the Cudoni brothers that was the best way for someone walking to reach the areas where most of the Italians lived.

It seemed busy men were everywhere, travelling between the harbor and the train station. Pittsburgh appeared quite compact for a regional city. To Filippo Cudoni, the inner city looked ugly and filthy. His mind went back to his beloved Calabria and his home on the mountainside, where the air was always clear. He decided that if he could live somewhere else rather than the place he saw before him, he would.

The Cudoni brothers were amazed at the amount of activity and the busy industrialized atmosphere that the Pittsburgh railway station area projected. It also appeared that numerous rail lines con- verged at this railway station.

The train was moving quite slowly, and soon it pulled to a stop at the huge Union Station in downtown Pittsburgh. The brothers collected their bags and stepped down onto the soot-laden platform. The old station seemed to have weathered into an ugly, hard-worn building, and it paled in comparison to the huge new station under construction a short distance ahead. While the new building was still only in its early construction, based on the size and sheer elegance of the rotunda and greyish-brown columns, which looked like brown stone and brick, it would be a massive building once it was finished. A young man ran up and down the platform, telling all passengers in English to collect their luggage and depart the train as the travelers gathered together on what was to them a huge platform.

With Batiste leading and explaining how things were here, they walked from the station towards the center of the city.

Batiste, his wife, their son, the four Folino men, and the Cudoni brothers made their way along the busy street to eat at a pizza place owned by a Napolitano, located next to a barbershop also run by an Italian. It was about one mile from the railway station. The pizza place was open when they got there and was busy.

The weary travelers put their luggage down and sat down. They ordered, and when they had finished eating, Batiste took the Folinos next door.

The city of Pittsburgh at this hour was a hive of activity. The steel and glass factories that had opened up in the area worked around the clock, but the shift that commenced work in the early hours of the morning had changed, and thousands of laborers were going home.

Pittsburgh was also the center for education in the area, and children were already heading off to the nearest schools.

When Batiste and the Folinos walked into the barbershop, the busy barber greeted him warmly. "*Compare* Batiste, how are you? *La moglio, e figlio,* how are they?" he asked in a mixture of Italian and English.

"Bene Grazie, Alfredo," Batiste replied in Italian. "I have brought them back to America with me, and they are outside. I also have some new friends with me, and I wonder if you could help me. These are the Folinos, and they have relations here. Do you know any Folinos?"

"Sure I do," Alfredo replied. "Natale and his boys live on the east end of Bloomfield." He turned to the man in the barber chair having his hair trimmed. "Dominico, do you know them?"

"Sure I do," the man replied. "Nice people."

The Folinos thanked them all for their help. They said, "Buon giorno" and left.

Antonia and her son and the Cudoni brothers, who had been waiting outside, came in when the Folinos left.

"Now, Alfredo, meet my good wife, Antonia; my little boy, Mario; and also my new friends, Filippo, Gennaro, and Antonio Cudoni," Batiste said, introducing them one at a time to the barber. After the introduction, Filippo asked Alfredo if he knew where Nicola and Theresa Cudoni and their five sons lived.

"Nicola was here about two days ago to have a haircut," Alfredo replied as he stopped cutting the man's hair. "They live, I think, on the west end of Bloomfield. Take the cable car to the top. It is the second boarding house on Idaho Avenue. It is about ten houses and one boarding house on the left side of Idaho Street, and Idaho Avenue is five more blocks that way and to the right." They walked to the door, and he pointed farther up the street.

The Cudoni brothers thanked him, told him they would see him when they needed a haircut, and walked outside. Batiste and his family followed them out.

They organized to meet at the barbershop the next day, and wishing each other a good day, they separated. The Cudoni brothers set off down the street towards the cable car with Batiste and his family. It was a new experience for the Cudoni's and for Batiste's family to ride in a cable car. Once they reached the top of Mount Washington, Batiste pointed out the way they should go.

The three young men set off—walking straight, tall, and determined and with an air of confidence—to find Idaho Avenue. This was going to be the start of a huge adventure and saga that was to be for all the members of the Cudoni family a turning point in their lives.

Forty-five minutes later, Gennaro knocked on the door of the boarding house. A plump woman in her early forties opened the door. She was holding a broom in one hand.

"What you want?" she said in poor English.

Filippo replied in Italian. "Cudoni famiglia?" At the same time, he indicated with his hands that he was looking for a person.

She took a long admiring look at the brothers, nodded, and headed down the hall. The Cudoni's followed her. She turned and signaled to them to wait.

She returned a short time later with a dark-haired woman in her late forties. Filippo recognized her as their auntie Theresa, who had left Italy nearly nine years ago.

"Zia Theresa," he called as she walked down the hallway. The three brothers waved cheerfully at her. "Do you know who we are?" he asked her in Italian.

Theresa looked at the three for a long moment. Then her face lit up into a huge smile. She ran to embrace them. "*Certo,*" she replied in Italian. "*Certamente.* Filippo, Gennaro, and this must be little Antonio Cudoni all the way from Sambiase."

After all the hugs and kisses were over, she led them into a big apartment where the family lived.

"Zio Nicola and the boys are at work, but they will be home this afternoon about five," she told them in her Calabrese accent. "Make yourself comfortable, and I will cook a big breakfast for you."

Filippo told his aunt they had already had breakfast, but a cup of coffee would be nice.

The boys sat down at the large timber table in the middle of the room while their aunt worked at the large wood stove. She soon had coffee ready. They talked for an hour, and then Filippo and his aunt went to see the woman who ran the boarding house to purchase an extra room and beds.

Filippo and his brothers carried their luggage to their room, and after each had a wash, they got several hours of sleep. Late in the afternoon, they went back to see their aunt.

Their uncle and his boys had not returned from work, so they talked to their aunt while she prepared the evening meal. Around five thirty, they heard voices in the corridor, and the door opened. A darkish-skinned man of about fifty-two years walked in first, followed by three much younger, taller men in their early twenties. They stopped in curiosity as they noticed the three young visitors in the house.

Zia Theresa stepped forward. "Nicola, do you recognize these three young men?" Zia asked her husband.

He shook his head. "No," he replied. Then he took a longer, better look at Filippo. "E Filippo, figlio di Francesco e Rosaria?" he asked.

Filippo chuckled. "*Si, si, Zio, sono* Filippo, Gennaro, *er* Antonio Cudoni, sons of your brother Francesco back in Italy."

Nicola introduced the three sons who were with him. "*Questo e* Michele our eldest, Benaldo the second, and Palmo, the biggest man in the family."

Half an hour later, the two youngest sons, Santo and Fiore, arrived. Their return from work was later than usual as they waited for the next train back from the city to return.

Nicola's five sons were aged from eighteen to twenty-six; Fiore was the youngest, and Michele was the oldest. Zio Nicola was born two years before his brother Francesco Cudoni. Francesco Cudoni had married when he was twenty-two years old.

Nicola had been in America for sixteen years. Nearly nine years ago, he had decided to bring his whole family to live in America. All of the younger American Cudoni's spoke reasonable to good Calabrese as well as English and were able to communicate with the cousins who had just arrived.

That night, over a large meal, the Cudoni family reminisced about old times and talked of the future in a new country. The American Cudoni's had much to tell of their life in the new country and the country itself. The younger members of the family had now learned to speak the English language fluently, and even Nicola had learned enough to get by. The only one who did not speak English well was Zia Theresa, but she was slowly learning.

Filippo and his brothers told Nicola and his family of their travels from Sambiase to France and then to America, including the help they had received from Batiste Raso and his family, whom they would be seeing the next day at the barbershop.

Nicola told them that Batiste's father and mother were actually their second cousins, but they had not seen them for a long time because they lived far away. He asked the boys to tell Batiste this and wish his family well.

That night, the three Cudoni brothers stayed with their cousins, uncle, and aunt at the boarding house.

The next day, Nicola and his sons had to go to work early and were gone by six in the morning—well before their three cousins woke up.

It was the first time in a while that the three brothers had had a decent night's sleep. When they woke up, they went to see their aunt, and she had breakfast ready for them.

At midday, they went to the barbershop to see Batiste. They told him what their uncle had said to them. Batiste was not surprised. He said that his parents had mentioned that they were originally from near Sambiase. Filippo, Gennaro, and Antonio took turns getting haircuts. Batiste told them of the sort of work available. Most of the Italian men in the area worked in the nearby mines of coal or iron ore. A good number worked in the steel factories around town, but the best-paying jobs were in either mining or building new railway tracks.

Most of the Italian men preferred the mines or the many factories littered around the city because they were able to live in Pittsburgh or the nearby towns around Pittsburgh, such as Sewickley. Most miners travelled by rail from town to the mines.

Work on the railways paid a little better, but workers had to live on the job, which meant they could be fifty miles from Pittsburgh.

Batiste told them he was going to return to work in the coal mine he had worked in previously as he would be with his family at night and would get good pay because he would also work as a liaison officer between the workers in his mine, mainly Italians, and the management. He had already been to see the company manager that morning and knew that there was extra work available.

"Get used to working long hard hours, boys. Mines and factories are close but full of smog and soot. Railroad work is out of town, also hard work, but has clean air," he told the brothers.

He told them that he knew the foreman/engineer at the Pennsylvania Railroad Company, and he could probably get them a job there together.

Filippo and his brothers decided to talk to their uncle and cousins about it that night. Their uncle had told them they could stay with him until they decided what they wished to do.

The next day Batiste took them for a long walk from Bloomfield, down to the cable car station, near the river across the big bridge, and showed them around Pittsburgh's city center. That afternoon, he took them to see the house he had bought for his family. Although it was a modest house, it was better than a boarding house; he would not have brought his young wife to America to live in a boarding house. Batiste's house was not far from where their uncle lived but was closer to the area known as Little Italy.

The three Cudoni brothers thought they remembered the way back, so Batiste did not go with them. On the way back, they stopped to sit under one of the many trees in the park to consider their future course of action.

It was a bit difficult to make any real decision without sufficient knowledge of the kind of work involved, but it seemed to Filippo that the work most suited to what they had been doing would be on the railway tracks. Antonio was of the same opinion, but Gennaro felt it would be better to stay in town, where at least he knew some people. He was not afraid of working on the railroad lines but felt the town offered him more and would provide a change.

"I have been on the land all my life," Gennaro told his two brothers. "I want to try town life for a change."

Filippo felt that the three brothers' main reason for coming to America was to make money and, when they had saved enough, return to Italy. The trouble with living in the city, he said, was that the lure of the hotels and saloons meant one spent more.

"That is up to you, but remember, Gennaro, it's quite easy to waste your money in the city."

"Si, I know, Filippo, but I'm going to give it a go," he replied.

That night, after much discussion with their uncle and the rest of his family, they decided that they would first find out what the job with the railway was about and how much it paid, and then talk again to Batiste about the mine job.

In the end, the freedom of the open country, where the Cudoni's preferred to live and breathe, won out. The oppression of the smoke, soot, and dust that continually drifted over Pittsburgh was more than they were willing to bear.

Chapter 11

Ten days after disembarking in New York, two of the three Cudoni brothers were due to start work for the Pennsylvania Railroad Company.

Batista who had learnt to speak some English had taken the two brothers to meet with the employment officer in Pittsburgh and convinced the man that these two were good hard workers and would not give any reason to be laid off. The man had explained the work needed and how much they would be paid.

The decision to go with the rail job meant that they would have to live in the rail barracks at Penn Hills or on site. The little town of Penn Hills was not far from Pittsburgh. The black smoke and smog that lifted up from Pittsburgh was visible from there, but it did not sit over the little town as it did over Pittsburgh. The little town had a clean, nice, homelike feel to it, and the Cudoni brothers could always return to Pittsburgh whenever they had time or felt a need.

The town was quite small, with only some three thousand people living in and around it. The Pennsylvania Railroad Company had one of its regional works and maintenance depots located there, and from there, the company was building a number of new railway spur lines connecting the outlying towns, in addition to maintaining and improving its existing lines.

Filippo and Antonio worked on the railroad construction sites, clearing and levelling the ground before the rails were set in place. At times, they also replaced rails and sleepers on existing tracks or improved the alignment of old tracks.

It was hard work, and the hours were long. The calluses and blisters on their hands at the beginning were painful, but after a while and with the use of gloves, they adapted, and their hands and fingers became as tough as old leather. Gennaro foundhis work was much heavier at times, but he travelled a lot. His task was to help load the sleepers and steel rail tracks onto the train wagons. He travelled with the train to wherever the sleepers and rails were unloaded.

The Cudoni brothers worked six days a week non-stop until mid-December. Slowly, they learned to understand words in the English language, and on his day off work, Filippo in particular would endeavor to learn to read and write in English. The only other breaks from work came when wild winter weather set in and held up work. There were several other Italians working on the rail, men who had been there much longer and knew the language a little better, and this helped communication.

It was not long before management noticed Filippo's and Antonio's work ethic and honesty, and they soon became trusted employees.

Twentieth of December to the early part of January, the company workforce on the line construction side took a Christmas break. The workers had a choice of staying in Penn Hills or going back to Pittsburgh or wherever.

The Cudoni brothers decided to move back to Pittsburgh to spend Christmas and the start of the new millennium with their relations there.

Nicola and his family had moved from the boarding house. They had purchased a house in Jackson Lane, which was in the suburb of Bloomfield, where Batiste and his family and a large number of other Italians, mostly Calabrians, lived. This suburb and its neighboring suburb of Little Italy had a large number of Sicilians living there as well.

They spent their first Christmas Eve in America with their uncle, aunt, and cousins. They boarded at the same boarding house where Nicola's family used to stay, but spent most of the afternoon with their relations. On Christmas Day, all the Pittsburgh Cudoni's planned to visit and have lunch with their uncle's family. Zio Cudoni asked his three nephews to go with them, but Filippo and his two brothers felt they would be imposing on them and decided it was best they not go.

"Filippo, don't be shy to come. I am sure they would be very happy to have you. Antonio and Catarina have three boys about your ages and a very pretty daughter as well. You three would have a great time with the boys," Zia Theresa told them. "I'm sure you would be most welcome, so if you change your mind, come here in the morning and come with us."

"The town is closed for Christmas Day," Palmo told Gennaro. "But if you come, we can play briscola as well."

Filippo spoke for the three brothers. "We appreciate your invitation to come, but I think it best that we leave it for another time." During the week leading up to New Year's, Filippo and his brothers spent some time sightseeing in the city and its surrounding area. They walked a lot and sometimes caught the new streetcars sightseeing around the city. Within a few days, they had learned their way around the city and the suburbs from their boarding house to their cousins' place.

A huge celebration had been planned for New Year's Eve in Pittsburgh. The city's civic center was, for three blocks, closed to all traffic. Fireworks in the small park where the two rivers met were due to go off at the stroke of midnight, and dancing in the street was to be an all-night event.

Zia and Zio Cudoni had arranged for Zia's brother and his family to join them for a New Year's Eve dinner. New Year's Eve fell on a Sunday night, and Filippo and his two brothers spent the day at their zio's home. During the previous day and that morning, the three brothers helped their uncle and cousins construct a large covered veranda area at the back of the house.

Later that afternoon, the family enjoyed a nice warm glass of red wine while they waited for the arrival of Zia's brother and his family. Just before five, they walked in. Zia's brother, Tomasi Folino Gallo, was fifty-two—a tall, once-dark-haired man about six feet three inches tall—and his wife of twenty-seven years, Catarina, was forty-eight. Her hair was black, but some grey was pushing its way through. She was still a tall, beautiful woman.

They had four children. The oldest, Giuseppe, or Joe, was twenty-five years of age and six foot six inches tall; Natale, who was twenty-three years old, was six foot one inch; and their daughter, Angelina, was twenty years of age. She was tall for a girl—even taller than her mother—dark-haired, and an absolute beauty. Angelina's long black hair was parted in the center and fell down both sides of her face, over her long, high, strong cheekbones. Her sparkling though dark eyes seemed cheery and full of life. She was a beautiful, strong, and irresistible sort of girl, but her height made her even more imposing.

Angelina's infectious smile and smooth complexion instantly infatuated and attracted Filippo Cudoni to the beauty of this lovely girl.

Sarino, who was the youngest, was nearly nineteen. He was six foot four and likely to grow some inches more.

Nine years ago, Tomasi had returned to Italy to pick up his wife and his children. The younger ones had learned to speak English well, but with a slight Italian accent.

They also had with them two cousins on Tommasi's side, Luigi and Natale Folino Gallo. Luigi, who was about six feet tall, had a wife and a small girl at home back in Falerna, Italy. Natale was twenty-six. He was six foot four tall and well built. He had a girl back home waiting for his return to get married.

Zia Theresa introduced her nephews to her brother and his family. "Tomasi this is Filippo, Gennaro, and Antonio Cudoni. You know their parents, Francesco and Rosaria Cudoni, Nicola's brother and his wife. Filippo, Gennaro, and Antonio, this is my brother, Tomasi; his wife, Catarina; their sons, Giuseppe, Natale, and Sarino; and my favorite niece, Angelina."

Filippo and his brothers shook hands with the Folino Gallo family. The Cudoni's were above average length in height, but the Folino Gallos were much taller people.

Filippo left Angelina for last. Her beauty had grabbed his heart like in a vise and he felt that he was mumbling as he spoke to her.

"Signorina Folino Gallo, it is such a great pleasure to meet one as beautiful as yourself," he told her as he held her hand.

Angelina blushed slightly as her heart stuttered and almost missed a beat. She too had noticed him, and now his charming smile and good looks pulled at her heart. In a city like Pittsburgh, it was not often that men paid young women compliments, and to hear one from this particularly handsome, good-looking young man appealed to her.

"It is a pleasure to meet you too, Signore Cudoni," she replied with a huge smile that lit up her beautiful face.

Her beauty and the sound of her voice sent Filippo's heart soaring higher than an eagle over the mountains. Filippo could instantly see that Angelina was a girl who spoke from her heart and her mind. Maria Valenci paled in comparison to this woman,

Filippo's mind told him. It also told him that he had been dumb not go there for the Christmas Day party. If only he had known.

"Please call me Filippo. I have never had a beautiful girl call me Signore Cudoni," he told her as he lifted her hand to his lips and kissed the back of it. "Can I be permitted to call you Angelina?"

"Si, si, Signore, come dice lei," she replied with a laughing smile. He caught the impish grin she gave him and smiled back at her.

The chemistry and fireworks that were later to embroil their lives had been ignited. He felt as if he could fly to the moon with her and make love to her, and he realized almost instantly that she attracted his male desires and instincts.

What a fool I was not to accept the invitation to go there on Christmas Day, he rebuked himself in his mind. *What a great week this could have been if only I had come*, he thought as he smiled to himself.

Angelina secretly felt the same. This smiling young stranger had set her heart on fire. Throughout the night, she stole quick glances his way. She liked his broad smile, strange blue-green eyes, and solid, manly appearance, and although quite a few young men had tried to approach her, none had made any impact on her. Not like Filippo Cudoni anyway.

When all the introductions were complete, the men sat around drinking wine while the women prepared the dinner.

Fiore and Sarino helped set up the tables, and the women brought the huge meal to the tables. Calabrese women could truly claim the title of the world's best cooks, and Zia Theresa and her sister-in-law, Catarina, could lay claim to that title as well. The aroma of freshly cooked food drifted through the house, and by the time they sat down to eat, they were all starving.

"Mangiare, mangiare e pronto," called out Zia Theresa. "The food is on the tables and ready to be feasted on."

The Pittsburgh Cudoni's were happy to have their relatives on their father's side join them for dinner that New Year's Eve.

Filippo could not remember having a Christmas week and New Year's Eve like this for four years. The last one with the Milano family in Marseille had been an enjoyable one, but this was as good as the old days back in Sambiase.

After the meal, they sat round the table, talking of life and events that had happened back in the old country, and then the talk moved to life in America. It was easy to see that some regarded life in America as the future, while others longed to return to the simple life that they knew existed back home. A new century was about to begin, and every person there felt it was going to be a fabulous future. By nine thirty, the younger family members were getting restless. They wanted to join the crowd at the city center and celebrate the new millennium with singing and dancing.

Angelina wanted to go as well, but it was only after all the young men promised to look after her that her parents relented and let her go.

The group—Michele and his four brothers, Giuseppe and his two brothers and sister, and Filippo, Gennaro, and Antonio— made their way to the corner of the street, where they hoped to catch a trolley car. Ten minutes later, one arrived, and all of them jammed into an already-packed car. Filippo did his best to remain as close to Angelina as he could, but there was barely enough room to stand, and talking was of no use. Still, he was close enough to help her down when the trolley pulled up near the cable car.

The weather outside was cold, but as everyone was rugged up in woolen clothing, nobody complained about the cold weather.

Filippo could not get Angelina out of his mind. She had such beauty and appeal. He searched for words to start a conversation. Angelina and Filippo had exchanged a few glances and smiles at each other back at the house, and both were keen to talk to the other.

"Do you remember much of Italy?" he asked her in Italian as they walked out towards the cable car.

"*Certo*, I was born in Italy too, you know." She smiled back.

"How old were you when you came over?" he asked her as they walked.

"I was nearly eleven. I suppose you want to know how old I am now," she said with a big grin on her pretty face.

There is nothing backward about Angelina, he thought to himself. "*Certo*," he replied with a laugh. "Zia Theresa said you were nearly seven when you came from Italy, and you have been here nine years, so you are sweet sixteen—and I bet you were the best-looking little girl to ever come to Pittsburgh as well." Filippo deliberately understated her age to see her reaction.

Angelina looked squarely into his greenish-blue eyes. "My zia never tells fibs, and I know she would have told you I was twenty."

Filippo laughed light-heartedly. "Nearly twenty, she said."

Walking near the rear of the group, they talked about some of the people they both knew back in Italy. Even after nearly nine years away, she still remembered some of the places and people and relatives she had left behind.

They walked to the cable car and, after waiting for their turn, rode it down to the bottom of the incline. Filippo managed to sit in the seat next to Angelina, and as the car sped down, Filippo's hand brushed Angelina's. His fingers locked around hers until they reached the bottom. With a steady hand, he helped her out of the cable car.

"Grazie," Angelina thanked him while still holding his hand.

"Tanto piacere," he replied with a smile, giving her hand a small squeeze.

As they approached the city center, the noise from the huge crowd that had gathered to celebrate the new millennium became much louder. The city center in that area had been closed to all traffic, and a huge throng of people were dancing and singing.

Harmony to the entertainers on a makeshift stage on one side of the civic center. A makeshift bar set up on the other side of the street was catering to the thirst of the crowd.

The group mingled with the crowd. At the bar, they purchased some stiff drinks to beat the cold and watched the entertainers per- form. Some of the entertainers had the crowd laughing with their funny antics, while some sang wonderful love songs, along with some folk and country songs.

A band of musicians was playing dance music from one corner of the stage, and when the carols and singing stopped, they continued playing dance music.

Even though he understood very little English and could not understand the words of the songs, Filippo asked Angelina if she would dance with him. They had watched some of the crowd dance before, and he thought he could do what they had done.

They danced to some romantic waltz music in addition to a touch of country music. For Filippo and Angelina, the time seemed to fly, and before they realized it, it was nearly midnight.

The crowd counted down the last ten seconds of 1899, and as the town clock hit midnight, a mighty roar went up from the throng. As the noise abated, the first of the fireworks commenced.

People in the street cheerfully hugged and kissed each other. Friends and strangers alike shook hands. There was laughter in the air all around.

Filippo and Angelina gave each other a long, lingering look. A warm and tender smile came to the face of each. The chemistry and the hormones in both bubbled to the surface, and they slowly moved into each other's arms and hugged each other tightly.

A sudden surge of desire and passion went through Filippo as he held her against his body. His arms pulled her tighter against him. She could feel his heartbeat through the heavy clothing against her breasts, and she pulled him closer to her. A long moment later, he released her, and holding one hand gently around the back of her head, he kissed her softly on the lips and wished her a happy new year. Angelina felt a huge flutter of excitement, love, and emotion sweep through her heart as they kissed.

For Filippo, it was as though he had come to heaven and was holding an angel in his arms. He did not wish to let go, but he knew he must.

They shook hands with the nearby throng, and some ten minutes later, they found the rest of the group.

As they had promised to bring Angelina back by one o'clock in the morning, they thought that they should leave straight away.

Some of the others wanted to stay, and in the end, Filippo said that he would escort her back as long as two of her brothers came as far as the house in case of any trouble.

Filippo, Angelina, and her three brothers walked back to the cable car and rode to the top of the incline. When the trolley car arrived, Filippo told them he was not returning to the celebration and would stay at the house.

"I am going to stay at the house, so if you boys want to return, you can."

When Angelina and Filippo had seated themselves inside the empty trolley car, the three Folino Gallo boys set off to rejoin the crowd in the city center. Filippo and Angelina watched as the three headed back towards the city. As they turned to look at each other, Filippo moved to put his arm around her shoulder, and it brushed against her breast and erect nipple. They looked at each other. She looked into his greenish-blue eyes and he into hers.

The passion that had been building up seemed to explode inside their souls. Slowly, he pulled her closer as she too moved towards him. They locked into each other's arms, and their lips met in a passionate kiss that seemed to last forever, though it was really only a moment. He could feel the beat of her heart and the firmness of her breasts against him as the warm sweetness of her moist lips sent his pulse racing. Desire raced through his body. She could feel the firmness of his manhood against her thigh as they held each other tightly. Filippo pulled away. "Please forgive me," he begged her. "I should not have taken advantage of you like that. I know we have only just met, but, but...I am sorry. Your beauty just seems to have taken over my heart."

"Please don't apologize. I wanted you to kiss me too," she implored. "Please don't make me feel cheap. I enjoyed it too much for that."

He relaxed and then smiled his charming smile. "I'm sorry. You are a lovely woman, and the last thing I want you to do is feel small. I shall remember this kiss forever," he told her. Then he smiled at her again with that big, toothy smile of his, and suddenly the world brightened, and they were relaxed again.

Angelina felt the first bliss of new love.

Holding her hand, he guided her up the stairs to the front door. After all the well-wishes and happy new years from those who had stayed at Nicola Cudoni's family home, Filippo left their house and made his way back to the city center to find his brothers and return to the boarding house.

Chapter 12

The next afternoon, Filippo Cudoni could not resist the urge to walk to the Folino Gallo residence. He was hoping to see Angelina, and with the pretense of wanting to talk to Giuseppe, he knocked on the door.

Catarina opened the door and was mildly surprised to see Filippo Cudoni standing there.

"I called in to talk to Giuseppe and the boys, Signora Folino." Filippo stuttered a little when he realized he must have appeared very foolish as the men would have been at work.

"I'm sorry, Filippo, but all the men are at work today. They didn't have the day off," she informed him.

Angelina came to the door at that moment and asked her mother, "Who is it, Mother?"

"It's Filippo Cudoni, Angelina. He thought your brothers might have been at home," her mother replied cheerfully with a slight grin and a knowing look on her face.

"Tell him to come in. I haven't thanked him for seeing me home last night," Angelina, still from inside the house, happily called out. A few moments later, Angelina squeezed her way past her mother, who was still standing in the doorway. She gave Filippo
a huge, happy smile when she saw him. "Buon Giorno, Signore Filippo. Come sta?" she asked cheekily, still smiling at him. Her

heart fluttered a little at his courage to come over and to see her, she suspected.

"*Bene grazia*, Signorina Angelina. I had nothing to do and decided to say hello to your brothers and your family and you," he told her with a beaming smile.

Catarina excused herself to attend to food on the stove, leaving Filippo and her daughter on the front porch. Filippo reached for Angelina's hand, which she instinctively gave him. He lifted it to his lips and kissed the back of it.

"I came to see you really, Angelina. I hope you do not mind."
"I'm really glad you came," she responded. "I really enjoyed last night."

He smiled widely, and his heart raced wildly within. "It was the best night of my life," he softly told her.

They talked for fifteen minutes about the events of the previous night on the steps of the house; then Angelina told him they should go inside.

Filippo's heart told him to accept the invitation, but he some-how felt uncomfortable going inside. "I would love to, but it might be better if I leave."

"Then you better go before Mother returns and wonders what we are doing."

"Can I see you again?" he asked her awkwardly.

"Si, please call again."

Filippo stood up from the step where they were sitting and looked around to see if her mother had returned. Not seeing Catarina, he leaned forward to give Angelina, who was still sitting on the top step, a kiss on the cheek. He put his arm lightly on her shoulder and around her neck, but Angelina pouted her lips, and he put his lips to hers in what was to be a quick kiss on her rosy red lips. Desire raced through his body at the sweetness of her lips and her sensuality. Her moist lips parted as he gently pushed his lips against hers. In his desire for her, he wanted to pick her up and squeeze her to him, but with difficulty, he resisted the urge and, smiling, took his arm away from her shoulder.

The image of her face and the feel of her lips on his stayed on his mind, and his heart told him he needed her forever.

Filippo and his brothers spent the next few days visiting some of the new friends they had made in Pittsburgh. With Zio Nicola and his boys busy at work in the coal mines, the three Cudoni brothers had time to stroll around the city. With time to waste, they decided to see the barber, Alfredo, and have a haircut.

The front door to Alfredo's barbershop was closed. This was strange for this time of day, and the three young men thought that Alfredo might have gone out on an errand.

"We can walk to the station and call in on the way back." Filippo, a little annoyed and scratching the back of his head, grunted. "If he's not back, then we might miss out on a haircut."

The three men started to walk away, but as they passed the window, Gennaro jumped up to look over the sill. A look of concern came over his face. "Hang on—something is wrong in there," he whispered to his brothers. "I think two men are trying to rob Alfredo."

Filippo motioned for his brothers to follow him and be silent. He tiptoed to the door. On his signal, the three men slammed the door of the little shop open and rushed in. The first thing they saw was Alfredo sitting in his barber's chair. A man was standing over him, holding the barber's shaving knife at Alfredo's throat and telling him he had not paid his monthly security fees. The back of the knife was rubbing hard against the skin on the front of Alfredo's neck, and it left a red welt as it moved back and forth. The other man, who had been standing behind the door with his back to it, went sprawling into the man near the barber's chair and onto the floor when the door flung open and hit him.

The man's gun flew from his hand and skidded to the far wall.

Filippo, who sensed that this was serious trouble, grasped a stool near the door, and in a voice filled with icy contempt, he looked at the man with the barber's knife and said, "One scratch to Alfredo and you are dead. Pick up your friend, and get the hell out of here. Leave—now."

The shock of three men bursting in, along with the tone of Filippo's voice and the fact that his companion was on the floor, temporarily made the man with the knife freeze. Both men were in their mid-thirties and both had dark complexions and long curly black hair. It was obvious they were of Sicilian descent.

Instinctively, the man with the knife moved closer to his friend and the gun on the floor and away from Alfredo. Gennaro had in the meantime moved a little closer to Alfredo, picked up a stool, and moved between the Sicilian and Alfredo. The man on the floor made a desperate lunge for his gun lying on the floor some six feet away.

Alfredo, in the meantime, was trying to find his voice, but the episode had left him speechless.

The man with the barber's knife looked at his friend, who was furiously crawling towards his revolver. Antonio's boot kicked the gun away towards Gennaro before the man could pick it up, and then, doing a full swing on his left foot, he kicked the man on the floor heavily in the ribs with his right boot. The boot made a thumping, cracking sound as it landed. The man bounced off the floor and then writhed in agony, groaning with severe pain with a suspected cracked rib.

Gennaro picked up the gun as the man unsuccessfully tried to get up.

Filippo's greenish-blue eyes seemed to burn a hole through the man's glaring rage as Gennaro pointed the gun at the side of his head. "*Compare mio*, drop it—slowly."

The man let the knife drop from his fingers.

"I don't know what you were up to, but get your stupid arseholes out of here before we decide to shoot you through them," Filippo told the pair in an ice-cold, angry voice.

The one who had dropped the knife looked furiously at Alfredo, who was still in the barber's chair, and, with a nasty snarl to his Sicilian voice, told him, "*Questi sono ignorante*. These stupid idiots will not be here next time. You get double as much money ready for us next time. We will be back." Then he growled, looking at Filippo, "If I was you three fuckin' idiots, I'd be disappearing fast, out of Pittsburgh, back to Calabria if you're not dumb enough to know what's good for you." He emphasized his point with a slash of his first finger across the front of his own neck.

Filippo looked at the man and then smiled. He took two quick steps towards him with the stool grasped in front of him in his right hand. Suddenly, the stool slammed upwards, hitting the man in the face and forehead. The man staggered back several paces but man- aged to stay on his feet. He glared in disbelief at what had happened and at the man who had hit him with the stool. Blood started to drip from his nose and mouth as he rubbed his face with the palm of his hand.

"*Mingia compare mio*, you're going to die," he hissed in Sicilian through his clenched teeth at Filippo. "I'll string you to a tree to rot and cut your testicles out to feed the dogs."

Filippo nodded, seemingly in agreement, but his right foot suddenly lifted off the floor and, with brutal force, landed on the man's pelvis area. The thud that followed made Gennaro wince at the very thought of the pain the Sicilian must have felt.

The Sicilian sank to his knees, his face inches away from the floor as his hands grasped at his testicles and penis. His face turned white as he groaned and writhed in agony.

"I said no threats, *caro amico*. There are a few of us, so next time, you and your friend better bring an army before you come here again, or you will be dead meat. Now, imbecile, get lost. Now," Filippo told him in an icy Calabrese tone as Gennaro waved the pistol in the man's direction.

The first man on the floor had, by now, painfully struggled to his feet with his right arm held tightly across the front of his chest. The man still on the floor tried to speak, but only grunts came from his throat. The other man moved to help his companion. His angry Sicilian snarl sounded ominous as he helped the other Sicilian man out the door. "I'll roast your dead hides to a cinder, you, you sons of bitches."

When the two were almost through the door, Gennaro's boot hit the last man flush in the rear. The impact sent the man forward, knocking over the other man he was trying to help, and both ended up sprawling into the street. Gennaro watched as the two men struggled to their feet and scurried up the street.

The three brothers sat Alfredo down in one of his chairs. His voice was slowly returning. "*Cari amici*, you saved my hide for today, but they will be back. I will still have to pay them. The problem has been that at the start, the money they wanted was reasonable, but now they want more than I can afford. *Amici mio*, those men belong to the Sicilian Cosa Nostra. They kill whoever gets in their way. In Pittsburgh, the Cosa Nostra throws a very long shadow over most Italians, but more so over all Sicilians and most Calabrese."

Alfredo was now starting to relax from his ordeal a little, but his concern for the safety of the three men who had befriended him was growing. "*Amici*, I think it is best if you leave Pittsburgh and go far away from here."

"We came here for a haircut, Alfredo. We are not running away from Pittsburgh," Filippo told him.

He gave them free haircuts a little later, and as he cut their hair, he told them what had happened to the Italian families in Pittsburgh, and in particular to the good Sicilian people.

"About ten years ago, we Italians in this area formed a group to be ready to protect each other from unprovoked attacks from other gangs and thieves," he told them. He went on to explain that a core group, mostly Sicilians, had banded together to show solidarity and strength. In recent times, the Italians in and around Pittsburgh were less molested as the Cosa Nostra dealt nastily with any person con- fronting them. The group started demanding money from their own people to survive; at the start, the fee was minimal, and the members were happy to pay for this security. The demands grew, and it was now at the point where the security payments were really extortion and were sending many people to the wall. They were demanding 10 percent or more of all the members' income. The Italians who refused to pay were robbed or mugged. The Cosa Nostra murdered some of the people refusing to pay the extortion monies to show the others the folly of refusal.

The stark reality of Alfredo's words slowly sank into their minds, and they became more aware of how harsh life could be in the city.

"Si, si, I understand." Filippo nodded as the realization told him they may not be there to help next time. "If they come back here, let the other Cudoni's know, and they will tell us. Maybe we can do something about it when we get back."

The day before they returned to Penn Hills, the three brothers arranged to send one hundred American dollars to the family back home from the post office in Pittsburgh to the little post office in Sambiase, Italy. In Italy, this was a lot of money.

Late that afternoon, they went to see Batiste Raso and his family. Batiste had just returned from work, and he invited them in for a glass of wine. They sat and talked for a short time. He told them that the Folinos had also gotten work at the coal mine where he was, and they sent their regards. Filippo told him to wish them well on their behalf.

Batiste walked to the front door with the Cudoni brothers and pointed out to them the house where the Folinos lived, down at the far end of the street.

The three brothers took their leave from Batiste and headed back to their rooms. When they got to the street that led to where the Folino Gallos' house was, Filippo told his brothers he was going to call in to say goodbye to the Folino Gallo family. Gennaro and Antonio decided they would continue home.

Filippo knocked on the front door of the house, and Angelina answered a moment later. "Just one second," she called from inside the house. Her face lit up when she opened the door and saw a smiling Filippo Cudoni standing there. "Come in. Come in," she said, and she quickly ushered him inside.

Once they were inside, she shut the door and moved over to him. She raised her arms. Filippo put his arms around her, and they kissed and hugged. Angelina did not want to let him go. She ran her hands up and down his back as she clung to him.

"I thought you were going away without saying goodbye to me," she half sobbed, tears of joy rolling down her cheeks. The sound of a boiling kettle made Angelina run to the kitchen.

The sound of the door opening made Filippo turn quickly around. Tomasi, his wife, and their two youngest boys walked in.

"*Buono serra, ciao, toti,*" Filippo told them. "Angelina opened the door for me, but I think she is back in the kitchen."

"We saw you come in from the other end of the street," Sarino cheekily told him. "We met your brothers going home."

Tomasi and Catarina invited him to stay for dinner. He declined, saying he had to go, but when Angelina heard, she popped her head around the door and told him if he left, she would not talk to him ever again.

He shrugged his shoulders and graciously accepted the invitation for lunch, thanking them and telling them not to go to any trouble for him. Inwardly, he could not have been happier.

Angelina had cooked a huge plate of pasta and crumbed steak, and by the time they were ready to eat, Giuseppe had arrived.

It was obvious to all that Angelina was in love with Filippo Cudoni and his charm, and she fussed over him during the meal. She kept asking him if he wanted more food and plied him with drinks. She sat on the opposite side of the table and could not refrain from stealing glances at him. Her mother, Catarina, noticed her daughter's attraction to this handsome young stranger and did not disapprove. Filippo stayed until ten o'clock that night and then took his leave. He wished them well and told them he and his brothers would be back at Easter.

Angelina took his hand. "I will show him to the gate," she told her parents, and before they could answer, she pushed Filippo out the door and closed it behind her.

"Please come back to see me. Don't make me wait till Easter to see you again," she begged him. "I can't think of anything except you lately. I want you to hold me so much."

For a quick moment, they hugged and kissed each other. Filippo Cudoni did not want her to get into trouble with her parents. He knew well the traditions of the Calabrese men. He knew how angrily the fathers disapproved if their daughters allowed male suitors to get intimate with their future spouses. He pulled away and, with one last quick kiss to her lips, dashed down the street.

Chapter 13

From early January to early March 1900, the three Cudoni brothers worked first in Penn Hills and then back at the railway construction sites. In early March, the brothers made a train trip to Pittsburgh one Saturday morning for an overnight stay. The trip was Filippo's idea, as he was keen to see Angelina again.

He called in to see Angelina that Saturday night at her parents' home. Angelina answered the door; her parents and his zia and zio were there playing cards.

She lit up with joy as soon as she saw him and was quickly in his arms. Almost immediately, her lips were on his. The sweetness of her tongue and lips on his was to stay with him for the rest of his life.

"Who's there, Angelina?" her mother called from inside.

Angelina was the first to pull away. "Coming, Ma," she called back, and then she put her lips back to his for a quick moment.

Filippo followed Angelina in and gave her his overcoat. The four playing cards were surprised and pleased to see him. He chat- ted with them for a while as they continued to play cards. Angelina offered him a chair at the table, and he sat down. Angelina was keen to know all about his work and his family as soon as she sat down beside him. As they talked, they secretly held hands under the table.

He could feel his desire for this girl growing stronger by the minute.

Eventually, Filippo told her he should go.

"You cannot go until you have at least had a cup of coffee," she quickly responded. "*Caffe?* Papa, Mama, Zio, *e* Zia?"

Thirty minutes later, Filippo was ready to leave.

Angelina walked out with him to the front porch, and they were able to share a few minutes in private. Angelina put her arms around him as soon as the door closed, and for several minutes, they hugged and kissed each other.

"*Ciao*, Angelina. I better go before your father comes to see what I might be doing to you. I will see you at Easter," Filippo laughingly told her as she hung tightly on to him, one hand over his rear.

Angelina kissed him again before he pulled away. "Come back as soon as you can," Angelina begged him. "You know how much I miss you, *amore mio.*"

Cudoni returned to work the next day. A few weeks after this, he was handed the responsibility of being in charge of a team of men working with bullocks and horses pulling the new ploughs and clearing the way for the tracks by the engineer.

His experience back at his father's farm and his temperament with animals convinced the man in charge to put him in charge.

There was a small language problem, but Filippo's friendship with the engineer grew stronger. The engineer invited him to dinner at the engineer's house near Penn Hills a few weeks later. This particular Saturday, the men had left the work site early to pick up supplies and personal items and were spending the weekend at the barracks in Penn Hills.

The engineer was Jack Benson. He was a third-generation American whose family was originally of English nationality. Jack, who had done a course in engineering, was a hard but honest man in his mid-fifties. He had come to really like and respect Filippo Cudoni as a soft-spoken young Italian who worked hard and minded his own business.

Jack had a wife, Jane, and one daughter living in Sewickley. His two eldest daughters were married. The eldest, Susan, was married to a miner named Bill Dixon, and they lived in nearby Glenfield; their daughter Kay was married to a lumberjack named Jim Morgan, who cut timber in the nearby mountains to supply the railroad company.

The youngest daughter, Tracy, was a teacher at the local school.

Filippo arrived at Jack's house about six thirty in the evening, and from the voices he could hear, he knew they had company. Tracy's sister Kay and her husband, Jim Morgan, had also come for dinner.

In the last seven months, Filippo had endeavored to learn as much English as he could so that he could hold a conversation in English.

Jack introduced him to his wife, Jane, to Jim and Kay, and to Tracy.

"His Italian name is Filippo, but we all call him Phil. That okay with you, Phil?" Jack asked him.

Filippo nodded and laughed. "Yes, Boss Jack, that okay," he replied.

"Don't worry about calling me Boss. Just call me Jack," Jack replied.

Filippo had a thoroughly enjoyable time with the Bensons that night. He enjoyed their company, and he thought they enjoyed his. Their quiet, unassuming nature was a pleasure, and they enjoyed teaching him to speak the American way.

Tracy in particular promised to teach him to read and write in English. She had noticed that he could write in Italian, and she told him if he would teach her Italian, she would teach him English.

On the way back to the barracks, Filippo mused that although they had not set a date, he would, no doubt, see a lot more of Tracy— and he did see more of Tracy in the coming months.

On Sunday afternoons when he was in Penn Hills, he would regularly spend a few hours getting lessons from Tracy on reading and writing in English. These lessons also improved his writing in Italian, and he regularly wrote to his family in Calabria.

Sometimes they went for long walks in the country and often sat with a lunch basket under a tree and conversed in Italian and English. Tracy realized after some time that she was attracted to this handsome young Italian, but he was not encouraging her, and when he realized her feelings for him, he thought he should try to avoid going to places where they would be alone.

He realized that he could easily be tempted to make love to this wonderful, charming person called Tracy. He knew when it came to pretty women he was a weak man, but he could not allow Tracy to be hurt with his weakness.

The pain from losing Maria had faded considerably since his meeting Angelina. He loved the fact the beautiful, tall, dark-haired angel was waiting for him. He realized that it was wrong for him to encourage Tracy when Angelina was constantly on his mind.

He decided to tell Tracy of his past involvement with Maria and of his current involvement with Angelina.

"I once had a girlfriend called Maria in Italy, and I have a wonderful girl here called Angelina!" Filippo started.

Tracy smiled. "I understand, Phil. All is well. No need to say anything more."

On Palm Sunday, he called over to the Benson house. He was surprised that Jack and Jane were not home, but Tracy was. She told him that her parents had gone to see Kay. Kay and Jim had called in during the week and informed Jane that her parents would have a grandchild by the end of the year. Jack could not wait to see his daughter.

Tracy invited Filippo inside. She could see he was a little quieter than normal and thought that something might be troubling him. Filippo decided he should tell her up front what was on his mind, and in his improving English, he told her.

Tracy listened in silence as he told her everything about Maria and what had happened then.

"I have met a wonderful lady named Angelina with whom I am very much in love. I intend to propose to her soon." He told her what a wonderful, charming person she was and how easy it would be for him to fall in love with her, but that it would be wrong of him to allow that to happen. She tried to tell him that it was too late, that she was already in love with him.

He tried to put his finger on her mouth to indicate that she should say no more, but she moved towards him, and he ended up with his arm over her shoulder and around her. She hugged him tightly for a while, and then she pulled her head back so they could kiss.

Instead of a kiss on the lips, he gave her a peck on the cheek. Confused and disappointed that he did not kiss her, she stepped back. "Please, Tracy, I may be going back to Italy. That is why I do not want to hurt you. I cannot bear the thought of you being hurt if I do not come back to America. It is not because I do not care for you. I could love you, but..." he confessed to her in his Italian-accented English.

He could see the relief that flooded her face upon hearing his words.

He can love me, she thought. She wanted to grab him, to hug and kiss him, to show him how much she cared for and wanted him. *But what?* Tracy wondered.

He spoke again. "But, Tracy, I have an Italian girl, Angelina, in Pittsburgh who wants me to marry her. I am not sure what to do. I love her too. I must decide what to do before my brothers and I return to Pittsburgh on Thursday. We will be back here on Tuesday afternoon. I will explain when I return. Please forgive me. It is better I go."

Filippo, Gennaro, and Antonio caught the last train pulling through Sewickley late Thursday afternoon and arrived in Pittsburgh around seven that night. They had sent their uncle a message to tell him they would arrive about eight that night. They called at the boarding house to arrange for an apartment to stay in for Easter. When they arrived at their uncle's place, their aunt had dinner ready for them.

Their uncle also had some good news from Sambiase. His brother Pasqualle's three oldest boys—Salvatore, Severio, and Dominico—were coming from Italy to Pittsburgh. The letter had arrived only two days ago.

The next morning was Good Friday. Filippo walked over to see Angelina and her family. The family was not at home. He guessed that they had probably left to go to Mass, and he decided that it was not too late for him to go as well. The church was full of people when he arrived, and Mass had been on for some ten minutes.

Inside, there was a mezzanine area above the rear of the church, and he decided that he might find a seat there. When he reached the top of the stairs, one of the first people to see him was Angelina. She waved for him to sit with her and made room for him beside her.

He made his way up to where she was sitting. Filippo shook hands with Fiore and then Angelina as he said ciao to both. Angelina held on to his hand as he sat down. She reached over and gave him a peck on the cheek. During the rest of Mass, she hung on to his hand as much as she could.

After Mass, most of the people—but, more particularly, the Calabrians—stood outside on the church grounds, talking in small groups.

Angelina took Filippo over to where her parents were talking to a group of other Italians and introduced him to them.

Angelina saw her two older brothers talking to two girls and three young men and dragged Filippo with her to talk to them. She introduced Filippo to the others. The older girl gave him quite an admiring appraisal and joked he was too good-looking for Angelina. She told Angelina that she had better watch out, or she would lose him. She had quite a sense of humor, but the others did not take her remarks seriously. One of the young men, whose name was Bruno Curcio, gave Filippo a long, curious stare as Angelina hung on to his arm.

The group was going for a walk down to the city center, and Angelina went to ask her parents if she could go as well. They gave her their consent, and she came back to tell Filippo she could go as long as they promised to be back by lunch.

Filippo, Angelina, Giuseppe, Natale, the older girl (whose name was Rosetta), Bruno, and the other man, who was Rosetta's brother, Giovanni, soon set of towards the city. It was obvious that Giuseppe was keen on Rosetta, and soon the two pairs were lagging behind the others.

The group was going to a coffee shop, but as Filippo and Angelina dawdled along, admiring the clothing and goods in the shop windows, they were soon lagging some distance behind. With the pretext of looking at some clothing, Angelina steered Filippo into an inverted shopfront.

Since that first kiss on New Year's Eve over three months ago, she had been thinking of him, and though she had seen him only several times, she was dying to be in his arms and held tight by him and kissed by him.

Once inside the shopfront, they hugged and embraced each other. She could not get enough of him. They kissed for what seemed only a few minutes but was much longer, with Angelina clinging to him as tightly as she could.

They continued to walk on. The others were some two hundred meters farther up the street, except for Rosetta and Giuseppe, who were another hundred or so meters behind the main group. Filippo and Angelina passed a menswear store that had some bright new shirts in the window. They stopped to look at them. Angelina pulled Filippo's arms around her from behind so that she was inside his arms, and as they looked at the shirts, he put one arm around her neck and over one breast and the other around her waist, hugging her against him.

Chapter 14

That Saturday night, Filippo went to see the Folino Gallo family. He wanted to speak to Tomasi, Angelina's father, in private to ask if Tomasi would allow him to court Angelina. It was the Calabrese way that if a man wished to court a girl, he would seek permission from the head of the family—in this case, her father.

Tomasi came to the door, and on the little porch of the house, Filippo asked for Tommasi's permission to court his daughter. Tomasi was pleased for Filippo to marry his daughter, but he had one reservation.

"You have my blessing to see Angelina," he told him, "but you need to know some things. One, I have only one daughter. Two, I do not want her to marry someone who is going to take her back to Italy to live as soon as they are married. If you really care for her, you will not take her away from her family."

"I respect your family very much," Filippo told Tomasi. "I know I am in love with your daughter, and I would never do anything to hurt her, but I will have to think very seriously about not returning to Italy. It was my intention—and that of my brothers— to return to Italy once we had made sufficient money to buy land near Sambiase." "That is something for you to think about, I am afraid. But I do not want you to take her back to Italy."

Filippo had not expected Tomasi to make this point or be so emphatic about it. "Will you approve for me to see your daughter while I consider this situation?" Filippo then asked Tomasi after some deep thought.

"I would be very happy for you to marry my daughter. And, yes, you can see her till you go back to work, but before you go, I want to know your decision," Tomasi told him after taking just as long to consider Filippo's question.

Early on Easter Sunday morning, all of the Cudoni families went to the same Catholic Church. The church was a twenty-minute walk from where Nicola Cudoni's family lived, and it was an additional twenty-minute walk to where Filippo and his brothers lived.

After the long mass on this holy day of obligation, the Calabrians gathered on the grounds outside the church in various groups. The large church had been full, with five hundred people crammed inside, and nearly all the people who had migrated from Southern Italy joined in the festive mood of shaking hands and wishing each other a happy and holy Easter.

Filippo, Gennaro, and Antonio saw most of the people who had travelled on the train from New York to Pittsburgh. They enjoyed the opportunity to renew their friendships.

Although the Cudoni's and the Folino Gallos had agreed to spend the day at the Folino Gallo house, the younger ones wanted to pack a lunch for midday, spend the day at the small park beside the creek running into the Allegheny River, and then go to the Folino Gallo residence late in the afternoon. Finally, the parents agreed. They decided that they would all return to their homes, and each family would bring a basket. Some of the other Italians were also going to spend the day under the trees in the park.

Filippo and his two brothers had purchased a dozen large bottles of good red wine, and they decided to give six bottles to their uncle and aunt and bring the other six bottles to the picnic.

They helped their aunt, who had already prepared some food, pack the baskets. In a short time, she cooked a huge saucepan of spaghetti as well.

On the way to the park, they called by the Folino Gallos' residence. The younger family members left early, except for Angelina and Filippo, who stayed to help. The parents, Angelina, and Filippo then set out for the park. Filippo and Angelina, carrying a basket each, set off briskly and soon left the others behind.

"I know a shortcut, *caro mio*," she told Filippo as they disappeared ahead of the parents. "Follow me."

Angelina handed him her basket, and he carried one in each hand. They walked quickly, with Angelina leading the way, until they could see the river and the park. They stopped under a tree full of spring blossoms. Angelina turned, put her arms around him, and kissed him, with Filippo still holding the baskets.

He put both baskets down and grabbed her by the arm. "Come back here, you little devil, and pay the price."

For several moments, they kissed passionately, and then with one arm still around her, his lips moved down her neck to the top of her covered breasts.

After a few more minutes of kissing her breasts, Filippo had to speak. "*Cara mia*, I better stop this before it arouses me too much."

Angelina pouted and then giggled. "Do you know what would happen then?"

Filippo, smiling, raised his eyebrows. "Let me guess." He dropped to one knee and pressed his lips into her lower pelvis, put- ting one hand around her buttocks and pulling her to him.

The park was between the river and the main railway line heading back towards New York. There were ten acres of land dotted with large trees in the park, and the green grass looked as pretty as a picture. A number of other people from Pittsburgh picnicked there on that day.

The two young lovers frolicked by the river for a while, and it was midday on a pleasant warm spring day by the time they returned and joined the others under the big tree.

Luigi and Natale Folino Gallo, Angelina's two cousins both about twenty, arrived and sat down to eat and drink. The women had placed two large tablecloths on the ground, and the older women then placed the food on top of these. They all squatted down around the makeshift table and helped themselves. The women had done a wonderful job preparing the lunch.

The Batiste Raso family had set up under another tree about one hundred yards away. They had a group of about fifteen, and the Folino families who had come to America with them were there as well.

After the meal, Nicola, Tomasi, Luigi, and Natale Folino, as he was referred to in order to avoid confusion with the other Natale, decided to play cards, while Zia Theresa and Zia Catarina put the remains of the meal away in the baskets.

Michele and Benaldo went for a walk right away after eating. Giuseppe Folino Gallo grabbed only a piece of chicken and left, and his younger brother, Sarino, joked that he and Michele had gone to see Rosetta, whose family was also somewhere on the other side of the park with their friends.

Filippo, Gennaro, and Antonio walked over to Batiste Raso and his family and all the other people who had come over with them on the boat across. Antonio and Gennaro then joined the other young men who were going for a look around the park.

Filippo slowly went back to where the rest of the family was. The two older women had finished putting the food away and were sitting and talking under the tree. Angelina had collected the dirty dishes and was contemplating what to do with them. The older men were still busy playing cards.

Filippo walked over to where Angelina was standing. "We can go over and wash them in the creek," he suggested to Angelina.

"That's the best idea you have had all day." She laughed at him.

Angelina put the dirty dishes in a small basket, and they walked over to the stream. She took her shoes off, pulled her long skirt up above her knees, and sat on a rock in the shallow water.

"You pass me the dishes, and I'll wash them," she told Filippo. Filippo took off his own shoes and folded his trouser legs up so that he would not get them wet. He picked up a dish and handed it to her. She had beautiful long white legs, he noticed as he waited for her to wash the dish. A lock of black hair fell across one side of her face, and she shook her head to send it back to its normal position. As she bent over to rinse the plate, he could see the formation of her breasts. She caught his glance as she looked up, and she laughed and splashed water at his face.

With a grin, he wiped the water off his face. He noticed that from where they were, the people under the big tree could not see them.

When he handed her the next dish, he bent all the way down until his mouth was just above her lips. "You have gorgeous legs," he told her.

She laughed softly again and then, with a cute smile, asked him, "How could you possibly know? You never saw them."

He moved until his lips were almost on hers. "You could show me," he suggested. At the same time, he scooped up a handful of water and then playfully dropped the water onto her legs, near the hem of her dress.

Her instant reaction was to pull her dress higher and wipe the water from her thighs. She really did have beautiful, long, rounded thighs.

"I told you, you have the best legs I have ever seen." He grinned at her.

She gave him a pretend dirty look. "It is probably the first time you have seen a lady's legs," she quipped.

When Filippo reached over to pick up the second-to-last dish, he reached down and splashed some water at her face. Angelina was too quick for him, and the water ended up at the bottom of her neck. With a huge grin on his face, he watched, fascinated, as the water trickled slowly down between her gorgeous breasts.

Angelina, in the meantime, scooped up a handful of water and threw it at him. He did not move as he continued to watch the water trickle down between her cleavage. The water she threw at him landed smack in the pelvis area. Against the light grey of his trousers, a big wet stain appeared in his groin area.

She could hardly contain her mirth. "You have wet yourself this time," she said with a laugh. She looked at him and realized it was not as funny as it had first appeared. The front of his trousers was wet, and it would be embarrassing to try to explain what had happened.

She went to the basket and took out a dry cloth. "Come here. I will dry it for you," she told him.

He leaned over and tried to take the cloth from her, but she pulled away. "I'll do it," she told him. She knelt down and tried to dry his trousers. Having her face so close to his loins and feeling her rub that particular spot with the cloth gave him an instant red face and an erection.

Her huge sense of humor knew no bounds, and seeing his embarrassment, she could not help herself from responding.

Her in-your-face sense of humor was more than he could take. He rolled over in the grass in a fit of laughter. On the bank of the small stream, she rolled over to sit on top of his lower pelvis. Her laughter slowly subsided as she looked down on his face. A look of anticipation and desire took hold of her body. She leaned down and brushed her soft lips over his for a long moment. He put his arm around her neck and pulled her down to him. Then his tongue was inside her mouth, searching for hers as they passionately kissed.

Filippo rolled her over onto her back and lay astride of her. She stopped laughing and eagerly waited to see what he would do next. He was infuriated that she was so up front with him. He wanted to punish her, yet he also wanted to make love to her. Emotion, passion, desire, anger, and frustration ran through his body. He wanted to show her who was the master, yet he knew he should get up and leave.

Angelina was at her most lovable when she was teasing him; it did infuriate him that she could read his every thought.

He pulled her long skirt up to her breasts and rubbed his chin and mouth over her stomach and down over her underwear covering her pubic hair. He heard her small groan of pleasure and desire as he pressed his nose and lips against her soft belly. He was about to pull her underpants down when a call from her mother to bring some water back made them freeze for a split second. Then he helped her up.

"You better bring the water to them," he told her. "I can't come like this. Tell them I am taking a walk or a nap or something."

She got a dishful of water and went back. Filippo lay on his stomach under the small bushy tree and decided he would wait until his trousers dried out a little.

He closed his eyes and, moments later, dozed off. Filippo Cudoni in his dreams could see the hills and mountain behind Sambiase. For a brief fleeting second, he vividly saw a picture of Maria and then the little girl by her side. *No*, his mind repeated. *She is not my daughter.*

He also saw images of Angelina, the woman he thought he now loved, but these beautiful images were somehow replaced by images of Tomasi chasing him with a shotgun and firing shots at him, shouting and telling him he could not take Angelina back to Italy.

Filippo Cudoni's heart was in turmoil; how he loved to be with this woman, make love to her; make her his wife, but...That *but* was that he had told his parents that he would return to Italy. His original dream was that he would make plenty of money in America and then return to buy land in Calabria. He would be the rich returned Americano. No more being the peasant he was back in and around Sambiase.

He had come to accept Pittsburgh and all its smog, but, but no, he could not live here. *I love Angelina,* he kept thinking. *But I want to return to Italy more. I have to tell her, I have to tell her now. It is time I talked straight to her.*

The consequences he knew were that Italian fathers and even brothers would shoot suitors who abused their daughters and sisters. As he dozed, a nasty bee kept landing softly on his face. He suddenly realized that something was actually on his face. He opened his eyes and saw her standing over him, gently rubbing a leaf over his cheek, lips, and nose. He snatched the leaf from her hand.

"Wake up, sleeping beauty," she said softly to him. "Everybody thinks you must have fallen into the river and drowned."

"How long have I dozed off?" he asked her.

"About two hours," she told him with a small frown.

Startled, he jumped to his feet. "Impossible. Can't be," he muttered. Then he saw the cheeky grin come over her face. "If I get my hands on you," he started.

"Catch me first, slowcoach," she quipped as she skipped away.

His trousers had now dried, and he re-buttoned them. He ran to catch her, and several hundred yards away, he did catch up to her. From behind, he wrapped his arms around her waist and pulled her backwards to him. "I have got you now, *cara mia*, and you cannot run away."

"So what are you going to do now that you have me?" she teased him.

Filippo did not answer; instead, he put his fingers around her breasts and kissed the back of her neck. She smiled in anticipation as his lips moved around her neck to her face and then lips. She turned to face him, and his arms pulled her tightly to him. By now, she had one arm around his neck, pulling his face closer to hers. His tongue found hers, and for several moments, they kissed passionately.

He was the first to pull away. He asked her if she would go for a walk with him. They walked towards the city and the junction of the mighty Allegheny River and the Monongahela River. On a small rise over the river, they could see the junction. They could see too the many riverboats that plied up and down the Ohio River and the trolley cars that moved along the countless miles of track that served the city and made Pittsburgh such a large and busy inland river port and railroad center.

The park stopped where it butted up against the University of Pittsburgh grounds, and they turned back once they reached the university. On the way back, they saw Rosetta's family. Giuseppe and Rosetta were sitting under a tree, talking. Filippo and Angelina stopped for a minute to talk to them, waved to the family from a distance, and continued back to their own group. They saw their brothers from a distance, kicking a ball around. A couple of girls were watching and waving to the boys, telling them what to do.

Angelina and Filippo did not join them. They came to a vacant bench in a secluded area and sat down. Angelina could not wait to tell him how much she adored him, and she was keen to know how serious Filippo was about her and when he would see her again. She was in a joyful, loving mood. She kissed and cuddled him when they sat down.

Filippo Cudoni wriggled out from under her. "Angelina, *cara mia*," Filippo started with a nervous croak in his voice. "We need to talk seriously about the future."

Angelina pouted her lips and then laughed. "I want you to, my love, but we don't have to go that fast." She giggled.

His serious frown put an uneasy feeling in her throat, and she stopped laughing. Filippo then made one of the most profound decisions of his life, the repercussions of which he was to suffer for the rest of his life. He told Angelina that he had spoken to her father about them.

Angelina reached over, pulled his head to her, and kissed him full on the lips. The news that he had told her father had made her think he wanted to get married soon.

"I love you so much. I knew you loved me too," she cried with joy as she hugged him tighter. "I can't wait to get married."

With a huge effort, Filippo pulled himself away and stood up. Dumbfounded and confused, she listened to what he had to say.

He told her what her father had said to him about marrying his daughter and taking her to Italy. He told her as gently as he could.

"*Cara mia*, I am unable at this point in time to promise that I will not return to Italy. I am intending to return as soon as I have sufficient money, and I cannot ask you to leave here and return with me."

He again remembered the promise to his parents that when he and his brothers had made sufficient money, they would return to Italy and live there.

Filippo told her, "I do love you, and I have loved every minute of time we have spent together. However, it has always been my dream to return to Italy at some point, and your father does not want me to take you away from your family, so your father has said no. I think it would be better if we did not see each other for a while."

Angelina could not hide her bitter disappointment. She hugged him, begged him to promise to stay with her, and told him just how much she loved him and that she would go to Italy with him if he wanted her to. "But… but I love you. I will go anywhere as long as I am with you."

"*Cara mia*, I love you too, but I cannot keep you on a string, waiting forever," he told her gently. "I promised your father I would not seek your hand unless I promised to stay in America."

Tears streamed down her cheeks. She was one of those people who showed all her emotions up front. She made no secret that she loved and adored him. Although they had only seen each other no more than seven or eight times in their lives, all her new dreams were shattered.

Her disappointment and his knowledge that she truly did love him tore at his heart and almost persuaded Filippo to change his mind and promise to stay. Filippo Cudoni knew deep in his heart that he would return to live in Italy one day, and he knew he could not ask her to leave her family behind and follow him.

Angelina's mind numbly went over what he was saying. It seemed to her that he and her father had cruelly decided what was good or bad for her. "How could you and my father decide what was best for me? How would—" she started to say when he cut in.

"Please, Angelina, do not cry. Maybe after I have been back to Italy, I will not like it and will come back here to stay," he tried to tell her. "Maybe we can get together again then."

This was the final straw for her. The words rolled around in her mind. *Might* and *maybe* meant little to someone who ten minutes earlier had been deeply in love for the first time in her life.

"*Might* and *maybe*," she mimicked him angrily. "Do you think that I will sit around forever on a *might* and a *maybe*? If you love me, you should love me now, not in a hundred years. You can stick your *might* right up your bum, you miserable bastard."

Angelina had never been as angry or disgusted as she was right now. She was in a fit of fury at the manner in which she had been led on, played with, and then scorned. She stood up and glared at him. When he did not reply, she brushed angrily past him and ran back to where her parents and relatives were. He wanted to run after her and apologize, to say that he was sorry, that he 0had acted like a cruel and selfish heel and led her on to believe he was seriously in love with her while knowing he was going to leave her, that he had made a mistake.

He knew his decision had not changed, and even if it had, he knew it would only make matters worse to tell her in front of every- body that he would now think about staying in America for her.

Filippo realized that it would not be a good idea to return to the group. He slowly made his way back towards the city center. He steered away from where his brothers and friends were playing. He knew he had made a total mess of the situation. He also knew that there would be no sympathy for him from anyone. He should have had enough brains to know he should never have led her on. She had been such a lovable, impulsive girl, and he had found her charm irresistible, but he knew he had treated her badly. He knew that his desire and urge to make love and be with her had overruled his head. He knew he had treated both Angelina and Tracy poorly—and in much the same way—and he should not have let his ego and lust rule his head. He also knew that Tracy and her family would somehow be more tolerant of his situation than the Folino Gallos would ever be. He wandered along the streets adjacent to the river, past the train station and the river harbor. On a Sunday afternoon, the city was usually much quieter than during the week, but on this late Easter Sunday, it was almost deserted. A city worker was walking along the streets, lighting the gas street lights.

As he was walking past a narrow dark alley, Filippo heard a call in Italian for help. He stopped walking. He was not in a good mood to worry about anybody else's problems, but he knew he could not walk away without looking to see what the problem was. Filippo took a few paces into the alley. He could just make out the figures of two men fighting. As he walked closer, he noticed that one was old and bald and the other much younger.

The young man had the older man in a headlock as he pounded his face and head with his clenched fist.

Filippo walked a few more paces closer and then called out, "Hey, stop it!"

The younger man stopped to look at the person who had spoken. Filippo's silhouette stood out like a beacon of light in the night against the background of the empty street behind him.

For a moment, the ruffian glared at him, and then with a growl of anger, the man let go of the older man and rushed full pace at Filippo.

Filippo nimbly jumped out of the way as the man charged past. Filippo's clenched backhand hit the man in the back of the neck, sending him sprawling headlong towards the street. However, as Filippo stepped back to avoid the attacker, his feet caught on a paving block that was slightly higher, and he fell backwards, hit his head on the wall, and almost knocked himself out cold.

Filippo's head blurred for a second and then cleared as he regained his full senses and stood up. The man had scampered off, and there was no one about. The old man was gone, and not a soul was in sight. He had a large nasty bruise on the back of his head, where he had hit the wall. He checked his wallet to see if while dazed he had been robbed. He found that nothing was missing from it. He figured the assailant must have been in a big hurry to get away.

When he returned to the boarding house, it was quite dark. He was unsure how long he had been groggy, but he guessed it must have been a few minutes. The back of his head was still sore, and a small lump had grown there, but he was probably in more stress from the scorn that Angelina had shown than the bump from the concrete wall. Neither Antonio nor Gennaro had returned to the boarding house yet, and he assumed that they would probably stay for tea at Zia Theresa's place. He did not feel any hunger and decided a wash and sleep would be better.

The next morning, still with a nasty headache and while Gennaro and Antonio were still asleep, he got out of bed early. He had been unable to sleep all night and had been awake when his brothers had arrived after midnight the night before. They had seen he was in bed and guessed that there may have been some problem but never asked. No doubt he would tell them in the morning if it was serious, they figured.

He decided that it would be best if he told his aunt and uncle what had happened. He thought his aunt at least would understand, and after a cup of coffee, he set out for their place.

When Filippo arrived, he saw that his aunt and uncle were at the back of the house, tending to the vegetable patch. They saw him approaching and waved for him to come to the backyard.

Nicola and Zia Theresa had been discussing what might have happened between them to lead Angelina to return to the group upset and on her own the afternoon before. They knew that Filippo and Angelina must have had some disagreement in order for her to come back alone and so upset.

Filippo quietly told his uncle and aunt what had transpired. They none too gently told him what a complete and utter fool he was for leading Angelina on the way he had if he was not serious about their relationship leading to marriage. Calabrese custom was very strict on why a man would court a young woman, and they did not appreciate him, their nephew, treating their niece poorly.

He knew they loved Angelina as the daughter they never had, and they would be upset to see her hurt in any way. They would know she would be heartbroken over the way he had treated her. They would understand why this nephew, whom they knew so little about yet had come to know and admire very much, had put a stop to the blossoming affair.

Filippo sought their advice on whether he should explain to Tomasi the reason he could not, under the circumstances, continue to see Angelina and why he had already told Angelina it was over.

His aunt told him that Tomasi would understand and that he should tell him man to man the reason why he had called it off with Angelina.

"I think Tomasi was wrong in putting those conditions on you, but don't just walk away and leave it as it is, Filippo. Go to see him, talk with Tomasi, and tell him why you put it off," Zia told him.

Filippo did go to see Tomasi after he left his aunt and uncle's place that day. Tomasi answered the door when Filippo knocked. It was an angry father, not a happy one, who listened to what he had to say. Tomasi knew his daughter was disappointed with both of them, but he was angry with Filippo for leading her on and then dumping her after getting her affections.

Tomasi Folino in no uncertain terms told Filippo Cudoni to never go to his place again. "Se tu vieni qui unaltra volta ti sparero, ignorante."

Chapter 15

For four weeks, Filippo worked on the rail site and stayed at the camp there, but at the end of the fourth week, he returned to the room he had in Penn Hills. Antonio also worked and stayed on the rail site, but on weekends, he returned to either Penn or Pittsburgh. Gennaro had gone back to his job carrying sleepers, but he returned to Pittsburgh every night.

Filippo and Antonio suspected that Gennaro had a girl somewhere, but he had said nothing, and they did not ask him. Filippo had told them that he was no longer going with Angelina Folino.

That week, Jack Benson, Filippo's boss and friend, did not return to work for the whole of that week. Filippo noted his absence. He asked the other workers why he was absent. They told him Jack was ill. They were unaware of what and how serious. He decided he should go see his friend.

Sunday morning, after he finished his chores, Filippo walked over to see his friend. Jane answered the door when he knocked, and she welcomed him in. She told him that Jack was in bed. Jack was having a severe bout of bronchitis, but the worst was well over now. She told him to sit while she checked to see if Jack was awake because she knew Jack would like to see him.

Tracy walked in while her mother went to check on her dad. "Hello, how are you, Phil?" she asked Filippo quietly.

"I'm fine, thank you, Tracy," he replied. "And how are you?"
"I'm fine," she replied as Jane walked back in.

"Jack is awake now, Phil, and he would love to see you," she told him.

Filippo followed Jane into the bedroom where Jack was. He was lying propped up in a single bed next to a larger bed. He tried to smile cheerfully when he saw Filippo, but it was obvious he had been very ill.

Filippo stayed with his friend for an hour. He informed him of the progress at work. Filippo could see that although Jack wanted to talk, he was getting tired, so Filippo took his leave.

He returned to the living room. Jane told him to sit down; she had a pot of water boiling and offered him a cup of coffee or tea. Tracy handed him a cup of coffee, and the two women had cups of tea.

"How is the line going, Phil?" Jane asked him.

"Si, si. Very good. Yes, we are on time," Filippo replied in his improving English.

After some more small talk, Filippo took his leave. "Tracy, can I talk with you for a bit?" he asked before he stepped out.

Tracy followed him to the front door and held the door open for him.

Filippo stopped and turned to her. "Tracy, I have stopped seeing Angelina, the girl in Pittsburgh I have told you about, and I am still not sure if and when I might go back to Italy. I think it is better that you know this," Filippo told her. He was unsure of just what he should or should not say.

Tracy noticed the uncertainty in his voice. *What is he really trying to say?* she wondered. Then she realized what he was saying. "What you're really trying to say to me, Phil, is that you are free, but do not want to be in a serious relationship with me. Is that right?" she asked.

"You must think terrible of me," he replied. "But until I know for sure that I am not returning to Italy to stay, I cannot ask you to be involved with me in any way."

Tracy now understood. He did not want to hurt her by promising love and then leaving her.

"Phil, you need to make up your own mind as to what you really want to do," she told him. "I care for you, and I understand what you are saying. But you must decide in the end."

She leaned up and gave him a peck on the cheek. "I hope you had a good and happy Easter. Bye." She opened the door wider as a sign that he should leave.

The following weekend, Filippo called in to the Benson home to see how Jack was. He was out, but Jane told him that Jack was back to normal and would be at work the next day. He did not see Tracy and did not enquire from her mother as to where she was.

That night, while the three brothers were eating at the local cafe, Gennaro told Filippo and Antonio that he had seen Palmo at the timber yard on Friday. Palmo told him his cousins Salvatore, Severio, and Dominico, sons of their uncle Pasqualle, had arrived from Sambiase the day before. Two of their cousins on their mother's side had also come with them. They were Augustino and Calmino Raso.

The three brothers knew both Augustino and Calmino Raso as they had been near neighbors near Sambiase, and they had met many times at their uncle Pasqualle's place. They also knew that Salvatore and Severio were married, but as far as they knew, Dominico was not, nor were Augustino and Calmino Raso.

The three brothers decided that the following Saturday, they would go to Pittsburgh after lunch to see their cousins and friends.

The following Saturday, they arrived in Pittsburgh at about three in the afternoon. They went to the boarding house where they normally stayed, only to find it was full and could not put them up for the night. The middle-aged woman they had met the first time they had been there directed them to a small boarding house on the next street, run by a Sicilian and his wife.

When Antonio knocked on the door, a woman in her mid-thirties opened the door. It was obvious she was Italian. Before she could speak, a male voice called out to her in a Sicilian dialect from within the house, asking who was at the door.

"Me scusi," she said to the brothers. "Abbiamo personi qui," she called to someone back inside the house.

Before she could say any more, Antonio butted in. "Si Italiano?"

"Si. Siciliano," she replied in her Sicilian accent as she took keen interest in her three young visitors. "What can I do for you?"

Gennaro told her they were looking for lodging for the night and asked if she had any rooms for the night. She informed a man named Geraldo, who was somewhere inside, that there were three men looking for rooms for the night.

A short bald man of about forty-five years came out. Geraldo introduced himself and his wife, Maria Torrisi, as the owners of the guest house. "We ah boughta this ah housa 'bout two years ago," Geraldo told them. "We ah fixa disa housa up ah plenty. You wanta room for ona night? We got ona big room with three beds." He waved three fingers at them. "That costa you one dollar fifty a week." "*Parla Italiano*," Gennaro told him in Italian. "I think it's better than your English."

"Si, si. Parlo Italiano," Maria Torrisi replied in a heavy Sicilian accent.

After cleaning up, Filippo, Gennaro, and Antonio went over to their uncle's place. Their aunt and uncle were home, and they invited them in. The boys had gone downtown with their newly arrived cousins.

Zio Nicola told them that their cousins had arrived just over a week ago and were still looking for work. They had looked at a couple of places, and Zio thought they would probably work at the steel factory not too distant so that they could all be together.

Zia asked them to stay for dinner because the new arrivals were also going to be there for dinner. The new arrivals and Zio Nicola's five sons came home about an hour later.

About seven thirty that night, Tomasi, Catarina, and Angelina Folino Gallo arrived. They had heard that some of Zio Nicola's family had come from Italy, but they had not been to see them yet. They were unaware that the Cudoni brothers from Penn Hills had also come to see their cousins. Zio Nicola introduced the new arrivals to the Folino Gallo family.

Angelina noticed that Filippo was there, but she did not acknowledge him. She gave a big smile to Dominico when she was introduced to him. From her very frosty glance in Filippo's direction, it was painfully obvious to Filippo that she was never going to forgive him for the shoddy and cruel way he had treated her.

Some of the younger men left early and went downtown. This included Gennaro and Antonio Cudoni. There was a band playing at the Pittsburgh dance hall that night, and as Saturday was also a big social night, many people went. The young men were going to check it out. The word was that many young women would be there.

The young Italian men had little or no opportunity to meet young Italian women as there were few in America. A dance night like this was an ideal way to make new friends.

Filippo left his uncle's place about ten thirty that night. He'd had a long discussion with Salvatore and found that his parents were in good health and spirit. They conveyed their love and well-wishes through Salvatore and his brothers. Salvatore said he had been instructed to tell them that they were missed back home.

Filippo went back to the boarding house and walked in. The Torrisis had told them the door would be locked at eleven every night and that they would need a key after that. Filippo had given the key to Gennaro and Antonio.

About ten minutes after arriving, he heard a light knock on the door to his room. It was Maria Torrisi. She told him she had come to check on him in case he needed anything. Her nightgown was almost fully open at the front, and her generous breasts had just the nipples covered. It was obvious that she was aware but unconcerned about her clothing—or, rather, the way it showed her breasts.

Filippo had been preparing to go to bed, and he had only his long johns on.

She walked over to him and rubbed the side of his chest. "*E bellissimo*," she told him in Italian. She picked up his hand and pressed it against one of her bare breasts, which had come out from under her open nightgown.

Filippo pulled his hand away, but he had felt the firmness of her breast. Very embarrassed, he quickly assured her that he did not need anything.

"Just remember, if you need anything, just call me," she said. She puckered her lips at him and then gave him a huge sexy pout as she closed the door behind her.

He locked the door, afraid she might come back during the night.

At two in the morning, his brothers returned and knocked on his door. Filippo thought for a moment that maybe Maria had returned, but then he heard Antonio's voice and opened the door. The two of them looked as if they had been hard at work. Their clothes were dirty and disheveled. Antonio told him not to panic. It had only been a fight at the dance.

They sat at the small table, and Antonio explained to Filippo what had occurred. Gennaro was dancing with a not-so-young American girl when the man who had held the dagger to Alfredo last Christmas tried to butt into their dance. The two soon got into a brawl. The bouncers soon expelled both out of the hall. Once they were outside, the brawl redeveloped into an all-out battle between Gennaro and his friends and the hood and his pals.

The fight did not last long as the Calabrians quickly flattened the daylights out of the other group. The ringleader of the thugs, someone called Ugo, promised they would get even soon or later and then disappeared.

Filippo told his brothers they should avoid going anywhere on their own and said it was possible that the person who had assaulted him at Easter was the same Ugo.

The next day, the Cudoni brothers returned to see their town cousins before catching the train back to Penn Hills. They had to laugh when they saw Fiore. He was sporting a huge black eye, and his nose was red and swollen.

Fiore laughed as well. "You can laugh, but you should go and see the other guy. I bet he's got two black eyes much worse than mine," he said.

Filippo, Gennaro, and Antonio told their newly arrived relatives that if they wanted jobs with the railway, they could call on them in Penn Hills, and they would help them. They said goodbye to all their relations and left.

Chapter 16

For the month of June, the Cudoni brothers worked hard on their respective jobs. They did not see Gennaro during the week while they were at work. Filippo and Antonio were now working on the same site, and Gennaro was delivering sleepers elsewhere. Gennaro was still living in Penn Hills, and his two brothers were returning to Penn Hills on weekends.

Gennaro told them that Palmo had called in to the timber yards and told him that Salvatore, Severio, and Dominico were working in one of the steel factories and living in Pittsburgh.

They received a letter at the post office from their parents that month. It had been four months since Filippo had written to them. In the letter, his parents said that they had been very happy to receive his letter. It appeared it took about six weeks for the mail to arrive, they said, and they wanted Filippo and his brothers to continue to write home. They informed their sons that everyone at home was well and that their younger brothers wanted to know how things were in America.

Their parents' letter explained that the brothers' presence was missed at home, and they asked Filippo to give Antonio a kick in the butt for leaving without telling them and not saying goodbye. Giovanni Trotta, who was the local postmaster, had written the letter.

Filippo had spent some time trying to teach Antonio how to read and write in Italian, and he was slowly able to read most of the letter. Gennaro had also tried to learn and was occasionally attending night school in Penn Hills to learn English. Filippo's English had gone no further since the last lesson from Tracy Benson.

It was now early July, and summer had truly arrived. It was hot, sweaty work on the track, and man and beast were feeling the heat.

The current construction site where Filippo and his gang worked was on a steep rocky hillside. They were laying a new track, cutting through the side of a steep hill. Once completed, the new track would save the train about ten minutes.

The original line had made a half-circle detour, going around this particular rocky hillside in a long, round, downward bend. The line had also dipped down and then climbed back up to follow the contour of the terrain.

Filippo's group was involved in blasting and preparing to cut out the hillside for a track about one kilometer long. This would cut about two miles from the old line. The engineers had decided it would be cheaper and quicker to build around the hillside rather than to blast through. Now, with more time and much better machinery, the engineers had come back to straighten this section of track.

It was hot, dangerous work, and the gang knew that any mistakes could be fatal. It was a fall of some one hundred feet to the bottom of the cliff. A new machine called a bulldozer was being operating on the site to push the rocks over the ledge. The machine had a big blade mounted to the front, which pushed everything in front of it farther ahead of it.

The specialist blasting team set off dynamite blasts in holes that they drilled into the rock, and the bulldozer then pushed the loose rock over the edge. The new machine now moved the loose rock much easier and faster than before when the work was done with men, horses, and the bullocks. However, the new machine was big and cumbersome and was slow to turn. One mistake by the driver, and men and machine would end up in the bottom of the valley below.

The bulldozer cut out the rock from the higher mountainside. This was pushed to fill or raise the lower areas. The bulldozer allowed the teams to clear the vegetation more quickly, and another machine—called a grader—that incorporated a movable blade sped up the time it took to level the new and old sites.

The engineer divided the team into two gangs at the start of the operation. Each team would work in from the opposite sides of the hill until they would meet. They had been working on this section for four months, and the two teams were now less than one hundred yards apart.

Slowly but steadily, the rock mound between the two gangs was disappearing. July turned into August, and the hot summer days were turning into nice, warm, sunny days.

On one weekend, when the three brothers had Saturday and Sunday off, the brothers took the early Saturday morning train back to Pittsburgh to see their relations and friends. They spent the first few hours shopping, buying items that were not available in Penn Hills.

They called in to see Alfredo while they were still in the city center shopping. Filippo decided that he could use a haircut, and while Gennaro and Antonio had coffee next door, Alfredo cut his hair.

Alfredo told him of the things happening around the city. He had paid the extortion money to the Cosa Nostra when they came back and promised to pay on time in the future. This time he said three men had come armed. They had demanded to know where the Calabrians were.

"I did not know those men, but I think they have gone back to Italy," he had stuttered.

There had been some problems with some Italians and the law, and although the issues had mainly concerned the group that called themselves the Cosa Nostra, the problems were not a good reflection on the Italian families. Alfredo had not received any more threats from the hoods who had tried to take his money forcefully that day, but he had also paid some more security money, which perhaps was the reason he, Alfredo, had been let alone.

Alfredo told him a Sicilian man who ran a small fruit and vegetable shop in an older area of Bloomfield nearer to Pittsburgh had been located dead near the river edge. It appeared he had received many stab wounds. The Pittsburgh police had found him a day after his wife had reported him missing.

The Cudoni brothers booked rooms in the same Torrisi guest house where they had stayed in early June. It was a little closer to the Pittsburgh Cudoni's than the place they used to stay.

Filippo was not overly keen on returning there after the incident with Maria Torrisi, but he did not want to make a big deal about it with his brothers.

That evening, they ate early at the pizzeria nearby and then later went over to see their cousins, zia, and zio. The uncle's place always seemed to be busy, and there was always someone coming or going. Some of the younger cousins were just leaving as Filippo, Gennaro, and Antonio arrived.

The city cousins, including Dominico, decided to wait a few minutes while Gennaro and Antonio said hello to the others inside, and then they all headed downtown. Filippo decided that he would stay awhile and then either take a nap or join them. He went inside. Zio Nicola was sitting, propped up on a pillow on a lounge chair, listening to Salvatore and Severio, his nephews, while Zia was still washing the dishes. Michele had left earlier.

Zia scolded Filippo for not coming over earlier and having dinner with them. Zio Nicola waved to him and pointed to his throat. He had a sore throat and the flu, Zia said. Filippo sat on a chair near his aunt and talked to her for a while.

Filippo asked her how the other relatives and friends there were doing.

Zia Theresa was an intelligent woman and was wise when it came to reading people. "You mean how Angelina is?" she asked him quietly.

Filippo nodded. "*Certo*," he told her. "How is Angelina, and is she still very upset with me?"

"Angelina was heartbroken when you left her. She wanted to kill herself," she told Filippo. "For a few weeks, she could not understand why you left her. She did not think it was for another woman. She thought you had loved her as much as she loved you. And I think you did. I think also, *caro mio* that you wanted to be honest and caring but could not resist leading her on before you called it off, and for you to hurt Angelina that way was unforgivable."

"Zia, I did not mean to hurt Angelina. She is beautiful and full of life, but everything just moved too quickly. I still love Angelina, but I could not take her away from her family if I go back to live in Italy," Filippo told his zia.

She gave him some sound advice. "Filippo, if you love her, you will need to make up your mind very soon. If you think you will go back to Sambiase, stay away from her. I am sure she would come straight back if you asked her to and told her you made a mistake and now intend to stay." She shook her head to show her disappointment in him as she spoke to him.

The message from his aunt was very clear. Filippo thought to himself, *don't go back to her if you later decide to return to Calabria, or you will find you won't have any friends here and possibly in Italy.*

Filippo talked to his uncle and two cousins for a while. They chatted about the Sicilian shopkeeper who had been murdered and discussed who might have done it. Filippo said that he would not have been surprised if the people who had been extorting the local Italian people for insurance on security had done it themselves. His uncle agreed.

Zia Theresa made some coffee for them, and after they drank it, the three cousins thought it best to let their uncle rest. They left together and walked down the street. It was still only nine thirty, and the air outside was pleasant. The two married men had no desire to go reveling downtown at this time of night, and neither did Filippo.

They talked at the street corner for thirty minutes or so, and then Salvatore and Severio went back to their lodgings. Filippo took a stroll down towards the city center. He decided to take the long way back to the boarding house as he was not in a hurry to get back. The city was full of life for this time of night. The hotels, saloons, and bars all looked busy. The sidewalks were crowded with people walking along the boardwalk. The loud sound of honky-tonk music could be heard from outside as it emanated from many of the catering establishments. Filippo was tempted to go in, have a drink, and waste some time but decided not to. He did not see his brothers and cousins, but he knew that they were going to a bar towards the other side of the city and on the other side of the boarding house.

He stopped at a coffee shop that had outdoor seating and had another coffee. He stayed there for half an hour, just watching people move about. He was absorbed and fascinated by the many different nationalities that went past his window—local Indian people, Negroes, Chinese, and Europeans. Pittsburgh was indeed a diverse city.

When he arrived back at the boarding house, it was almost eleven. This time, the brothers had asked for two keys and two rooms. Filippo let himself in through the front door. The lamp in the hallway was low but still on, and he had no trouble finding the door to his room. He opened the door, went in, and locked it behind him. The high window was letting a little moonlight in, so he did not bother to light the lamp on the table. The moonlight was hitting the small dressing table, and he had no trouble finding a pair of long johns in his bag.

He took off all his clothing and was about to put his long johns on when a voice nicely told him in Italian that he looked better with them off and would not need them in bed.

Filippo got the shock of his life. *Who and where the hell is she?* He wondered as he covered his genitals. For a split second, he half prayed it was Angelina, but he knew she would never approach him in this manner. Something moved on the bed, and although it was in the shadow, he could make out someone's head, long hair, and shoulders sitting in bed.

"Maria Torrisi!" he said angrily. "Whata the hell are you doing in my bed?"

"Don't be angry with me. I just wanted you and to give you a great thrill for a while," she pleaded with him. "There is no one else, and I thought you would understand and enjoy it."

Filippo put his trousers back on as she gently rubbed the point of one of her exposed nipples.

"Come over here and sit down on the bed," she ordered him at first. When he did not respond and with a sexy look of desire, she implored, "*Per piacere per mi.* I want you."

Filippo was getting extremely annoyed with this patronizing and demanding woman who thought that any man who saw her naked body and large breasts would never dream of kicking her out of his bed. He had a wry smile, which quickly turned into a frown, spread over his features as he realized that most men would not waste the opportunity to give her what she wanted and then kick her out.

He thought of Angelina, Maria, and even Tracy, and to think of Maria Torrisi in the same breath as those women was worse than comparing chicken manure to cheese.

"Before I get really mad, you better leave," Filippo told her, pointing to the door.

She seemed to take no notice of what he had just said and kept waving to him to get into bed with her. "You don't have to worry about Geraldo," she told him as she pulled back the bedcovers to reveal her naked body. The black hair on her head and pelvis high-lighted her olive complexion. She swung her shapely legs towards him and sat on the edge of the bed, facing him. "He's gone to play cards at his cousin's place and won't be back until one in the morning."

As she spoke, she started rubbing her right breast with her left hand and the inside of her right leg with her right hand. The sensuous movements of her hands and body had the desired effect of quickening his pulse. A flicker of desire raced across his mind and body, but it was gone just as quickly.

He walked to the bed and reached down to her with one hand. She smiled, thinking that her lustful dreams were to be happily received. She stood up to put her arms around his bare upper body. He brushed her aside, and with a vise-like grip on her arm, he marched her to the door.

She screamed with anger when she realized he was throwing her out.

"You bastard, son of a bitch!" she screamed at him. "Let me get my clothes. They are on chair."

Filippo turned and saw the dress on the chair. He let her get her dress, expecting her to retrieve it and put it on. She looked at the dress and then suddenly turned, put her arms around him, and started kissing him.

"I want you. I want you to make love to me," she mumbled to him as she tried to kiss and hug him. He could feel the firmness of her bare breasts against his bare body. "Don't turn me away now."

He swore at her frantic attempt to cling to him and wrap herself around him. Picking up her dress in one hand, he marched outside the room with her still clinging to him. When she realized she was outside the room, she let go, and swearing profanities at him, she slipped into her dress and disappeared down the hall.

Filippo allowed himself a chuckle. *What a lustful and demanding woman*, he thought as he locked the door behind him. Worried that she might return and try something again, he jammed a chair under the door handle. *This will be the last time I stay here*, he promised himself.

The next morning, the three brothers decided that they would go to see Batiste Raso before they returned to Penn Hills. Batiste and his family were just returning from church when they arrived.

Antonia invited them in for a cup of coffee, and while the men talked, mainly about what was currently happening around Pittsburgh, Antonia made the coffee. She also brought out a big platter of cakes and sweets for them to eat with their coffee. The boys really appreciated the cake and sweets and complimented Antonia on her great cooking.

Chapter 17

It was now late August, and the work on the connecting section of track was almost complete. Heavy rain over the last two days had put a temporary halt to the work, but on this particular day, the sun was shining, and Jack thought that the bulldozer might be able to finish pushing away the last of the remaining rock formation against the cliff face. The blasting crew had detonated the last charges the day before the rain set in.

The bulldozer moved into position, and the task of pushing the last rock from the cliff edge above the track began.

Filippo and Jack were discussing in a loud voice the amount of bedding sand needed on this section of track. Jack was listening to Filippo but watching and directing the bulldozer driver as to where he needed to clear.

Filippo's attention moved to the fluttering and squeaking of birds that flew out from the cliff face above where the bulldozer was working. The birds swooped down to the valley below.

Out of the corner of his eye, Filippo noticed that from where the birds had come, something was moving. It was a small shower of medium to large rocks. Instantly he thought the blasting and the rain overnight must have loosened the rocks, and the bulldozer had now totally dislodged.

Cudoni knew the rocks would certainly create a rockslide and crush Benson under it as it landed on the rail line.

Jack was now watching the driver and how close to the edge the bulldozer was and could not hear Cudoni's loud warning above the roar of the bulldozer.

Filippo rushed towards his boss and shoved him forcefully away. This sent Benson sprawling onto his back some yards away from where he had been.

The leading big rock bounced off the small rocks that the bull-dozer was trying to push over the edge. One of the smaller rocks bounced out from under the bigger rock and towards Cudoni. It hit Filippo a glancing blow on the side of his chest and sent him flying sideways over the edge of the cliff.

Jack heard the sound of rock hitting rock as he hit the ground. He rolled away from the rockslide and then stood up. He looked to see were Cudoni was and could not see him. He realized what had just happened—that his friend had saved his life at the cost of his own and that Filippo had gone to his death over the edge. The bulldozer driver, in a state of shock at his own near miss, stopped his machine and jumped down.

Jack crawled to the edge of the ledge and looked down. The rocks had reached the bottom of the valley, and everything looked calm and peaceful except for a little dust slowly settling where it had been disturbed. He screamed to the men, who had come to see what had happened, to get ropes because a man had gone over the edge.

Antonio was the first man to go over the edge to look for his brother. Meanwhile, Benson ordered two men with a team of horses pulling a wagon to go back along the track until they could get to the valley floor to pick up the body if he had gone all the way down. Two other men joined Antonio going down the ledge face.

The cliff face dropped almost straight down. At the end of this drop was a tiny ledge. To his utter relief, Antonio saw that someone was lying on this tiny ledge, held back from falling farther by a small thorn bush. It seemed to Antonio that by some small miracle, his brother Filippo Cudoni had fallen no farther."

Antonio scrambled cautiously towards him. He knew any slight movement could send his brother right over the ledge. He worked his way down slightly below Filippo and to one side. He gestured to one of the other men to do the same alongside him in order to try to prevent Filippo from falling down and over the tiny ledge. The other man was to try to perch on the ledge alongside Filippo and tie him with a rope so that if he fell, at least he would not fall to the bottom. Antonio and the first man made sure that if Filippo moved, he would not roll off the ledge.

Filippo Cudoni was alive but unconscious. The tedious and risky task of safely bringing him back up commenced. He needed to be stretchered up to the ledge above. Jack Benson took charge.

It was a dangerous and delicate operation. They knew that any mistake or slip could mean death to some or all of the men endeavoring to bring Cudoni back up to the top of the cliff.

Antonio guided the stretcher with his brother on it slowly up the face of the cliff until the stretcher eventually reached the top.

It took half an hour to bring the stretcher to the top. Filippo did not move. Once Filippo got to the top, Jack checked his pulse and knew that his friend and lifesaver was still alive, but by what slim thread he had survived both the impact from the rock and the fall, he was not sure. One thing Jack knew was that Cudoni had to be taken to a hospital as quickly as possible. Jack ordered the men to carry the stretcher to the spot where the rail line was operational.

Jack had seen enough accidents to know that it was important for his friend not to be moved or rolled over until it was ascertained there was no internal damage. He knew that a broken rib could puncture a lung and that any damage to the vertebrae could cause severe back problems, paralysis, and even death if he was moved without due care and attention. He ran his palm over Cudoni's ribcage and found no signs of internal breakage.

He checked his schedule of trains going through on the main line to Pittsburgh. He calculated that the freight train from Cleveland was due to pass this way at any time. He immediately dispatched a leading hand and two others on the trolley car to pull up the first train heading to Pittsburgh. They then laid some blankets on the other trolley car and, with Filippo still strapped to the stretcher to stop him from moving, placed him on the blankets.

The trolley car was driven along the finished line to a point where it would connect to the main line.

Jack and Antonio could see a train slowing down as they approached. The men on the first trolley car had succeeded in stop- ping the train going to Pittsburgh. They put Filippo into the guard- room and rode with him to Pittsburgh.

Cudoni was still unconscious two hours after the accident when he was admitted into the Pittsburgh hospital. Three hours later, a doctor came out to tell Antonio and Jack about Filippo's condition. "Your brother has a severe concussion from a blow to the head, most likely caused during his fall. It is still too early to tell what dam- age that may have done and whether he will recover from it. He also has three cracked ribs and severe bruising to his side and back. There is no doubt that his physical strength saved him, and if you had not strapped him up as you did, there could have been more fatal damage done internally by his ribs to other organs," the doctor told them.

"How is he now, Doctor?" Jack asked him.

"He is still unconscious," he replied.

"The next few hours are critical. We are doing everything we can, and we hope and expect that he should regain consciousness. We have operated on his broken ribs and cleaned up the internal bleeding. I will be back in a few hours to check him again. The main worry at the moment is the blow to the head."

At five, the doctor came to the waiting room to see them. "Philip is breathing a little better. He is still unconscious, but we think that he should regain consciousness sooner rather than later. "But" he stressed, "you can never tell absolutely for sure. You can see him for a few moments."

A nurse took them into the room where Filippo lay strapped onto a single bed. Bandages covered most of his face and all of his upper body. He lay motionless on the bed.

Gennaro arrived at the Pittsburgh hospital at 6:00 p.m. Antonio had informed him that Filippo had been seriously injured at work and was now in the hospital in Pittsburgh.

It was eight that night before the nurse came to tell them that Filippo had regained some consciousness. The nurse told them they could go in to see him; however, the doctor had told her to tell them he did not want them to talk to Filippo.

She said he was still in and out of consciousness and probably would not recognize them anyway.

The three men stayed overnight at the nearest hotel and returned in the morning to see their brother and friend.

Filippo was now fully conscious but obviously in a lot of pain. The three were overjoyed to see he had his eyes half-open.

His head throbbed, and the whole of his left side from his hip to the top of his shoulder ached like hell. He indicated to them with his right hand as he slowly nodded. He was in too much pain to talk, and with the bandage around his head and chin, it was almost impossible to talk anyway.

Jack squeezed Filippo's right hand. "Thank you for saving my life, my friend. You just hurry up and get better. I need you back at work." He looked at his friend as he spoke. "On second thought, take a few weeks off and get better."

Jack returned to Penn Hills late that afternoon.

Gennaro and Antonio stayed until the next day. Filippo was still in a lot of pain, but at least the throbbing of his head had eased a little. The doctor informed them that his biggest concern was any internal bleeding that might have taken place. He told them that the broken or cracked ribs were mending, but if any small splinter of bone remained inside, then these could cause more damage.

The doctor told them it could be some weeks before Filippo would be well enough to leave the hospital. He suggested that it would be best for them to return in a few days and let him get some rest.

Gennaro and Antonio called to see the Pittsburgh Cudoni's and informed their aunt about what had happened. Zia told the two brothers that she and their uncle would keep visiting Filippo while they were away.

"Don't worry too much about Filippo because we will all go and see him in the hospital," she said. "If you like, come back on Saturday and stay with us for the weekend."

Gennaro and Antonio returned early on Saturday morning to see their brother and were surprised at how much better he looked. He still could not sit up; however, the bandages around his chin were gone, and at least he could now talk a bit without getting too tired.

Filippo told them that Zia and Zio had been to see him every day and that Batiste Raso and some of their cousins had called in the night before.

Gennaro and Antonio stayed with him for a while and then left him to sleep and get some rest. They returned late that afternoon and found that Salvatore, Severio, and Dominico were going in to see him as well. They found Filippo awake but in considerable pain. The throbbing in his head had returned, but the worst pain was in the whole of his side and left shoulder. He was still unable to move his left arm.

The visitors left early to allow him to rest. Gennaro and Antonio returned after lunch the next day. Filippo was awake and feeling his best since he had been admitted to the hospital.

He was for the first time able to talk freely without any throbbing in his head.

"Antonio, can you tell me what happened? I remember seeing some rocks tumbling down the side of the hill above the bulldozer and trying to get out of the way and then falling down, down—is that right?" Filippo asked his brother. "What happened?"

"The rock or rocks that hit you pushed you over the edge, and you went over. Very fortunately, you were caught up in a thicket on a tiny overhanging ledge. Otherwise, it would have been goodbye. Incidentally, you saved Jack's life when you pushed him out of the way," Antonio told his brother.

Gennaro and Antonio stayed and talked to their older brother for an hour, and then they left to return to Sewickley that night.

Filippo was tired and drowsy and drifted back into an uneasy sleep. In his mind, he kept seeing visions of Angelina at his side. She even kissed him lightly on the mouth and held his hand for a while. She told him she would always love him and to get better. He tried to move. He wanted desperately to tell her that he would never forget her, but he could not move or talk.

Angelina did go and see him. She had left work at the bakery early and found him asleep when she got there. She gave him a little kiss on the mouth and decided to wait by his side for a while. She held and kissed his hand as she waited. She could see that he was in a lot of pain and, even in his sleep, was somewhat stressed. She had agonized for a few days over whether she should go see him or not. In the end, her heart had won, but now she had second thoughts. Maybe she should not have come to see him. Maybe he still felt that it was better they did not see each other anymore. She looked around. No one had seen her come in. *What would happen if his relations or mine found me here with him?* she wondered. *What would they say?*

She had been there only fifteen minutes, but suddenly it seemed like hours. She stood up, looked around the room, and then quickly walked out; she almost collided head-on with a nurse coming into the room.

Sometime later, Filippo awoke and found a packet of red apples on the side dresser that he had not seen before. When he asked the nurse who had brought them in, she told him, "I suspect it was a very tall dark-haired young angel who was in a big hurry to leave. She nearly knocked me over running out of here." She let out a small giggle and smiled warmly.

He knew then that it was a live Angelina and not an angel from heaven who had come to see him. *If only she had stayed,* he thought to himself. How much he would have loved to hold her soft hands in his.

Chapter 18

By the tenth day of September, Filippo had been in the hospital for two weeks exactly. The doctor called in to see him early that morning and told him he was happy with Filippo's progress. Filippo was now able to take a few paces at a time, and the nurses fussed over who should be helping him walk.

The swelling on his back and the side of his ribs had started to come down. His ripped skin was mending but did occasionally weep. The tight bandages around his chest required daily changing so that no infection would set in.

His uncle, aunt, and cousins and the Rasos regularly called in to see him. Some of the Folino Gallo family, except possibly Angelina and her parents, also visited. He suspected that she must have been the dark-haired young woman who had nearly knocked the nurse over, but he could not ask to make sure.

On Friday morning, the doctor told Filippo that if he wished, he could leave the hospital the next day as long as he came back every day for treatment. He recommended the small hotel next door so that Filippo could be close to the hospital and could walk back and forth.

That afternoon at about five, he was lying on his bed, staring at the ceiling above the door, when a gorgeous woman walked in wearing a knee-length, low-cut dress and a new pair of shoes. He could hardly believe what he saw. Her long blonde hair had been slightly trimmed, groomed, and permed and set about her face.

She had applied some makeup to her face and cheeks, highlighting her great looks. She looked like a beautiful doll—too good to be true. It was Tracy Benson.

Filippo's mouth dropped open in surprise and disbelief.

Tracy walked right up to him and planted a huge kiss on his open mouth. "I thought I would surprise you," she said. "How do I look?"

"Beautiful. But is it really you, or am I just dreaming?" he asked.

"It sure is, Phil. Anyway, how are you? I am very sorry I did not come to see you earlier. I was to come to Pittsburgh last week for a week's training course, but it got deferred to this week, so I will be in Pittsburgh until this Friday. And this is to thank you for saving Dad's life," she told him, and she bent over and planted another big, lingering kiss on his lips.

"Hmm, that was nice. I loved it. At this rate, I hope they never let me out." He grinned at her. "Can we do it again? Please?"

Tracy gave him another little kiss and then stayed and talked to him for an hour before she left. She told him she was doing a study course at the teachers' college to learn new teaching methods. The course started at eight on Monday morning, and she had taken Friday off to come earlier to see him and also do some shopping and finalize lodging at the college.

Filippo told her it was his last day in the hospital and that he was moving to the hotel down the road, on Penn Avenue, the next day because he would still have to call in to the hospital every day.

Tracy told him that her father and mother were coming to see him the next day. She had arranged to meet her parents at the rail- road station at ten and would then come with them to see him at the hotel.

She gave him another big kiss on the mouth before she left to return to the college.

At nine the next morning, Allegheny General Hospital discharged him, and he left carrying a small bag with his spare clothing. He made his way slowly to the small hotel and booked a room there for the next week. The room he got was on the ground floor and not far from the dining room. Gennaro and Antonio, who were going to bring him some extra clothes, would also be there sometime that day.

At about ten thirty, he went to the dining area and had a coffee while he waited for the Bensons to arrive.

Jack, Jane, and Tracy did arrive a short time later. Jane Benson had not seen Cudoni since the accident, and she was relieved to see that he was now much better than what she was first told.

Cudoni's two brothers arrived some fifteen minutes later.

"Jack has told me how you saved his life, and we are all extremely grateful to you for risking your own life to do what you did for Jack," Jane told him. "We will be eternally in your debt, Phil."

"Do not worry about that, ma'am," Filippo said. "He is the best boss I have ever had, and we could not afford to lose him."

Filippo suggested that they sit in the lounge room and have something to drink. A waiter took their orders and later returned with the drinks.

"It's good to see that you are much better," Jack told Filippo. "If you are up to it soon, I am putting a team together to go to

Canton to do some work over there for two to three months. We should be finished with this job by the end of next week. Just think about it and tell me when you get back. By the way, I have arranged for the company to pay the bill for you at the hospital and for you to stay here at the hotel until you are fit to leave."

The Bensons stayed until twelve forty-five and then left. Tracy told Filippo she would come to see him soon as she was staying at the college. Jack and Jane were taking the late train back to Sewickley.

Gennaro and Antonio stayed and had lunch with Filippo at the hotel. They stayed with their aunt and uncle that night after going out with their cousins earlier. They called in to see Filippo the next day before they returned to Penn Hills.

That Sunday afternoon around five thirty, Tracy turned up at the hotel. Filippo was resting comfortably on his bed when he heard the knock on his door. Thinking it was hotel staff, he told them to enter. He was mildly surprised but happy to see it was Tracy Benson.

Filippo was wearing trousers only. His chest and back still had bandages around them. A few hours earlier, a nurse at the hospital had replaced the old bandage.

"Hi, Phil," Tracy greeted him warmly. She walked over to him and sat down next to him. "How are the ribs and back? Still sore?" She ran her hand over his left arm.

He nodded. "A little, but not too bad," he responded.

Tracy slipped her right hand around his waist, still softly rubbing his left upper arm. "Anyway, I've come to take you out for dinner," she told him, "and I don't want to hear any buts about it. The question is, where would you like to go?"

"For you and with you, I would go anywhere," he replied gallantly.

She smiled at him. "Let's start with dinner first. Let's see...we could stay here at the dining room or go around the block to the restaurant there. Can you walk that far?"

"Of course I can. So we go to the restaurant then," he said.

Filippo asked her how the college teaching course was doing and where she was staying. The hotel was not far from the college, she told him. She had caught a lift on a streetcar, and it had taken only about twenty minutes to get from the college to the front of the hospital. They talked for another thirty minutes and then decided it was time to go.

Tracy took a shirt out of the wardrobe and held the shirt open for him to get into. After she helped him get dressed, they set off.

Tracy slipped her left arm around his right arm, and arm in arm, they slowly walked along the street, around the block, across the street, and into the restaurant. The waiter found them a small table in a nice, quiet, dimly lit corner. There was a quaint, romantic feeling in the place. The waiter took their orders for drinks. Filippo ordered a glass of red claret while Tracy asked for a glass of champagne.

It was more of a Western-type dining place than a restaurant, specializing in huge steaks and helpings of mashed potatoes and cooked vegetables.

The two left the restaurant at about nine and returned arm in arm to the hotel. Filippo asked Tracy to sit and talk, but she said she should go as she had an early start and still had something to prepare for the morning.

Filippo asked Tracy if she would like to have dinner again before too long.

"Sure, why not? I will come Tuesday night about six thirty," she told him.

Tracy walked up to him and gave him a thank-you goodnight kiss on the lips. He put his good arm around her shoulders briefly and gave her a gentle kiss on the lips in return. With a quick good-bye, she left.

The next morning, the hospital's nursing sister gave him plenty of exercise routines to do and, at the finish, changed his bandage. She told him to return the next day for more of the same.

His ribs were no longer stiff and sore, and he was slowly responding to the treatment and exercise. He could now move his left arm to just above the horizontal position.

Tracy turned up at twenty to seven that evening, and they decided to dine in the dining room of the hotel. The meal was not as lavish as the one at the restaurant two nights earlier, but it was quite appetizing. Tracy spent most of the time talking about what she had been learning over the last two days, and although most of what she said was way over Filippo's understanding, Tracy tried to keep it as simple as possible.

She asked him what he had done over the last two days, and he told her about the exercise.

"This hospital is very modern, new, and up to date. It is best to do the exercises recommended," she told him.

"Yes, it is very much modern," Filippo agreed.

"Your English is improving. Are you still trying to learn to write as well?" Tracy asked him.

"I am trying a little," he replied, "but I do not have a good teacher anymore." He looked at her as he spoke and then winked at her.

Tracy smiled as she remembered their days by the riverbank.

"It's getting a little late, and I have plenty to do tomorrow," she told Filippo, "but I want to ask you something. Phil, I might be able to get two tickets to the opera for Friday night, and as I don't know anybody in Pittsburgh, do you think you might like to come with me?"

"It will be my big pleasure, and I would love to come to the opera with you, Tracy," Filippo told her.

"I will call to see you Thursday afternoon about five thirty to let you know," Tracy told him.

Filippo stood up and pulled her chair out to let her leave. He reached forward, and she gave him her hand. He gave the back of her hand a kiss, and she responded by giving him a quick kiss on the lips.

Then she was gone.

Filippo's shoulder and ribs were responding well to the treatment and exercise, and by Thursday afternoon, he felt strong enough to go for a walk down to the river.

He was back by five to make sure he did not miss Tracy, but she was late and did not arrive until after six. When she did come, she was quite excited.

"Sorry I'm late, Phil, but it took me over one hour to get the tickets. There was such a long queue of people trying to buy tickets. You're looking much better today," she added.

"No need for you to be sorry that you're late, Tracy," he told her. "You're right—I am feeling very much better, thank you. You know, you always make me feel better when I am with you. I went for a big walk along the road down to the river this afternoon. Tracy, can you stay for dinner tonight, or do you have to go?" His voice turned soft.

"I was going to eat at the college, but I think it will be too late for that by the time I get back," she told him. "Maybe we can get something to eat and take it back here."

"I know a little place to eat not too far from here. We can have something to eat there," Filippo said. "It's not far at all."

Hand in hand, they walked over to the little cafe, and it wasn't long before they had finished eating. With their arms around each other, they walked back to the hotel.

Once back in Filippo's hotel room, they sat on the edge of the bed, holding hands. Slowly, Filippo pulled Tracy to him, and with his good arm around her, he hugged her tightly. His lips searched passionately for hers. She made no resistance to his advances, and soon her lips were searching for his. They continued to embrace and then lay on the bed for a long while, kissing, petting, and hugging.

Tracy told him she had to study on her return, and the next day was going to be a long day for her, so it was not long before she had to leave.

They agreed to meet at the front of the Pennsylvania Opry Theatre at seven that Friday evening, and Filippo was there by twenty to seven. He had taken a streetcar and arrived earlier than he had wanted. Slowly, he read all the notices about the coming plays and opera singers, and he realized that that night's show was by a European tour group that included a famous Italian baritone.

Tracy arrived fifteen minutes later. She looked beautiful in a new mist-blue chiffon frock, and her blonde hair was in a new hairstyle. The show was not due to start until seven thirty, so they decided to have two drinks at the theatre bar before going to watch the show.

To Filippo, the show was magnificent and unbelievable. He had never seen anything like it in his life. During the romantic early part of the show, he held Tracy's hand in his. She sat on his right-hand side, and he put his good arm around her shoulders at the start of the show. During the romantic scene, he placed his hand around her breast and let his fingers rest lightly there, and he kept them there 'til the interval. During the second half, Tracy snuggled in against his chest, and during the dimly lit scenes, they stole a few quick kisses.

The show was in two parts. It was a romantic yet sad and tragic story of a beautiful soprano who fell in love with a singing lay about gypsy who was always in trouble with everybody but who also helped everybody else. The gypsy was killed by a gang of thieves he owed money to in the final scene. It was a few minutes past eleven when the show finished.

During the show, the drink waiters had been constantly around, and Filippo and Tracy had had a few more glasses of wine. They had thoroughly enjoyed the show, and they were in a jovial, romantic mood when the show ended. They took a tramcar back to Filippo's hotel. Arm in arm, they walked back into the hotel and up to Filippo's room.

Once they were inside, they kissed as passionately and as wildly as they could. Their desire had reached fever pitch. Filippo helped Tracy out of her dress, and she helped him out of his jacket and trousers.

With Filippo lying on his back so as not to strain his healing injuries, they made gentle love.

Tracy went to the college on Saturday morning to pick up all her books. When she returned to Filippo's hotel, she found that Filippo's brothers had arrived from Sewickley and were with him, but she did not see them until after she had addressed Filippo as *cuore mio*. They were a few of the words Filippo had taught her.

Gennaro and Antonio were glad to meet Tracy. They knew she was Jack Benson's daughter and realized Filippo was a little sweet on her. They stayed for a short while and then left.

Filippo had already been to the hospital to have his bandage changed that morning and had gotten back just as his brothers had turned up to see him. They had noticed the happy change in him but did not have time to find out what might have happened until Tracy breezed into the hotel room.

Tracy had agreed to stay with Filippo again that night and had left her gear there. Filippo told his brothers that the doctor had told him he could leave the hospital and that he would be returning to Sewickley on Monday afternoon after he had his final check that morning. He was also going to see his uncle and aunt on Sunday afternoon to thank them for what they did for him while he was sick.

Tracy and Filippo decided to take a coach tour of Pittsburgh for the rest of the afternoon. Pittsburgh was a bigger city than either of them had thought it was, and they took all afternoon to see some of the wonderful sights of the city. Hand in hand, they took a stroll through one of the many river parks.

They returned to Filippo's hotel at six in the afternoon. The two shared a leisurely warm bath in the huge cast-iron bathtub in the common bathroom not far from Filippo's room. While it was a common bathroom, it was lockable from the inside.

Refreshed and in clean clothes, they went out to eat at the restaurant they had been to the previous Sunday night. They dined quietly, both immersed in their own thoughts.

They realized this would be the last night for a while that they could spend together. It was improper for her as a schoolteacher to be sleeping with a man without being married.

In a place as big as Pittsburgh, she could get away with it, but in a small town like Sewickley, it would be impossible. The parents of the children would have her run out of town. Filippo had made no comment to her that he was even remotely interested in marriage. She knew that if he asked, she would jump into his arms. She also realized that they were like a pea and a bean trying to fit into the same pod. Filippo had already told her that he expected to return to Italy at some point.

Filippo's and Tracy's minds were focused on much the same thing. She could love this man. He had an aurora of strength, yet he seemed so gentle and loving. He was different from most of the men she had dated. It was these differences that she found interesting and to be admired. His desire to return to Italy was a worry, but she would learn the language if she had to, she felt.

Filippo felt he could love the warmth of this woman for the rest of his life. She was beautiful—in fact, gorgeous—intelligent, and sophisticated, as well as educated. He was an uneducated Italian country peasant boy with no real means of providing her with the things she deserved. Their backgrounds, nationality, and upbringing were different, and he felt that he could neither change his way of life nor ask her to change hers.

Filippo Cudoni was beginning to like America, but could he live there forever? No. He was a country boy at heart, and his ambition had always been to save sufficient money to go back to Italy and buy plenty of land.

He thought of his cousins who were making America their home. Could he do the same? And what of his parents and the rest of the family? Anyway, where would—or, more precisely, where could—he live that could suit both his parents and Tracy's? If he decided to live here, then it would be with Angelina.

He knew in his heart that his parents would find it most difficult to communicate with Tracy and would therefore distrust her without giving her a chance to prove otherwise.

He knew if he stayed in America, then the girl for him was really Angelina. Nobody aroused in him the same passion, desire, and love as she did. Tracy was beautiful and sophisticated, and she had a great body. Making love to her would be terrific; other men would kill to be with her, and he knew he would too. No, that was not correct, his brain told him. He would kill to stay with Angelina, yet returning to Italy somehow seemed more important.

Filippo Cudoni's inner thoughts were interrupted when the waiter asked if he wanted another drink.

"Yes, please, I would like another red wine. Tracy, would you like another glass?" Filippo asked her.

Tracy, who had also been absorbed in her own thoughts, was slow to hear and then decide. "Yes, please. Make it the lucky last for the road." She smiled at Filippo and the waiter when she realized she had been slow to decide.

Her smile had an instant effect on Filippo. Suddenly the light shone more brightly, and the gloom he had felt a few moments ago vanished. He smiled back at her, and her world suddenly brightened as well. It was their night, and they both wanted it to be perfect. Their desire for each other was not going to be denied—not that night anyway.

They slowly walked back to the hotel a little later with their arms around each other. They made love that night—not as passionately or wildly as the night before, but with deeper meaning and a more somber intensity. They slept in each other's arms for the rest of the night and made love again the next morning. They felt like a honeymoon couple—but without the wedding. They felt somehow fully satisfied with each other, but somehow they did not feel right.

Perhaps they felt a touch of recrimination or maybe just sadness at having to continue to live apart, but when Tracy left, it was in a somber, sad mood. Both had tears in their eyes when they hugged and kissed before Tracy left to board the train back to Sewickley.

"I will cherish and treasure you in my heart and memory forever," Filippo whispered to her as they hugged quickly for the last time before she boarded the train.

She left with tears streaming down her face. She knew that the night before might have been the last time they would make love to each other. That night, she confided to her mother, whom she felt very close to, everything that had happened between her and Filippo. Her mother comforted her, saying, "Whatever will be, will be."

Chapter 19

The job at Canton took until mid-December. Both Filippo and Antonio transferred to Canton, and although Antonio made one trip back to Pittsburgh, Filippo stayed there full-time. Jack Benson, whose specialty was clearing difficult, rocky terrain, was in charge. This particular task was to put a pass through a small, low, rocky ridge. With the new machinery and better blasting methods, the job took just eleven weeks.

Jack Benson was an astute judge of people. He knew his daughter Tracy very well, and he had come to know Filippo Cudoni well also. He sensed there had been something between them on a personal level—how much and how personal, he was not sure. He knew that whatever it had been, something had eroded it away. On his last trip home, Tracy had told him that she was transferring to a larger school in Pittsburgh at the beginning of the coming year in order to expand her teaching capability and knowledge.

Jack mentioned this to Filippo, whose short reply was "Wish her the best of luck for me, Jack."

Neither Filippo nor Antonio cared to stay in Canton, and as soon as the job was finished, they transferred back to Penn Hills. From there, they asked Jack if they could work out of Pittsburgh.

Gennaro had already transferred from the railroad to the timber mill, which supplied the railroad with sleepers and timber. He also delivered timber to Pittsburgh customers. With the amount of building going on in Pittsburgh, he was working out of Pittsburgh almost full-time and travelling between there and the main timber supply mill in Penn Hills.

That Friday, Jack told Filippo and Antonio that a major realignment of the existing railroad line just west of Greensburg was to be constructed. This new work consisted of building a new bridge and then laying some five miles of new track, plus cutting a new pass over and through a large ridge and following this ridge back to the main rail- road. The realignment would cut some twelve miles of distance from the current line. His superiors had put Jack in charge of this job, and he would have a say in bringing a gang together to do the work. He had recommended the gang he already had.

Jack told Filippo and Antonio that the men were to live in Pittsburgh but would work out of Greensburg during the week. He and his wife would also relocate to Pittsburgh if he took the job. The company would give him a house in Pittsburgh. The men would have barracks in Greensburg, but if they wished to live in Pittsburgh on weekends, they would have to organize their own accommodations. Weather allowing, work would commence in January. Jack asked them to let him know of their decision as soon as possible.

That night, the two brothers decided that they would transfer to the new job and stay at the boarding house in Pittsburgh where Gennaro was staying when they were in town. They also decided that they would relocate to Pittsburgh as soon as possible if Jack was taking the job and wanted them on the team.

Saturday afternoon, Filippo and Antonio went over to Jack's place to inform him that they were ready and happy to go to the new job.

Filippo spoke to Tracy on the Sunday morning that the gang going to Dayton had left. She had come to the station with her mother to see her father off. Tracy and Filippo had gone for a short walk away from the others to have a talk. Both had found that denial of the yearning for each other was frustrating and intolerably painful. However, both were inwardly strong people, and they had agreed that what had happened between them should in their memories for the time being. They had departed as good friends, and Tracy had given him a kiss on the cheek before he boarded the train.

When Filippo and Antonio arrived at the Benson house to tell Jack that they would go to Greensburg, they found that only Jane and Tracy were home. Jane and Tracy welcomed them inside. Jack, they said, had gone to see the bulldozer driver to make certain he was ready and willing to go to Greensburg as well. Jane said he had left about an hour earlier and should be back soon.

Tracy told the two brothers that she was transferring to a bigger school in Pittsburgh and that she hoped her parents were going to Pittsburgh as well. Jane said she was looking forward to living in a larger city after living in a small town like Penn Hills.

Jack arrived home a short time later, and seeing Filippo and Antonio there, he smiled and wagged a finger at them. "You better say yes." He grinned at them.

For all his toughness at work, he really was a nice person at heart. It seemed to Filippo the rest of the family members were just as nice. Filippo mentally reminded himself that he would never do anything to hurt this family.

Filippo turned to him with a slight frown on his face.

"Huh, Boss, uh, we really don't thinka we can, but uh, uh, say, uh, no." He laughed as he spoke and grinned at Jack. "How could we say no to a bossa lika you?"

Jack turned the wagging finger into a fist and waved it at him. "Don't you bloody well frighten me like that," he told them sternly. Then he laughed, and everyone joined in. "I'm really glad you two are coming."

Antonio told the Bensons that they would be leaving for Pittsburgh the next day and spending Christmas with their relations there. Jack replied they would be in Pittsburgh about the fourth day of January and would see them at the works depot in Pittsburgh on the seventh.

"I will be in Pittsburgh on the second, but at this point, I'm not sure where I will be staying until Mum and Dad know where they are staying," Tracy told them, looking at Filippo.

Antonio shook hands and wished Jack and his family a merry Christmas and a happy new year. "You hava a gooda Christmas anda new year."

Filippo also shook hands with Jack and gave him a hug and a pat on the back.

"All the besta for Christmas and a happy new year, Boss. Take care," he said, and then he turned to Jane. She reached out to shake hands. He took her hand and kissed the back of it. He put his left arm around her shoulders and gave her a quick kiss on the cheek. "You are just like my own mama," he told her, and with his right arm, he pulled Tracy to him as well. He planted a big kiss on her cheek as well. "The besta schoolteacher in the world, and I lova you both. My very best wishes to you both for Christmas and a happy new year." He gave them a peck on the cheek each, and then with a nod to Jack, he walked out, following his brother.

Jack walked out to the front yard with them, leaving Jane and Tracy inside. Jane put her arm around her daughter as Filippo walked out the door.

"I understand what you mean. At heart, he is a great guy," she said. "I am sure your dad and I would love him as a son-in-law, dear, but who knows—maybe one day."

Chapter 20

The Cudoni brothers spent Christmas Day 1901 and most of the night at Zio and Zia Cudoni's place. The Folino Gallo family, including Luigi and Natale, were there as well. Both Giuseppe and Michele were there during the day, but late in the afternoon, Giuseppe went to see Rosetta, and Michele went to see his fiancée, a girl Filippo had not met.

They had lunch under the veranda at the back of the house. Although it was winter, it was not that cold during the day. Filippo and some of the young men helped the women put the leftover food and dishes away. Nicola took out his bagpipe while Tomasi went and picked up the squeeze box he had brought with him, and together they played some soft Calabrese music. The younger men sat around and talked, mainly about the demands of the Cosa Nostra in and around Pittsburgh. Benaldo and Palmo stated that they had heard at work that the group had connections to other groups in New York and Chicago. The Cudoni's decided that if any threats were made by the Cosa Nostra against any one of the Cudoni's, that person should contact all the others.

Angelina was, of course, also there and at first avoided Filippo by staying in the kitchen, drying the dishes. While the others sat out- side talking, Filippo went inside. He had waited for an opportunity to speak to her when she was on her own, and when the older women went out to the back of the yard, he went into the kitchen.

"Angelina, can I talk to you for a bit?" he asked her.

She was about to tell him off, but something in his tone made her hesitate. "Yes, what about?" she said in a dull, flat voice.

"I wanted to thank you for coming to see me when I was in the hospital. I'm truly sorry I was not awake," he regretfully said to her.

Angelina's cheeks turned pink with embarrassment at the recollection of that moment. She regretted going to see him, but worse still was for him to have found out. "I-I-I never came to see you," she sputtered.

Filippo politely cut her off. "I know it was you. Please, I know I did not deserve it, but I really did appreciate that you did come. If one day you can forgive me for what I did to you, please forgive me, and if you ever need help, just call me," he begged of her, and then he gave her a smile and a wink. "The nurse saw you, and anyway, thanks for the apples. Every time I ate one, I remembered those beautiful, long white legs." He turned and went back to where the other men were.

Angelina's heart did a complete circle. His sincere consideration and charm in thanking her had made her heart flip and awakened in her a slight desire for him, but his flippant remark about her legs was a message that she should not consider him for any serious relation- ship. The stinging retort she had ready for him died in her throat as she realized it was his way of saying that nothing had changed and that he was not ready to make a commitment. For them, life was to remain as it was before.

After the women finished cleaning, they joined the men, listening to the music and sometimes joining in the tarantella and other Italian dances. Angelina joined in the dancing as well. She was quick on her toes and was an extremely good tarantella dancer. It was great to see the way in which she skipped from one foot to the other. Filippo played a few tunes on the bagpipe, but he did not do any dancing.

Christmas passed, and it was now time for the New Year's Eve party downtown. The party was not as huge as last year's, but nearly as many people turned up as the previous year. There was singing and dancing in the city center and a fireworks show at the stroke of midnight. All the Cudoni's were there other than the married ones.

Giuseppe and Rosetta were there, and Filippo and his brothers met Michele's fiancée, Marietta Zappalla, for the first time. She was an honest-looking young girl who seemed very down to earth. She was the sort of girl who would make some lucky young man a great wife.

Some of the boys decided to go to one of the local dance halls and party 'til the early hours of the morning. Salvatore, Severio, Calmino and Augustino Raso, and Filippo decided that they would go home and have an early night.

The job at Chestnut Ridge was due to commence on January 14, 1901, but due to a blizzard and some heavy snowfall in the high country during the week leading to January 7, the job was delayed for several weeks. The crew organized for that realignment work was stuck in Pittsburgh. The area supervisor asked Jack to carry out repairs and maintenance work on existing tracks in and around Pittsburgh until the weather cleared.

Jack and his wife were given a nice house to live in by the Pennsylvania Railroad Company; this was on the eastern side— the Bloomfield side—of Pittsburgh. It was less than three miles from the main station, but only about one and a half miles from the works depot. Tracy was now living with her parents. The location also suited her as she was close to the school where she taught. Their house was also close to all the educational centers located in Pittsburgh.

The three Cudoni brothers lived in a boarding house nearer to the center of town and not too far from Bloomfield. They were a little farther from the works depot.

Every morning at six, they would make their way to the railroad station. Gennaro would go to the passenger section, while Antonio and Filippo would join the rest of the crew at the works depot and would set off from there on a trolley car to whatever site they were working on. Filippo was in charge of this work gang. This usually consisted of about seven to eight men, and he was in charge as the head ganger. Jack would sometimes go out if any special work needed his attention.

Filippo and Antonio would normally return to the Bloomfield works depot by six o'clock at night. The hours were long and the work was hard, but the pay made it all worthwhile. The three brothers were quite frugal in their living and saved most of the money they earned.

In mid-February 1902, Filippo and Antonio, together with the rest of the construction crew, moved to Greensburg. This was a much bigger job than the last few jobs the crew had carried out. Thirty men were recruited from the Greensburg area to help complete the work on schedule.

Jack had estimated that the job would take about eight months with the extra men. Besides, he had needed experienced bridge builders to carry out some of the work. The bridge spanned a small tributary creek of the Loyalhanna Creek, east of Greensburg. While some guards camped on site, the main crew stayed in Greensburg.

During March, two more cousins of the Cudoni brothers arrived from Calabria. They were Severio and Bruno Mercurio, whose mother was a sister to their mother, Rosaria. Gennaro found them at Zio Nicola's place one night while visiting there after work. He talked to them for some time and then left.

The two brothers and their cousin later found work at the Pennsylvania coal mine where some of Zio Nicola's boys also worked. Filippo and Antonio did not return to Pittsburgh until the Wednesday night before Easter. They had a week off for Easter and decided to return and spend it with the rest of their relations. Gennaro informed them that night that Severio and Bruno Mercurio and their cousin Nicola Raso had come to America, and they were in Pittsburgh working in one of the mines.

The next day, Filippo and Antonio went over to see their zia Theresa. As Thursday was still a workday for most people, the rest of the family members were at work. Zia was on her own, busy washing her men's dirty work clothes. She was glad to see Filippo and Antonio, whom she had not seen for several months. She said that Nicola had received a letter from his brother Bruno and his family back in Sambiase. Zio Bruno had three boys and three girls back home, and two of his boys were keen to find out how things were in the New World. Bruno had asked for Zio Nicola's opinion on whether he should allow his two boys to come to America or not.

She said that Zio Nicola wanted to ask Filippo for his opinion.

While Zia did the washing, she talked and listened to her nephews' thoughts about this new land. She sensed that both of them were not happy here and badly missed their family back home. She already knew that was the main reason that Filippo and Angelina had split up. She thought that Gennaro was the one most likely to stay in America.

"That's the main reason that you stopped seeing Angelina. It is because you still want to return to Sambiase. Am I right?" she asked him.

"That's right, Zia. I truly did love Angelina. And although she's a headstrong young lady, if we lived in Italy, I would marry her today," he replied.

"What about you, Antonio? Do you have any girlfriend here, or do you want to go back to Italy as well?" she asked Antonio.

"Zia, I like everybody here very much, but my heart is still back in Calabria. I don't think I would stay here forever," Antonio replied. "I still miss my little brothers back home." He paused a while. "I particularly miss Giovanni and Giuseppe and little Theresa." He did not mention a certain young lass in Marseille.

"I understand," Zia said. "If your family was here like mine, I think that maybe you would stay."

"I think that maybe you could be right," Filippo said.

On Good Friday, Filippo and Antonio went to see Severio, Bruno, and Nicola Raso at their boarding house. It was about half a mile away from their boarding house, and they found the new arrivals were still in. Calmino and Augustino Raso were also visiting them. They had all been the best of friends in their young days, being cousins and growing up in the same area, but they greeted each other cordially. It had been nearly three years since they had last seen each other.

Severio and Bruno were both married. Severio had a baby girl nearly one year old, while Bruno had been married only six months. Both were unhappy about the economy back home and the lack of opportunity to earn a decent living in Calabria. Both resented the fact they had to come to America to get ahead, but at home, they had little or no possibility of providing for their families.

They brought news that the Cudoni family was well and sent their regards to their sons and brothers and all their other relations.

Filippo asked Severio how Maria Pasqualle was, and Severio told him that she now had two little children.

They talked for another hour, mainly about the hard work and the long hours. It appeared to all of them that the pay in America was roughly equal to about three times the pay in Calabria, not that work in Calabria was available. Severio told them that many men from Calabria were talking of going to America to work and to make money.

Filippo and Antonio then went to see the other Cudoni men. Gennaro, Benaldo, Palmo, and Santo went into town. Filippo and Antonio went inside and talked to their zio and zia. Zio Nicola asked Filippo if he had thought any more about what his aunt had spoken to him about the day before.

"Zio, I see it this way. If one is wishing to start a new life in a new country with plenty of opportunity, then America is the place to come and live. If one wants to come here and is prepared to work hard and make some money, then he should, but if he does not want to work, then it is better to stay in Sambiase. They all have to decide for themselves," Filippo told them.

Antonio nodded in agreement. "It's not easy work, but if you want to get ahead, America will give you a great opportunity to do so."

Zia Theresa asked the brothers to spend Easter Sunday with them and the boys. If the weather was good, she said, they could go to the park again; otherwise, they could meet at the house. Filippo accepted and said they would bring the wine.

Easter Saturday night, the three brothers met with the rest of the unmarried Cudoni's, Folino Gallos, and Nicola Rasos in the city center. Some of the men wanted to go to the strip area, and eventually they went to the High T Saloon first and had a few drinks there. There was promise of a great floorshow to come, so they waited for it. The show went on at nine o'clock, and it lived up to their expectations.

An array of beautiful dancing girls with great costumes had the audience on the edges of their seats for most of the time.

Although most of the audience was male, it was not a raunchy show—but not the next show. This show was for the men only. The female dancers showed plenty of flesh, and the erotic dancing had the men panting for more. A well-proportioned blonde woman took off her panties, but to the dismay of the aroused men, she had a smaller pair on. She threw the first pair into the crowd. Gennaro was the man with the dubious honor of catching them.

They stayed there drinking and watching the dancing girls until midnight. Filippo was becoming bored with this kind of entertainment and told the others he was going back to the boarding house.

"I'm a family man at heart, and this I'm getting tired of," he offered as an excuse. He had tried comparing the dancers with Tracy and Angelina, and the dancers were a poor second best.

The next day, the three Cudoni brothers went over to their uncle's place. The weather, which had been miserable and wet, appeared to clear a little by midmorning; however, it did not totally clear away, and they decided to stay home for lunch. The Folino Gallos were coming that night, and there was no point in going to the park, getting wet, and having to rush back anyway.

That afternoon at about five, the Folino Gallo family arrived. Michele was missing, but in his place was Bruno Curcio, whom the Cudoni brothers had met the previous Easter. Salvatore, Severio, and Dominico Cudoni also arrived some fifteen minutes later.

Zia Theresa had prepared a huge meal for everybody, and her sons had set tables in the dining room and in the open area at the back of the house. The older members stayed in the dining room while the younger ones ate in the back.

Angelina, with Bruno Curcio hanging around her skirt tails, went to the back. Filippo decided that it would be better for him t o stay with the group in the dining room, but when he went, there were no vacant chairs in the dining room, and he was obliged to sit with the younger group. He had to sit at a table slightly opposite to Angelina, who still had Bruno alongside her. Angelina was up most of the time, helping her aunt carry food and things to the tables.

Angelina pointedly avoided any contact with Filippo, but, as if to spite him, she was all smiles for Bruno Curcio, who at times could not resist a gloating glance in Filippo's direction. Filippo choose to ignore him.

The early night was pleasant enough, but with the threat of more rain and a chilly breeze showing signs of becoming worse, everyone left early in the night.

Chapter 21

The coal mine where most of the Italians worked now operated two eight-and-a-half-hour shifts, with the first shift commencing at 6:00 a.m. and the night shift at 3:00 p.m. Each shift allowed a half-hour break for lunch halfway through the shift and a five-minute break for changeover at 2:55 p.m. This shift finished at midnight.

The work in the coal mines was physically hard and demanding. The night-shift hours of work were also demanding on the wives and children of the married men whose families were with them. Most of the Italian men working in the area had left their wives and families back in Italy. Those who had taken their wives with them lived with the constant worry that while they were at work, their workmates on the other shifts who had no wives would be pestering someone else's wife for sex.

Several brothels were operating on Pittsburgh's main strip, one by the Cosa Nostra, but this was not enough to stop some of the violent arguments that erupted at times between even supposedly the best of friends over women.

One Wednesday morning, Filippo was in his room writing a letter to his parents back home when screaming from a woman and a man shouting threats in Italian invaded the previously peaceful morning. The shouting and screaming reached fever pitch. Filippo put down his pen and raced up the flight of stairs to the floor above. The door to the room that the din was coming from was open, and Filippo walked in.

A man in his mid-thirties was wielding a knife and stalking a dark but good-looking younger man, who was completely naked, around a table. The younger man was bleeding profusely from several knife wounds and trying desperately to keep away from the man with the knife. A young dark-haired woman in her mid to late twenties, also completely naked, was lying on the floor near the door to the bedroom. She was slowly trying to get up. Her long disheveled dark hair barely covered her shoulders and her bare breasts. It was obvious that the man with the knife had caught the pair making love. There was no doubt that he intended to kill the naked man and possibly the woman as well.

Filippo took a pace into the room, calling to the man with the knife to stop. "Hold it—stop!"

The enraged man with the knife stopped in his tracks at the sound of Filippo's voice and turned towards Filippo. "Get the hell out of here, *paesano*, before I kill you as well!" he screamed at Filippo. Filippo took another step towards the man, who started to wave the knife towards him and screamed again for Filippo to get lost. The naked man moved painfully to a chair and, picking up the heavy wooden chair, watched horrified and half dazed as Filippo took another step towards the angry man, thus distracting him further. The younger man smashed the chair against the head and shoulders of the would-be assassin. The enraged man collapsed to the floor; the blow almost knocked him out cold. He fell several times as he tried to stand up.

Several other people had now gathered at the door, and some had seen what had occurred. The naked man staggered into the bed- room and attempted to put his trousers on. He slipped on his own blood and fell to the floor. He staggered to his feet but passed out before he had his pants completely on and fell awkwardly to the floor.

Filippo walked over to the bed, pulled up a sheet, and spread it over the woman, who was bleeding from a split lip. A huge red bruise was spreading over her right eye and cheek, and blood was seeping from a cut above that eye.

The owner of the boarding house walked into the room. He told those present that he had sent for the police and was sending for a doctor as well. He asked Filippo to wait with him until the police arrived, just in case the man should start trouble again. He told Filippo and those who waited that the woman was married to the man who was dressed, but she obviously had been having an affair with the naked man.

Some fifteen minutes later, two Pittsburgh policemen arrived, and they took over. A doctor arrived a few minutes later. One of the policemen asked Filippo what had happened. He told the police in his poor English what had occurred, and the owner of the boarding house confirmed much the same thing.

The knife-wielding man was regaining his senses, and he started to curse and scream again. One of the policemen put handcuffs on him while the doctor announced that the other man needed to be taken to a hospital to be treated for knife wounds and loss of blood. The sobbing woman was now sitting in a chair and complaining that her husband was going to kill them both. She kept babbling that it was okay for him to screw around but not for her to do the same. "Anyway, why wasn't he at work? He shouldn't have been home until after three this afternoon," she kept repeating.

Filippo went back to writing his letter, but the incident had left him with the sobering and sour thought that it was not a good idea for a husband to leave a young wife cooped up in a boarding house all day while he went to work. In many growing wild towns like Pittsburgh, with a shortage of women, keeping a woman at home with little to do was just asking for trouble to occur.

Later in the day, he went to the post office to post the letter. He included some money in it to his parents and family back in Sambiase.

That afternoon, Filippo and Antonio were sitting in their room talking when a knock sounded on the door. Antonio opened the door to find two burly Italian men standing there. One of them asked in a heavy Sicilian accent, "Are you one of the Cudoni men working in Pittsburgh?"

"Si," Antonio replied. "I am Antonio Cudoni, but I do not work in Pittsburgh. What can I do for you? Would you like to come in?"

The two men scowled at Antonio but followed him into the room.

"My brother Filippo," Antonio said, pointing to Filippo. "I did not get your name."

The one who had spoken before did the talking. "You don't need our names. We are from the Cosa Nostra, and we look after all the Italians living and working around Pittsburgh. We understand that you and your brothers live and work here. Our group is responsible for your security, and to carry this out, we charge everybody who has a job a commission equal to 10 percent of their income. We calculate that you three brothers are in arrears to about fifty dollars each. We want payment by the end of week."

Filippo was still sitting on the bed. He had not yet spoken. A blanket was over his knees. He had his hands under the blanket and around what appeared to be a long rifle or shotgun. One hand appeared to be on the trigger of something.

"With due respect to you, sir, we have not asked for any protection, nor do we want any from you or your group. Nor do we wish to pay you any money you claim we owe you. We have our own group and do not need yours. Please leave us alone, and we will leave you alone," Filippo told him matter-of-factly with no sign of any intimidation. There was, however, a hint of mockery as he raised his eyebrows towards the heavens.

The man who had done all the talking scowled, laughed, and then took a few steps towards Filippo. "*Ma sei propio ignorante.* We didn't ask you if you wanted to pay or join, arsehole," he snarled at Filippo. "We are telling you. You will both pay, or we will smash your stupid heads all the way back to Calabria. Now you have one week to pay. *Comprendi*? We will be back on Friday."

The man raised his right arm to reach inside his jacket as he spoke. Filippo reacted instantly. He stood up and pointed the blanket with what looked like a shotgun inside it straight at the man's head.

"Steady, steady, *compare mio*. Put your hand down. You will not be collecting anything but a head full of shotgun pellets. Your arsehole friend might just collect what is left of your head if he still has his. *Comprendi*? The next time you try to blackmail any Cudoni's to pay you shit money, you better bring an army,"

Filippo Cudoni told him coldly as he solidly jammed the pointed end of the blanket into the man's pelvis. As the man doubled over in agony, Filippo pointed the gun at the other man's abdomen.

Antonio stepped forward one pace towards the man who was doubled over in pain. He slammed down his closed fist on the man's head. The man fell in a heap to the ground, groaning in pain. Antonio reached into the man's coat and pulled out a revolver. He twirled it in a small arc and then, laughing, pointed it at the man who was still standing. The man froze as he thought he was about to be shot.

Antonio stepped around the man, still pointing the revolver at his head. He reached around and under the man's coat. Stuck inside his belt was a Colt .38, which Antonio brutally yanked out from inside the man's belt. The sights of the pistol left a welt on the man's stomach as the gun pulled out.

"Leave fast with your friend, shithead, before you get carried out without your balls and legs," Filippo told the one standing, his voice cold as ice.

The second man's face had turned livid with rage, and the fingers on his right hand itched to reach inside his coat, but with Antonio pointing a gun at him and Filippo pointing what appeared to be a shotgun under the blanket at him, he swore under his breath.

He then helped his hurt friend to the door, but not before the one who did the talking snarled at them, "You will hear from us again, and next time, there will be hell to pay."

The two brothers watched as the pair struggled to the top of the landing. Filippo turned and went back inside the room. Antonio watched, laughing, as the hurt man slipped down the stairs, his friend taking a few steps after him.

Antonio was about to turn his back on them but noticed out of the corner of his eye that the man had stopped going down the stairs and was turning around. He saw the man's right hand swinging back towards him and realized he had pulled a gun from somewhere. A bullet shattered the doorframe beside him.

Antonio pulled the trigger of the revolver in his hand, pointing towards the man shooting at him. The first bullet hit the would-be thug high in the upper right arm; the second missed the man as he screamed and fell down the stairs.

"What the hell did you have under that blanket?" Antonio demanded as soon as they had made sure the thugs had disappeared. "I didn't like the sound of the voice when you spoke to them at the door," Filippo said with a laugh, "so I got the *scobeta* shotgun Papa gave me from under the bed. It sure is and looks like a shotgun under this blanket." On a more serious note, he continued, "Anyway, there is going to be plenty of trouble to come out of this. I think that we better go and buy a shotgun or two so we can go shooting foxes or crooks. We need some more guns straight away, and we can leave them with Gennaro when he is on his own. I think we better tell the others to be as careful as possible. These Cosa Nostra people are trouble—big trouble."

That afternoon, the three brothers went to the gun shop near the main railroad station and purchased one double-barreled shot-gun, a Winchester rifle, and a six-shot .38 Smith & Wesson handgun and a box of bullets for each of them.

They walked over to their uncle, aunt, and cousins' house to tell them about what had taken place. Zio Nicola and his family were all home. Their aunt implored them to pay up and to not take any risks.

The three brothers decided that they would not pay anybody any money; they would talk to all the Cudoni men and the Folino Gallo, Raso, and Mercurio men and back themselves into their own group. The next day, they all got together at Zio Nicola's place. Gennaro, who, because of his job, did more travelling than the others in the group, was elected to represent everyone in the group. He was, in a sense, elected to oversee the group.

They felt they could get at least twenty-two men in the group with just the relations. Filippo thought that Batiste Raso might be able to pick up a few more men to join the group. The group calculated that over twenty men could join them.

The next Monday morning, Filippo and Antonio, together with the other men living in Pittsburgh but working at Greensburg, left and decided that they would return to Pittsburgh on Friday night and go back to Greensburg on the late Sunday afternoon train.

It was seven thirty that night when Filippo and Antonio got back to the boarding house. Gennaro had finished eating and was washing up his dirty dishes.

"Glad to see you boys have come home," he told his brothers when they came in. "I'm thinking that we should expect the Cosa Nostra boys for a visit this weekend."

"That's what me and Filippo were thinking," Antonio replied.

"I think it will be tonight or tomorrow night," Filippo added, "but I don't think they will knock first. I have a plan."

At two in the morning, a shotgun blast ripped through the room where Antonio and Filippo normally slept. Seconds later, a multitude of shots rang out as four masked intruders' pumped bullets into the beds where Filippo and Antonio normally slept. Then a deadly silence followed. A few minutes later, one of the intruders crept up to one bed, and another approached the other bed. To their horror, they found both beds were empty and realized they had been shooting at shadows.

They raced down the corridor and down the stairs to the ground floor. A thin rope stretched knee-high across the middle step sent all four tumbling to the ground. The two men following behind landed on top of the first two already on the ground. A gun from one of the first two discharged into the floor, while a gun from one of the second two men blasted a hole in the ceiling of the boarding house. The guns of the other two men flew from their hands and slid along the floor towards the back door to the boarding house.

Swearing profanities, the four picked themselves up, grabbed their guns, and raced out the back door. They knew that at any minute, guns would be blazing at them. They were four paces from the door, and as they raced away, that they were again tripped by a tightly strung knee-high rope. Again all four fell untidily to the ground.

This time as they picked themselves up, bullets started to fly around them. One man was shot through the backside by a revolver, while another copped a backside full of buckshot. The man in the lead was shot in one of his shoulder blades as he ran.

Then a voice in Calabrese floated over the air as the four intruders raced away. "Come back and see us during the day if you have the courage."

Coming home on the third weekend after that episode, Filippo and Antonio were met at the station by Gennaro. Antonio had seen him through the window of the train, and they were concerned to see him waiting for them at the station. They quickly got off the train and went to greet him.

"Gennaro, what's the matter? Is there a problem?" Filippo quizzed him as soon as they were out of hearing range of the others. "Yes and no," Gennaro told them. He explained that the Cosa Nostra had been concentrating on terrorizing the Sicilians over the last few weeks, and one family had had their house burned down. Luckily, no one had perished in the blaze. The father had been able to save his wife and three small children only because the neighbor's dog had barked and awakened him once the fire started. The man had not tried to be a hero; he simply had been short of money and unable to pay.

Another Sicilian, about twenty-five years of age, had tried to be a hero. They had broken one of his arms and one leg and had cracked several ribs, and then they had left him for dead. The man was badly battered but recovering in a hospital. The man told the police that he had been bashed by thieves, and when the thieves had found he had little money on him, they had bashed him up some more and then left him lying in the street for dead.

Gennaro took them through several side streets to a large, old, unused grain storage shed, which had later become part of a newer, larger warehouse. He took a key out of his pocket and opened the small front door next to a larger door. The door was made from thick, solid timber, and the walls were made of concrete. There was a table and ten chairs standing in the middle of the room. The floor was made of thick timber boards, and it was obvious that this facility had originally been used for storing sacks of grain. A small pile of straw lay scattered in one corner.

Gennaro closed the door behind them, and then he went to the corner where the straw lay and, with his foot, pushed the straw to one side. As Filippo and Antonio watched, Gennaro got down on his hands and knees, and as he pushed down and towards one wall, a small section of the floor slipped away to reveal steps leading down to a cellar. The three went down the short set of steps and into the cellar. It was not large, but there were several large boxes on the ground, and on top of them were boxes of bullets, along with several rifles, shot- guns, and handguns. A door was at the other end of the small cellar. Gennaro told them that the door led into a short tunnel that eventually led out to the back of the building. The Calabrese group had decided to rent the building so they could use it as a place to meet.

Gennaro told them that he had gathered, including his relatives, about thirty-seven people to join the group, and everyone had contributed three dollars. This had paid for the guns and the small monthly rent.

The Pittsburgh police had learned that so-called protection groups had been formed in New York and Chicago. They were also of the opinion that a so-called extortion gang existed in

Pittsburgh, and the police suspected that this same gang was involved in the recent fires and bashings that had taken place within the Italian com- munity. However, there was a stony wall of silence from the Italians, and the police were unable to obtain any information that linked the Italians to such a group. Sergeant Stewart Russell, who was in charge of investigations, was frustrated and angry.

Several months passed with no members within the Calabrese group being approached by the Cosa Nostra to contribute towards the Cosa Nostra. At least, no one was aware of any approaches made towards anyone in the group.

It was now well into summer, but one particular night, darkness fell over the city early. A late afternoon thunderstorm had passed over the city earlier and left a blanket of thick, cumulous clouds hanging over the early night sky. With only the bare outline of a new moon low over the eastern skyline, darkness came much earlier than normal in Pittsburgh.

To starry-eyed, lovesick Bruno Curcio, the dimness of the Sunday night was nothing. His mind was too full of lovemaking and longing for Angelina to worry about the early darkness. He had spent several hours with her that afternoon, during which he had asked her if she would be his fiancée and marry him. He had held her hand for a moment when he had sat beside her and asked her. She had rested her hand on his thigh for a few minutes and replied that she would let him know by the end of the following week.

He had felt her breast brush against his arm as she stood up, and he had felt the point of her nipple against his arm. He dreamed of what it would be like to make love to his beautiful Angelina, to have his face between her two beautiful breasts, and to kiss her rich red lips.

If he had been more alert, he might have seen the darkish figures following him home. He might also have noticed that at first there were three of them following him, but later there was only one.

Bruno came to an intersection and decided to take the longer way home rather than cut through an alleyway that he sometimes used. This decision might have saved his life, as events later proved. The three shadows split up, and while one followed him, the other two took the shortcut through to the other side to cut him off on the other street.

Bruno walked halfway around the block until he came to the next street, where he paused for a while near a streetlamp. A friend of his who lived in a house across the street still had his house lights on. The man was sitting in a chair on his porch, smoking a pipe. Bruno could not see anyone but thought of dropping in and saying hello.

He did not hear the man sneak up on him from behind. He was about to step across the street when he felt something hard press into his ribs. He knew instantly that it was a gun. He froze on the spot.

"Don't move, you miserable bastard, or you will have a new hole to get fresh air from," a male voice told him in Sicilian. "Just step back this way, and we will go the way you should be going."

Bruno did as told. He knew it was the Cosa Nostra. They had warned him two weeks ago to pay them their security money or else. They had warned him that if he told anyone, they would harm his beautiful girl, and he had kept it to himself. But he had refused to pay and had not handed over the money.

He started to shake. He knew that they would kill him. He knew now that he should have told the others. He had not joined the group that he knew Angelina's brothers had formed. He had not thought that the Cosa Nostra would do anything then.

He stopped walking and got on his knees. He pleaded with the man behind him with the gun. "Don't shoot, don't shoot me. I will pay. I'll pay you—I'll pay you anything. Anything you want," he pleaded.

Down at the other end of the street, two men were walking towards them.

This is it, Bruno thought to himself. *These thugs are going to kill me.* He thought about running, but he knew he would only get shot in the back if he tried. Maybe he could talk his way out of it.

"I have the money at home. I will get it for you. There is no need to do anything. I'll get it now," he pleaded again.

"Shut up and walk," growled the man standing behind Bruno. Bruno was about to get up when a shotgun blast blew the shop-front window behind him into little pieces. He thought, *I'm dead*, and he dropped down to one knee.

Reacting to the shock of the shotgun blast that had come from behind him, the thug pulled the trigger of his revolver without really looking. The bullet that was meant for Bruno's back passed through his side and hit his ribcage. Then the barrel of a handgun crashed into the back of Bruno's head, and he slumped to the ground. Blood seeped from the wound in Bruno's head and more profusely from the side of his chest.

The man on the porch had seen Bruno and had been about to wave to him when he had noticed the man creeping up behind him with a gun. He had sneaked inside, and after calling his brother, they had picked up a shotgun each and slipped out the back of the house and into the street.

The thug, who had been distracted when Bruno went down on his knees, had not seen them. When Bruno's friend thought that Bruno would be shot, he had deliberately shot into the shopfront glass. His brother had shot just above their heads a moment after the man shot Bruno. The thug had then belted Bruno brutally on the head with his revolver and, before the two friends could reload their shotguns and fire, bolted down the street, joined the other two, and disappeared into the night.

Bruno Curcio was left lying almost dead on the dirty street.

Filippo and Antonio heard about the incident when they returned to Pittsburgh the next Saturday afternoon. They also heard that the thug called Ugo had mysteriously met with foul play two nights later. Someone had cut off most of his tongue, cut off his right index finger, and smashed his right hand to a pulp. They had also cut off a piece of skin around one of his testicles and warned him that next time there was any foul play involving a Calabrese, he would lose the lot as well as his head.

Filippo asked Gennaro how Bruno Curcio was now.

"He's still in the hospital in a coma. His bullet wound is no problem, but he may have internal head injuries. His family is constantly with him, praying that he will pull through," Gennaro replied. "Was Bruno part of the Calabrese group of Italians?" Antonio asked Gennaro.

"No, he had said that he and his three brothers were thinking of joining, but they had not done so," Gennaro replied.

"What does the group think about this, and more importantly, what does it intend to do?" Filippo asked him.

"The group does not intend to do anything about it," Gennaro said. "However, it seems that something has been done about it."

Gennaro told his brothers that the group advised everyone connected to it to make sure that group members did not travel alone. It was unlikely that the gang would attack more than one. The members of the group spread the word that any harm to the Calabrians would mean worse harm to those who caused it. With the number of new people coming to America, it was obvious that the Cosa Nostra had many more potential victims, and it was easier to leave the Calabrians alone.

Filippo wondered how Angelina was managing with this latest problem in her personal life. It was none of his business, he thought, and anyway, it was best if he stayed away. The last person she would like to see now would be him. In his heart, he felt no enmity towards Bruno Curcio, and he did genuinely hope that he would be all right.

That Saturday night, all of the single or unattached Calabrese men went downtown. They visited several bars and went to a social dance hall. Thirteen of them walked along the street from the city center to the strip and back. They had a few drinks and had a good time but caused no trouble. The point of the whole exercise was to show anyone from Cosa Nostra who might have been watching that they were a solid group and would not be pushed around by any other person or group.

Natale Folino Gallo told Filippo that Bruno had come out of his coma, but his speech was still slurred, and he could not say any- thing coherently at this point. However, the doctors were hopeful that he would make a full recovery.

Chapter 22

The Cudoni brothers received another letter in mid-August from their family in Sambiase. The letter said that the family was well. Even their grandparents were fine, although their grandmother was having hearing problems. Their father told them that Giovanni and Peppino were impatient to come to America. Even Carlo wanted to go to America. However, Giovanni had received his military call-up and had now been in the army for several months. His parents wrote that they had received the letter from Filippo in which he told them about how much money the brothers were making and all the new friends they had made.

They were glad to hear that all their relations in America were doing well. Papa Francesco had informed his brother Pasqualle that Pasqualle's boys had arrived safely in America and that his sons had seen them and that they were staying in Pittsburgh.

Giovanni, they said, had been upset that he had to report in for his twelve months of military training. The day he left, he'd told his parents that he would go to America as soon as he returned.

Filippo and Antonio worked at the site near Greensburg for the next six weeks. The work was progressing quite well, and Jack estimated that they had about another four weeks of work there. Jack had also been promoted to site general manager, and he had made Filippo foreman in charge of his land-clearing team. Jack was given other projects to oversee as well, and he was not always on this site.

One particular week, Jack had been away since Tuesday afternoon. Filippo's gang had completed all of the land clearing and road- bed preparation, and only the sections close to the bridge approaches remained to be completed. Filippo needed to know if Jack wanted those sections done next, so upon returning to Pittsburgh on Saturday, Filippo decided that he should go see him.

He arrived at the Benson house at about one in the afternoon. Jane was in the garden when he arrived. She was happy to see him and scolded him for not coming over more often. She invited him in but also told him that it might be another hour or so before Jack would return. This was the first time that Filippo had been to their new home. Filippo followed Jane into what was a bigger and better house than the one they'd had in Sewickley. The entry led into a large lounge area, and a hallway led into the rest of the house.

"Please sit down, and we shall have a chat," she told him. Then she called out to her daughter. "Tracy, we have a visitor! She's in the study, working on a school project," Jane told Filippo.

A few minutes later, Tracy walked into the room. Filippo stood up to welcome her. *How beautiful she looks*, he thought.

Jane also stood up. "I'll go make a cup of tea while you say hello to each other," she told them, and then she turned and left the room. Filippo watched Jane leave and then stepped towards Tracy, his right hand outstretched. "It's really nice to see you again, Tracy. How are you?" Filippo said as he reached for her hand.

Tracy leaned up to give him a kiss on the cheek as well as hold his hand, but at the last moment, she put her arm around his neck. She hugged him while she lifted her face and pressed it against his. Filippo put his arms around her and hugged her tightly to him.

"I miss you so much," she whispered into his ear. "I can't bear to be without you. I love you so much."

"I will cherish you also forever, *cara mia*," Filippo told her. "But I will never do anything to hurt you."

They sat down on the sofa, still holding hands. For a long moment, they just stared into each other's eyes. Then Filippo asked her about her new school. "Your new school—is it a big school? Your new student children—are they nice to you?"

He smiled wryly. "You tell them that if they make you upset, a Calabrese man will come and smack their bottom."

She laughed lightly as she wiped the tears from her eyes. The moment of emotion between them had passed.

A few minutes later, Jane came back carrying three cups of tea and handed a cup to each. She noticed the slight flush on Tracy's cheeks, and she thought that her daughter was possibly still in love with this handsome, young Italian man and would follow him to any part of the world if he should ask her to.

They talked for a while about life in Pittsburgh, how different it was from Sewickley. There was much more to do, and there were many different places to enjoy. Tracy mentioned that a new show was on at the theatre where she had been with Filippo and that she was taking her parents to the opera house in two weeks' time to see it. Filippo remarked that the show he had seen with Tracy was magnificent and that he had greatly enjoyed it.

Jane looked at Tracy. "Perhaps you could get another ticket, and Phil could come again, dear," she said.

"Phil, would you like to come? There is one on next Saturday, the twelfth of October," Tracy said as she looked at him. "We would love you to come."

Filippo was surprised that he had been asked to join the family at what he thought was an important family social event, but he really had enjoyed the show last time, and even though he felt that he was out of his depth with such an occasion, he did not want to say no to them.

"I would be extremely honored to come to the theatre with your family," Filippo replied to Jane and Tracy.

"That's settled then," Tracy said. "I will get the extra ticket for you, Phil. The show starts at 8:00 pm sharp. Do you wish to come here first, or shall we meet you at the theatre?"

"If you don't mind, I will come here, and we can go together from here. Is that all right?" Filippo asked.

"Yes, come here, and we will go together. That way, Jack can't find any excuses not to come." Jane smiled as she answered.

Jack got there a short while later, and after he briefly discussed the work on the track, Filippo took his leave from the family.

The following Saturday, Filippo and Antonio arrived back from work at about three in the afternoon. They had worked for the first half of the day and then left work to catch the train back to Pittsburgh. Gennaro was not at the boarding house when they arrived, but he returned at about five that afternoon.

Gennaro had some unexpected news for them when he did arrive. Young Bruno Curcio had been out of the hospital for a month and was to marry Angelina Folino Gallo early in January. Gennaro told them Bruno had proposed to her before being shot, and she had now accepted his invitation to marry him.

Gennaro also told them that Zia Theresa and Zio Nicola, the parents of Michele, and the parents of Marietta Zappalla had announced that Michele and Marietta were to be married on the seventh day of December. They had expected this news as the couple had been going steady for some time. There had been few weddings in America among the Calabrese community because there were not many young Calabrese women, particularly in Pittsburgh. This was a mixed marriage in that Marietta was Sicilian, but regardless of that, everyone was looking forward to it.

Filippo had a visit from Michele on Sunday morning. After exchanging pleasantries and small talk, Michele asked Filippo if he would do him a favor. *"Cogino,* will you be a groomsman for me and Marietta at our wedding in December?" Michele asked Filippo.

"Si, si, *perche no.* Of course I would be honored to be in your bridal party. Who is the unlucky girl to be my partner?" Filippo asked without it giving it much thought.

"Well, it is Angelina Folino, and I know she has already agreed to be your partner," Michele told him.

"If Angelina is happy to do it, I shall be just as happy to do it for you, and I would sincerely like to congratulate you and Marietta. I think you two will be extremely happy and have a large and great family. You a papa—ha ha," Filippo teased him with a wink and a grin.

Michele told Filippo that his cousin, Giuseppe Folino Gallo, was going to be his best man, and Giuseppe's fiancée, Rosetta, was the maid of honor.

"I was going to buy a suit anyway," Filippo said. "At least now I will have somewhere to wear it."

The following weekend, Filippo and Antonio did not have to work on Saturday and decided to catch the late Friday night train coming back to Pittsburgh. The train got into the Pittsburgh station at nine that night, and carrying a bag each, they were out of the station within fifteen minutes. They stopped at a saloon on the way for a few drinks before they went back to the boarding house. Pittsburgh at this hour on Friday night was alive and vibrant. People of all descriptions were everywhere. Music coming from some of the more elaborate establishments seemed to float over the night air.

A steady stream of men on horses and horse-driven carriages passed on the streets. There was no doubt that there was a busy nightlife Pittsburgh.

Saturday morning, Filippo decided to see an Italian tailor he had heard some good reports about. There were two other men talking to the tailor when he arrived. The tailor welcomed him in and introduced himself as Napoleone Sirianni. He introduced the other two men. Filippo introduced himself and said that Alfredo, the barber who had given him a haircut earlier in the day, had mentioned he made a quality suit.

Napoleone laughed. "Alfredo and I were on the same boat when we came to America. We are very good friends. I recommend him, and he recommends me. You are Calabrese?" he asked Filippo. Then he added, "I'm a Napolitano. And don't mind these two. They are only here to talk and make me waste time."

It was obvious that Napoleone did not waste one second of time. The only time he stopped working was while he shook hands with Filippo. The rest of the time, his nimble fingers kept sewing or cutting the material in his hands.

"I take it you want a suit made?" Napoleone asked Filippo.

"I would prefer one already made if that is possible—and in a dark color if possible," Filippo replied.

Napoleone put down the cloth he was working on and showed him a number of tailored suits he had on a rack. Filippo picked out a few he liked, and then he went behind a drape and tried them on.

Eventually he settled on a charcoal-colored suit. Filippo put it on and showed it to the experienced Napoleone, who pinned it where it needed alterations.

"If you call back for it next Saturday, I will have all the alterations done for you," Napoleone told him.

"Sei mi fate il piacere, o bisogno del vestito questo sera, perche devo portare una bello donna al teatro," Filippo begged him. "I can- not take her in my old suit. Please."

Napoleone laughed. "It's always the same story. Every man that needs a suit needed it yesterday. Can you come back at four this afternoon? I will see if I can have it ready for you. I won't promise, as I already have two others to alter before yours."

Filippo returned just before four that afternoon. Napoleone waved him to come in. He finished sewing the trouser leg that he was working on and then handed the trousers to Filippo. He picked up the jacket and handed that to Filippo as well. "Try them on," Napoleone told him.

Filippo Cudoni thanked him for doing the alterations on such short notice and left. Filippo took a streetcar as far as it would take him, and then he walked the rest of the way. He arrived at the Benson home at six thirty. Jack came out the front door to meet him.

"Are you the same person I know working for the Pennsylvania Rail Company?" Jack laughed good-naturedly at him when he saw him all spruced up in his new suit and bow tie. "Come in, Phil. The ladies are nearly ready."

Jack was smartly dressed as well. The ladies had made sure he looked the part of a modern theatregoer. When Jane and Tracy came out, the men both stared in amazement. They looked like two sophisticated sisters going to the annual ball in their long gowns. Jane had a fur coat on, while Tracy was carrying hers on her arm.

Jack had ordered a carriage for seven, and it arrived a few minutes to seven. Thirty minutes later, the carriage stopped outside the Pennsylvania Opry Theatre.

They mingled with the crowd slowly making their way in. The House Full sign was up, and a large crowd built up as they made their way in. It was a large theatre with seating for some five hundred people. Filippo and the Bensons were ushered to their seats. Jim and Kay joined them later due to the late train times. They arrived a few minutes after eight, but the show had not commenced. Filippo and Tracy made room for them to sit next to Jane and Jack. They seemed excited, and Kay soon informed her parents that she was pregnant.

"Mum, I think the baby will be due mid to late March," Kay told her mother and everybody else. Tracy, at the thought of being an aunt again, was nearly as excited as was her sister Kay. Her sister Susan already had a little boy, Timothy.

Filippo reached over, shook hands, and congratulated Kay and Jim, and also Jane and Jack on being grandparents again. He sat down and then reached for Tracy's hand and congratulated her on being an aunt again.

At the interval, Filippo and Tracy went outside for a walk in the dim streetlight. Tracy was longing for a kiss, and as soon as they were away from the crowd, she turned towards Filippo. "I miss you so much," she told him. "Those two nights with you, I was in heaven."

Filippo looked into her eyes. He saw the passion and love for him there. His resistance melted to nothing. He pulled her to him, and they kissed passionately for a brief moment.

It was a great show, and everyone, with the possible exception of Jack, really enjoyed the performance. Jack, who suffered from a mild touch of indigestion, was a bit uncomfortable towards the end of the show.

The parents invited Kay and Jim to stay the night with them at the end of the show. The four of them took the first carriage available while Tracy and Filippo waited for the next available carriage. While they waited, Filippo held Tracy's hand. It was another thirty minutes before they were able to get a carriage.

Filippo knew that it would be better if they did not get too inti-mate. As a red-blooded male, his great desire was to make love to her, to hold her close to him. He remembered what he had told her and his desire to return to Italy. Having sex with her would be wrong, but how he longed to do so.

Tracy's mind was also working overtime. Should she have sex with him if he instigated it? She knew she had just had a wonderful evening, and he was a very handsome young man. She smiled to herself. Yes, she most likely would have sex with him if he wanted to.

These thought were on both their minds as they rode back in a horse carriage. Soon they were back at the Bensons' house. Filippo helped Tracy down. He motioned to the driver to wait while he walked Tracy to the door. Tracy opened the door and walked in. She had asked him to come in and have coffee, but he had refused. Jane came out when she heard them come in. Filippo asked her how Jack was, and on being told that he was okay and had gone to bed, he wished them good night and then went back to the coach and left.

Chapter 23

On Sunday morning of the weekend before the wedding, Michele called on Filippo. Filippo was helping Antonio write a letter to their parents while Gennaro had gone over to the Calabrese meeting place. After a bit of friendly banter, Michele told them that the wedding was to take place at the Roman Catholic Church not far from where Michele lived, and they had booked a large hall close by for the wedding reception.

The priest at the church had asked that a rehearsal take place for the wedding group on the Friday evening prior to the wedding.

"Can you leave work early enough to get to the church by seven?" Michele asked him.

"Don't worry about my getting to church," Filippo told him. "I have already asked to have the day off. I will be coming home on Thursday evening so that I can help you all day Friday and Saturday as well."

"I knew I could depend on you," Michele responded. "If you would like to come to our place sometime Friday morning, we will work it out from there."

They chatted a while longer about the wedding arrangements. Antonio offered to take Friday off as well, but Michele told him there was no need to waste a day off work and that it would be great if he could help on Saturday.

On Thursday, Filippo came back to Pittsburgh as he had promised. That night, Filippo and Gennaro went over to see their zia and zio to offer to help in any way. The Zappalla and Folino Gallo families were there, and they were all busy making *torrone* and other confectioneries for the reception. Filippo met the Zappalla family, who appeared to be nice people. Angelina Folino was also there, but she endeavored to avoid any direct contact with Filippo, and he like- wise avoided her as much as he could. However, he could not avoid her when he had to take his turn stirring the *toronne*.

"Hello, Angelina, how are you?" Filippo enquired politely.

"Very well, thank you," she replied with a haughty and curious but steady look at him.

For a brief moment, their eyes met. Neither one's eyes flickered. Inwardly, Filippo's heart wrenched at his soul. *How I love this woman in a way I have never loved anybody*, he thought. Not even Maria Valenci, his first love, whom he had thought he would never get over but was now just a distant memory of the past. Not even Tracy Benson, for whom he had a passionate desire. Tracy was a wonderful, beautiful, and loving woman whom any man could be justifiably proud of, but she was not Angelina Folino Gallo. This woman tore his heart out. He wanted to pick her up and smack her behind; he wanted to carry her off to the nearest bedroom and make love to her day and night for the rest of his life and show her that he was the master. Her rebellious spirit of life kindled a kindred spirit in his soul. However, he showed none of these feelings. He just wondered what she felt for him. Was it just loathing at the scandalous manner in which she believed and he knew he had treated her?

Angelina had learned quickly after her episode with this man to hide her inward emotions. Inside, her heart churned at a great pace. She hated him, but even though she had promised to marry Bruno Curcio, she knew that if this man asked her to follow him to hell and back and meant it, she would. She would, just as long as she was his. Her whole body ached for him to make love to her. He infuriated her with his cool, steady, charming manner and those eyes. *Why on earth did God give him those greenish-blue eyes?* she pondered. It appeared to her that he could see right through her with those eyes as if she were a naked ghost just floating on her back in the air in front of him, with her long black hair streaming to the ground—someone he could just reach out and touch whenever he felt like it. *But why doesn't he?* her body cried. If only Filippo cared enough, Bruno Curcio would become a past memory.

The Cudoni family house was a hive of activity on Friday morning when Filippo arrived. Michele and Giuseppe were waiting for him so that they could go check that the carriages to pick up the bride and bridesmaids and take them to church, along with the carriage to pick up the groom and his men, were organized.

The girls had prepared ribbons and other decorations to go on the carriages before they left for church. The same carriages would later take them for a short tour of the city and then to the reception hall.

Michele had also arranged for a carriage to pick up Marietta, Rosetta, and Angelina later that afternoon to bring them to the church for rehearsal. Giuseppe was to go with them to help. Michele and Filippo would meet them at the church.

After the rehearsal that night, the group decided that they should go for a quick cup of coffee before they returned home, and although Filippo and Angelina were not keen, neither objected. They walked from the church to a small coffee shop close by. Michele bought coffee for everyone. He and Marietta had to return to her place as there was still plenty of work for them to do before the wedding, and they left soon after.

Giuseppe asked Filippo if he would drop Angelina off on his way home as Giuseppe was going over to Rosetta's place. His sister gave him a venomous look, but Giuseppe looked at Filippo.

"Please, will you? I'll do you a favor one day," Giuseppe said with a pleading look towards him.

"I will chaperone Angelina home anytime. There are too many crooks and villains about for her to go home alone. But only as long as it is all right with her," Filippo replied gallantly. "I don't want to upset or impose on Angelina or anyone."

Angelina said no more about it, but she seemed upset with her brother for leaving her with Filippo.

Giuseppe and Rosetta decided to take a quick stroll downtown before returning to Rosetta's place. Filippo hailed the first carriage that came past. The driver stopped, and Filippo put up his hand to help Angelina get up.

She refused his helping hand and told him, "I do not want to put you out, and I can go home on my own. You may have other things to do."

"I promised your brother that I would make sure you get home safely, and I could not leave a beautiful young woman such as your- self on your own, alone, at this time of the night," Filippo returned gallantly as he stepped onto the carriage step. He directed the driver where to go and closed the coach door behind him.

Filippo was surprised at the amount of traffic and the number of people about at this time on a Friday night. Angelina sat on one seat, and Filippo sat on the other side. Neither spoke.

The coach had moved down the street two blocks and was about to enter an intersection when a crazy fool on horseback trying to race his horse down the street clipped the nose of the horse pulling Filippo and Angelina's coach. The startled horse reared up on its hind legs and then galloped down the street with its driver trying desperately to pull it to a stop.

The passengers inside the coach bounced from their seats. The sudden jolt threw Angelina towards the back seat, where Filippo was. Filippo managed to put his arm out and catch her just as she was about to hit the rear seat. He hung on to her as the frightened horse galloped on. Fearing more sudden jolts, Filippo braced his feet. He could feel Angelina stiffen in his arms as well. He could feel the pounding of her heart as her breasts pressed into his chest. With the swaying of the coach, she clung tightly to him. He turned his face to look at her, and then they were cheek to cheek, then his lips were close to hers.

Angelina did not attempt to pull away from him as the coach driver slowly pulled the frightened horse back to a slow canter.

Filippo could hold himself back no longer. Still holding Angelina tightly to him, he slowly moved his face until his mouth was over hers. Her mouth slowly opened, and they locked into a desperate, longing, passionate kiss and clung together as if there would be no tomorrow.

By the time the coach driver had totally calmed the horse down, Angelina was sitting on Filippo's lap. They were both exhausted and out of breath, but they were still tightly hugging each other, her head resting on his shoulder.

The driver was reluctant to get down from his driver's seat, fearing the skittish horse would take fright again. He called out to his passengers in the coach. "I'm very sorry. Are you all right in the coach? Did anyone get hurt?"

"What's a matter, you fool? You have scared the young woman. Don't you know how to drive a coach? Whatsa hell happened?" Filippo demanded angrily.

"Some crazy guy racing his horse down the street smacked my horse in the head as he raced past," the driver said. "If I find out who it was, I will blow his head off." The driver could now afford the luxury of being angry. Then he added, "If you don't mind, I will walk the horse for a while till he is totally settled down."

"Sure, okay," Filippo responded.

Angelina pulled Filippo's head down towards her. "Stop talking and kiss me again."

Their lips locked in wild abandonment. They kissed like never before as they held each other tightly. She had hated him for what he had done to her, but still she loved him and wanted him, and she moaned with sensual pleasure at his touch. He realized he was going too far and that they would eventually be unable to control their wild desire. They kept kissing until they were close to her house.

The next day, those in the groom's party collected at the Cudoni house. At two, the carriage arrived to take them to the church, and once there, the groom and his two groomsmen went into the church to await the arrival of the bride. When she arrived, the bride looked beautiful, as all brides do. The bride wore a long white gown that trailed behind her. The bridesmaids were dressed in long light blue gowns, and both looked stunning, but Filippo thought that one of the bridesmaids looked completely out of this world.

Angelina was in a happy but confused frame of mind. Her long proud legs, her upright stance, and her long neck made her stand out from the rest of the girls.

Bruno Curcio, who was sitting in a pew with one of his brothers, thought he must have been the luckiest man in the universe to be marrying the smiling bridesmaid as he watched her follow the bride proudly to the front of the church. Little did he know that her whole mind and world were being torn apart and that the biggest part of her thoughts revolved around another man—a man he had once felt jealous of.

Angelina was so preoccupied with her own thoughts and looking for Filippo that she almost did not see Bruno waving to her. She gave him a small wave and smile as she moved on.

That's my girl, thought Bruno, but he missed the quick frown of confusion that followed as she turned her face away.

Angelina knew she was marrying Bruno, but in her heart, she also knew that she would drop him cold for Filippo. Filippo Cudoni had her heart, but he was choosing otherwise at this stage anyway. She knew he wanted to return to Sambiase, but she could not work out why. He seemed to like America and he got on well with its people, yet something in him yearned to return. Her thoughts returned to the present. She assisted Marietta, and eventually Marietta and Michele were ready to take the official vows.

The bride and groom took their vows before God and the church. Afterwards, the priest, Father Sebastiano, who was of Sicilian background, told Michele he could raise the bride's veil. He did.

"You may now kiss the bride," the priest told Michele. Michele kissed Marietta.

Standing behind Father Sebastiano and behind Michele and Marietta, Angelina pressed Filippo's hand to the side of her thigh. The bride and groom were now ready to walk down the aisle as husband and wife. The bride and groom walked arm in arm down the aisle, followed by Giuseppe and Rosetta, who were also arm in arm, and then by Angelina and Filippo. As they started to follow the others, Angelina slipped her arm around Filippo's arm so that they too walked down the aisle arm in arm, but she dared not look at him.

Once the bridal party was outside the front of the church, their relations and friends showered them with confetti. They all wanted to be the first to congratulate the bride and groom on their wedding.

The many well-wishers had plenty to say and abundant advice to give. Eventually the bridal party got into the carriages to take them for a tour of the city.

The bridal party left the church in three separate coaches: the bride and groom in the first, Giuseppe and Rosetta in the second, and Angelina and Filippo in the third.

The coaches took the road down to the Monongahela River; they were to follow the river as far as Squirrel Hill and then eventually drive back to the hall where the invited guests would be waiting. About five minutes after the coaches left the church, a light rain shower started. The lead coach stopped, and Michele got out as the driver lifted the canvas cover over his coach. The other drivers followed suit. Michele told the other drivers and passengers they would still like to go as far as Squirrel Hill and back unless the rain got too heavy, in which case they would go straight to the hall.

The coaches set off again. The air became cooler as the breeze picked up. In the third coach, Angelina snuggled closer to Filippo, who put his arm around her shoulders. She melted into his arms, her lips hungrily searching for his. How she loved this man; her inner body ached for want for him. She put his hand between her thighs and held it tightly between her legs. Angelina could not get enough of him. As they kissed, she ran her hand over the front of his pants until her hand reached his penis. She gently pressed her fingers over it.

The rain did not get any worse, and the coaches continued their journey past the hill, around it, and past the park. Angelina and Filippo were both sexually aroused to the point where both would have had an orgasm if they did not stop.

Filippo was the first to pull back. "*Amore Mia*, this is too much. You will kill me if we don't stop," he whispered as his lips brushed softly against her ear.

"I don't care. I want you to make love to me so much that I can't think straight anymore," she told him as she fondled his penis a little more. "I need you, I want you, and I don't want to wait. Tonight at the wedding, we can slip away, and I will be yours. Bruno need never know what was between us."

Filippo smiled ruefully. "Angelina, my little angel, I'm dying to make love to you more than anything in this world, but you are to be married soon, and we would need to be very careful not to get caught." As much as he knew he should not do such a thing, his desire was too great to allow his head to overrule his heart.

Angelina was too happy to notice his rueful look.

The coaches were now getting close to the reception hall. They had originally decided to pull up at the park, but because of the light rain, Michele had waved them on, and they were going to arrive at the hall some thirty minutes early.

Angelina quickly brushed her long black hair. As she did so, Filippo, grinning at her, lifted her dress up and kissed the inside of her long white thighs and her pelvis. She responded by pushing his head down harder between her legs to a place where he had never been before.

The coaches pulled up at the front of the hall, and the bridal party got out. The bridesmaids helped the bride out as the groom and his groomsmen watched. The rain had ceased before the bridal party arrived, and they now made their way into the hall. The guests were seating inside the reception hall when the bridal party made their way in. As Michele and Marietta appeared at the door, the musicians—a man with a guitar, a woman on the piano, and a middle-aged man of Italian nationality on the piano accordion—played a short wedding tune.

The middle-aged man was also the emcee for the night, and he announced the bridal party as they came in. The bridal party tables were set up at the head of the hall so that everybody could see the bride and groom. Michele and Marietta sat at the middle table. Next to Marietta sat Rosetta with Giuseppe, whose table was slightly for- ward and facing the bride and groom's table. Next to Giuseppe sat Marietta's mother and father; their table was slightly forward from Rosetta and Giuseppe's table. On the other side of the room, with the tables in the same format, Filippo sat next to Michele, with Angelina next to him, and Zio Nicola and Zia Theresa were at the other table.

Each table had a stiff white tablecloth that reached halfway to the floor. The girls had painted a pretty decorative board that sat in front of the bride and groom. It had the word *Wedding* at the top, *Of* in the middle, *Michele* on one lower side, and *Marietta* on the other lower side, with the colorful impression of a heart and two arrows drawn over most of the board. The artistic hands of a florist had arranged a vase full of roses and other assorted flowers in the center of each of the main tables.

The emcee, one of Marietta's uncles called Batiste Cristaldi, began some of the formal speeches as soon as everybody sat down. Father Sebastiano said grace before partaking of the meal.

During the speeches, Angelina and Filippo held hands under the tablecloth. Nobody was aware that these two had made up and were now secretly friends, let alone would-be lovers. Angelina maintained a composed, smiling face towards the guests and rarely glanced at Filippo, but under the tablecloth, her hands were far from relaxed.

As Filippo was listening to Michele answer a toast on behalf of himself and his new bride, Angelina ran her hand over the inside of his leg and over his penis. He nearly choked on the glass of wine he was drinking when she gave it a hard squeeze. It gave her great pleasure to feel it grow almost instantly under her fingers. He stole a quick look at her, only to see that she was staring straight ahead and smiling at the crowd. He returned the compliment a few moments later. When Michele was toasting the bridesmaids on the wonderful assistance they had given the bride, Filippo reached under her dress and under her underwear and pressed his fingers along her vagina.

Nobody on the floor could tell these two were playing games under the tablecloth, except maybe Zia Theresa. She had detected a small, well-concealed look of satisfaction on Angelina's face, and she did not think it was towards Bruno Curcio. She was sure it was towards Filippo Cudoni. Later, while dancing to the bridal waltz, Angelina seemed to be dancing a little closer than necessary to Filippo. In fact, Angelina was not missing any chance to press her firm, well-proportioned breasts and body against Filippo. Zia Theresa knew some things were not what they seemed to be.

Michele had been able, through a friend going to Philadelphia, to hire a professional piano accordion player who also sang in Italian and in a more traditional Calabrese style. The man, who was in his early thirties, had never been to Pittsburgh and had agreed to come at a reasonably priced rate. He had only been in America for six years, but he had become an adept singer in English as well.

Zio Nicola was an accomplished bagpipe player. Back in Italy, he used to make bagpipes. He had made a few bagpipes in America, and he had brought one to the wedding. He took it out and joined in the music-making. Filippo was also an accomplished bagpipe player, and while Angelina went to have a dance with Bruno Curcio, he had a go at blowing the bagpipe. The guests appreciated his style and rhythm and asked him to play another tune. This time while he played, another guest played the squeeze box. It was a great night of fun and entertainment, and everybody got into the swing of dancing early in the night.

Angelina avoided Bruno as much as she could by using the excuse that she was in the bridal party. She did have several dances with him during the night, but mainly when Filippo played the bagpipe.

At ten, the cutting of the cake ceremony took place. The bridal party again went as a group to dance, and after the first bracket, the musician from Philadelphia teamed up with the squeeze box player and picked up the pace by playing the tarantella. All of the people on the dance floor were again full of energy with this quick-stepping Italian dance.

Filippo and Angelina did not take part in this one and stayed sitting at the bridal table. The tablecloth reached the floor. The two were sitting poker-faced at the bridal table, remaining outwardly cold towards each other. Angelina took her shoes off under the table and rubbed his leg with her toes. He had reached under the cloth and was rubbing the inside of her leg.

By ten thirty that night, both Angelina and Filippo did not want to wait any longer to slip outside and make love.

During some loud tarantella dance music, she whispered to him that in the passageway to the women's toilets, there was a door that she thought would lead outside. She would tell Rosetta that she had to go to the women's. She would slip into the alley and wait there for him. He could pretend to go for a smoke and walk out through the front door.

Two women were having a quiet chat inside the reception center but keeping a wary eye on everything taking place. One noticed Filippo Cudoni was standing up. They saw him walking towards the front entry.

'I wonder how he is coping having to partner Angelina all night?'

"It looks most of the time that they are not happy being with each other," Zia Theresa said as she brushed a strand of hair from her face. "But I get a twinge in my bones that says I think they are actually enjoying it."

Catarina nodded. "I think you may be right. I feel that as well." Filippo left first, quietly and slowly slipping outside into the street. He lit his pipe as he walked, and nobody took any notice. Once outside, he quickly went to the side of the hall, opened the gate there, and then quietly closed it behind him. It was dark inside the narrow lane, but once his eyes adjusted a little, he walked to the end of the lane. It stopped at a door. He found the door was locked from the inside. It was the only door there, and he really hoped that Angelina could somehow get to it from the inside. He waited for what seemed an eternity, and still no one turned up. He thought maybe Angelina was getting even with him and playing him for a fool, but he doubted that as she appeared too sincere for that. Then he thought he heard a noise coming from the other side of the door.

A moment later, the door opened. It was even darker inside, but he could barely make out a figure in the doorway.

"Angie," he whispered softly.

"Fil," Angelina whispered.

Then she was in his arms. They clung tightly to each other for a brief moment, their lips and mouths locked on each other. In the dark, he unhooked the buttons at the top of her gown, and she let the gown down to her feet and stepped out of it while he took off his jacket. With one hand, she quickly took off her underwear and put her dress and underwear on his jacket, which was on top of a large box. Filippo undid the buttons on his shirt and put the shirt on top of the other clothing. Angelina bent down and undid his belt and the buttons on his trousers. She pulled his trousers down to his feet. The touch of his lips on her breasts sent a flush of warmth coursing through her entire body. She wanted him as badly as he wanted her. They locked into a passionate kiss for several minutes.

They realized they were in a laneway where items were stacked.

Filippo pushed the clothes to one side and sat Angelina on the edge of the box, her legs around him. He pulled her buttocks in towards him. He could feel the firmness of her breasts and nipples against his chest, while she could feel the hardness of his large erection against her virginity. With her legs wrapped around his backside, she pulled him tightly against her.

She felt the pleasure and joy of her first love. It was something she would never forget. Her body strained for as much of him as she could get. She moaned with pure pleasure and sheer ecstasy as she orgasmed. Nothing that she had ever done in her life before had given her as much pleasure as reaching an orgasm with this man. Nor would she ever forget the man who gave it to her.

However, the twenty minutes they were absent from the hall had been noticed, and although they came back from different directions, Zia noticed that Angelina was much too happy and wearing just a little too much color to be coming back just from the women's room.

Filippo Cudoni came in ten minutes later looking quiet and a little glum and smoking a cigar, but Zia Theresa noticed a new brightness in his greenish-blue eyes when he got close. *I would bet money those two have been to see each other somewhere,* she thought to herself.

She had also noticed that Bruno Curcio had kept his eyes in the direction of the women's room.

Chapter 24

Filippo did not see Angelina again for several weeks after the wed- ding. No one knew that the two had made love on that wedding night. There had not been any opportunity for them to meet, and as neither wanted anyone to know, they had resisted any urge to visit each other.

He had returned to work on the job just west of Greensburg, but that had been only for a few days. With the work completed, the group that Filippo supervised had returned to Pittsburgh. The two weeks prior to Christmas, Filippo and Antonio worked out of the Pittsburgh area and returned to the boarding house every night.

The group now paid Gennaro a small fee to coordinate the Calabrese group's security, and this task, on top of his regular job, kept him quite busy.

Both Antonio and Filippo suspected that Gennaro had a woman somewhere, but he did not say anything, and his brothers did not ask.

Antonio was the quiet one, and there was no mention of any woman in his life. Filippo suspected that Antonio did not have any particular girl in America in mind; she was in France. On the other hand, Antonio knew that Filippo had gone steady with Angelina for a while, but they had called it off. Antonio had noticed that Filippo had spent some time with his boss's daughter, Tracy.

The Saturday afternoon before Christmas, Filippo was in his room at the boarding house when he had an unexpected but welcome visitor. It was Tracy Benson. Antonio and Gennaro were going with Benaldo and some of the other boys to the club. They met Tracy at the front of the boarding house as they were leaving. The two brothers told her that Filippo was in his room writing and that she should go on in.

Filippo had written a letter to his parents and was trying to translate it into English, as much to improve his English as anything else. He was better at reading English than at writing it.

"Hello, stranger," Tracy greeted him as she walked in, adding, "Have you missed me as much as I've missed you?"

"A most beautiful lady like yourself? I miss you all the time," Filippo replied gallantly as he gave her a huge smile and stood up. "Please come in, Tracy, and how are you anyway?"

"I'm heartbroken like Cinderella," she replied. "My prince never comes to see me or court me. I want so much for him to make love to me, but I never see him. I decided to see if he still remembers me." Tracy walked up to him and pinched him in several places. "At least you are still alive," she chided him.

"Forgive my bad manners," Filippo told her as he looked deep into her blue eyes. They looked longingly at each other for a long time. Filippo Cudoni realized that while Tracy may want him, he should refrain from making any sexual advances.

He put his arms around her shoulders and pulled her towards him. She put her hands around his waist. For a long moment, he held her close to him, her heart beating against his, their cheeks firmly pressed to each other.

"It is better we remain good friends," he told her as they pulled apart.

Tracy looked into his eyes. She did not speak. Her woman's intuition told her he was desperately stopping himself from pulling of her clothes and holding her tight to him.

Before she left, Tracy remembered why she had come, and it was not just to seek to have sex with him. "Mum asked me to ask you if you would like to come over for dinner at our place on Christmas Eve, Phil. Will you come? I want you to," Tracy begged him.

"Tell your mother that she is a wonderful lady to have a daughter like you, and I will do anything she asks me to," Filippo told her. Tracy gave him a quick kiss on the mouth. "Liar," she told him and then left.

On Christmas Eve, Gennaro and Antonio went to see their cousins, Zia and Zio Cudoni. Filippo took a streetcar and arrived at the Bensons' at six. He was welcomed at the door by Tracy, but before she let him in, she gave him a quick kiss on the lips.

"Have you been having any dreams of me?" she asked him as she ran her hands over him.

"I keep dreaming of your hot lips and what might have been the other night," he told her jokingly as he closed his eyes and pretended that he was still in heaven. "What do you dream of, Tracy?"

"Never you mind," she lectured him, as if he were a schoolboy. Filippo Cudoni followed Tracy inside. Jane walked across to Filippo. She wished him a merry Christmas, and Filippo wished her the same. Jack came in a few minutes later carrying two glasses of wine.

"Here, get this into you, Phil," he told Filippo, and handing him the glass of wine, he wished him a merry Christmas and a happy new year. Filippo returned the good cheer.

Ten minutes later, Jim and Kay arrived to join them, and a few minutes after them, the Bensons' other daughter, Susan, and her husband, Bill Dixon, arrived. Filippo was helping the women set the table when Bill, Susan and their little boy arrived. He had not met the Dixon family before, so Tracy introduced him to Susan, Bill, and little Timothy.

"Phil, this is Susan, my oldest sister, and her husband, Bill, and my little nephew, Timothy. Susan, Bill, and Timothy, this is Phil, the man I told you about who saved Dad's life and always gives me a hard time." Tracy smiled as she said the last part.

"I'm glad to meet you, Phil. Dad and Mum have said some very nice things about you, but I didn't know that you were giving Tracy a hard time," Susan said, winking at him. "But I find that hard to believe. Tracy, are you sure you're telling the truth?"

Tracy laughed again. "Only some of the time."

By this time, Filippo had shaken hands with all of the Dixon family, including little Timothy. He liked Bill Dixon. Bill was a big man but seemed like a gentle giant, and he had a handshake like that of a gentle giant. Filippo knew the power was there, but Bill did not need to show it.

By seven, the family had tucked into the roast turkey and vegetables. There was no doubt that Jane Benson knew how to roast a turkey. By the time dinner was over, Filippo had polished off two bottles of wine, and his head was a little dizzy. He had really enjoyed the home-cooked meal, and with the great company, it had tasted even better.

After the meal, he helped Jane and the women clean up, and although they would not let him wash, they gave him a tea towel to dry the dishes.

With the cleaning done, everybody retired to the lounge room. Jack had the huge fireplace going, and the room was cozy and warm. Outside, the weather was cold. Snow had fallen on the high country, and the snow on the mountains was visible in the distance.

The Bensons had acquired a piano when the girls were young, and Jane, who could play the piano, had made sure that all her girls also learned to play. The family had spent many a winter night playing the piano and singing folk songs. Jack, who played the violin, sang a mixture of folk and country songs. Jim, who yodeled, was the guitar player. That night, the girls took turns playing—generally Christmas carols—and the whole family pitched in to sing; even the booming voice of Bill burst high at times. Tracy, who taught music to some of her schoolchildren, was good at both playing the piano and singing some of the popular ballads of the day.

Tracy had written a song of her own, "Light in My Night." Bill, who knew the words, joined the three sisters in singing it.

Female Duet

My loving darling, you came to me
Like a bright flame in the night;
You became the smoldering flame in my heart.
You played the game;
You lit the flame and set my heart burning bright.
You are the bright light in my night.

Male Voice

I came to you; you set my heart alight
Like a bright burning light in my night.

Chorus

One day you may return
And rekindle the light,
But for now, all that is left is the
Flickering flame in my heart and
the Smoldering light in my night.

You lit the flame and left me to my fate,
And for a while, my heart glowed bright.
But you loved me and left me,
And now all that is left is the
Flickering flame in my heart and
The smoldering light in my night.

Male Voice

I left you for another who came in the night,
made me burn brighter, more bright in the night.

Chorus

One day you may return
And rekindle the light,
But for now, all that is left is the
 Smoldering flame in my heart,
Smoldering light in my night.

You lit the flame in my heart, then put it right out.
You left me for another; now all that is left
Is the flickering flame in my heart and
the Smoldering light in my night

Male Voice

She left as she came—in the middle of night.
She left me for the hustle and bustle of city

life With a rich cattle rustler who splurged her with dough.

My darling, you were the bright light in my night And the smoldering flame in my heart. You lit the love light to my sheer

delight. You were the only light in my night, But the flame flickered and burst, and Now my heart burns with sorrow and hurt.

Chorus
One day you may return
And rekindle the light,
But for now, all that is left is the
Sorrow in my heart and the last
Flickering flame in the night

Male Voice

My darling, I know I made a big
mistake, But I hope one day you will let
me return And

Chorus

Rekindle the light, put it back right.
But for now, all that is left is the
Sorrow in my heart and the last
Smoldering light in my night.
And slowly the light fades into the night.

    As the hands on the big grandfather clock showed eleven o'clock approaching, Filippo took leave of the Bensons. He wished all a merry Christmas and a prosperous new year. Tracy walked out- side and down to the gate with Filippo. The air was still but cold.

Tracy snuggled up to Filippo and put her arms around him, her firm breasts pressing gently against him. She bent her head slightly so that he could kiss her on the lips. He responded, and for a brief moment, they held each other in a tight embrace. Then they separated.

Filippo had decided that if he had time, he would go to the midnight mass at the church where Michele had been married. He walked the two blocks to where he could catch the streetcar. He had to wait twenty minutes before the car arrived, and he was getting very cold. He thought of going home, but once he was in the streetcar, he changed his mind and rode the car to the street close to the church.

Chapter 25

The midnight church bell was ringing by the time he arrived, and nearly all the people had already packed into the church. Filippo thought that his uncle's family would probably be inside and maybe his brothers as well. The seats in the main part of the church seemed full, so Filippo decided to go upstairs. That area was also full of people. As he looked at the kneeling people, he noticed that the Folino Gallo boys, Natale and Sarino, and their sister were sitting with Santo, Fiore, and his brother Antonio. He also noticed that there was a spare seat behind them.

He moved over to that area and sat down. As he sat, his fingers slipped along the back of the pew in front of him and gently and quickly brushed along the back of Angelina's shoulder. She casually glanced up and backwards to see who had touched her, and when she realized it was Filippo, her heart skipped a beat. For a split second, she looked into his eyes, and then she looked forward.

It was well after one in the morning by the time Mass was finished. At the end of Mass, Tomasi and Catarina Folino Gallo and Zio and Zia Cudoni came out together and joined the younger family members, who were talking outside. Tomasi invited Antonio Cudoni and his brothers over for Christmas Day lunch at midday.

The next morning, Antonio told Gennaro about the invitation to the Folino Gallos' and said that all the cousins had been invited go there this year instead of going to the Cudoni home. Filippo

Cudoni had heard Tomasi tell Antonio to tell his brothers to go, but he was unsure if he would be welcome.

Tomasi had told Filippo he would shoot him the next time he went there. However, he decided that Angelina would never forgive him if he did not go, so he decided he would go.

They arrived at the Folino Gallo residence at about eleven thirty. The three brothers had purchased a large flask of good quality wine they had intended to give their uncle and aunt for Christmas, but they decided to give it to the Folino Gallos instead.

Most of their relations had already arrived by the time they arrived. Filippo took the flask and, wishing all the family a happy and joyous Christmas, presented the flask to Tomasi, who thanked him. He wished Filippo Cudoni and his brothers a happy Christmas. Filippo, however, noticed that Tomasi did not look directly at him when he spoke, and he thought he was only being nice because it was Christmas Day.

Filippo, Gennaro, and Antonio shook hands with all the relations and friends there. When Filippo got to Angelina, she looked coldly at him for a moment before she offered him her hand to shake. He took her hand, but instead of shaking it, he quickly kissed the back of it and then let it go. Zia Theresa caught the faint edge of satisfaction on Angelina's face before Angelina pretended to pull her hand away. The pretend annoyed look on Angelina's face came too late to fool Zia Theresa, but no one else seemed to notice anything unusual.

Catarina and Angelina had prepared a truly great meal in the typical tradition of Calabrese cuisine. They feasted on huge helpings of homemade long pasta topped with grated homemade cheese and tomato sauce; eggplant filled and stuffed with small pieces of meat, flour, and egg; chicken pieces roasted in a frying pan; homemade bread; several varieties of homemade salami; and capsicums roasted on the stove with a dash of olive oil and garlic.

The Folino Gallo residence was a modest timber house. Natale and Sarino had set up a row of tables from the kitchen into the lounge room, and all of the guests squeezed into the chairs around the tables.

The jovial group of relatives, along with a few friends, enjoyed a great Christmas Day lunch.

Filippo sat next to Michele and Marietta, and they had plenty to say about the places they had been to on their two-week honeymoon. They looked like the honeymoon couple they were, and everyone enquired about their honeymoon in Philadelphia. They had been the last to arrive and would likely be the first to leave.

Angelina and her mother, Catarina, served the sumptuous meal. During the meal, Angelina asked Marietta if she had enjoyed her honeymoon, and when Marietta said that it had been a great time, Angelina gave Marietta a kiss on the cheek and then turned to Michele and, with her arms around their shoulders, gave Michele a kiss on the cheek as well. As she started to move away, her foot seemed to catch on the edge of the chair, and she nearly fell onto Filippo. It seemed that only his quick reaction saved her from falling.

Near the end of the meal, Filippo went to the toilet to pay a call of nature. The bathroom was located off a small passageway that also led outside. Once in the bathroom, he quickly pulled out the note that Angelina had slipped him when she "fell." The note was simple: "Go to the second window on the right as you go outside."

Quickly, he walked out and around to the window. It was slightly open. He pulled on the hinged window and opened it a bit more. He could see that the window led into a woman's room. Ten seconds later, Angelina arrived. With a finger on her lips to signify silence, she leaned out the window and embraced him in a passion- ate, loving kiss. She could not get enough of him. She ran her hands over his cheeks and neck and into his shirt as they kissed. Then she forced her hand down into his trousers and searched until she found his erection.

Filippo slipped his hand under her jacket and into her warm blouse and gently squeezed her breasts. He kissed her gorgeous nipples, and after a quick kiss on the lips, they pulled apart. He returned to the toilet. It was still empty. It had taken only a few minutes, but it had seemed like an hour.

After the meal was over, Zio Nicola took out his bagpipe and played a few tunes while the women and some of the younger men cleaned up the dishes and leftovers. Zio Nicola handed Filippo the bagpipe to play a tune on it as well. Tomasi got a squeeze box and joined Filippo in playing. They made a pleasant musical combination. When the women finished their work, they joined the men.

Natale and Sarino shifted some of the tables to make room for dancing. The combination of Zio Nicola on the bagpipe and Tomasi on the squeeze box got everybody in the mood for dancing. Some of the young men started doing the tarantella, and soon the girls joined in as well. As was the custom with the tarantella, each dancer dropped out as he or she tired, and someone else took his or her place, or there was one less on the floor. The better and fitter dancers kept going until just two dancers remained on the floor. The last two on the floor ended up being Angelina and Filippo. They held hands as they stepped in unison to the beat of the music. It was at this point that Bruno Curcio walked into the Folino Gallo residence. He was not amused to see his future wife dancing with a past boyfriend. He said nothing as he realized that the dance was the tarantella and that their pairing would have been simply the way the dance turned out. Angelina was so absorbed dancing with Filippo that she did not notice Bruno arrive. The dance lasted a long time, as neither wanted to be the one to stop first. When Filippo Cudoni saw Bruno Curcio arrive, he decided it was time to stop dancing with Angelina and let her go to Curcio.

Filippo avoided having any direct contact with Angelina, and although Zia Theresa suspected that something was not what it seemed, she kept it to herself. It did occur to Filippo that having an affair with a woman who was soon to marry someone else was not a wise thing to do, but when Angelina offered him love, wisdom was generally the last concern on his mind. He decided that he should make an effort to avoid Angelina in the future. He had too much love and respect for her to wreck her impending marriage to Bruno Curcio.

He made an obvious effort to be nice to Bruno, but it was only for Angelina that he did it. Bruno was obviously still jealous of him.

It was after midnight when the three Cudoni brothers left to return to their boarding house.

The following day, the weather showed signs of turning nasty. A cold wind picked up from the north-west, and although there was no rain or snow in the morning, by early afternoon, the sky turned a dull grey color. In the dim light of the next morning, one could see that the snow line had moved considerably lower down from the high country, and it was only a matter of time before the blizzard would move through the whole area.

Pittsburgh missed the major fury of the blizzard that Christmas and New Year's period, but some areas to the north-east of Pittsburgh were cut off for weeks. The states to the north and west were totally snowbound.

The Calabrians gathered that New Year's Day at Zia and Zio Nicola's place. They had a great meal for lunch. Zia Theresa, as always, had prepared a great feast. The Folino Gallo family arrived well after everyone had eaten. Zia Theresa and Zio Nicola were a bit concerned when they did not show up in time to eat but were relieved when they finally did arrive.

They explained they had been waiting for Bruno to arrive so that they could come together. One of Bruno's brothers had eventually turned up to say that his brother was suffering from a bad headache and was running a fever and that the Folino Gallos should not wait for him. His brother said to tell Angelina he would go over to see her within the next day or two.

It was easy to see that Angelina was unhappy when they arrived. Little did anyone know that the distress she felt was not because of Bruno's sickness but, rather, her happiness that he was not coming and that she would once again see Filippo Cudoni. Never in her life had she contemplated that she would be in a position where she had agreed to marry one man while her heart and soul yearned for another man. How she missed his touch, his kiss, and the feeling of his manhood inside her. She had felt as if she were in heaven when they had made love. She just could not marry Bruno, and now he was sick. She knew that a good fiancée would rush to his bedside to make sure he was okay. These thoughts had hounded her mind as her family had walked over to the Cudoni place. She knew that if Filippo asked her to marry him, she would leave Bruno standing at the altar, but she also knew that Filippo would not ask her to marry him. He would make no promise that he would ever marry her—and especially not until he returned from Italy if he ever did.

Angelina knew it was only two more weeks to her wedding and that she must make up her mind. She could not confide in anyone about her predicament. No one knew just what Filippo meant to her. She was also acutely aware of the fiery tempers that the Curcio men had and felt she would be placing Filippo's life at risk if she now cancelled the wedding. Anyway, she did like Bruno very much, and if she could not have Filippo, she figured she might as well marry Bruno.

Filippo and Angelina kept out of each other's way for the rest of the afternoon. Filippo had also decided that their secret was not ethical, and morally, he felt guilty that he had allowed himself to take advantage of Angelina's feelings towards him. He knew that Angelina adored him and would do anything to get him to marry her. He thought she had too much dignity to throw herself at his feet and beg him to marry her. Filippo thought that she would rather marry Bruno instead. In this regard, he might have underestimated her love and passion for him. He hated to admit it, but he felt conceited that two of the most beautiful women in Pittsburgh wanted him.

The brothers stayed for dinner. Their three other cousins as well as the Mercurio brothers also came for dinner. Michele and Marietta, who had spent the day with her parents, also arrived in time for dinner. The party had now grown to about twenty-five, and there was a lot of dancing after they cleaned up the dinner dishes.

By eleven, everyone had left to go home. The weather outside was chilly and wet, and by the time they got home, the Cudoni brothers were glad to change and go to bed.

Chapter 26

The next day, the railroad sent out a messenger to call on all employees to report to work. The blizzard and accompanying rain had caused widespread damage to railway lines and bridges. Some train services were rescheduled; even the main line back to Philadelphia was in urgent need of repair. The company had cancelled all staff leave, and all railroad staff had been required to return to work as soon as possible.

Antonio and Filippo were still at the boarding house when the messenger called early that morning. They were at the works depot by ten thirty. They worked twelve-hour shifts for the next two weeks, and by Friday night of the second week, they were more than glad to have a break.

They had received word that Bruno Curcio was better and that the wedding would still be on that Saturday night.

Gennaro gave Filippo a letter that Angelina had written to him. The letter simply said that she bore no grudge against him and that she wanted him, if he would accept, to attend the wedding, along with his brothers.

Gennaro told Filippo that Sarino had dropped the letter off the weekend before, but because Filippo had not been at home, Sarino had left it with him. As far as Gennaro knew, the wedding was at three in the afternoon, and the reception was at six thirty that night. Gennaro and Antonio were definitely going to both the ceremony and the reception. Filippo decided that he would go to the reception but that it was not a good idea for him to go to the ceremony.

Filippo did go to the reception the next night. He was extremely nervous, and he felt angry with himself. For the past three weeks, he had questioned his own intelligence. Was he really such a fool as to allow this beautiful woman to slip through his fingers like water slipping through sand? He knew he loved her as much as he knew she loved him, yet something intangible held him back from rushing over and telling the world that she was his and only his.

He found that he had no answers to his questions. He wondered if the fall down the cliff had damaged his brain. He was the one who had broken things off with Angelina well before that occurred. He knew that he loved Angelina Folino Gallo a lot more than he had ever loved any other woman in his life. Yet he was happier to see her march down the aisle with someone else than to marry her himself. Was he really that determined to return and stay in Italy, or had he simply lost his brains? He was unsure.

Tomasi Folino Gallo had not stated that if he married his daughter, he could not go to Italy; he had just said he did not want her taken to Italy to stay there.

Filippo sat with his Mercurio and Raso cousins at the reception. At twenty minutes to seven, the bridal party made their grand entry into the hall. It was the first time Filippo had seen Angelina since New Year's Day. She looked more beautiful than he could ever remember her. Yet her face looked a little gaunt, as if she had lost a lot of weight and sleep. She smiled at all the people as she cheerily waved to everyone. Yet he noticed that she did not really see them, and she did not look at him when she moved by. His hand waved to her as she passed, but his mind was on a distant planet.

Angelina looked like the beautiful young bride that she was, but her thoughts were also far away. She saw his hand waving at her, and she saw the look of anguish on his face. She wanted to rush over to him, to comfort him, to hold him, but she also wanted to get a gun and shoot him. She forced herself to look forward and ignore him and to smile and be cheery; it was, after all, her wedding day, and she had every right to enjoy it. There was one thing she did know—that Bruno Curcio worshipped the ground she walked on.

During the meal, Filippo's cousins noticed that he was unusually quiet. They had heard that Filippo had been interested in Angelina himself and that he might feel out of place at the wedding, but that was his business, so they were not going to worry about it.

Later in the night, while Bruno and Angelina were cutting the cake with her bridesmaids, Filippo decided to walk over and congratulate her and Bruno. As he walked over to them, Bruno walked away with some friends of his, and Angelina was standing alone.

Angelina was surprised and confused when Filippo suddenly appeared in front of her. He held out his hand to her. "Angelina, I would like very much to congratulate you and Bruno on your wed- ding," Filippo said to her. As he spoke, Bruno returned. Filippo turned to Bruno and raised his hand to shake Bruno's hand. Dumbfounded, Bruno reached out and shook hands.

Smiling ruefully at him, Filippo asked him, "She looks wonderful, and she is a wonderful young lady. You are a lucky man, and I mean that sincerely. Do you mind if I kiss the happy bride?"

Bruno was speechless after hearing those words come from someone he had been very jealous of. *It's odd that he thinks I am lucky to marry her, when she was Filippo's girl to begin with*, he thought. "Uhhh urrr, okay. I mean okay," he blurted.

Filippo leaned forward and planted a small but lingering kiss on her cheek. He took her hand. With a solemn look on his face, Filippo Cudoni wished her well. "Angelina, congratulations and best wishes to you and Bruno. I hope you both find the happiness and love you both deserve," he told them both.

Angelina bowed slightly and gave him the quizzical look that she sometimes gave. He knew it was time he left.

"Thank you very much, and thank you for coming to mine and Bruno's wedding," she told him politely.

Filippo did not stay long at the wedding after that. Before he left, his zia Theresa got hold of him.

"You know that should be you by her side, not Bruno Curcio," she told him bluntly. "I have been watching you both. I am sure you are both in love with each other, but you are both too stubborn to admit you have made a mistake. Tell me, *nipote*, what is the problem?"

"Zia, one day I will tell you, but I think tonight is not the right time or place," he told her. "If you will excuse me, I think I will go home."

For the next four weeks, the gang that Filippo supervised was busy repairing damage done by the New Year's blizzard to the rail-road tracks, particularly to the north of Pittsburgh. He would see Jack Benson, who was supervising the overall repair to all lines, in the morning and then go to the relevant area as directed by Jack. With the damaged rail tracks repaired, the trains started services again.

For the first time in four weeks, Filippo and Antonio were able to return to Pittsburgh late on a Friday afternoon instead of a Saturday. Gennaro was still in when they got back to the boarding house. He was in the process of cooking spaghetti for himself, and he added a little more when they arrived so that the three of them could have dinner together.

When they were halfway through the meal, Gennaro remembered that the woman owner of the boarding house had told him that she had a letter there addressed to Filippo Cudoni and that only he could pick it up.

After the meal, Filippo went to see the owners, Ron and Betty Howard. They were sitting on the back veranda of their house, which was adjacent to the boarding house. A walkway connected the house to the boarding house.

Betty saw him coming and stood up. "I suppose you want to pick up a letter?" She winked at him.

"Yes," Filippo replied. "Gennaro said that you had a letter for me." "I sure have," she replied. "Just for you."

Betty went to a cupboard inside, took out a letter, and brought it over to him. "I promised the young lady that I would give it to you personally. There you are." She handed him a handwritten envelope. Filippo put the envelope in his pocket and thanked her for it.

"Aren't you going to open it?" she enquired.

Filippo shrugged his shoulders as he left. "Maybe," he replied.

There was no mistaking that the handwriting on the envelope was a woman's handwriting. He knew it was not Tracy Benson's handwriting, and he felt he knew from whom the letter may have come from. In the privacy of his bedroom, he opened the envelope. Filippo's heart pounded as he confirmed that the letter was from Angelina. He returned to the start and read the letter.

My dearest love,

How are you? I am very sorry that I have to write to you, but I cannot see any other way of contacting you. I love you, and I miss you. I know I am married to Bruno, but my life now has many problems. I do not know anyone else to whom I can talk. I need someone I can trust to talk to. I cannot talk to my mother or trust anyone else apart from you. Please, I must talk to you, or I will go mad. We live in the boarding house located at 10 Bridge Street. It is the first door on the left as you come up the stairs to the first floor. Bruno works from three in the afternoon to midnight. Please come after eight at night.

Please come urgently, or I will go mad.

From the only person who loves you dearly. x x x x x x

Filippo read and reread the letter a number of times. It was without a doubt from Angelina. It was also clear that she was very worried about something and that the letter could get into the wrong hands.

Gennaro and Antonio went out for the night. He decided that he would go over straight away. He caught a streetcar to the corner of the street where the boarding house was and walked from there to the boarding house. It was nine by that time, and he was about to walk up the stairs when he heard voices coming down from the top of the stairs.

He recognized Angelina's voice and that of her mother's. By the tone of the voices, it appeared that there was some disagreement over something. Filippo searched desperately for some- where to hide as the voices came down the stairs. He could hear Tomasi telling his daughter that it was a tough world and she had to live with it.

Filippo went down a corridor and ducked behind a closet. He found that the door was unlocked, and he hid inside. After a while, he could hear the voices receding and the sound of Angelina's foot- steps going up the stairs. He slowly opened the door and peered out. No one was in sight. He quickly but quietly ran up the stairs. He heard Angelina's door close behind her.

He tapped three times on her door, and then it opened.

Angelina could not believe her eyes. Hurriedly, she pulled him inside and locked the door. She put her arms around him and hugged him tightly. She was sobbing as she did so.

For five minutes, Angelina hugged him as tightly as she could. Slowly, she stopped sobbing, and then she turned her face so that they could kiss. It was not a passionate kiss; rather, it was a bitter yet sweet kiss that had more meaning than any words could ever convey. When they eventually sat down, Angelina started sobbing softly again.

"What a mess of things I have made," she sobbed. "I should never have married Bruno. I was so angry that you did not want me that I would have said yes to any man who proposed to me. Bruno does not understand. He blames me for all his troubles. He has fits and headaches. I think the blow to his head is making him go mad." Filippo cut her short. "Angelina, please. Hang on a moment.

Come here." He helped her to her feet and put his arms around her. "Slow down, and start from the beginning. Just what is the problem?" he asked as he held her close to him. "The start of our problem was at the end of the wedding reception," she told him. "Bruno was nearly drunk by the time we left the hall. The carriage took us to the hotel where we were staying, but when we got there, he had some more to drink. When we went to bed, he tried to make love, but he was too drunk to do anything. The next morning, he was very angry and upset. He tried again, but he could not do anything.

He keeps blaming me, saying I am cold to him. Maybe I do compare him with you in my mind, but that should not stop him, and I have never mentioned you to him. What am I to do? He now gets upset and violent, and it only makes matters worse."

Filippo wiped away her tears gently with his finger. "You must not compare him with anyone, let alone me," he told her softly. "But first I want to see you smile." He gave her a quick kiss on the cheek.

She gave him a wry, faint smile.

"See, you can still smile a little," he told her.

She tried to smile, but it came out more as a frown. He reached forward and put his cheek on her cheek for a while longer.

"See, no trouble," he said. "Try again."

This time, she smiled a bit more. She was starting to warm up. His arms gently went around her shoulders, and he could feel her firm breasts against him as she responded.

"Angelina, please tell me to leave. Please? If I stay one moment longer, I will want you worse than you ever wanted me," he told her. Angelina's thoughts had totally shifted from her problems with Bruno. All she could think about was her love for this man. She smiled as she looked into his face. She looked at him and said nothing; then she reached over and put her hand on his crotch. She could feel the bulge of his erection.

"It's too late, my love. You cannot leave me now," she told him. "I do want you to make love to me."

His heartfelt desire was driving him insane. How he wanted this woman, but he remembered what he had told her and her husband at their wedding.

"No, Angelina, I promised myself not to interfere with your marriage. Go get some sleep now and rest. I will come another day to see you," he told her, and he walked out. His body ached badly for her, but his head ruled for the moment, and he knew he should walk away from her.

Gennaro and Antonio were not back at the boarding house when he arrived, and they were not to know that he had been anywhere since they had left. A week later, the brothers received a letter from their parents and family back home. They wrote that they had received the letter that Filippo had written to them and were glad to find that the boys in America were in good health and spirits. Back home, they said, things on the land were much the same as when the boys had left. However, the boys back home were missing them, and the two older ones were serious about wanting to join their brothers in America. Little Theresa said she wanted to see Filippo, and even Giuseppe wanted to know how things were in America. The brothers talked it over, and they all felt that maybe one of them should make a quick trip back to assure everyone at home that they were all right, and if Giovanni really wanted to come to America, he could come back with his brother on the return trip. They were unsure as to whether he was back from military training. They decided to make a decision later as to who should go.

Chapter 27

In Pittsburgh, the situation between the Sicilian Cosa Nostra and the other Italians was slowly becoming more and more intolerable. Since the Bruno Curcio incident, there had been little con- tact between the Cosa Nostra and the Calabrians. The Sicilians had given them a wide berth. However, between the Cosa Nostra and the rest of the Italians, there were many battles, which the Cosa Nostra quickly settled, resulting in people disappearing and/or turning up dead. The police suspected that the local Sicilian Mafia was responsible, but it was extremely difficult to obtain any concrete evidence to charge anyone. The Sicilians themselves would not talk, and the others were too dead to talk.

Gennaro's group quietly spread the word around Pittsburgh that if the Cosa Nostra molested, injured, or hurt any Calabrese people, their group was well armed and ready to use force in retaliation.

The *Pittsburgh Times* carried regular stories of brutal bashings and killings in the area. The police suspected that the Cosa Nostra did not commit all of these crimes, but that some were.

The Sicilian Cosa Nostra opened up a bordello in the strip area of Pittsburgh. Although the police thought it to be legal, it was a known fact to the Sicilians that the bordello was a front for the Cosa Nostra and that the profits went to the people running the group. Because it was the only Italian-speaking brothel in Pittsburgh, Italian men from various parts of Italy frequented the joint. As there was a shortage of Italian women in Pittsburgh, it was very popular with Italian men and other European men.

The police questioned the Calabrians as to what they knew about the Cosa Nostra, but hardly any of them really knew much, and anyway, reporting the Sicilian Cosa Nostra to the police would have been the quickest way to start a war that no one wanted.

Gennaro and his friends in the Calabrese Club did have an idea which Sicilians were the ringleaders in the gang. However, there was no way Gennaro and his friends were going to get involved between the Sicilian Cosa Nostra and the Pittsburgh police.

One Friday morning, Filippo went to see Jack at his tiny office before his team left for work. The two men discussed the work Jack wanted Filippo's team to do the following week. Filippo was about to leave when Jack passed on a message from Tracy. She said that she had been over to ask him if he would like to go with her to see the circus that was in town, but neither he nor his brothers had been home. Jack said the circus was on the following Friday and Saturday nights. "Sure, Boss, I will be happy to go with Tracy to the circus. I will try to see her over the weekend. Maybe Saturday."

That night, Gennaro asked Filippo if he wanted to go out with Antonio and him. Gennaro told him that he and some of the boys played five-card-draw poker on some Friday nights, and they had organized a game that night. Neither Antonio nor Filippo played poker for money. They knew how to play but were too cautious to play for money. Antonio decided he would go out with some of his younger cousins. Filippo decided to stay in his room at the boarding house.

After dinner, the two younger brothers wanted to leave early, so Filippo cleaned and washed up. The night was still young, and a bright full moon had come over the greater Pittsburgh sky. There was a cold nip to the air, but a brisk walk would do no harm, and Filippo relished the idea of a good walk. He felt good and set off. He passed groups of people walking along and a young couple sitting on a park bench, oblivious to the rest of the world, hugging and kissing. The sight of the young couple stirred his feelings of want and desire. He would not admit it, but his body eventually led him to 10 Bridge Street.

He knocked on the door of Angelina's room. Nobody answered, then Angelina was at the door. She seemed tense and agitated, but she gave Filippo a quick kiss on the lips.

"Shh, Bruno is asleep inside. He's been sick in bed for the last three days, but I've missed you so much, my love," she whispered to him. How she missed his strong personality, his strength, and his touch.

Filippo returned her kiss. He missed making love to this beautiful, sensuous young woman in the prime of her life. He thought he had been an utter fool to let her go. He wondered if he would ever find a woman who would love and arouse him more or even as much. He doubted he ever would. Tracy loved him too, but she was a different type of woman. Tracy's love was great, but her heart was under the control of her head, whereas Angelina's heart ruled her head. He knew though that she did understand more the ways and customs of the Calabrian people.

The sound of Bruno's sick voice pulled them back to reality. "Is someone here, Angelina?" he called faintly from the bedroom. "You better go, my love. Please come back Monday or Tuesday.

I want you so much," she implored. She pushed him to the door, and at the same time she called back to her husband, "Somebody got their door wrong."

Cudoni pulled her tightly to him for a brief moment. He could feel her body and breasts press against his own body. Then he left.

The next afternoon, Filippo went to see Tracy. Tracy and her parents were home. Jack was in the garden, pruning his roses and planting some fresh late-winter flower seeds, while Jane was in the kitchen baking some scones and a cake. Filippo talked to Jack for a while and then went in and said hello to Jane. Tracy poked her head out from her room and told him to go in when he was ready. Jane offered him a small scone to eat and offered to bring him a cup of coffee shortly.

Filippo tapped on the door to the study, where Tracy was. "Come in, stranger," Tracy reproached him. Filippo walked in.

Tracy was dressed in a light, loose white cotton shirt and an old pair of riding pants, which highlighted her well-shaped posterior. The top button of her shirt was undone, and the top of her cleavage looked tantalizing to Filippo when he walked in.

"Hello, Tracy. How are you? Long time I no see you," Filippo flippantly replied.

Tracy stood up and walked over to him. She put her arms over his shoulders and around his neck. "Have you forgotten about me and"—she put her lips to his and kissed him—"that I love to kiss you?"

"Forgive me, Tracy, but I don't really deserve your love. I have been so unkind and cruel to you. You need someone who deserves you more than me," he told her.

"Just hold and kiss me for a while. And be quiet," she ordered him.

He did as told, and for a long moment, they stayed in each other's arms, just hugging and kissing. When they sat down, Filippo asked Tracy if she still wanted him to go to the circus with her.

"I would love you to come to the circus with me on Saturday night. Will you?" she asked him.

"Tracy, I would love to take you to the circus," Filippo said as he scratched his lower chin.

"We won't have time for dinner at a restaurant," Tracy said. "But we could maybe get something to eat at a cafe."

"What if I come at five that afternoon? We can go for a walk first and then have something to eat and then go to the circus," Filippo suggested.

"It sounds like a great idea to me," Tracy agreed.

They talked for a while longer, and then Jane called out that she had some tea, coffee, and cake for them. She had also called Jack in, and when Tracy and Filippo went into the kitchen, Jane had every- thing on the table. Jack was already sitting, drinking some coffee.

"Phil's taking me to see the circus next Saturday, but I think I will feed him to the lions when it's finished," she joked to her parents. On the way home, Filippo called in on his zia and zio Cudoni.

He had not been to see them for some time, and he wondered if they thought he had gone back to Italy or something. His uncle was in the backyard, planting potato seed and looking after his vegetables. His aunt was preparing the dinner for that night.

Filippo smiled as he thought that it was obvious in Pittsburgh, like in many other places around the world, that vegetables planted in the backyard indicated the home of Italians.

She welcomed him in and then scolded him for not calling in before. "Your zio and I have been a bit concerned about you," she told him. "What have you been up to?"

For a moment, Filippo thought, *What does she mean? Does she know about Angelina and me? No, she could not.* "Well, I have been busy at work. But I have also been a bit lazy. I have not been going out much at night anymore, and I am sorry—I should have been to see you a lot sooner," he responded.

"I have been looking forward to talking to you since the wedding, and yes, you should have been to see your zio and me much earlier. Anyway, how are you first?" she asked him.

"I'm fine, just great, zia," Filippo told his aunt, and then he asked, "How are you and Zio?'

"We are okay. Now tell me, what is the answer to what I asked you at the wedding? About you and Angelina, that is," she said.

"Well, Zia, what can I say? Angelina is now married. I have always liked her and, yes, been in love with her. However, as I told her, until I have been back to Italy and made up my mind about whether to stay here or stay in Italy, I cannot ask any woman to marry me. Tomasi was and is right. No man should ask a woman to marry him if he cannot decide where he is going to live. I could not promise Tomasi or Angelina that I would be happy to stay in America. Angelina was not happy to wait and see what would happen. I do not blame Angelina in any way. She is totally right to kick me out of her life on the conditions I put on her. She is entitled to marry any man she chooses. She picked Bruno Curcio, and that is her choice. I think she could have done better, but that was her choice, and we all have to accept that. I did love her, Zia, and I think you are right. I have been foolish, but it is too late to change that now. I am still going back to Italy, possibly in a few months," Filippo quietly and patiently explained.

"Filippo, will you stay for dinner with me and your zio?" his aunt asked him. "I think he would like to talk to you." She had completely changed the conversation.

He knew she would not question him about this matter anymore; whether she believed him or not was another story.

During the early part of the following week, Filippo went to work as usual. On Wednesday night, he decided that he would see Angelina one more time. After telling Antonio and Gennaro that he was going for a stroll and possibly going to see an acquaintance, he left at about seven thirty.

At eight that night, he was tapping quietly on Angelina's door. He tapped very lightly. She did not hear it. On the second go, she heard the faint tapping. She had guessed it would be him, and she was in his arms as soon as the door closed. She hugged and kissed him as though he were the first person she had seen in years.

Bruno, she said, had gotten over his sickness and returned to work on Tuesday afternoon. It would be at least midnight before he returned. Angelina told Filippo that her personal problems with Bruno were getting worse. His fits of rage and depression were more frequent and severe. His attempts to consummate their marriage we're becoming more desperate and less successful. He constantly complained of severe headaches. Angelina had convinced him that he should see a doctor, and he had an appointment set for the following week.

Filippo told her that she should do everything she possibly could to make sure that her husband got better. It could very well be that the blow he had taken to the head had done significant damage.

Angelina appeared to be in a much better frame of mind than the last two times he had called on her. He thought that maybe she was coping better with her husband's condition. He did not realize that the only reason that she felt better was because she believed she would be able to have a relationship with him without her husband knowing. They talked for a while about things in general. Angelina got a bottle of wine out and poured herself and Filippo a glass each.

She was first to propose a toast.

"To my only love—you," she said to Filippo as she raised her glass to his. "May our love last forever."

"In my heart, I will love you forever, my sweet," he told her. "However, you must accept that you have married Bruno, and he is your husband. We cannot restart this affair and keep it going forever. We must put an end to it now."

Angelina took one drink from her glass and then put her glass down on the table. She walked around behind him and put her arms over his shoulders and around his neck as he spoke. She kissed his ear and then the side of his mouth.

He enjoyed the sweet taste of the wine on her breath near his mouth. His resolve to call an end to the affair was taking a battering. Her tongue searched for his as her lips and mouth clung to his. The sweet saliva of her tongue on his sent a second wave of desire pounding through his body. Angelina knew his very soul. She knew how to excite him, to get the biggest erection out of him. Her hand went down to his trousers and over his erect penis. How she loved to see and feel it swell under her touch.

Filippo's intention to call an end to this affair had vanished. He wanted this woman now, and he wanted her whole body and soul.

He wanted his penis inside her body, and he wanted to show her he could give as much as she could give and take.

"Angelina," Filippo said quietly to her, "that was heaven, but that will be the last time I will visit heaven with another man's wife. I will not come to see you again. Please say nothing. I love you too much to have a fight with you. I want to remember you just as you were tonight—my own special earthly angel."

Angelina knew then that this would most likely be the last time the two of them would ever make love—while she was married, anyway.

"I thought I was in heaven too. I always want to remember you as you were tonight. You are my love from heaven as well. No, I do not want to fight with you. You are too precious to my memory to destroy it now," she told him just as quietly.

Chapter 28

On Saturday afternoon, Filippo went with Tracy for a walk, as they had agreed. He got to her house at about four thirty. The afternoon breeze was still a little cool, and it would be quite cold later that night. Each carrying a coat, Filippo and Tracy set off arm in arm for a walk down towards the Allegheny River. It was probably about a two-mile walk down to the river, and if they wanted to eat first and then go to the circus, which was closer to town, the trip would be too far on foot.

They walked as far as the small park that ran towards the river. The trees in the park had all shed their leaves for the winter, but with the approach of spring in the air, the early flowering trees and bushes were starting to form the first buds of the season. The pair found an empty park bench and sat down to have a small rest. The fresh chilly breeze on their faces, combined with the effort of the long walk, had turned Tracy's cheeks a deep pink.

Filippo put his hand to her cheek and gently pinched her cheek with his fingers. "Tracy, you would not want to be a mountain climber, or you would turn into a beetroot, and then every time I kissed you, I would have red lips," Filippo teased her.

Tracy swung her feet onto the empty part of the bench and lay with her head on his lap. "Show me how you would get red lips," she dared him.

With one arm around her, he reached down and firmly kissed her lips.

"I don't see any beetroot on your lips," she quipped. "Maybe you don't know how to kiss me."

He gave her a deeper, more passionate kiss. When he finished, he pulled out a handkerchief and pretended that his lips were beet- root-red and she had caused it.

"It's your fault. Look at my face. I've turned into a beetroot," he joked. Then, on a more serious note, he said, "Tracy, we better move our legs. It will be getting late and dark."

They headed back towards the city center to where the circus was. After having something to eat at a small cafe along the way, they made their way to the circus. They arrived early and sat for a while on a bench in the darker area of the park. They talked, hugged, and kissed as they waited.

After the circus, they took a ride in a coach to Tracy's house. Inside the coach, they hugged and kissed some more before they arrived at the Benson house.

They agreed to go out again the next Saturday night.

Filippo Cudoni hesitated before leaving. "Tracy, I am not sure how to say this. I really enjoy your company and the fun we have, but!"

"I know, Phil. It is not serious." Tracy cut him short. "However, I will still teach you how to dance the modern waltz next Saturday."

A Napolitano who worked at one of the bakeries owned by an Italian from Florence was robbed and badly beaten on Thursday morning. His boss found him in one of the back alleys close to the bakery where he was to work that night. The owner was a little concerned when he did not show up for work, but he did not have time to go look for him during the night. He was also a little apprehensive about the possibility of what might have happened to him.

With the light of dawn, the owner ventured out to the back of the bakery and down the back alley. He saw the man's feet sticking out from behind a pile of rubbish about one hundred yards away from the bakery. The man was still alive, so the owner carried him back to the bakery and sent for the police and a doctor. The man was still in a coma when the doctor examined him, so the police had him taken to the hospital.

The police suspected that the attack had been the work of the Italian Cosa Nostra; they extensively questioned the owner but had no success confirming who might have committed the deed. The other Italian staff also denied any knowledge of who might have instigated the crime.

Gennaro told Filippo and Antonio on Thursday night that the information their group had was that the Napolitano had refused to pay the security fee (extortion) the Cosa Nostra had demanded. Although no one could prove it, the police believed it had been the work of the Cosa Nostra.

During that night, the three brothers discussed who should return to Italy and bring back their other brother or possibly two younger brothers. They knew that nothing had changed in Italy, and the younger brothers were prepared to come to America to work hard and make and save money. Both Gennaro and Antonio insisted that the one to make the trip should be Filippo. He was the oldest and also the one who most deserved to go home first.

Gennaro joked that Filippo would probably find a woman and get married while he was at home in Calabria and possibly not return to America. Filippo promised to make some enquiries as to what it would cost and what he needed to organize a trip back to Italy.

The Mercurio brothers had said their trip had taken them four weeks from Naples to New York. They had said that a new boat under construction in New York was going to cut that time down to just three weeks. The newer bigger steamships were better equipped than the older steamships that the three brothers had travelled on.

The brothers had another talk the following night about who should return to Italy. Antonio told to Filippo and Gennaro that he also would like to return for a quick visit, especially after the way he had left last time.

"I want to see Marcella in Marseilles," he told Filippo, who reminded him that although the Italian government had relaxed the military call-up period from two years to twelve months, he would certainly be at risk of the Italian military enlisting him.

On Saturday night, Filippo went to pick up Tracy at seven as arranged. He had his new suit on, as Tracy had told him most people at the ball would be well dressed. Filippo was met by her mother when he arrived at Tracy's house.

"She is still getting ready, Phil," Jane said. "But she should not be too long."

A few minutes later, Tracy appeared. She was wearing the same mist-blue frock she had worn when they had been to the European concert, but with a navy blue jacket over it. The jacket added a touch of class to the outfit.

Filippo bowed when Tracy approached. She looked like a fairy princess with her stylish blonde hair. "Your coachman waits to escort you to the ball, madam," Filippo told her light-heartedly after bowing slightly.

The ball was in the large school hall not far from the Bensons' home, and Filippo and Tracy decided to walk. Although there was a cool nip in the air, they were both quite happy to walk to the hall. Arm in arm, they set forth and only stopped in the shadow of a small fir tree for a quick hug.

Filippo had never done any dancing like this. The orchestra played as professional musicians, and although Filippo knew none of the steps, Tracy was a good teacher. He was light on his feet, which helped Tracy guide him about the dance floor. He enjoyed the quick- steps as they reminded him of the tarantella. There were people of all ages at the ball. Tracy knew most of the people there as she taught their children, and she knew most of the women in particular as they were mostly mothers who came regularly to the school with their children.

There would certainly be some tongues wagging at the school gate on Monday morning about Tracy and the handsome young Italian she had taken to the ball. She introduced him to several couples that she knew, but she generally kept him to herself. They stayed until eleven thirty and then left. They were at Tracy's front door by a quarter past twelve. After a tight embrace and a long, lingering kiss, Tracy went inside, and Filippo went home.

Filippo did not see Tracy again for several weeks. He went to see her the Saturday before Easter. He called over to the Benson home early in the afternoon. Both Jack and Jane were busy in the front garden. The Bensons always had a beautiful, well-manicured garden, and it was obvious that it took skill and plenty of hard work to keep it that way. They both seemed to have green thumbs. Filippo wished them both a happy Easter and enquired if Tracy was home and if he may talk to her.

"Sure, Phil, Tracy's inside. Just call her when you go in. She may not know you are here," Jack told him.

Filippo walked inside and called out, "Hello, anyone home?"

"Just a moment," Tracy called out from somewhere inside the house. She acknowledged him with a faint smile when she saw him.

Filippo could tell that she was a little annoyed and disappointed in him as she had not seen him for some weeks.

"Tracy, will you come for a walk with me? There is something I would like to talk to you about," he said quietly.

She could see that there was something on his mind. "Sure," she replied. "Have a talk to Mum and Dad. I will be a few minutes."

He went outside, and she came out a few minutes later. "Mum, we're going for a walk. We won't be too long," she told her parents.

They walked towards a small park close by. Both were silent as they walked. They sat on the ground near a small tree once they were there.

"Tracy, I thought that it was best that I tell you myself that I will be returning to Calabria in the summer. Antonio and myself will be going. I think I will be returning. We have several brothers back in Italy who want to come to America, and I might come back with them. The bad news is that we do not know how long we will be in Italy," Filippo told her.

Tracy seemed to cheer up at the news. "Does that mean that once you come back to Pittsburgh, you will stay in America?" Tracy asked him with a flutter in her heart.

"It is better I answer that when I return," Filippo replied. "I do not know how things will be when I return to and maybe from Calabria. I do not know for sure how my family is coping back home. We will see."

Filippo was deep in thought. Filippo really did like Tracy, and he thought he could easily fall in love with Tracy, but he was still not sure that it would be wise for him to marry her. Anyway, he could not offer her anything definite until he returned. The old ways and customs of the Calabrians were still entrenched deeply in his soul, and his parents would not approve of someone they could not understand.

Tracy was also deep in thought. She knew that she would marry this unassuming yet strong-willed Italian if given half a chance. She did not have any hang-ups about his nationality, and she was certainly attracted to him sexually. She wondered how he would cope with returning to Italy and then leaving his family again. Would he leave his family and return to America? One thing she had learned was that although there was a great bond in her family, there was a greater bond and more family unity among the Italian families.

"Tracy, I am still making enquiries about passage back to Italy, and at this point, I do not have a definite date as to when we will leave. I will tell your father this afternoon that I wish to go back and ask if it is possible to get work with the Pennsylvania Railroad when and if I return," Filippo explained to her.

"How long do you think you may be away?" Tracy asked him. "I don't know. But I think it will be for at least four months,"

Filippo told her sincerely. "Tracy, there is also one thing I wish you to know. Tracy, I do not expect you to wait for me. I do not want you to waste your life waiting for me. You are one of the most beautiful and nicest women I know, and you have every right to get the best of life. I love to go out with you and be with you. I love you as a beautiful woman, but you deserve better than I can give you. I want you to be happy. I know you will find a very nice man like your brothers-in- law and have many children. I know you love children. Tracy, if we are meant to be, it will happen, but in the meantime, please do not depend on me."

Tracy and Filippo returned slowly to the Benson home. They walked back hand in hand, but both of them were preoccupied with their own thoughts. They had been through this routine before, and both had been well aware that this was going to happen. Tracy did not blame Filippo for circumstances being as they were. Filippo had never encouraged her otherwise.

When they arrived back at Tracy's house, Filippo told the Bensons about his decision to return to Calabria to see his family and the possibility that he may return with one or two of his younger brothers or that he may stay in Italy and not return. Filippo asked Jack about the chances of him and Antonio coming back to Pittsburgh and getting a job with the railroad.

"Well, I don't know," Jack commented. "I would say that if I was in charge, they would be…reasonably good, Phil." He grinned. "Let me know when you set the date to leave, and I will organize leave for you and Antonio."

The next day was Easter Sunday, and the Cudoni, Folino Gallo, Raso, and Mercurio families had previously decided that if the weather permitted, they would spend the day in the same park where they normally went. After the morning mass was finished, they got together at the front of the church and decided that they would indeed go to the park. There were no low clouds in the sky, but there was a thin cover of high stratus clouds. The sun, hidden behind the high clouds, appeared as a round ball of orange flame in the grey early morning sky.

The family groups went home to pack lunch baskets and drinks after agreeing to meet at the park sometime between eleven and eleven thirty. The three Cudoni brothers had purchased some wine and food from the delicatessen downtown on Saturday. All three decided to go together to the Easter gathering, and they arrived at the park at about twenty to twelve. Most of the families were already there.

By twelve thirty, everyone had arrived, and they sat down to eat, some on the park table and benches that were there, and the rest, mainly the younger ones, on the ground. After a leisurely meal, the younger set decided to go for a walk around the park. The older men played cards. Filippo watched the men play cards for a while and then decided to go for a stroll.

As he walked, Filippo took a deeper, longer look at the world around him in Pittsburgh. There was a feeling of progress here. There was a sense of constant movement towards the future— an exciting, changing future. It really was a case of the new getting newer. The pace of change and progress towards the future there would be unbelievable to someone back in Calabria. In Italy, no one worried about any change, let alone the pace of change.

He missed the peaceful, quiet life and the clean air in the countryside around Sambiase. The lifestyle in Sambiase was very relaxed if you had money. The land barons there had the peasantry doing all the hard work. The lives of the rich were better in Calabria than in America for young men of his background. Sure, it was easier to make money in America, but what would he do with it here!

Anyway, the only reason he had come to America was to make money to go back and buy the biggest block of land he could afford in Sambiase.

Chapter 29

Filippo was so absorbed in his thoughts that he did not notice he had come within hearing range of an Italian couple. It was only when he heard raised voices in Italian swearing at each other that he realized where he was. A man was obviously berating his wife, and she was none too pleased about it. As he listened, it suddenly dawned on Filippo that the voices he heard belonged to Angelina and Bruno Curcio, and the woman sitting on the ground with her back to him was Angelina. There was a line of small trees and shrubs between him and the couple, and he could not clearly see what was going on. Filippo walked along the hedge until he was a little closer. He could now see and hear them quite clearly, although they could not see him.

Bruno had in the meantime become very agitated and was losing his sense of reason.

"You always want to go to your fucking family. We are never good enough for you. You're my wife, and you will do what I say, when I say. You're not going to see your fucking family, you fucking bitch. We're going home," he kept repeating to her.

Angelina tried to tell him that she had told her parents that they would be joining them later in the day, and she insisted that her parents would wonder what might be holding them up and that they should go see them. Bruno was getting more and more agitated, and in frustration, he bent down, grabbed a handful of her hair, and slapped her across the face a few times. Then he tried to drag her along the ground. "You're coming home with me, bitch. If you can't screw with me, you can't go anywhere else."

Filippo had seen and heard enough. He stepped out from behind the hedge and started to walk towards them. Neither saw him coming. Angelina swore at her husband to let her go while he tried to drag her kicking and screaming along.

"Let her go, you ignorant, filthy bastard," Filippo told Bruno icily, "or you will never touch anyone else again."

Bruno was too enraged to take any notice of who had spoken and did not even recognize him. "Get the hell out of my business before I blow your stupid brains out. This is my family problem," he hissed without looking up.

Filippo was standing behind Bruno, and he gave him a huge, stinging backhand to the side of his face. The force whipped Bruno's face around, and he let Angelina go.

"Take her to see her family now, and I will forget this happened," Filippo told him coldly.

Bruno straightened up, turned around, and saw who had slapped him. The rage and fury returned to his face. "It's the *cunnuto* who used to be her lover boy. Arsehole, I will rip you to pieces!" he screamed at Filippo.

Angelina had, in the meantime, dragged herself to her feet. "No no no, don't fight. Please don't fight," she begged them. "I'll go back with you, Bruno. I won't go to see my parents."

Bruno took no notice and instead whipped out a knife from inside his jacket. He waved it at Filippo. "Go on—run away, you smooth piece of shit. Run, and I will cut her up into little pieces as well." As he spoke, he grabbed Angelina by the hair and rubbed the knife against her long black hair, cutting a lock off.

Filippo took two paces closer to Bruno. "Look, you're a piece of chickenshit. Look at you. You're such a big wanker that you threaten girls," Filippo told him. He sat down on the grass nearby. "When you finish threatening girls, I'll be here to kick your arse in," he added.

Filippo Cudoni knew that he had to distract Bruno from taking his anger out on Angelina. He had to get Bruno to come over to where he was and move away from her.

"Why don't you come here and stick that knife of yours into me if you can, or are you going to show everyone who goes past that you can hold a knife at a woman's throat? Stick that knife into me if you have you got the balls, or do I have to lie on the ground with my hands tied up first? Curcio, you're just a gutless arsehole."

The stinging rebuff worked. Bruno let go of his wife's hair and threw her to the ground. He rushed at Filippo, the knife in his hand ready to slash at Filippo's chest and head.

Filippo had anticipated this, and he was ready for it. He lashed out with his foot at the hand with the knife in it. Somehow, Bruno Curcio managed to avoid the impact of the foot on his arm by pulling back and up. He managed to hang on to the knife. Filippo had barely enough time to rise to his feet before Bruno lunged forward again, thrusting the knife at his chest. Filippo moved back and to one side, but it was not quick enough to miss the knife completely. The knife opened up a wound just under his left breast. The cut ran the whole length of one of his ribs.

Bruno sensed that he had cut Filippo around the chest. He rushed forward to finish him off. This time, Filippo was ready. He dropped down and forward onto his fingertips and on one leg. As Bruno rushed past, stabbing at the air, the point of Filippo's boot hit him hard, sinking into his stomach just below the bottom rib.

The knife went sailing forward as Bruno doubled over in his tracks, his head snapping forward onto his chest.

Filippo jumped to his feet and landed a huge right-handed punch to the side of his bottom rib, just above where his boot had landed. Bruno hunched over with more pain in his chest. Filippo threw a quick left jab to the side of Bruno's head, but he missed as Bruno wobbled about. A ferocious right uppercut, however, found its mark on the side of his jaw, and Bruno was out cold and on his back.

Angelina had stood up and watched in horror as her husband and her not-so-secret lover fought in deadly seriousness. She knew her responsibility as a wife was to her husband, but she also knew his hot temper and ruthlessness to anyone who upset him. She knew that in his rage, Bruno would have killed them both if he could have.

Then she saw the blood oozing through Filippo's shirt. She was at his side in an instant.

"Core mio, you are bleeding. Let me have a look," she implored. "It's just a scratch," Filippo replied vainly, but the blood was saturating his shirt and jacket. He was starting to feel nauseated as he spoke. He looked at Bruno, who was still motionless on the grass. "I think he will be all right. I did hit him pretty hard on the jaw, but he should be all right soon." He wobbled on his feet as he tried to walk over to Angelina. "I think you should go to where your parents are," he told her, but he nearly collapsed at the same time.

She managed to hold him up. "Come on, hang on," she urged him. "I better get you out of here before Bruno comes to, or he will kill both of us."

With Filippo's arm over her shoulder and her arm around his waist, she half carried him as they stumbled towards where her family was. Angelina was now a woman—and a strong one at that—and she needed all her strength to carry him.

It took them twenty minutes to get to where the Folino Gallo and Cudoni families were. By the time they got there, Angelina was as covered in blood as Filippo was. She called out to them when she was close enough, and the men came running. At first, they all thought that both had stab wounds, and Catarina nearly fainted at the sight of her daughter covered with so much blood. Angelina quickly told them that her husband Bruno had stabbed Filippo when he interfered in an argument they were having.

Filippo had lost a lot of blood by then, and he was extremely weak. Zia Theresa took over. She had him placed on his back where she removed his shirt and saw that, luckily, most of the cut was over a rib bone; only towards the end of the cut had the knife slashed between two ribs. She took a clean tablecloth out of her lunch basket and cut it into strips. She laid some of the strips against the wound and wrapped the rest tightly around his chest. She soon had the bleeding stopped.

Angelina explained to the families what had happened as her aunt worked on Filippo. She told them Bruno had been so angry that he would have killed Filippo and probably her if he had been able to.

She told them she should go check on Bruno, whom they had left lying on the grass.

Her father cautioned her against going to see Bruno at the moment or that night. If he was in such a rage, he might still do something drastic.

Filippo Cudoni lost consciousness as his zia cleansed the wound. The men were still debating whether they should go check on Bruno when the younger men returned. They quickly told the young men what had happened. Gennaro took charge immediately. He told Antonio to get a carriage to take Filippo to the nearest home and said it was better that no doctor or police be called. The nearest house was that of the Folino Gallo family, and they agreed that they would take Filippo there. Gennaro asked Benaldo and Natale to go with him to check on Bruno. The three men went to the spot that Angelina directed them to, but they could find no sign of Bruno anywhere. It was obvious that he had left.

Antonio returned with a horse and carriage and, with help from the other men, laid Filippo on one of the seats in the carriage. Antonio, Sarino, and Angelina sat on the opposite seat as the driver took them back to the Folino Gallo residence. Palmo sat up front with the driver. Soon they were at the house, and the three men carried Filippo inside and laid him on a bed.

They took off his boots and bloody jacket and shirt. Angelina retrieved an old sheet and cut it into large bandages to put tightly around his chest and ribs to stop the bleeding. Palmo fetched a bottle of scotch. He drank some before he poured some more into the cut on Filippo's chest. Angelina then wound the bandages around his chest as Antonio and Palmo held him up.

Angelina fetched a small container of water, dipped a cloth in it, and sat on the edge of the bed, gently wiping the moist rag over his forehead. Filippo showed no signs of pain, but he was still unconscious. Zia believed when the bleeding stopped with him resting, he should wake up within a few hours.

The rest of the families followed the coach back to the Folino Gallo home on foot; when they arrived, they found that Filippo was still out but seemingly okay. Angelina explained in more detail to everyone what had happened to start the fight. She did not mention that Bruno suspected that she might still love Filippo more than him. It was apparent to all there that Bruno was extremely jealous and that he might be suffering from some problem if he did not want his wife to go see her parents.

Several hours later, Filippo regained some consciousness. The first person he saw was Angelina. Concern came quickly back to his face. "Are you all right?" he struggled to ask.

She barely heard him, but she knew he was going to be all right. Filippo had no idea where he was or how he had gotten there.

He closed his eyes for a moment and then reopened them. "Where am I, and how did I get here?" he asked Angelina.

"I helped you back to where our families were, and then our brothers brought you here to Papa's place. Antonio is here with you now," Angelina told him.

Antonio walked around from the other side of the bed so that Filippo could see him. "General, Bruno cut you up a bit with his knife. Lucky for you, most of the cut is over a rib and not between ribs. You lost a fair bit of blood while you were fighting, but you should be all right as soon as you get your strength back," Antonio told him.

Gennaro had heard talking and looked in through the door. He saw that his brother was awake and looked all right. "Get some rest, Filippo. You will be feeling a little better by the morning, but you are going to be very sore."

Filippo heard some of what he said but drifted back to sleep. It was an uneasy sleep, filled with nightmares; he saw Bruno doing unthinkable acts to Angelina, and Filippo seemed to be powerless to do anything to stop him. He awoke during the night and realized that his visions had only been bad dreams. He was well aware that he had a severe cut on his chest, and the pain was becoming acute. He tried to move, but the movement brought a sharp groan of pain, and the more he moved, the heavier the pain became.

Angelina, who had fallen asleep in the chair beside the bed, woke up. She picked up his hand and held it. "It is okay, don't worry, and try not to move. I am here with you," she told him. He felt reassured. He squeezed her hand.

Angelina stood up, and holding his hand against her breasts, she put her lips against his. "Try to sleep, my darling. We will talk in the morning," she told him.

Angelina stayed with him until about two in the morning. Her mind was in turmoil. Where was her husband? What was he doing, and what was he thinking? She knew she should also be looking after Bruno. He was her husband, but he had threatened to kill her and Filippo.

At seven that morning, Gennaro and Antonio returned to the Folino Gallo residence to check on their brother. They had stayed with him until ten thirty the previous night and had left only when they believed that Filippo would be all right. Angelina had promised that she would stay by his side for the night, even though her parents had protested that she should get some rest herself.

When they arrived, Filippo was awake but in some severe dis-comfort. Tomasi and Natale were talking to him. Angelina had gone to her room to get some sleep a few hours earlier.

"I am very concerned about Bruno's state of mind," Filippo was telling the two men. "He appeared like someone who had lost control of his senses. I think, in his condition, it would be much too dangerous for Angelina to return to their house until you are sure he is all right." He tried to wave to Gennaro and Antonio with his right hand, but the sudden, sharp pain across his chest stopped him. Slowly, he continued, "Si, I know it is none of my business, but I think it is best if one of the men goes with you, Tomasi, to talk to him first before Angelina goes back."

Tomasi nodded in agreement. "I think that I will go over with Giuseppe and Natale and talk to him before Angelina goes anywhere near him," Tomasi said. "I don't want my daughter having to live with an animal who pulls a woman by the hair. He will need to learn that no one mistreats a Folino Gallo woman and lives to brag about it."

"I did not intend to come between Angelina and her husband," Filippo told Tomasi. "But I could not stand by and watch him dragging her by the hair as he was. He could have taken her by the arm. But he seemed like someone who had gone mad to me. He seemed to have lost all sense and reason."

Zio Nicola and Zia Theresa arrived at the Folino family house soon after. They too were concerned about what had happened the day before. Zia Theresa had come to check that the wound was not infected. She chased the others out of the room except for Antonio, who helped her get Filippo up to open his shirt.

Angelina came in as Antonio was removing the shirt, which had a big bloodstain on it. As Antonio and Angelina held Filippo up by his arms, Zia Theresa slowly removed the strips Angelina had tied around his chest. Gennaro also came back into the room.

Zia and Gennaro inspected the wound. The cut stretched from just under his left breast to his side, some six inches. The bleeding had stopped except for a small, fresh trickle caused by them moving him.

Gennaro looked at the point where the knife had first hit. He pointed it out to the others. "Filippo, you are extremely lucky to be alive," he told him. "If the knife had hit just half an inch higher or lower, it would have slipped between the two ribs, and the damage could have been a bit more drastic—even fatal."

The news that the stabbing could have been fatal really upset Angelina. "You mean he could have been killed?"

"No, no, he's too tough for that," Gennaro laughingly said, changing the line of thought.

Zia cleaned the wound up while Angelina went to find some clean cotton rags to use as bandages. She returned with a clean sheet and a pair of scissors.

"If he was in the hospital, a doctor would sew the cut up to help it heal. You have tough skin. Otherwise, it would leave quite a scar," Zia told Filippo. "I think you will be all right, but you will need to stay still and not move, or the cut will reopen and could get infected."

With Angelina's help, Zia wound the strips they had cut from the sheet tightly around Filippo's chest. When they finished, they put a clean shirt on him.

Catarina came in carrying a steaming cup of coffee for Filippo. "I have fried you a couple of eggs and some bread. You better eat while you are still sitting up," she told Filippo. "We don't want you to starve now."

"No, no, don't worry about me. I will be fine. If Antonio and Gennaro help me up, I will be able to walk home. Don't worry about cooking me anything to eat, Mrs. Folino," Filippo said to Catarina.

His aunt let out a big snort. "You will do no such thing. You cannot move for at least several days, or the wound could become infected. If your brothers try to move you, I will clobber them on the head with a rolling pin," his zia told him. "Now eat your food like a good man, and be quiet."

Tomasi, Natale, and Giuseppe went to the Curcio residence to see if Bruno had returned to his parents' place. When they arrived, Mr. Curcio Senior invited them in. Bruno, he told them, was not in. They had a brief discussion about what had happened the previous day. Mr. Curcio told them that all he knew was that Bruno and Angelina had had a big row over going to the Folino Gallos' Easter party and that Bruno had stormed home late in the afternoon in a rage. Tomasi told him the rest of what had happened. He pointed out that the Folino Gallo clan would not tolerate any ill treatment of its womenfolk because of someone's ill temper. He asked Mr. Curcio to tell Bruno he needed to call in to the Folino Gallo house to talk to him before he would allow Angelina to return to live with Bruno. As it was the Monday after Easter, most workers had the day off work. Antonio and Gennaro returned to the boarding house while Zio Nicola waited for Tomasi and his boys to return from the Curcio residence. Catarina had given the plate of food to Angelina, and she fed it to Filippo; the others returned to the kitchen.

"I'm so confused," Angelina told Filippo quietly but with a look of resignation. "I love you so much, and I want to thank you for what you did for me. At the same time, Bruno is my husband, and I do not even know where he is. I want to be honest with him, but I am so afraid of him and what he may want do to you and even to me. He has changed so much from the fun-loving boy he was before he was mugged. He is now constantly in a foul mood. He has fits of rage and depression. I don't want to make love to him, but if I dare say no, he flies into a rage, and then he has trouble doing anything anyway. My darling, if only you had married me, how happy I would have made you, and you me."

Angelina broke down, and after putting the dish on the floor, she wept with her head on his good shoulder. Filippo put his good arm around her and tried to comfort her. Angelina quietly fell asleep, feeling at peace in the safety of his arm. Her mother found her asleep on his shoulder twenty minutes later. Both had drifted to sleep.

The next morning, Gennaro came to pick Filippo up and walk him home. The swelling and most of the pain had eased off a bit. The wound was showing good signs of healing when Angelina changed the bandages, and provided he took things slowly, there was no rea- son that it would bleed again.

Angelina had been to see Filippo early that morning. She had planted a long, lingering kiss on his lips and fervently assured him that she would never forget him and that if he ever wanted to leave with her, she would go to the end of the world with him. As she had looked at him lying there, her body had longed for him. However, she could not forget she was married, and she already had more problems than she could deal with.

Tomasi and his sons had gone off to work, as had Antonio, who was going to tell Jack that Filippo would need a few more days off due to a small mishap where he had cut himself with a knife.

Angelina had helped Filippo to the kitchen table, and they were having breakfast with Catarina when Gennaro arrived.

"Hi, big brother. I see you are well enough to have breakfast with the beautiful signorinas. How are you this morning?" Gennaro greeted him. He nodded hello to Angelina and her mother. "Hello, Mrs. Folino, Angelina."

"Pretty good, actually, Gennaro," Filippo responded. "Angelina and Catarina have been kind enough to cook me breakfast again—for which I would like to thank you both very much."

"Don't worry about food. We just want you to eat it," Catarina told him.

"I have come to see if you would like any help getting back to the boarding house this morning, Filippo. Or do you have other plans?" Gennaro enquired.

"Thanks, Gennaro, but shouldn't you be at work this morning?" Filippo asked.

"Well, I should be, but I didn't think it would be a good idea for you to try to get home on your own," Gennaro answered.

"You are probably right," Filippo replied. "I suppose I better hurry, or you will miss the next train as well."

"If Gennaro has to hurry to catch the train to work, I can help get you back to your boarding house," Angelina cut in, as if she had not been there until that point. "I would be happy to make sure he gets home after what he has done for me. In fact, I insist that you go to work, Gennaro, and I will make sure he gets back to your boarding house."

"I have enough brains not to argue with a lady." Gennaro winked at her. "But are you sure you want to get this stupid Calabrese home?" he light-heartedly joked.

"Sure, why not? I will help him get home. We can get a trolley car so he won't have to walk much. This way, you will not miss your train to your work," Angelina stated pointedly.

"Okay, okay," Gennaro replied. "I know when I'm not wanted. However, big brother, I will go with you to the trolley."

Gennaro walked with them to the trolley car. From the point where the trolley would bring them, it was not far to the boarding house. They had not seen anything or anyone who could pose any risk to Angelina or Filippo. "I think you should be okay now," he said, and with that, Gennaro left.

At ten in the morning, Angelina and Filippo walked to Filippo's room at the boarding house. They had walked slowly so as not to reopen the cut; nevertheless, Filippo was a little tired when they got there. He sat down on the edge of the bed.

Angelina sat down beside him. "Lie down, and I will make both of us a cup of coffee," Angelina told him. She stood up and went to the stove.

Fifteen minutes later, she returned carrying two cups. He had drifted into a light sleep. She put the cups on a chair and sat on the bed beside him. She bent over and kissed him lightly on the lips. The warmth of her lips on his woke him up. He sat up and looked at her as she handed him the coffee. Slowly, they drank the coffee.

"I'm so mixed up, Filippo," Angelina told him. "I just don't know what to do anymore. The only thing I can think of is how much I want you."

"I want you too, Angelina. But I have made a vow to myself that I will never touch another man's wife again," Filippo told her.

Angelina picked up his cup and took it and hers back to the kitchen. She picked up his hand and held it against her heart when she returned. "You are so sweet and always considerate. My heart is yours," she told him.

She pushed his hand across her chest until it was over her breast and his fingers were on her nipple. He could feel the firmness of her breast and the hardness of her nipple under the palm of his hand, and he instinctively squeezed her breast to feel it better. She held his hand there for what seemed an eternity. Slowly, a wave of passion and longing came over them as they stared into each other's eyes. She could feel the desire for him reaching fever pitch, and she could not hold back any longer. She stood up, and looking down into his eyes, she opened the top of her dress and showed him her breasts. She put her hand on his shoulder and gently pushed him back so that he lay down on the bed. She reached down and started kissing him on the lips.

Filippo did not resist at first, thinking that Angelina was only thanking him for what he had done for her and that it would not go much further. Anyway, a kiss was just a kiss and not a big problem, he figured. Her mouth opened his, and her tongue searched for his. The pure sweetness of her tongue on his tongue sent his pulse soaring.

Angelina certainly knew how to arouse the animal lust in him. "I'm sorry, *amoro mio*. I thought you would like to see them," she murmured to him.

"I always love to see your breasts, but I am of no use to you today."

Angelina lay half-dressed near his good side for a few long minutes. Then she sat up, put one arm on his face, and gently caressed his pubic hair with the other hand. Her breasts pressed against his upper arm; her legs were wrapped around his leg.

"You have no idea how much I've been wanting you to make love to me," she said. "Take me away from this place, Filippo. I will follow you to any part of the world. I know my father does not want me to go back to Italy. But I don't care as long as I am with you. I will go anywhere. There is no way I will go back to that sick Bruno," Angelina pleaded desperately.

Filippo was silent; he stared at the peeling paint on the ceiling. He was not happy about what had nearly happened. He had sworn he would never again touch a married woman, yet he had allowed Angelina to bare her all. He had wanted this married woman, and he had let her control him after he had said no. He knew it was only the pain that had stopped him, and he would have thoroughly enjoyed having intercourse with her—probably more than he had ever enjoyed sex with anyone. But he felt guilty, weak-minded, and dishonest with himself when he realized that if he had been capable, he would have gone through with it. It was the first time in his life that he had looked at it that way, but that was the truth of it. He had allowed himself to be dishonest with his own conviction. He knew he honestly loved this woman more than any woman he had ever loved before, but he told himself he would never allow this to happen with a married woman again. He decided that the sooner he left for Italy, the better.

Filippo finally brought his gaze back to Angelina. It was not easy; he did not know where to start. "I am nothing but a useless, idiotic *norante*. I say one thing, and yet..." He paused. "I do the opposite." After another long pause, he said, "I will not see you again until I return from Italy. Please go."

Filippo knew he had saved about 850 American dollars. It was now April 8, 1902, and by the end of June, he figured he could save maybe another fifty dollars. That would pay for the fare and any small expenses he might have. That would leave him with about twenty-five thousand lire. His mind was lost in accounting when he realized Angelina was talking to him.

"I'm sorry, Angelina, my mind was many miles away. What did you say?" he asked her.

"I said, can I live with you here? I won't go back to Bruno. I don't care what my parents say. He frightens me to death, Filippo. I love you—only you. I want so much to be with you. Please say yes. I can't bear to leave you now or ever," Angelina implored. She started kissing him all over the face and neck.

"Angelina, at this moment, you cannot stay here. If the Curcio family found out that you left him for me just three months after getting married, there would be a war. I cannot allow myself to be the reason that your family went to war. I was supposed to help you, not be the reason for war. And we would both lose the respect of all our friends and relations. No, you must understand that at this point, you must first resolve your problems with your husband. You need your family to help you sort out this problem," Filippo pointed out to her.

"But you are my problem," she said. "It's you I love. That is the problem."

"Angelina, I may be the one you love, but I never told you that I would marry you or tell you to marry Bruno. That was your choice, and you must now sort that out. I do not want to be seen as the rea- son that you are leaving Bruno, or there will be a war between your families. People could get killed—your relatives and mine. I am sure you do not want that to happen. You must go back to your parents and sort this out," Filippo told her sternly.

He regretted that he had not been sterner earlier, but somehow he could never be stern with this woman who loved him so much. It was now midday. *She should go back now, and quickly*, he thought, *before anyone finds her still here.*

"Angelina, it is best that you go now before anyone starts to worry for you," he told her abruptly.

Chapter 30

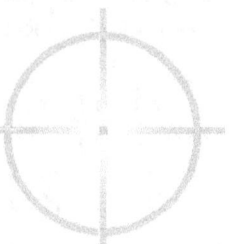

His zia and zio came to see him several times in the next few days to make sure he cleaned and changed the bandages daily. It had been a clean wound anyway, and no infection had set in. The scotch that Palmo had poured had made sure of that.

The second time his aunt and uncle came to see him, Zia told him that Bruno, along with his father and brother, had been to see the Folino Gallo family and Angelina. Bruno had apologized profusely and apparently honestly for the shameful way he had treated Angelina. He had promised that he did love her and would look after her forever. He had also apologized for any harm he had done to Filippo Cudoni and said that he had become very jealous when Filippo had turned up, and as a result, he had lost his senses.

Angelina's father had been unaware of what had happened between Angelina and Filippo and had strongly encouraged her to return and give Bruno one more chance. Tomasi had told him very clearly that if he mistreated Angelina one more time, he had better leave America instantly, or he would join those who had passed away before him. He had indicated with his raised right hand, fingers pointing to the throat, that Bruno's head would go if he tried that again.

Zia and Catarina had said nothing of what had happened between Filippo and Angelina, but Zia Theresa knew that Filippo was the reason that Angelina was not happy with Bruno. She made the remark that some women should make up their minds on who or what they wanted before getting married. Zio was not sure he under- stood what she had meant, but Filippo knew.

On Monday of the following week, Filippo returned to work. He saw Jack that morning and apologized for not being at work for the last ten days. He told him he had accidentally cut himself with a sharp knife in the side of a rib. He asked Jack if there was any extra work available because he wanted to make up for the time he had been away. Jack assured him he would get back to him and let him know.

Jack did get back to him and told him there was extra work available. He also told Filippo that he was a granddad again. Kay and Jim had had a little boy they called Benjamin. Filippo congratulated him and asked that he congratulate Jim, Kay, and Jane for him. He told Jack he would go over one afternoon and visit the family.

For the next month, Filippo worked every day from 6:30 a.m. to 5:30 p.m. At night, the three brothers discussed the upcoming trip to Italy. Antonio took a few hours off work one day to organize rail passes to Philadelphia.

Filippo finally took one Sunday afternoon off and decided that he should go congratulate the Bensons on the arrival of their new grandson.

He got to the Bensons' around five o'clock in the afternoon. Jack and Jane were inside when he arrived. They welcomed him in, and they sat in the lounge room and talked. Jane commented that they had heard he'd had a small mishap and asked if he was all right now.

"It was nothing really. Yes, just a scratch. I am all right now. Thanking you very much, Mrs. Jane," Filippo told her. "I have not seen Tracy for some time. How is she by the way, Mrs. Jane?"

"She's very busy now, Phil. She has been promoted. She is a school education coordinator now, and she works extra-long hours— sometimes even on weekends," Jane told him. "She has gone to see another teacher regarding a new school project she is working on."

"That's wonderful," Filippo replied. "Will you congratulate her for me on having a new nephew and for her promotion? I would also like to tell you that we are thinking of returning to Italy in early July. We are going to Philadelphia on Friday to book our passage back."

Tracy walked in as Filippo was telling them about going to Philadelphia. "Hi," she said to Filippo. "Are you going for a holiday to Philadelphia?" She joked, "Can I come too?"

"Hello, Tracy. It is nice to see you. Yes, we are going to Philadelphia, but not for a holiday. We are going to book fares back to Italy in July," Filippo told her. "I think we will be back from Italy about October or early November if I return."

Tracy seemed excited about her new project. "Phil, did Mum tell you I have been promoted?"

"Yes, Tracy, and congratulations are in order to you for your work and for being an auntie again." Filippo stood up and gave her a little peck on the cheek. "I have to go, but I will see you again before I leave. You will be the school boss soon, Tracy," Filippo joked as he left.

Antonio found that people working for the company got free rail travel to other towns and cities where the company rails passed. They decided to take one Friday off work and catch the train to Philadelphia on a Thursday afternoon; that way, they would be in Philadelphia on Friday to organize boat fares to Italy. They decided they would return on Sunday and, in this way, lose only one day of work.

That Thursday, Filippo and Antonio caught the late afternoon train to Philadelphia. They arrived there the next morning and went straight to the offices of the shipping companies. By two in the after- noon, they had organized two boat tickets from New York to Naples, Italy, departing July 7, 1902. They stayed in Philadelphia until early Sunday morning and caught the six thirty morning train back to Pittsburgh.

They arrived in Pittsburgh during the early part of Sunday night. Gennaro was still up, and they told him that they would be leaving Pittsburgh the fifth day of July, travelling from Pittsburgh to Philadelphia and then to New York, with the boat leaving from New York on the seventh on its way to Europe. It would take them as far as Naples via Marseilles.

Gennaro reminded them to say hello to the Milano family if they had time. They had seven weeks to go before they left.

The following night, Antonio and Filippo went to tell their zia and zio that they would be returning to Italy via New York on the seventh day of July. All the family was home except for Michele and Marietta, who lived not far away. As they were talking, Natale and Luigi Folino Gallo called in to say hello. They came in, and Filippo told them that he and Antonio were going back to Italy in July. Natale was a little excited.

"What day are you leaving?" he enquired. "I want to go to Italy as well. I have not seen my little lady for a long time, and I want to go back for a visit."

"We are leaving on the fifth of July from Pittsburgh," Antonio told him. "You may still be able to get a passage for that day."

"That would suit me perfectly," Natale told them. "I have to stay till the end of June to go to the wedding, and then I can leave."

"Who's wedding?" several of them asked at once.

"Didn't you know? Giuseppe and Rosetta have set the date as the twenty-eighth of June for them to get married," Natale told them. "The company we are going with is called the Flotta Napoli. It is obviously an Italian group, and you could contact them and come with us," Filippo told Natale. Natale promised to make enquiries about joining them on the same boat.

A few nights later, Gennaro and Antonio went to see some of the Folino Gallo boys. They all decided to go down to the city center for a night out. The next morning on the way to work, Antonio told Filippo that he had confirmed that Giuseppe and Rosetta were to marry in June and that the three brothers were invited to the wedding.

Chapter 31

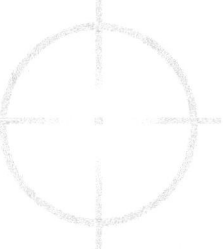

The days quickly sped by. The Cosa Nostra had not bothered the three brothers for some time, and the brothers thought that maybe they had decided to leave them alone. The Cosa Nostra was very active against other Italians and, in particular, the Sicilian people. They robbed, bashed, and mugged them. The police found people of Italian origin, most of whom were men dead in and around Pittsburgh, sometimes for strange unknown reasons.

Filippo called in to see Jack, Jane, and Tracy two weekends prior to his departure. It was about three in the afternoon when he arrived at their home. Filippo could hear voices speaking from inside when he knocked on the front door. Jane answered the door.

"Hello, Phil, it's nice to see you. How are you? Come in," she greeted him.

"I'm great, thank you," Filippo told her as he followed her through the doorway.

Tracy was talking to a young man who looked to be about twenty-seven.

"Hi, Phil." Tracy cheerily greeted him and introduced him to her friend. "Phil, this is John Russell. John, this is Phil Cudoni. Phil,

John is a science teacher at the same school where I teach. John, Phil works for the railroad with my dad."

John Russell was a tall, athletic, good-looking, and friendly young man. "Nice to meet you, Phil. Tracy has said some nice things about you," he warmly greeted Filippo.

"It is nice-a to meet you too, John," Filippo told him in his improving English accent. "Anyone who is a friend of Tracy's has to be a nice-a guy. I am glad to meet you." Filippo reached out and shook John's hand.

"Jack's not home, Phil, but take a seat, and I will go and make you a cup of coffee," Jane told Filippo. "I'm already making a cup for John and Tracy."

"John and I are working on a school project together, Phil. Anyway, how are you? I haven't seen you for a long time. I thought you might have already departed for Italy," Tracy cheerfully said.

"Good, yes, I am good," Filippo replied, "but I would never leave without saying goodbye to you, Tracy. You are one of my best friends here in Pittsburgh. How could I leave without saying good- bye to you? And my boss would never give me a job again if I did that. Actually, that is why I have come, Tracy. In case I do not see you again, I have come to say goodbye till we meet again."

Jane came back carrying cups and saucers and some cake. She handed everyone a cup and invited the two men to have a piece of cake. She sat on a spare chair close by.

"Well, Phil, when are you leaving us, and are you coming back?" Jane asked him.

"We are leaving on the seventh of July by boat from New York and leaving Pittsburgh by train on the fifth. It is only two weeks to go now," Filippo told them. "But next Saturday night, I will be going to a friend's wedding. I wanted to make sure I came and thanked you for all the wonderful things you have done for Antonio and me. I thank you from the bottom of my heart. I will try to call in again before I leave."

They talked for a while longer, and then Filippo took leave. Tracy excused herself from John and followed Filippo outside.

"If I don't see you again, Phil, I would like to tell you that you are one of the nicest people I know, and I will never forget the good times. I would like to wish you the best, whatever you choose to do. I will always cherish you. I hope you return one day, and I hope you find what you want," Tracy told him sincerely. She leaned up and gave him a lingering but passionless kiss on the lips. Filippo put his arms around her and gave her a giant, brotherly hug.

"No matter what happens, you will always be one of my best friends, Tracy. I wish I could have stayed here forever with you and your family, but this was not meant to be. I will always cherish you," Filippo responded. "I hope to see you again before the end of the year. Goodbye for now, Tracy." After giving her a quick kiss on the cheek, Filippo was gone.

That weekend, Filippo went to see a few of the people he wanted to say goodbye to. He called in to see Batiste Raso and his family. Batiste and Antonia had had a little sister for young Mario since Filippo had last seen them. They were glad to have Filippo and Antonio call on them. Batiste told Filippo to call on his parents if they went to his little home region. He knew they would be happy to see him.

Late in the week, Filippo and Antonio called in to see their zio and zia, who scolded them for not calling in more often. It was late when they arrived, and the younger sons had gone to see the Folino Gallo boys. Zio offered them a glass of wine. They sat and talked for a while. Zia left to go do something, and then she called to Filippo to give her a hand. "Filippo, can you carry this box into the other room for me, please?" Zia asked him.

"Sure I can," Filippo replied. He picked up the empty box and followed his zia to the other room.

"What did you want to talk to me about, Zia?" Filippo asked her as he put the box down. "You didn't really want me to carry an empty box around."

"Sit down for a minute, Filippo. I want to talk to you about Angelina," his zia told him. "What is going to happen to you two now?"

"Zia, what about Angelina? I told Angelina that time back on Easter that I could not promise her or her father that I would not go back to Italy to stay. I am going back to Italy, and I cannot guarantee that I will be coming back. She is married, and she is back with her husband, where she should be. Is she in some trouble with Bruno again or something, Zia?" Filippo asked his aunt.

"Filippo, I do not want to be a busybody, but I do not want either of you hurt. I know that on the outside, you both pretend not to be friends, but I am sure you are more than just friends. I think you both still love each other very much, more than what Bruno Curcio thinks too. Am I right, Filippo?" His aunt wanted to know. "I am sure that Catarina also thinks that, but her daughter will not tell her."

"Zia, if Angelina tells her mother there is nothing going on, do you think I will tell you that there is?" Filippo asked his aunt.

"No, I suppose not. However, will you tell me if you have had an affair with her during the last six months?" his zia demanded.

Filippo smiled ruefully. He knew he had to tell her a lie. "Zia, I am not in the habit of having affairs with married women, and anyway, why do you ask me this now? Do you think I am going to Italy because I am running away from her or something? Zia, is there a reason for this question?" Filippo asked.

"I have my reasons, Filippo. Are you telling me that you have not had an affair with Angelina?" she persisted.

"I have not told you anything, Zia, and with all due respect to you, I do not see why there should be anything to tell you. Has anything happened to warrant these questions, or are you just guessing that there may have been something? Zia, I am not trying to be smart, but if there is any problem, please tell me."

"There is no problem to worry about. Forgive me for asking," his aunt said quietly. "Can you carry the box back, please?"

Filippo felt that his aunt and Angelina's mother both suspected the truth and had discussed that Angelina's problem lay with her love for Filippo. They might also have suspected that there was a physical problem with Bruno, but if Angelina had not told her mother, then he was not going to either. His zia was too cagey to ask any further on the subject. They joined Antonio and Zio Nicola in the kitchen. "Antonio, I have asked Filippo to tell my relations that we are doing well and are in fine health if he sees any of them. Please give them our regards," Zia said to Antonio.

"Filippo, I would like you to give our best regards to your parents, grandparents, uncles, aunts, cousins, and friends back in Sambiase," Zio said, echoing the words of his wife. "And please give a hug to your grandparents for me, and tell them we miss them very much. Tell them that I will try to come to Italy to see them soon."

Zia made them coffee and biscuits, which they enjoyed. They talked about a variety of things, particularly about life back in Calabria. At ten, the Cudoni brothers went home.

On Saturday afternoon, the three brothers went to the wedding of Giuseppe and Rosetta. The wedding ceremony was at three in the afternoon. It was a hot, sticky afternoon, and the threat of storms lay in the air.

Giuseppe and Rosetta were getting married by Father Sebastiano in the same church where Michele and Marietta Folino Gallo and Angelina and Bruno Curcio had been married.

Benaldo and Natale were Giuseppe's best man and groomsman, respectively. The wedding guests waited for half an hour before the bridal party arrived. Rosetta and her father led the way in. Rosetta looked her usual cheery and bubbly self.

Filippo had seen the bridesmaids before but did not know their names. The matron of honor was Angelina. She had no partner and followed at the rear of the group. She was an imposing figure behind the other two girls. She seemed at least eight inches taller than the other girls in the wedding group.

To Filippo, she seemed more relaxed, somehow more at peace with herself. She looked more mature, more filled out, more radiantly glowing and beautiful than she ever had. There was something different about her that Filippo could not understand. He could sense it, but he could not fathom what it was. It played on his mind for the rest of the night.

The wedding reception was in the same hall where the other two receptions took place, but the decorations and the layout were different. The hall looked as pretty as a picture, and the atmosphere was cheerful. Filippo could detect Rosetta's hand in it. It was a great night and truly enjoyed by everyone. The only person who seemed to have a scowl on his face was Bruno Curcio, which contrasted his wife's new happier look on life.

Filippo kept away from Angelina and her husband during the early part of the night. He tried to say goodbye to as many people as possible during the night. Natale Folino Gallo, Tommasi's nephew, caught up with Filippo at one point.

"Filippo, I have some great news. I checked with the company you and Antonio are leaving with to go to Italy, and they had one spare fare. I'm coming back to Sambiase with you and Antonio, my friend," Natale told him excitedly. They spoke at length of what was to be done and when. They agreed to see each other before departure time.

Just before the bride and groom were ready to leave, Filippo decided to say goodbye to Angelina and her husband. They were sitting at a table on their own when he walked over.

Filippo walked straight over to Bruno and offered him his hand. "Let's forget the past, Bruno. I would like to say goodbye to you and Angelina and wish you the best for the future. Let bygones be bygones and look to the future. What do you say?" Filippo asked him, looking him straight in the eye, sounding extremely sincere.

Bruno had stood up as Filippo spoke. Alarmed at the possibility of confrontation between them, Angelina also stood up. Concerned, she watched her husband's reaction to this new development. He looked Filippo in the eye. "Can you forget the past—forget what has happened between us?" he asked Filippo.

"Bruno, I don't deny that we haven't been the best of friends, and I have been very much in love with your wife and her with me. That was in the past. She is married to you. You should consider yourself the luckiest bastard under the sun. I want Angelina to be the happiest woman in the world because I still care for her, but she is your wife now, and I will respect that. I want you to look after her. I will totally forget the past as long as you look after her. If you do not look after her, I will be back, but not as a friend. *Comprendi?* Shake?" Filippo told him slowly.

Bruno thought he could now understand a little better where Filippo Cudoni was coming from and why. Maybe he had overreacted before, he thought. He realized that to Angelina, he would probably never mean as much as Filippo Cudoni, but Filippo Cudoni accepted that he, Bruno Curcio, was her husband and should be the one to look after her.

He slowly put out his hand and shook hands. "Si, I understand," Bruno replied. "As long as you understand I am her husband."

Filippo understood the subtle insinuation. Angelina recognized that it was also a way for Filippo to tell her that the love affair between them was truly over.

Angelina's face showed her relief at the lack of confrontation, but in her heart, she knew she had lost her lover. Still, the two most important men in her life were no longer at loggerheads. Far more than that, her husband now accepted that Filippo had been the most important person to her in the past.

She embraced her husband, but she saved her biggest hug for Filippo. "I will always love you," she whispered in his ear. Then louder she said, "Thank you. Thank you for what you have done for us." She let Filippo go and held her husband's hand.

Some of the guests looked a bit surprised at them. Angelina's mother and Zia had seen Filippo walk across to talk to them. For a moment, both had been concerned that there could be another fight. Then they had seen them shake hands. They had seen the relief on Angelina's face and the hugs that she gave her husband and Filippo. They knew that most of her present problems were over, but not all. There would be at least one more to come.

"Arrivederci, amico," Filippo said again to Bruno as they shook hands again. He leaned forward and gave Angelina a quick peck on the cheek. "Arrivederci, cara mia," he said to Angelina.

Filippo left them and walked away. He knew that he had not been completely honest with Bruno and that Angelina would feel shut out of his life, but it was better for Angelina and Bruno to go forward on their own from now on. He was pleased he would be leaving no enemies behind and felt satisfied that Angelina had an opportunity to be happy.

Zia Theresa caught his eye and made a sign for him to go over. He went over and sat beside her.

"Lei come sta, Zia?" Filippo asked her.

"*Molto bene, grazie*," his aunt replied, "but tell me, what did you say to Bruno to make him shake hands with you and to make Angelina happy as well?"

"Not much. I told him that what had happened between Angelina and me was in the past and for all of us to forget it. I told Bruno to look after Angelina, or I would be back to talk to him. More or less, that's it," Filippo told her.

Catarina, who was listening intently, spoke up. "For whatever you said to them, thank you. They at least now look relaxed with each other. I thought their marriage was *finito*, but now they have a chance."

"*Signora*, I wanted Bruno to know that Angelina was his wife and to look after her. I still care enough for Angelina to want the best for her, and that means Bruno looking after her. I thought it was best that I do that before I left, and I think he will do that," Filippo explained to Catarina.

Filippo returned to the boarding house as soon as the bride and groom left.

Filippo and Antonio worked until early afternoon the following Friday. They collected their pay and said goodbye to Jack and the rest of the crew they had worked with. Jack shook hands with them and told them goodbye and to come see him about jobs when they got back. The rest wished them well. They packed their bags for the last time when they got back to the boarding house. As soon as Gennaro got back from work and cleaned up, they went to their zio Nicola's place to eat. Zia had invited them for dinner.

Most of their friends and all of their relations came to say good-bye to them there that night. They were catching an early train in the morning, and it would be too early for most to see them off at the station. Natale and all the Folino Gallo families were there at the Cudoni residence as well. Angelina and Bruno came too. Everyone said ciao and wished them a bon voyage.

A few tears were shed, but most were happy with the knowledge that the brothers were returning. The one who shed the most tears was Angelina. Her tears flowed freely, but this time, Bruno did not get upset because he now understood what this man had meant to her. Angelina tried to make light of her tears by joking to Filippo that he would probably come back with a little fat Italian wife. She gave Filippo a huge, long hug, and although he could feel those beautiful breasts pressing into his chest, the instant passion they had aroused in him in the past did not occur.

The next morning, Gennaro and Luigi went with them to the railroad station to see them off. It was strange to Filippo and Antonio to be leaving Gennaro behind, but they both thought they would be coming back and would be back before Christmas.

They were in Philadelphia by early that night and stayed the night in a local hotel. They left the city by train early Sunday morning and were in New York by midafternoon. The next morning, they were at the wharf early, and soon the ship was leaving.

They departed the wharf at nine that morning, almost three years to the day since they had arrived. The world of the three Cudoni brothers had certainly changed a bit since the day they had left their town of Sambiase, and changes would continue.

Chapter 32

Three weeks later, the boat anchored at Marseilles. It was an over-night stop, and the passengers had a choice of staying on the boat or going ashore. The Cudoni's and Natale decided to go visit the Milano family. It was 3:00 p.m. when they arrived at Milano's Restaurant.

Antonio walked in first. There were still a few customers in the restaurant, but most had finished eating and were just sitting around talking. Siesta time was almost over, and they were preparing to return to work. Marcella was handing some customers their last glasses of wine. She looked up and saw the three men walk inside the restaurant. She handed one man his glass of wine and was ready to hand the other man his glass when it suddenly dawned on her who the men were. The last glass slipped through her fingers and crashed to the floor as she let out a shriek of delight.

"Antonio, my Antonio!" she called out in a loud voice. She dropped the tray she was carrying and raced over to hug and kiss him. The noise and clatter of breaking glass had startled her father, and he came racing out to see what the commotion was. He saw his daughter hugging a stranger and wondered what had gotten into her. Then he saw Filippo and recognized who it was. He came striding over with a huge grin on his face.

"Filippo Cudoni, well, I'll be damned," Luigi said. "I'm glad to see you."

The two warmly greeted each other and shook hands.

Filippo introduced Luigi to Natale. "Luigi Milano, this is Natale Folino Gallo, a family friend. Natale, this is Luigi."

Antonio managed to free himself from Marcella and shook hands with Luigi, who had not changed much since they last saw him. Other than a few extra grey hairs on his head, he was the same old Luigi.

Luigi sat them down at a table and brought them some glasses of wine. He called to his wife, who was washing dishes in the kitchen. She came over, said hello, shook hands with the three men, and then returned to the kitchen to finish washing. Luigi wanted to know all the things they had been up to since they had left France and gone to the New World. Meanwhile, Marcella had dragged Antonio off somewhere, maybe to share an extra hug and a private kiss or two.

Luigi told Filippo that Alberto and Brigitte were both married. Alberto was out buying stores for the restaurant, but Brigitte no longer worked at the restaurant. She and her husband had a shop not far away on the same street. Marcella was not married, although she did have a couple of young men chasing her. Alberto had married, and while he worked at the restaurant, he lived with his wife and baby girl not far away.

Filippo knew that Luigi had to prepare for the busy night ahead. He told Luigi that he wanted to show Natale the city but said they would return early that night to eat and see Alberto and talk some more.

Antonio and Marcella had disappeared, so Filippo and Natale left to see the city sights. They came back at seven that night and found Antonio sitting in the restaurant. They sat down with him. He told them he and Marcella were going out together that night. She was getting him something to eat, and afterwards, they were going out on the town. He told Filippo that if he did not see him during the night, he would see them at the boat in the morning. Marcella brought him something to eat and told her parents that she and Antonio were going out, and a short time later, they left.

Antonio and Marcella went for a stroll around the city, but all they really wanted to do was hug and kiss. Marcella suggested that they go up to her room above the restaurant through the back stairway. No one would see them at this hour if they sneaked in through the back alley, up the flight of stairs, and into Marcella's room. Once they were in her room, she locked her bedroom door. They sat on the bed, kissing, hugging, and petting. It was not long before both were naked in bed and making love. Around eleven, Marcella dressed and sneaked back out through the rear stairway. She walked around to the front and into the restaurant.

Filippo and Natale had returned to the ship, Luigi told his daughter, and she said Antonio had also returned to the boat. She told her parents she was going to bed and said good night. She went back to Antonio, who was waiting for her. Antonio stayed the night with Marcella, and in each other's arms, they slept. They made love several times during the night and early morning, but before the early sun was ready to rise, Antonio sneaked out of Marcella's bedroom and into the street. He wandered around the street until full daylight and then returned to the ship.

The boat was due to depart about midday. The three men decided to take a stroll downtown and then return about ten thirty to the boat. When they were near the restaurant, Antonio decided that he would go see Marcella first.

He told Filippo as they walked there that he was thinking of staying a week or so in Marseilles with the Milano family. The other two decided to have a cup of coffee there in the meanwhile.

The restaurant was just opening when they arrived. Alberto was sweeping the front of the premises, Luigi and Josephine were in the kitchen, and Marcella was replacing tablecloths on some of the tables. Alberto, who knew Filippo was back in Marseilles, was happy to see his friend and shook hands with the three men, who then went inside. Marcella was happy to see them, but her eyes were for Antonio mainly. Filippo and Natale sat down at a table while Antonio went to talk to Marcella privately.

Antonio told Marcella he would like to stay an extra week with them if they would put up with him. She was over the moon with joy but told him that she would have to ask her father if he could stay with them. She went to make coffee for them and asked her father about what Antonio had proposed.

Luigi came from the kitchen and sat with them. "*Buon giorno,*" he welcomed them. "Antonio, you would like to stay for a week or so, Marcella tells me."

"With your permission, sir, I would like to stay here in Marseilles until the next boat is here in about a week's time. That is, with your approval, sir," Antonio said.

"We do have a spare room where Alberto used to sleep. If that suits you, you can stay," Luigi told him.

"*Grazie tanto,*" Antonio told him. In his mind, he wondered if Luigi would have let him stay if he had known that he had spent the night making love to his daughter in her bed—or if, with that knowledge, he would have preferred to shoot him instead.

Filippo and Natale left France that day and arrived in Naples six days later. The next day, their little train pulled into the railway station in Sambiase. On Wednesday, August 6, 1902, Filippo returned to his native Calabria and Sambiase.

The little station looked the same. It was the same. Nothing had changed since the last time Filippo had ridden the train in from military training. Natale commented on how small it looked compared to the stations at Pittsburgh, Philadelphia, and New York.

No one greeted them at the station because no one knew they were coming. Filippo and Natale walked down to the piazza. They stopped for a cup of coffee at the little cafe where, just more than four years ago, Filippo and Gennaro had handed out a hiding to an overly jealous waitress admirer and his friends.

Natale and Filippo agreed to meet later in the week in Falerna, where Natale,s parents lived. Natale's mind was on the girl he had left behind, and he was anxious to walk the eight kilometers to her place. He lived in a slightly different direction from Filippo and set out as soon as he finished drinking his coffee. Filippo paid the owner, who did not recognize him, picked up his bag, and walked out into the street. He looked down towards the railway station, and then he turned around to head towards his parents' farm.

As he turned, he nearly ran into a woman with a baby in her arms and two other children following behind her. He apologized to her for his clumsiness and moved aside. As he stepped around the children, it suddenly dawned on him that he knew this woman.

"*Aspetta un momento*," Filippo called to her. "Maria Valenci."

The woman stopped in her tracks. In Sambiase, it was common for a woman to retain her maiden name; however, the sound of his voice made her stop. No woman forgets the voice of her first love.

"Filippo Cudoni, the Americano now," she said in amazement. "Maria, it is a long time since I last spoke to you. How are you?" Filippo said. "These three lovely children are yours?" Filippo was looking at the eldest child, who was now an active young girl of about five years of age. "Your little girl is very pretty, and she reminds me of you."

"Yes, and it is a very long time since you last spoke to me—about six years. And for two years, I waited to hear from you, but you must have found someone else," she said.

"Maria, please forgive me, but I never had anyone else then. I found out after I returned from the military service that my messages to you were not getting to you. I thought you got sick of waiting for me and went with someone else. I was very angry when I found out what had happened. However, you were married by then, and it was too late. So I went to America, and I just returned today," Filippo told her.

"What do you mean your messages were not getting through?" she asked him, anger and curiosity in her voice.

"I mean that I left plenty of messages for you, but you obviously never got them," Filippo replied. "Anyway, you are married and have three lovely children. You must be very happy and proud. How are your parents?"

"My mother is good, but my father passed away two and a half years ago. To whom did you give the messages?" she asked.

"It does not matter now," he replied, "but my heart was in pieces when I saw you with this little one, that day in front of this cafe three years ago. You were a lady with a family, and that was that. That is when I decided to go to America. Good luck, and good day to you and your family, Maria."

"Wait, you hypocrite. You did not seem too upset to me before you left. In fact, you looked like you were going to make love to the mayor's granddaughter in the piazza if I remember correctly.

So your talk about being heartbroken is just rubbish like the rest of you," she quickly retorted before he could leave.

Filippo looked at her and considered explaining to her just what had happened that day with Gina. He opened his mouth but could only stutter a sound before he realized it would be better to say nothing. It dawned on him that Maria had seen Gina kissing him that morning at the front of the shop, and nothing he could say would change the way it would have looked to someone watching. There was something else he wanted to say but thought better of it.

He gave her a wry smile. "Maria, as I just said before, you have a very pretty young daughter who looks to me to be about five years old. Am I right? So you say you were forced by your parents to marry the baker because they were worried you were getting old. Timing seems very strange. You must have made love with him well before you got married. Good day, Maria."

Maria's face turned almost red, a very angry red, and for some- one with olive skin, the color showed brightly against her smooth face. "I-I-I, eh. It is a long story, I know, but, but…" Her voice trailed off. Filippo Cudoni had already walked off.

With a suitcase in each hand, Filippo set off for his father's farm. It was now four in the afternoon, and it would be some thirty-five minutes before he knocked on his grandfather's door on his way home.

His grandparents were overjoyed to see him. His grandfather was now in his early eighties but still very alert. His grandmother, who was seventy-five, had lost some of her hearing. He told them he had just arrived back from the New World and still had not seen his father's family. He talked to them for some time before he bid them ciao and set off for his father's house.

As he went out, he noticed a small group of people gathered outside his father's house. He set off quickly towards them. He was glad to see his parents and siblings waiting for him.

Giuseppe had noticed a man go into their grandparents' place and had told his mother, who had called his father. They had all come out to see who it was.

Little Theresa, who was no longer little, came running down the path to meet him. She was now fifteen and almost a full-grown woman. "Filippo, my Americano. You have come back to stay with us."

His mother, Rosaria, was overjoyed to see her eldest son return home and kept embracing him. His father, who was normally reserved, embraced him and kissed him on the cheeks as well. His younger brothers were extremely happy that he had returned, and they wanted to know as much about the New World as possible.

"Eh, Americano. Tell us about America," the younger brothers kept asking.

Giovanni and Peppino were already planning what they should take and how long it would be before they left.

Giovanni had grown a little taller and much broader since Filippo had last seen him, but he was just a little shorter than Filippo. Peppino, on the other hand, was nearly as tall as Gennaro, but he was very lean. Both had black hair, brown eyes, and a light olive complex- ion. Giuseppe was the only other member of the Cudoni's to have the blue-green eyes of their grandfather, Pietro Antonio Cudoni.

Filippo told them that Antonio was also coming back and would be in Sambiase in about seven or eight days. Carlo, who was nineteen years old and nearly the same build as Filippo, also wanted to be included in any trip to the New World. Giuseppe, the youngest male in the family, was still undecided about all this talk of America. He was close to his parents, and the idea of leaving them was not encouraging to him.

There were many hugs, kisses, and tears of joy that night. Filippo had brought presents for the whole family. He brought with him things that the family back home had never heard about. All of the family wanted to know how things were in the New World.

"How is Gennaro? Where was Antonio? How were all the Americanos back in America?" Giovani kept asking.

It was late before they eventually went to bed that night.

Chapter 33

For the next few days, Filippo helped his parents and brothers on the farm. On Sunday, he decided that he would go see Natale Folino Gallo, whose parents lived on a farm near a town named Falerna. It was just over an hour and a quarter's brisk walk from his parents' place to where Natale's parents lived, and he left early in the morning to avoid the hotter part of the day. It was about nine when he arrived at the Folino Gallo farmhouse. The outside walls of the family's simple cottage had stone walls, and the roof was covered by hard-baked earth shingles.

There was nobody around when he knocked on the front door to the house. After having walked this far, he did not want to return without talking to Natale. He looked around to see if they were in the fields. A search revealed that no one was around. He remembered that it was Sunday and that Natale had mentioned that his parents were devout Catholics who went to Mass every Sunday. He had no idea what Mass times were in Falerna, but he figured that was where they were. It was only a fifteen-minute walk to the little mountain town of Falerna. He could actually see the town from the back of the farm.

Filippo decided to go to the church. He could see it as he walked towards town. The town of Falerna was not very big. It sat compactly on the top of a mountain ridge. The road Filippo took passed through the town and out the other side and then wound its way down to the Mediterranean Sea. The town was some seven hundred meters above sea level.

The piazza in Falerna looked out and over a ridge that dropped steeply to a stream well below the town. The stream flowed past the town, down to the coastal land, and then out to the sea. The magnificent view from the piazza down to the sea was not unlike that from Filippo's family farm near Sabiase, except this piazza was closer to the sea.

Filippo left the piazza and went up the road to the church. The church bells had rung as he had walked towards the town, so he knew that Mass had started, and he would be some ten minutes late. The little church, he noted, was quite full, so he stood up in the back. It was during the giving of Holy Communion that he was able to spot Natale with his family, sitting towards the front seats.

Three women sat on one side of Natale, and one much younger woman sat on the other side. All wore veils on their heads, and it was a little hard to make out any features. There were also two younger men with him.

When Mass finished, Filippo, who had been at the back of the church, was one of the first out. He waited until Natale and his family came out and then approached them. Natale had not noticed him in church, but he spotted him outside when Filippo waved to him.

Natale came over to talk to him. "Ciao amico Americano. Buon giorno, Filippo. Come stai?"

"Bene grazie," Filippo told him. "I didn't know it was Mass time here in Falerna, or I would have come earlier."

"How long have you been here, or did you go to the farm first?" Natale enquired politely.

"I did go to the farm first, but then I thought you might be at Mass, so I came here about ten minutes after Mass started," Filippo replied.

"It doesn't matter now, Filippo. Come over, and I will introduce you to my family," Natale told him.

Natale led him over to where his family was. He introduced him to his father first. "Papa, this is Filippo Cudoni, u Americano. He is another nephew of Zia Theresa and Zio Nicola. Filippo, this is my papa, Antonio; my mama, Rosa; and my younger brothers, Pietro and Paulo. Our sisters—Rosina, Carmela, and Fiorina—will be here soon. Rosina looks a lot like her cousin Angelina in America."

Antonio Folino Gallo was a big man, and Filippo could see from which family side his relations in Pittsburgh and the Folino Gallos there had inherited their tallness. His wife, Rosa, appeared to be a gentle and caring woman, still dark haired and above-average height.

Filippo shook hands with everyone as Natale introduced them. A very tall young woman and two younger but shorter girls dressed in the traditional Italian costume of red, white, and green were making their way towards them. They also wore bright red scarves over their heads and around their faces. As they approached, the tallest girl removed the scarf from her head and face. Filippo nearly fell over backwards. Although Natale had warned him that Rosina looked like Angelina, he was surprised at just how much. Rosina was maybe a fraction taller and more slender but had exactly the same facial features. Filippo Cudoni noticed that while Rosina did not have breasts as large as Angelina did, they could easily have been twins. Her long black hair was parted in the middle of her head and fell around her long, high cheekbones.

She was about twenty-two and had piercing dark—almost black—eyes. She, however, did not have the dominant, cheeky, devil-may-care attitude that made Angelina who she was. Rosina had a gentler, kinder, and more considerate look, which appealed to Filippo's inner perception of what a good wife should be. His mind returned to the present.

Carmela, a pretty dark-eyed, dark-haired girl, was nineteen, and she was slender as well but was only about five foot six in height. She had a much bigger bust than Rosina. Fiorina was seventeen and had dark hair and dark eyes, was lighter skinned and a little shorter and had a bigger bust than Carmela.

"I told you she looked a little like Angelina." Natale laughed, seeing Filippo's reaction when she took off the scarf. "Rosina, Carmela, and Fiorina, come and meet Filippo Cudoni, the Americano who is a cousin to our American Cudoni cousins in Pittsburgh," Natale called out to his sisters. He then introduced his sisters to Filippo. "Filippo, my sisters. This is Rosina, Carmela, and Fiorina."

Rosina smiled and gave him her hand. She had a wide smile and even white teeth. She curtsied as she offered him her hand. Filippo was impressed with her action and gave the back of her hand a quick kiss. His action brought a red flush to her cheeks as she quickly with- drew her hand.

"I am very pleased to meet you, Ms. Rosina Folino Gallo and Ms. Carmela and Fiorina Folino Gallo," Filippo said, a little embarrassed at his own action.

"I am very pleased to meet you too, Mr. Cudoni," Rosina replied almost timidly.

Carmela giggled a little at her older sister and then cheerfully told Filippo, "Buon giorno, signore." She was the giggly type and had a mischievous look to her face.

Fiorina was the sensible one. "Ciao, le come sta?"

"Bene grazia, Fiorina. Tanto piacere di conoscervi," Filippo responded.

Filippo realized from the sound of Rosina's voice that her resemblance to Angelina was only an outward, physical one; in reality, Rosina was nothing like Angelina and certainly not a domineering and happy-go-lucky person like Angelina. She was a much shyer, timid, and quiet sort of young lady, who would rather listen than be the one to give orders—or so he thought.

"Please, you must call me Filippo. *Signore* makes me feel so old," Filippo told the girls.

"Please call me Rosina as well," Rosina said quietly.

"Papa, Filippo and I have plenty to talk about. Can I invite Filippo over for lunch today before he goes home? We are going to the cafe for a coffee first," Natale told his father. "I am going to see Natalina later this afternoon, and Filippo can stay till then."

"Filippo, you are very welcome to come to our house. And we would be pleased if you would stay for lunch," Natale's father said.

"I would be honored and happy to come and share lunch with your family at your place, sir," Filippo replied politely.

"We will be home before midday, Mama. Promise," Natale told his mother. "Pietro, do you want to come with us?" he asked his younger brother. Pietro was twenty-five years old, three years older than Rosina.

"Sure, I would love to come and hear some more stories about America," Pietro replied.

The three set off for the local coffee shop while the rest of the Folino Gallo family made their way home.

The three went to the cafe and had their coffee and a long chat about life in America compared to Sambiase. Natale said he was going to stay for a while in Sambiase and maybe get married as soon as his lady friend set a date. Pietro told the others he wanted to go to America as soon as possible, and if Filippo was going soon, he wanted to go with him and his brothers.

At midday, the three returned to the farmhouse to be there early for lunch. The meal was almost ready when they arrived, and as Natale finished showing Filippo around the farm, Rosina came to tell them that lunch was ready.

The entry into the house led straight into the kitchen-cum-dining-room, which was quite large. From the inside, the Folino Gallo house was bigger than it looked from the outside.

Filippo enjoyed the meal with the Folino Gallo family. Before the meal commenced, the father said grace with all the family joining in. It was obvious that the family was very religious and no immoral nonsense would be tolerated. The family was respectful of other people and their rights. There was no idle gossip about other people. The family did enquire about the health of Filippo's family in Sambiase and in Pittsburgh. Antonio told Filippo that he and Rosa knew his parents quite well; the families had met when Zio and Zia from Pittsburgh lived in Calabria.

During the meal, Filippo occasionally stole glances at Rosina while she served the food and when she sat down to eat. She was a quiet girl and did not have much to say unless spoken to. Filippo found himself admiring this quietness in her. Near the end of the meal, he caught Rosina looking at him, but she quickly looked away, and he noticed that she appeared slightly embarrassed about it.

Rosina, in fact, had noticed this handsome friend of Natale's from Sambiase, and he appeared to her to be a decent man, much along the lines of Natale, her brother; she realized that was probably why they were such good friends.

After the meal, Natale was in a hurry to go visit his beloved Natalina Mercurio, who lived on the other side of Falerna. Filippo and his friend Natale left the Folino Gallo farm at the same time.

On the way home, Filippo could not help but reflect on the differences between Angelina and Rosina. Angelina was headstrong and impulsive; Rosina was quiet and orderly—the sort of woman who would respect and be true to any man she married. Both were beautiful women, but they were certainly different in character. He had only just met Rosina, yet here he was thinking about what sort of wife she would make. She looked like the kind of woman who would make a good wife and mother right there in Calabria.

It struck him that maybe he was missing Angelina more than he had expected. He realized that comparing Angelina to her cousin was a little odd at this point in time. Maybe it was the love life he had shared with Angelina that he really missed, and perhaps Rosina reminded him of that.

Somehow he could not get Rosina out of his mind. He had seen her for only an hour, but already he was convinced she was a nice girl who was friendly and decent at heart. He resolved that he would go see Natale more often.

On Wednesday afternoon, Antonio arrived from Marseilles. His younger brothers were overjoyed to see him. He had always been a favorite with them. Giovanni and Peppino in particular wanted to hear his version of life in America. His parents had also missed him, and while they had been upset with the way he had left over three years ago, without telling them anything, they were glad to see he was fit and well. That night, the Cudoni family, other than Gennaro, was back together again. Giuseppe was sent to ask their grandparents to join them for dinner, and he returned with them a short time later.

The grandparents had seen Filippo again after the first time he had called in to see them. They and Filippo's parents had so many questions to ask about all their relations now living in America and the way of life in America. Francesco had, fifteen years earlier, nearly gone to America with his brother Nicola. It was only the difficult times and hardships that Rosaria would have had with the eight children that had caused Francesco to abandon his intention to go to America at that time. If he had gone to America, he most likely would have done the same as Zio Nicola and eventually taken the whole family across to Pittsburgh.

Filippo had told his parents that Antonio had made some friends in Marseilles and had stayed behind to see them; they suspected that a girl might have been involved somewhere. Giovanni ribbed him that she must have been a beauty to keep him in Marseilles all that time. Giovanni had been away to do his eighteen months of military training near Rome and was wise to the ways of the world. Antonio pretended to punch him in the head and missed.

Filippo walked home with his grandparents that night. His grandparents were getting old and a little fragile, although his grandfather still had his vegetable patch behind the old house. His grandmother was more fragile. Her hearing was almost gone, and she needed a little support to walk the three hundred meters to her home. His grandfather, who was now approaching eighty, walked with a straight, upright stance, but Filippo could see that it was his pride and dignity that would not let him show pain or age. Filippo had heard many stories about his grandfather Pietro Antonio.

Pietro had been a rebel, or brigante, during his earlier days. He had clashed many times with the soldiers of the kingdom of

Naples and the small princedoms that dotted Southern Italy during the period up to the sixties. He had never been a regular soldier, but he had teamed up with groups of other dissatisfied locals, robbing and avenging scores with corrupt officials and the brutal soldiers of the many princedoms. Pietro Antonio Cudoni had never been captured by the carabineiri or the prince's soldiers. He had built up a reputation as one not to offend or to make fun of.

The story was that on the night of his wedding, as a young groom of twenty-two years, he refused to allow his bride to sleep with the local prince. The law proclaimed that the prince had the right to sleep with all new brides on their wedding nights. Only the prince or the king could take away the virginity of the young brides. Pietro and his new bride sneaked away after the wedding ceremony and spent the night in a goat herder's shack in the mountains.

The next day, when the young couple was walking down from the mountain where they had spent their honeymoon night, the pair were ambushed by some of the prince's soldiers. During the ensuing fight, the prince's soldiers shot the young woman dead. Pietro saw his beautiful bride killed before he escaped. He made it back to the mountains, and there he teamed up with other men who had grievances against the prince.

The group called themselves the Mano Rosso Della Calabria, meaning the Calabrian Red Hands. As a brigante, for the next three years, he avenged the brutal death of his one-night bride. The story continued that every soldier who took part in that ambush that day died at the hands of the brigantes. The brigantes killed any soldiers who were picking up newlywed brides for the prince's pleasure. The ranks of the Mano Rosso at times suffered casualties from attacks by the soldiers, but as soon as one brigante died, at least two more were ready to take his place.

One year later, Pietro Antonio Cudoni sent a message to the prince that the next time the prince took a virgin bride away from her husband on her wedding night, it would be the last time that he would see daylight after this. He made it a promise to him that the prince would die without mercy. The outraged local people sup- ported the brigantes as much as they could without risking their lives.

The story went on that the prince, in his usual bluster, did take the next virgin bride to his bed on her wedding night. The next day, after the bride lost her virginity, she returned to her home. The prince was walking in his garden when a sniper's bullet hit him in the lower groin, and although he did not die then, he was never able to walk or lie down straight. He was never able to have an erection, and he never again slept with another woman. The prince lost any respect he might have once commanded, and he spent his last month riddled in pain and terror that the brigantes would come finish him off before he died.

It became a saying that if small children misbehaved or disobeyed their parents, the brigantes from the Mano Rosso would punish them. It was known that when the famous Giuseppe Garibaldi passed through the area in August 1860, he asked to meet Pietro Antonio Cudoni. Giuseppe Garibaldi was impressed with the manner in which Pietro Antonio Cudoni carried himself and, although he was now married, offered him a position as captain in his army. Pietro Antonio thanked Garibaldi for his offer but refused, saying that he now owed his services to his family and told him his days of scourging corrupt officials and sadistic princes were over.

By this time, Pietro Antonio Cudoni had met and married Rosa, and they had four sons and two daughters. The couple had lived in the same house since then. Filippo's grandfather never spoke much about those days, except at times to Filippo, but his father told him that most of the stories were true, and people had not interfered with Pietro Antonio's life again. Now he was just an old granddad like anybody else's grandfather, but his grandfather had many times repeated his philosophy and Cudoni creed to Filippo: "No man who kills a Cudoni should live to die of old age."

Chapter 34

Filippo and Antonio worked hard alongside their father and brothers for the next few days. The hard manual work on the small block of land never seemed to finish. While they worked, the brothers made plans to return to America. Giovanni, Peppino, and Carlo all wanted to go to America. However, they realized that they could not all go and leave their father and mother and brother Giuseppe to handle all the work on the farm. They decided that Carlo would stay for a while longer and come out to America later.

Filippo told them that while the chance to make money was there, the work was hard; it was a rough and tough life in the States. It was different from life in Sambiase, Antonio told them. He personally would prefer to live in Sambiase once he had made enough money, he told them.

On Sunday morning, Filippo and Antonio left for Falerna. They knew that this Sunday was the feast of the Lady of the Rosary at the small church in Falerna. Filippo was sure that Rosina and her family would be going. He did not know what time Mass would be, but he assumed it would be early, so he and Antonio set off at seven that morning. They arrived at the Folino Gallo farm at about eight thirty. The Folinos, as they were commonly referred to, were just leaving for the church.

Natale introduced Antonio Cudoni to his family, and they all set off for the church. Rosina was wearing a long bright Sunday dress, but she had not put on her shawl. Antonio too could see that she was the spitting image of Angelina back in Pittsburgh.

Filippo walked with Rosina for part of the way. She told him Mass was at nine and would be followed by a procession along the road from the church to the outskirts of town to a large olive tree where the Blessed Virgin, holding rosary beads in her right hand, was supposed the have been seen. Every year, the priest blessed this tree, and numbers of local people hung rosary beads on its branches. According to local legend, this was done so that the Lord would pro- vide good harvests for the people.

"Can I walk with you during the procession?" Filippo asked Rosina.

"Carmela and I will be at the front of the procession, reciting the rosary," Rosina told him. "If you don't mind saying the rosary, I would be happy to have you walking with me."

"My family and I go to church nearly every Sunday as well, so I know the rosary too," Filippo told her. "I will be there."

When they were nearing the church, Natale left them to call at the Mercurio household to pick up Natalina. He left Filippo and Antonio talking to Pietro, who also had made up his mind to go to America. He asked Filippo if he could travel with them, as Natale was hoping to get married to Natalina soon and would not be going back to America for a while.

"Sure, we would be happy for you to come to America with us. At this point, we do not know for sure when we are leaving, but we will let you know so that we can work it out to leave together," Filippo told him.

They arrived at the little church of Saint Tomasi in Falerna fifteen minutes before Mass was to start. Natale's parents, Carmela, and Fiorina went inside. Pietro, Rosina, and Paulo waited with the Cudoni brothers for Natale and Natalina to arrive. After a few minutes, they still had not arrived, so the rest of them went in. Rosina sat with her parents, Carmela, and Fiorina, while the four young men sat in the seat behind.

Mass lasted an hour and a half. Afterwards, all the people who wanted their rosaries blessed took them to the front of the church, and Father Pio blessed them. A group of worshippers placed a statue of Our Blessed Lady on a timber frame. This frame had four handles so four people could carry it around. The rosary beads were placed on the statue or on top of the small tray. Four strong young men came forward and picked up the tray by the handles.

The four men carried the statue down the aisle to the front of the church, followed by Father Pio and a group of people, mainly women, reciting the rosary. Filippo joined Rosina and her sisters in this group as it set off. The four bearers carrying the statue led the way down the road. Two men collecting donations moved around the statue, putting donations into the tray. Father Pio followed behind, and then came the group leading the chanting of the rosary. The rest of the congregation followed behind them.

Rosina had given Filippo a spare set of rosary beads, and he walked alongside her, chanting the rosary too. The procession moved down and along the road. The people lined both sides of the road. As the procession moved past, people threw money and donations to the men collecting them. The front of the procession eventually halted at the foot of a large old olive tree, which the procession had been coming to for the last hundred years or so. The olive tree was some five hundred meters from the church. The crowd spread around the tree, then Father Pio blessed the tree and prayed that the olive harvest and all the other crops that year would be good. The priest and his helpers took the blessed rosary beads off the statue and placed them on the tree. The procession, still chanting the rosary, then returned to Saint Tommasi's church.

The procession arrived back at the church at midday, and the helpers carried the statue of Our Blessed Lady back inside the church and put it back in its original place. A magnificent feast had been prepared in and around the church grounds. There were many food and entertainment stalls set up.

During the procession, Filippo and Rosina became separated from their family members. They went to a food stall where Filippo purchased something to eat. Filippo was quite impressed with Rosina. She was not very educated, yet she was very intelligent. She had such a quiet manner about her; nothing seemed to upset her.

While Filippo and Rosina were eating, Natale arrived with his fiancée. Filippo had not met Natalina before, so Natale introduced her. Filippo could see why Natale was attracted to her. She was of medium height and had a bubbly twinkle in her brown eyes, black hair, and an infectious smile that won friends wherever she went. He paid Natalina a compliment of sorts.

"Natale, what have you been doing in America? If I had a lady like Natalina here, I would be worried sick in America that all the young men here would be trying to take her from me. No won-der you don't want to go back to America," Filippo said to Natale as he shook hands with Natalina. "I am very pleased to meet you, Natalina," he told her.

"I am pleased to meet you too." Natalina laughed as she spoke to Filippo. "That's what I say to myself—why am I waiting for him when I have so many offers from so many good-looking men?"

"Natalina, I think you have made a wise choice with Natale. I know he doesn't look like much, but he is a great guy," Filippo joked. "But he is nowhere near as good-looking as his sisters."

Rosina's eyes lit up slightly at the compliment that Filippo had paid her and the rest of the family while she laughed at the friendly insult to Natale.

"And where were you," Natale quickly quipped, "when the good looks were being handed out? Out minding the sheep and goats or something?"

"Touché." Filippo grinned.

Rosina's parents and sisters arrived as they were talking. Her parents told them that Antonio and Pietro had gone down to the piazza. There would be another procession at two in the afternoon, and when that finished, there would be singing and dancing in the piazza later in the afternoon.

The same men who had carried the statue before led the second procession, and even more people joined in. Filippo joined Rosina and her sisters in chanting the rosary, following the statue carriers and Father Pio. This time, several thousand people followed the pro- cession through the streets of Falerna. Two hours later, the procession returned to the church, and the statue was returned to its place to the left of the main altar.

Filippo told Rosina he had greatly enjoyed the whole day and that Falerna had a great fiesta in honor of the Virgin. Rosina replied that she too had enjoyed the day and that he had a great voice and could come again if he wanted to. She gave him a reserved but warm smile as she spoke.

The smile seemed to implant itself in Filippo's heart, and it stayed with him for a long time. He smiled back at her and her sisters, who were still with her.

"Ciao, Filippo," Rosina told him with an even warmer smile. "Ciao, Rosina," he said, and then he remembered the sisters. "Ciao, Camila, Fiorina."

Filippo and Antonio made some new friends that afternoon, the main one being Pietro Folino Gallo. Filippo did not see a lot of Rosina as she left with her parents to call on other relatives, but he liked what he did see of her, and although she reminded him of Angelina, he liked her for who she was.

Late in the afternoon, Filippo and Antonio left to return home. On the way home, they decided to go into Sambiase to have a glass of wine. They went to the same place where Filippo and Gennaro had handed out a hiding to the four card players three years earlier.

A number of card players were there that afternoon, but Filippo was not sure he recognized any of them. He and Antonio had two glasses of locally made red wine and then went home. Although Filippo had not recognized any of the card players, Giovanni, the card player who had instigated the trouble last time, had recognized him.

For the next week, Filippo made a number of enquiries regarding land prices and land for sale. Some of the rich land barons did have land for sale. The situation in southern Calabria had reached a point where it was more economical for them to sell their land than lease it out to peasants to work it. However, it became apparent to Filippo that the brothers would need to raise more money to buy enough of the better land. He and Antonio decided that they would wait until they came back from America in a few years before they bought any property.

That Saturday, Natale called in to see them. Filippo introduced Natale to his parents and brothers and sister.

Francesco told him that he knew his father and mother quite well. Natale came bearing some exciting news—at least for himself. Natalina had agreed to marry him in four weeks' time. They had already been to see Father Pio at the church in Falerna, and he was preparing the necessary papers. Natale had come to ask Filippo if he would be a groomsman for him and Natalina. The wedding was to be at two in the afternoon at the church, with a reception party later at the Folino Gallo house on the farm. He also invited Antonio to the wedding. Natale told Filippo that his partner would be his sister Rosina.

Filippo and Antonio congratulated Natale and told him they would be happy to be at his and Natalina's wedding. Filippo did not say so, but he was happy at the prospect of seeing Rosina and being her partner at the wedding.

Filippo, Antonio, Giovanni, Peppino, and the family spent many hours talking about when they should leave for America. Their parents, while unhappy at the prospect of losing five of their sons to America, understood that if the boys were to get ahead in their lives, they had no choice but to go there. They decided to leave on September 28, 1902.

The Mafia in Calabria, while disorganized, was very active. More and more young men had been getting involved in crime over the last few decades because of the lack of opportunity to improve their lives. While most of their activities were towards robbing the rich and the officials, quite often the poor became the casualties.

The Cudoni's, while regarded as peasants and therefore poor, were left alone. The reputation they had for not taking any nonsense from anybody had also kept the Mafia from posing any problem or harm to them. Woe to any man who molested a Cudoni family member. The older people in the area certainly remembered the stories of the brigante Pietro Antonio Cudoni. The brothers also felt that their family would be safe while Carlo and Giuseppe were there with their father.

For the last two seasons, the region around Calabria had been suffering a dry period. The olive trees had less than an average crop, and some of the local streams were starting to dry up. The grass on the mountainsides was getting sparse and dry, so Francesco decided to sell a few of the goats. He gave most of the money to Giovanni and Peppino to pay for their trip to America.

Early one morning, Filippo and Antonio made a trip to Catanzaro, which was the largest city and the provincial capital of the south, and had the services of a bank. They converted their American dollars into Italian lire. They deposited what they wished to leave behind in the bank and took sufficient funds to meet all the costs of the trip to America. They gave their parents more than what the sale of the goats had earned to help the family carry on.

As the day that they would be leaving got closer, Giovanni and Peppino became more excited about the future and what they would do in America and how much money they would make. They would come back to Sambiase and buy lots of land.

Chapter 35

On the Saturday of Natale and Natalina's wedding, Filippo and Antonio left home about nine o'clock in the morning. When they arrived at the Folino Gallo house, the family—apart from Rosina and Carmela, who had gone to Natalina's place—were still home, working and preparing the dinner for that night before leaving for the church.

It was the custom that the groom would not see the bride until she arrived at the church on her wedding day, so none of the brides-maids were there. Natale's best man, his compare, a cousin on his mother's side named Gino Vescio, had been there all morning helping him. Most of his relations who had come over to help had left and were going to meet them at the church before the wedding.

Rosa and Fiorina prepared lunch to eat before they left for the church at one. The Folino Gallo family and the friends and helpers who had come to the house made a jolly party as they walked along the road to Falerna.

Fiorina, dressed in her new dress, looked chic and pretty and more grown-up as she skipped along the road with the group. The young men of Falerna would soon be lining up at her door to be the lucky man to win her hand.

They arrived with plenty of time to spare at the church. Natale, his *compare*, and Filippo went into the church. Natale had a present for Father Pio, and he gave it to him before the wedding.

Father thanked him and wished him and his future wife a happy life together.

Natalina and her two bridesmaids arrived a short time later. Her infectious smile had everyone in good humor from the start of the ceremony. Rosina, one of the bridesmaids, was her quiet, beautiful, and unassuming but self-assured self. The maid of honor was Natalina's younger sister, Concetta. After Natale and Natalina said their wedding vows and became husband and wife, Father Pio congratulated them and wished them a long, happy, and prosperous life blessed with many little ones.

At the conclusion of the ceremony, Natale and his beautiful bride walked down the aisle arm in arm. Gino and Concetta followed the bride and groom down the aisle, and next came Rosina and Filippo, who also walked arm in arm to the front of the church. All the many friends and relations who had come to wish them well did so at the front of the church. Many of Rosina's friends at the wed- ding had not met Filippo, but they told Rosina what a good-looking, nice couple they made.

Among the wedding party were a squeeze box player, a mouth organ player, and a bagpipe player, and while the wedding party walked, the three entertained them with song and dance all the way to the Folino Gallo residence. The normally twenty-minute walk took forty, but no one cared.

Rosa had prepared the ingredients for a big meal, and with the help of a few of the older women, she soon had the wood stove reheated and a fine meal in the making.

During this time, the others sang and danced to the music of the three musicians. It was simple yet enjoyable entertainment. The young bride and groom led the way with the dancing, and Gino and Concetta and Filippo and Rosina joined in. Rosina was a good dancer—not as accomplished as Angelina, but a good dancer anyway. Natale's father had killed and cut up a young lamb the day before and had roasted it in the brick oven early in the morning, so there was plenty of young lamb, pasta, home-made bread, salami, and salad when the ladies called everyone to come eat. Natalina's father had brought along twenty liters of his best wine, and they thoroughly enjoyed the meal.

A few speeches were delivered during the meal; these kept to a minimum for the most part. Natale was not one for public speaking, but he did thank all those he could think of, particularly Natalina for marrying him. Natalina's father had plenty to say, and he gave a lengthy speech. Night was fast approaching, and with no moon, it was soon going to be very dark. Antonio Folino had prepared a pile of hardwood, and as everyone ate and sat around, he lit the fire. Soon a large bonfire was going, and there was plenty of light for the people to return to dancing.

It was an exciting night; everyone got into the spirit of dancing, and the men drank plenty of *vino rosso*.

During the night, Filippo asked Rosina for a dance, and soon he was monopolizing her. Rosina was a wonderful dancer, but more importantly, she seemed to be a wonderful person. She was a quiet, reserved person. Filippo Cudoni was amazed at how different Rosina was to Angelina, who virtually looked like her twin sister. He could not believe how alike they were in looks but so different in attitude.

He could not stop himself from comparing them. *Rosina was the sort of woman who would commit and follow her man forever*, he thought. Her gentle touch and her softly spoken voice sent a shiver of passion and thrill through him. *This was the sort of woman who would make any man—Filippo Cudoni—a wonderful wife*, he thought.

Late in the night and while dancing, Filippo asked Rosina if she would give him the honor of being his girl.

"Tu sei la piu bella signorina qui. Mi fai lonore di essere la mia ragaza?"

Rosina had been thinking about her future and with whom that future would be. She was enjoying the night dancing with this newly returned Americano. *Could he be the one?*

"I...I don't really know anything about you. Will you, will you, err, give me some time to think about it? I don't know what to say," she replied.

"Of course I will, Rosina. I do not want to rush you. Take as much time as you want." Filippo smiled as he replied. "But I will keep asking until you say yes."

Rosina blushed before she replied "Hmmm, hmm, one week?"

Filippo did the tarantella with Rosina, and at the end of it, both were exhausted. They decided to move away from the light and get some fresh air. Filippo led Rosina to the side of the house. He held her hand as they walked. Once they were in the dark, he kissed her hand. It was obvious to Filippo that Rosina had no experience with men at all.

"You are such a beautiful girl. How is it that you are not married?" Filippo asked her softly. In the dark, he thought he could see her blushing. "Has your father promised to shoot anyone who comes close enough to kiss you?"

"No, no, he hasn't shot anyone. I...I wasn't really ready to marry, that's all," she replied, a little embarrassed by his question.

"Then he won't shoot me if I kiss you," Filippo replied quickly. Before she could answer, he had his arm around her shoulder, and he drew her slowly to him. Softly, he put his lips to hers. She did resist a little but did not draw back, so he put his other arm around her waist and drew her closer until she was tight against him. He could feel her nipples and breasts pressing against him. Her mouth opened, and their tongues met.

She felt a warm glow spread through her body. She could also feel something pressing against her thigh and suddenly realized it was his erect penis. She backed away. She had never been this close to a man before, and she was a little wary of men. However, this man seemed different; she still held his hand in hers.

"We better go back before Papa comes out with his shotgun," she told him jokingly.

"Rosina, do you mind if I come and see you again next Saturday?" Filippo asked her. She squeezed his hand to show she accepted.

Around midnight, and after the wine was finished, most of the guests started to leave and walk to their homes or the homes of nearby friends. Antonio, Natale's father, had told Filippo and Antonio during the afternoon that if they wished to stay the night, they could sleep in the lean-to next to the animal stables. They had accepted, and when everyone had gone, Pietro got two blankets for them and showed them where to sleep. There was plenty of hay and straw on the ground, and it was remarkably comfortable.

The next morning, Filippo and Antonio waited until they could see that some others were awake before they went over to the house.

Antonio Folino had been up earlier and fed the two bullocks that he owned and with which he worked the land. He had also milked the goat and fed the few dozen chooks they had.

Rosa and Rosina had, in the meantime, cooked some breakfast for everyone. In addition to Filippo and Antonio, Gino and a few other friends had stayed as well. Rosa called everyone in for break- fast except the honeymooners, who had not come out. Rosina served them fresh home-made ricotta and bread, plus some salami and coffee. As she served the coffee, when she got to Filippo, she rested her hand on his shoulder.

"Would you like some more coffee, Filippo?" she asked him. "Yes, please, Rosina," he replied.

By eight, they had finished having breakfast. The Folino Gallo parents and the three girls were going to Mass at nine. They quickly cleaned up the remains of breakfast.

Filippo and Antonio said thank you and goodbye to everyone. Filippo had just finished saying goodbye to Rosina when Natale poked his head around the door leading to the bedrooms.

"Thanks very much for coming to our wedding, Filippo and Antonio. I will come and see you guys before you leave for America," Natale told them.

Filippo and Antonio returned home to Sambiase. It was mid-morning when they arrived back home. They found that the rest of the family had gone to church.

A few afternoons later, Filippo and Antonio went into town to buy some things for themselves and the family. Filippo was not happy about taking Antonio into town during the day; he was afraid the authorities would become aware of who he was and take him away for national service. However, Antonio insisted, so there was little point in arguing. Antonio did not think that anyone would know that he had skipped out on national service. Filippo knew that Antonio was not the sort of person who wanted to be noticeably visible, and Filippo thought that as soon as they finished their business in town, they would go home.

Just as they finished all their errands, Antonio met some old friends of his. His friends suggested that they go have a glass or two of wine. Antonio reluctantly agreed and went with his two friends to the pizzeria, which also served wine.

Filippo decided to have a stroll around town instead. The town's small shopping area was generally between two roads and several blocks. Filippo had walked over most of it and was getting close to the post office when he met his old flame Maria Valenci. Although Maria was much more mature these days, she was probably more beautiful now; however, the old torch that Filippo had carried for her had diminished, and he was now more interested in other women. He was older and wiser, but she still looked like a very desirable but mature young woman.

"Good afternoon, Maria." Filippo saluted her and continued on his way.

"Filippo Cudoni!" Maria called after him.

He turned and walked back with an inquisitive look on his face. "I want to talk to you, Filippo," she said to him.

"What about?" he remarked quickly but quietly.

"I have talked to my mother about what happened those years ago between you and me," she said. "She told me what Papa did— that he promised to tell me what you had said but did not. I totally blamed you, and I was wrong. I would like to apologize and say I am sorry for what I said and thought of you."

Filippo screwed his face into a little smile. "A lot of water has passed under the bridge since then. We were both young then. Sure, we had a great time, and maybe I did let you down by not having intercourse with you, but I would not worry about it now. I was very upset when I returned from the army, but now you are married, and I am returning to America. It would be nice, but we cannot go under the oak tree again. So we must forget it," he told her.

"That's the point," Maria said. "I spent many nights dreaming of us and how it would feel to have you inside me—and then upset and angry that you had dumped me. I wondered what I had done to you to deserve that. Now I understand it was not your fault, and I can see why you were angry too. I would like to make it up to you, but I do not think my husband would approve of us going under the oak tree and doing what we did or did not do then—even though you made better love to me without making love than he does. I will never forget that time under the tree. I wanted you then, and I still do, so can we at least still be friends?"

"Maria, in the army I used to dream of coming home and making love to you all the time, and I still remember the afternoon under the oak tree near the fountain and what I should have done to you. Sure, we can be friends. The best to you and your children," Filippo told her as he started to walk past.

Maria reached out and grasped his arm. "I want us to be good friends, Filippo. Will you forgive me?" she asked him. The flame that he had once ignited in her seemed to have flickered anew at their chance meetings, and it appeared Maria was asking him to renew that friendship.

"Sure. I did that when I found out it was your father to blame. But now you are married, and I also have a lady. So as I said, I wish you and your family well," he told her, and he walked away.

Maria stood there gazing after him. His casual attitude towards her implied wish of somehow renewing their past relationship left her a little disappointed and angry. The desire he had aroused in her in the past had not totally gone away, and she resolved that another day was still to come for them. Although she had three children, Maria felt her marriage was an empty cage with her slave-to-work husband. She still fantasized about making love to Filippo Cudoni.

Filippo went to the pizzeria where Antonio and his friends had gone. It was the same pizzeria where Filippo and Gennaro had had the run-in with the card players. Antonio and his friends were ready to leave when Filippo walked in. There were several groups of men playing cards. Filippo thought that one of them could have been Giovanni, but he was not sure. He walked over to Antonio and his friends and had a glass of wine with them.

The man called Giovanni stood up and walked around the table where he was playing cards with his friends. He took a long, hard look at Filippo. He said something to his mates and walked out.

Filippo saw him walk out and had no doubt that the man had recognized him. He wondered what the man did for a living. Every time he had seen him, he had been playing a card game with his friends. *If I had a suspicious mind, I would say he is most probably mixed up with the Mafia*, Filippo thought.

He walked over and told Antonio that he was in an urgent hurry to leave; he told him to finish his drink so that they could go and promised him he would explain later.

Within five minutes, they were at the edge of town on their way home.

"One of the men playing cards left when I came in," Filippo explained to Antonio as they walked home.

Antonio gave him a quizzical look and shrugged his shoulders. "And?"

"He was the same guy that Gennaro and I had a run-in with four years ago. I am sure that he recognized me. On that afternoon, I was told that he has a brother who is a carabinieri, and he may have gone to tell the carabinieri to check on us. I didn't want to hang around in case he came back with the carabinieri, or give him any reason to check and find out about your missing out on doing national service."

"National service," Antonio replied. "I don't want to hang around for them to find that out. The sooner we leave for America, the better."

Filippo and Antonio both knew that if the carabinieri checked with the army, they would find out that he had not done his national service. There would be no punishment for not doing it; however, Antonio would be enlisted and moved to the nearest army barracks and forced to do his required twelve months of duty.

That Friday, Giovanni, Peppino, and their father went into town to buy the boys some new clothing to wear on the trip to America. Francesco knew it would be the last time that he would be buying them anything for some time. He was upset and emotional that five of his boys would be gone, and he knew he would miss them terribly. He put on a brave face, and in the excitement, the two boys hardly noticed. While in town, they mentioned to several acquaintances and relations that Giovanni and Peppino were going to America.

On Saturday, Filippo returned to the Folino Gallo residence in Falerna to see Rosina. He arrived in the early afternoon. As he approached the house, he noticed that Mr. Folino Gallo was working in the vegetable garden, and he decided that he should tell him the purpose of his visit. He went over to talk to him.

"*Buon pomeriggio*, Mr. Folino," Filippo said to him. "How are you?"

"*Bene, bene,* Filippo, *e tu*?" Antonio replied.

"*Bene grazie,*" Filippo replied. "Mr. Folino, I would like to ask you if I might be allowed to see and court your daughter Rosina.

I like your daughter very much, and I would like to get to know her better with an honorable view to marriage."

"Is that your intention, Filippo Cudoni?" Antonio Folino Gallo asked him, looking him straight in the eye.

"Si, Signore—in all honesty, it is. Some of my brothers and I are going to America on the twenty-eighth of this month for several years to try to make some more money to buy land. I cannot ask Rosina to marry me now, as there is not enough time. However, if she is still unmarried when I return, I would like to ask for her hand then. In the meantime, I would like to know her better," Filippo told him.

"I am very happy for you to meet my daughter, provided that nothing is definite until you return from America," Antonio replied. "Natale has many nice things to say about you, and your family appears to be nice people. I think Rosina likes you too, but do not rush things until you return. At the moment, she is inside."

Filippo thanked him for his courtesy in allowing him to see Rosina and then went over to the house. He knocked on the front door. Carmela came out to greet him. She said hello to Filippo and then let out a loud call to her sister.

"Rosina! There is a man come to see you," she called out. Rosina came to the door. When she saw Filippo, her eyes lit up, as a light pink color spread over her cheeks.

"*Buon giorno*, Filippo. Take no notice of my sister. Sometimes she is a little silly," she said, a little embarrassed that her sister had called so loudly for her. "Please come in."

Filippo gave her a big smile, said, "Buon giorno," and followed her into the house. Mrs. Folino Gallo was at the kitchen table. It was obvious she was knitting a blanket; there were spools of wool on the table as well as a half-finished blanket on her lap.

She welcomed Filippo in. "*Buon giorno*, Filippo. If you have come to see Natale or Pietro, they are not in. Natale and his wife have gone to see her parents, and Pietro has gone into town."

"*Buon giorno* to you too, Mrs. Folino, but no, I came to see Rosina. I have talked to Mr. Folino outside, and he has said it is okay for me to talk to her. But I did need to talk to Pietro about America and tell him that we are leaving soon," Filippo told her.

"I think Pietro said that he will be gone for about two hours, so he will be home in the next hour or so," his mother replied.

Rosina wanted to get out of the house and asked, "Filippo, do you want to go for a walk to see our vineyard? There might still be some grapes."

"Sure, I would love some fresh grapes. Ours are finished at home," Filippo responded.

Rosina followed Filippo outside. They walked around to the back of the farmhouse, up a small rise, past some olive trees, and then to the vineyard. The red grapes, known as Isabella grapes, were too old to eat, but there were still a number of fresh green grapes on one row of vines.

Rosina picked a nice-looking bunch and gave them to Filippo to eat.

"Very nice. These are better than the ones we grow at our place," Filippo told her after he had tried a few. He handed a small bunch to her.

Rosina ate them. "These are very tasty," she agreed.

"It takes a wise, beautiful lady to pick the best grapes," he responded gallantly.

She looked away a little shyly. She had an inkling of what he was going to ask her next.

"Rosina, I have been thinking of you all of the time since I last saw you. I cannot get you out of my thoughts and your lovely face out of my mind." He reached out for her hand and held it to his face. "I have thought very much about what I am asking you, and I realize I am possibly asking for too much. I will be leaving in two weeks' time with my brothers and Pietro, and we will not be back for at least two years. I cannot expect you to wait all that time for me, but if you will wait for me, I will be back as soon as I can, and I will love you forever," he proclaimed to her.

"I would love to wait for you to come back to me," Rosina said shyly, "but I cannot ask you to be true to me for that long either."

Filippo pulled her slowly to him. "Does that mean that you would be happy to be my *signorina*? I promise I would write to you every day," he said.

"I would love to be, ah, your *signorina*, and I could—ah, can— wait for you to come back," she nervously but emphatically told him.

He could see that she was nervous but that she was trying hard to convey her new feelings for him.

"This is the happiest day of my life. I love you, love you," Filippo told her excitedly. He pulled her closer in a tight hug. Then he started to kiss her, first on the cheeks and forehead, and then slowly on the lips. They had moved under a large olive tree while they had been talking, and they were not visible to anyone in the house.

It was a long, lingering kiss. She gave him her mouth voluntarily, and soon she was returning his kisses with some passion as well. This time, she did not object to the feeling of his penis through his trousers on her thigh, and she enjoyed the feeling of his chest pressing on her breasts.

Filippo knew that Rosina was not wise to the worldly ways of romantic couples, and he did not prolong the kissing. He knew that Mr. Folino would not expect him to do anything to hurt his daughter in any way.

They talked for a while about life in America. Rosina asked when Filippo thought or expected to return. He told her he would only stay for as long as it took him and his brothers to make the money they would need to buy some farmland.

They agreed to be just boyfriend and girlfriend until Filippo returned from America, but Rosina agreed to let Filippo keep seeing her until he left for America.

Slowly, they walked back to the house. They were inwardly happy, but they also knew that there would be a lonely and harrowing time ahead for both of them. Three years was a long time to wait for someone you knew well, let alone someone you had just recently met. Yet strangely, both felt that they had known the other for a life-time and felt that they were indeed soul mates from the heart.

Rosina and Filippo returned to the house to tell her parents the understanding they had reached. Rosina explained that both of them had agreed to wait for the other.

Her parents were quite impressed and agreeable to the decision. Antonio warned them that three years was indeed a long time to wait for anyone. They would need to be strong and true to each other to make it work, her parents told them.

Her parents wished both of them the best of God's love and hoped everything would one day work out. They both knew that

Rosina's strong religious belief would keep her strong and faithful, but life would not be that easy on Filippo Cudoni.

The family was enjoying a cup of strong black coffee when Pietro returned from town. It had crossed his mind that Filippo might return to see them that day, so he had come home early as he could, just in case.

Filippo told Pietro that his brothers had purchased everything they needed and were very much looking forward to the day they would be leaving. Pietro also had been busy preparing and was just as keen to leave. He also had a girl in town he was seeing a lot. She had been upset when he had first told her he was going to America, but after he had explained the reasons why, she had been accepting of his decision.

Pietro asked Filippo where the best place to leave from was. Filippo told him he could walk down to the marina where a small train stop was, or walk to Sambiase and catch the train with the Cudoni's.

Filippo suggested that it would be much safer to go to Sambiase and purchase a ticket there as he could not recall whether the train had stopped at the marina stop; if they left from Sambiase, they could leave together. Pietro agreed as he remembered that Natale had also left and returned from Sambiase.

With the threat of rain in the air, Filippo decided that he should take his leave of the Folino family and return home. Rosina held his hand as she walked to the road with him. As they walked, Filippo told her he would be back to see her on the following Saturday. Once on the road, she gave him a quick kiss on the lips and then skipped happily back to the house.

From the roadway outside Falerna, Filippo could see to the south-west of him a huge storm cloud moving in over the bay towards the mountains. He doubted that he would get back before the storm hit, but he did not care. Rosina had at least told him she would wait for him if he wanted her to for when he returned to Italy in a few years.

She had told him she cared enough to give him hope she would. He knew that he had to see her as much as he could before he left, and he would return at least on Saturday—maybe earlier. He expected that as Pietro was leaving from Sambiase, maybe the family, including Rosina, would come to see him off on Sunday.

Filippo did not wait until Saturday to go see Rosina. He returned on Thursday afternoon. The storms that were around the area caught him again. He was drenched by the time he arrived. The storm had also caught him on the previous Saturday while he was returning from the Folino Gallos' home. It was still raining when he knocked on the door of the house.

Rosina answered the door and was surprised to see him standing there all drenched. She quickly let him in. The rest of the family was also surprised to see him. Rosa got him a towel to dry himself and then went to get some of Pietro's clothing for him to change into. She gave the clothes to Filippo and told him to go into a room to change. Pietro was a little taller than Filippo; otherwise, the clothes were a good fit.

When Filippo returned, Antonio had a large glass of red wine for him.

"Drink this. It will soon warm you up," he told him.

The whole family, including Natale and Natalina, were home. Natale could not resist a small joke at Filippo's expense.

"It is good to see you, *compare*, but don't you people from Sambiase have more sense than to walk around in the rain?"

he joked. "In Sambiase, it only rains when we want it to," Filippo quipped.

"But it is still good to see you and Natalina and all the family."

Filippo sat with the family in the large kitchen-cum diningroom, talking until late in the afternoon.

The rain outside had settled into a steady, monotonous downpour. By late afternoon, the rain showed little sign of easing. Filippo knew he would have to leave soon; otherwise, it would be dark before he returned to Sambiase.

However, as time passed, the rain showed less sign of abating. Antonio advised him that he should stay the night and leave the next morning. Filippo decided to wait awhile longer and then decide.

When the rain did not let up, they convinced Filippo to stay the night. He had dinner with the Folino Gallo family. This Folino Gallo family was no exception to the tradition of good cooks carrying that name, and he really enjoyed having dinner with them. In the pale light of the kerosene lamp, with ten adults around the dining room table, the house seemed full of people, but they all got on so well that the time went quickly. The parents went to bed first while Natale and Filippo recounted stories of life in America. Filippo told them he was leaving early in the morning and thanked them for their hospitality.

At ten o'clock, Natale and Natalina decided it was time for them to go to bed, and they retired to their room. Rosina said she, Carmela, and Fiorina should go as well. She said good night to Filippo, and as she walked past him, she squeezed his hand. The three young men decided to go to sleep as well. Filippo went with Pietro and Paulo to their room, where Mrs. Folino had prepared a mattress and two blankets on the floor for Filippo to sleep on that night.

The next morning, after a cup of coffee and a farewell to Rosina and her parents, he left for Sambiase and walked the two hours it took to get there.

Chapter 36

Some unexpected and unwanted visitors arrived to see the Cudoni family that afternoon. Two carabinieri and an army-type man walked up the road to the Cudoni house.

Giuseppe saw them approaching the house and called his father and some of the brothers. By the time the visitors got to the front of the house, nearly all of the Cudoni family was there.

Antonio and Peppino were in the garden behind the house hoeing some soil and were not aware of visitors.

"Mr. Antonio Cudoni?" the person who was presumably in the army asked Giovanni as they approached the family.

"No, that is my brother. I am Giovanni Cudoni. What do you want my brother for?" Giovanni asked him.

"Where is your brother now?" the army man asked. He looked around at the family. "I want to know where your brother is— now." Francesco Cudoni came to the front. "I am his father. Tell me, what do you want with him?"

"You son is nearly twenty-four and has not yet done his national military training. You know it is compulsory. We need to know from him why he has not enlisted. I repeat, where is Antonio Cudoni?"

"I am Antonio Cudoni. What can I do for you?" Antonio had been coming from the back of the house and had heard his name mentioned, though he had not been able to see who was asking. If he had seen that they were from the military, he might have chosen to run. He answered before he had seen the army man, and now it was too late.

"Antonio Cudoni, I am Sergeant Fronzo Muoio from the king's military polizia, and I am here to notify you that you are called up to enlist and make sure that you serve your time in military training. You are to collect what you need and come with us now," the military sergeant announced as though he had done this a thousand times before. "You have five minutes to collect your things and say goodbye to your family."

"Wait a minute. Hang on. What do you mean I have only five minutes' time to leave? I need at least a couple of days to organize my affairs before I can leave," Antonio spluttered as the enormity of what was happening to him sunk in.

"It has come to our attention that the reason you have not attended military training before is that you have been out of the country. Our concern is that if you are granted time, you would leave the country again, and you would then be charged with desertion. We do not want that to happen, nor would you. You have five minutes to pack a bag," Sergeant Muoio told him. "Constable Menoli, you go with him. You go to the back of the house. If he tries to run away, shoot him."

Antonio could see that he had no choice but to collect what he needed.

His brother Filippo was taking a good look at one of the carabinieri. He thought that he looked vaguely familiar, as if he had seen him somewhere before. Then it dawned on him that he looked similar to Giovanni, the card player who had vowed to get even.

"Did someone report Antonio being here to the army, Sergeant?" Filippo asked him quietly.

"Yes, it was brought to the attention of the army that your brother was back from America and had not volunteered to carry out his national duty. However, the army never discloses its source of information. You have done your time. You should know that," he told Filippo.

"How long does he have to serve?" Filippo asked him.

"It is not my job to know that. You will need to contact command to find that out," the sergeant told him. "You have been in the army. You know how to find out."

Filippo had already found out what he wanted to know. Someone had informed them that Antonio was back in Italy and might not have served his military training. It was easy to guess who, out of spite, had done it.

A few minutes later, Antonio came out carrying a small bag. He said goodbye to his mother and father first and then to his brothers and sister. When he came to Filippo, Filippo whispered in his ear, "I think that Giovanni person from the pizzeria told his brother, who I think is one of the carabinieri. When you finish, you might come out with Carlo to America. Take care."

"You too, big brother. Say hello to Gennaro and the boys in America for me," Antonio told Filippo.

Antonio and the three officers set off down the road towards Sambiase. Not far down the road, he stopped, turned around, and waved to his family, who waved back at him and watched as he dis- appeared down the road.

Francesco turned to Peppino. "If and when you return, you may find that the same thing could happen to you as well," he told him. "I will make enquiries on Monday as to how long he will need to stay at military training. I think that there should be no trouble, and I see no reason that you three cannot still go to America. Antonio can join you once he has finished his training if he still wants to go to America."

That night, the Cudoni family discussed the new situation now that Antonio had gone to do his military training. Filippo told his parents that the brothers still needed to go to America to raise the money to buy land. There was no way of making money in Calabria or Italy without joining the Mafia, and they had no wish for that. The brothers left Antonio's gear and money behind for him for when he completed his military stint.

Filippo told his parents about Rosina Folino Gallo and said that her brother Pietro was going with them to America. His parents knew the Folino Gallo parents well and thought well of them.

Francesco told his son that Rosina should make a good wife when he returned to her.

His mother agreed and said that she thought they were good people and that any daughter of theirs would make a great daughter-in-law. Filippo was quick to point out that were no promises, only that Rosina had said she would wait for him to return.

The next morning, Filippo made a quick trip to Falerna to say goodbye to the Folino Gallo family and Rosina in particular. She was glad to see him and went up the road to meet him when she saw him coming. He gave her a quick kiss on the lips when they met.

They went back to the house where Rosa was preparing lunch for the men, who would soon be coming in from the vineyard.

Filippo told them he was preparing to leave and wanted to make sure he saw the whole family before he left. It was not long before Antonio and Paulo came in, and soon all were sitting down to a fine lunch.

Rosa said she was unsure whether she was fit enough to walk all the way to Sambiase on Sunday morning to see Pietro off and thought that maybe she would not see him again until he returned from America in several years' time.

After they finished, Filippo told them he needed to go.

Filippo took his leave, wishing the family all the best until he could see them again. Rosina walked outside and a small way up the road with him. She held his hand as they walked along.

"I wondered if you would come to say goodbye to the family before you left. And to me," she added a little shyly.

"I could never leave without saying goodbye to my bella ragazza," Filippo teased her. "I needed one more *bacio* before I could leave you."

Rosina stopped and gave him one more kiss. There was a lot more passion in this one. Rosina seemed to have grown more confident in her womanhood in the last few weeks.

Filippo left and went to Falerna to say goodbye to Natale and his wife, who were not coming to Sambiase. The rest said they would see him in Sambiase.

The train was due to leave about ten thirty in the morning, but they were hoping to get to the station about nine or earlier. Filippo told them they could meet in the piazza, which was close to the station. He wanted the Folino Gallo family to meet his parents, sister, and brothers again before they left.

He set off for Sambiase, and soon he was approaching the spot where he and Gennaro had found the Bartocchi brothers robbing the mayor and his wife some years earlier. It was a place where the road, surrounded by trees, crossed a small stream.

He remembered the sweet kiss Gina had given him for saving her grandparents from a beating and possible death.

He was smiling to himself as he stepped onto the small narrow bridge over the stream when a man jumped from behind a large stone near the bridge and confronted him. The now older man was Mario Cirillo, the man he had fought with years ago. It was obvious the man recognized him and was not about to wish him a good day. Filippo stopped just a few paces on the little footbridge and looked straight at the man before him. Cirillo did the same, a small laugh coming from his mouth. "Well well well, it's the same bastard Americano who did not want to share his woman with us at the procession, eh, Cudoni? And you ran like a sick dog afterwards," he added.

Filippo sneered back at him and then laughed. "You want the same hiding I gave you then by the look of it."

"I'll kill you before you do that," a voice behind Filippo answered. "You may have given my balls a pain for a month, but yours will be permanent."

Filippo recognized the voice as that of Pugliese, the third member of the Mafia group with whom he had the fight over Maria—the man he had kicked in the balls at the time.

Slowly, Filippo turned around to look at the man behind him. It was Pugliese, and he did not look any better than he had five years earlier. The man held a small handgun in his left hand, and the gun was aimed straight at Filippo's chest. Pugliese was about four meters away.

"Did Maria tell you we went to see her one day after you left for army training?" Cirillo jeered at him.

Filippo did not answer. His mind was whirling inside his head.

What the hell is he talking about? I wonder what they did to her.

Cirillo laughed loudly as he sneered. "Yea, we went to see her— me and Puggy. Guess what, Cudoni? She was home all alone, and we gave her a real great time." He laughed again. "Boy, was she glad to see us. Me, anyway."

Filippo looked at Cirillo. Maria might not have been his girl anymore, but she had been at the time, and he was getting the sickening feeling these two animals had had their way with her. *That was why she seemed so bitter towards me when I first saw her on my return from military training. This mongrel dog had his way with her, and in her guilt, she blamed me*, he thought quickly.

"You fucking mad animals. What did you do to her?" Cudoni screeched as his mind raced back. He was now livid with rage. That was why Maria had a child so soon after he left for his military training—her little girl was this animal's offspring.

That was why the Valencis had pushed her to marry the nutty baker.

Cirillo sneered back at him. "Not Puggy—he was still unable to do anything with the ladies, but boy, did she give it to me, especially after you had knocked her back at the fountain. I had to encourage her a little at the start, but once she warmed up, she really went for it. Ah, Puggy. All he could do was watch after what you did to him, and boy, I gave it all to her. I went back to see her many more times after that, and then she had to go and get pregnant—the stupid bitch— and then marry that dumb-arse baker."

Cirillo sneered and laughed again. "I don't think Pasqualle can give it to her like I can, so I go and see her occasionally."

Filippo could only imagine what sort of encouragement Cirillo would have offered her. He had probably offered to shoot her father while holding a gun to her head—who knew—but it did explain why she had suddenly married Pasqualle.

"So? So what? Do you want a medal for using a gun on her, you poor, miserable sick bastard?" Filippo angrily asked. He knew the way people in that area reacted to a girl getting pregnant. Family pride was much more important than any feeling the girl might express, and as soon as she told her parents, they would force her to marry the first man who asked for her hand, regardless of the fact she was raped in the first place, and she had been.

"Just wanted you to know what happened and how much me and Maria loved doing it. She just could not wait to spread her legs for me. Now you know, we can blow your miserable brains out," Cirillo taunted Filippo. "But first I've got a small score to settle— like breaking your neck." He was wearing a twisted grin from ear to ear, and Filippo could see that this man, who was part of the Mafia in Calabria, would have no hesitation in killing him.

Pugliese butted in. "You can break whatever you like, but I'm going to finish him off dead as a stone wall."

Filippo realized that while these two thought it was a huge taunting joke to tell him what they would do to him in retribution, they would actually do it, and death was that end. They were involved with the Mafia, and it was more than likely they had already killed more than once.

While Cirillo had informed Filippo of his assault and then rape of Maria, Pugliese had asked him not to raise his hands, and Filippo had crossed his arms in front of his chest. Pugliese was the man to worry about because he had the gun in his hand. There was no doubt Cirillo would also be carrying one, but if so, it was still in his pocket. After the encounters that Filippo had been through both in Italy and in the USA, he too now carried a gun. He fired through his jacket at Pugliese, hitting him high in the shoulder and knocking him over the side of the road and onto the small slope leading to the stream. Just as he fired, Cirillo hit him in the ribs with his shoulder, sending both down onto the floor of the bridge. Cirillo heard the gun go off as he launched himself at Filippo, and he thought it was Pugliese shooting. "Hold off, Puggy. I told you I want to break his neck first!" he screamed as they hit the road.

The blow knocked the wind out of Filippo Cudoni as he hit the ground, and he hit his head on the road as Cirillo landed on top of him. Cirillo was the first to get to his feet, and he kicked Filippo in the ribs for good measure. Filippo rolled over to avoid more kicks and rolled over the side of the bridge into the small stream, clutching at his bruised ribs. Cirillo pulled a small Colt revolver out of a pocket and jumped into the stream to finish Filippo off.

Frantically, Filippo tried to get to his feet, ignoring the pain in his ribs. He tried to roll under the bridge, but he was too late. Cirillo was standing fewer than four paces away, his gun in his hand, ready to shoot.

"I told you I would get you, you miserable, ugly bastard, and you're going to die," Cirillo growled harshly through his teeth.

Filippo knew his time on earth was probably up, but he had a burning rage to kill these two if he could. He stared with pain-filled eyes at Cirillo for a split second and then dived to his left. A shot rang out followed by another as Filippo tried to roll away, but it was Cirillo who tumbled head first into the water.

"I told you it would be me who would shoot that miserable Cudoni, not you!" the voice of Pugliese screamed from near the stream bed.

Filippo had come to his feet as he watched Cirillo hit the water and then watched as Pugliese desperately tried to reload his revolver to shoot Filippo. Filippo pulled his gun out and, before Pugliese could reload his pistol, shot him through the head.

Filippo checked to see if either man was still alive. Cirillo was probably still alive, but Pugliese was dead. Both had their guns in their hands, and he thought that anyone coming onto the scene would assume they had shot each other. Filippo Cudoni decided to leave both men where they were and not say anything to anybody. He climbed back onto the road after making sure no one was around and then set off for his parents' place.

Filippo did not follow the advice his grandfather had given him. The advice, which was based on Pietro Antonio's life experience, was simple: a dead enemy was no danger, but a live one could turn out to be fatal.

The fact that he had possibly left Cirillo alive was very much on his mind as he walked, but he had been unable to shoot Cirillo while he lay in the water on the verge of dying. A few hundred meters down the road, he stopped and was about to turn back, thinking he should heed the advice of his grandfather, when he saw someone on a donkey coming towards the little bridge. He knew it was too late and now better to keep going.

He returned before lunch to his parents' place. There was still so much to do, and there were so many people to say goodbye to. He called in to see his grandparents on his father's side on the way home. After lunch, the three brothers went to see their uncle Pasqualle and aunt Fiorina. Three of their boys were already in America, and they had three more boys and three girls at home.

They chatted for a while, but they still had their uncle Bruno and aunt Maria to see before they went home. None of their children—three boys and four girls, who were all adults—had gone to America. The two youngest boys were considering going to America, their uncle informed them, but could not make up their minds about when to go. On Wednesday, they had been to see their uncles and aunts on their mother's side.

On Saturday afternoon, some of the neighbors and more relations and friends called in to say goodbye to Filippo and his two brothers. This time, more people were aware that the brothers were leaving, and subsequently, more people came to see them off.

Sunday morning came quickly, and the family was up early. A number of chores required doing before they could leave. The three brothers did a final check to make sure nothing was overlooked, the younger brothers fed the few sheep and goats, and their father checked and fed the bullock. The family sat down for breakfast at seven. It was unusually quiet around the table for a short while, and then suddenly everyone wanted to talk. Rosaria had plenty of advice to give her boys about housework.

Francesco realized that with Antonio at military training, he would have five of his sons away from home. Rosaria was thinking the same thing as she handed out the breakfast. The three youngest were doing most of the talking. Even Giovanni and Peppino, who were normally talkative, were silent.

With breakfast and the cleaning done, the three brothers set off earlier than the rest of the family to say goodbye to their grandparents.

When the rest of the family arrived at their grandparents' home, they all set off for the railway station.

They arrived at the little station in Sambiase early in the morning. A few people were about on this Sunday morning, but the people Filippo wanted to see had not yet arrived. The Folino Gallo family arrived some ten minutes later. All had come except Natalina.

Filippo presented the Folino Gallo family to his family and then all the Cudoni family to the Folino Gallo family. The parents, who had seen a lot of each other when Zio Nicola and Zia Theresa were in Italy, had not seen each other for some ten years or more.

Filippo asked if anyone cared for a cup of coffee at the coffee shop close by, which had just opened. The parents decided to sit, rest, and talk. Filippo, Rosina, his brothers Peppino and Giovanni, Natale, Pietro, and Carmela went for a cup of coffee while the younger ones went for a walk along the piazza.

As they enjoyed their cups of coffee, Natale and Filippo told them stories of America. Natale recounted how, at one stage, he had been being attacked by the Mafia in Pittsburgh and had managed to steal a horse and ride out of town, only to be attacked by marauding Indians. After shooting about a dozen, he said, he had managed to slip back to town, where he had shot a few more Mafia thugs before they ran away.

Rosina was aghast at what her older brother had just said. "Surely you did not kill all those people, did you, Natale?" she asked disbelievingly.

"No, Rosina. Luigi was with me, and he killed half of them," Natale replied calmly. "Did you think I killed them all on my own?"

"But...but surely you would not be so barbaric," Rosina said.

Filippo thought it was time to stop. "Rosina, your brother likes to make jokes. Sometimes he exaggerates a little. There have been no Indian problems for some fifteen years now, and he keeps well away from the Mafia. Would you like to come for a short walk with me please?" Filippo asked.

Rosina pretended to hit Natale in the head as he laughed. "Just joking, little sister. We did not see too many Indians at all," Natale told her.

Filippo paid for the drinks and helped Rosina up, and they left the others to finish their drinks while they took a short roundabout walk to the piazza.

"Rosina, I dream of you all the time," Filippo told her. Then he asked, "Do you think of me a little when you dream at night?"

Rosina blushed before she spoke. "I do think of you sometimes," she answered shyly.

"I mean, do you think of me when you are dreaming at night?" Filippo asked again with his arms held wide and high.

"I don't dream, but I do think a little of you sometimes," Rosina answered slowly and modestly, but there was a definite brightness in her eyes, which indicated to Filippo that romantic thoughts were on her mind.

"Then I shall go away for a while a happy man, but I shall return as a man in love with you. Please wait for me, Rosina," he implored. "I will wait for you, Filippo. I promise you, I will wait for you to return to Italy and to me," she said.

He had waited all week to hear this beautiful woman say these loving words to him. He gathered her in his arms and hugged her. Then he kissed her on the lips with her parents watching. Her shy-ness disappeared with her knowledge that she would not see him for a long time to come, if ever at all.

Filippo Cudoni realized he now had a tall, beautiful, dark-haired young woman here in Italy who was falling in love with him and was prepared to wait several years for his return from America. He knew he needed to return to America for financial reasons, but he also knew a part of him—a large part—still wanted to see the tall dark-haired young woman who adored him in America, Angelina.

He knew Rosina would make the best wife and mother to his children—not that Angelina would not, but she was now married, and that was now over.

The little train chugged into the station, and the whistle tooted as the train ground to a screeching halt. A few passengers disembarked from the passenger cabin. The stopover was a twenty-minute one during which the steamer's water tank was replenished and the coal room restocked.

Four young men—Filippo returning to the New World, his brothers Peppino and Giovanni, along with Pietro Folino Gallo, set-ting off for the first time—were about to leave for a strange country in a faraway land. The excitement of leaving was somewhat tampered with the knowledge that they would not see loved ones for some years.

They all said goodbye to their loved ones and slowly boarded the train. Filippo was the last to board. He hugged Rosina tightly to him. He now knew that he had come to love this soft-spoken but lovely young woman.

The four stayed on the train's step as it left and waved goodbye for the last time. Filippo stood there until the station was no longer visible, and then he joined the others inside the cabin. It was October 5, 1902.

Chapter 37

They arrived in Naples early the next morning. They had little sleep and were stiff and sore all over.

"Nothing has changed much," Filippo told them.

The train ride was just as bad as the first time he had left three years ago, and even before, when he had gone to army training. That day, they arranged to depart on a ship leaving in two days' time from Naples.

Filippo closely inspected the ship from the wharf. He knew he had not seen this ship before. To make matters worse, it did not look like much from the wharf. However, their decision was to either take this one or wait for the next one, leaving in about a week's time. They decided to leave on the current one rather than wait for the next one, which could be in worse shape or delayed.

They searched for and found a boarding house that would give them a room for two nights.

Filippo warned his brothers and Pietro not to go anywhere alone, particularly around the wharf and fountain area. The pickpockets and thieves in the area were among the best anywhere. Beggars, he told them, were the eyes of the common thieves who preyed on the unsuspecting traveler.

The four young men spent the next two days sightseeing around Naples. However, they kept a close eye on the movements of the *Alexandria*, the boat on which they were departing. Plenty a passenger ship had left without having its paid passengers on board. Filippo had heard stories in America about ships deliberately overbooking and then solving the problem by leaving people behind.

They were vigilant, but the ship nearly left them behind. That morning, when they contacted the captain of the ship, he told them they could not board until one o'clock in the afternoon and said they should come back after lunch. They agreed and left. Filippo could see that the sailors were still loading supplies and figured it could be a few hours before they would be ready. They walked away, but Filippo did not like the shifty look in the captain's eye. They walked out of the wharf area carrying their suitcases. Filippo told the others of his suspicions and sneaked back into a local coffee shop from which they kept a close eye on the small ship.

He noticed at 11:00 a.m. that no more stores were being loaded on board. In fact, one of the sailors was preparing to undo the mooring ropes. They raced the 150 meters to the wharf and tried to get aboard just as a huge sailor was about to pull up the gangplank. The burly Roman sailor tried to stop them, but Filippo stood on the plank.

"Fuck off. We are still preparing the ship, and it will not be ready until one. So get your shit off the plank and come back then," he snapped gruffly at Filippo.

"That's all right, *amico*. We will just wait on board," Filippo told him casually without stepping off the plank. "No need to worry. We won't get in the way."

"You too stupid to understand? I said come back at one. Now off before I throw you overboard," the surly sailor repeated in a thick Roman accent. No one had dared to cross him before, and he was not about to let some shithead country bumpkin do so.

Filippo moved a step closer and looked the sailor squarely in the eye. His blue-green eyes had turned cold and angry. "*Marenaro*, I and my friends are coming on board now. We have paid our fares, and we are boarding this boat. If you believe you have been on this world long enough and you do not need your balls to think with, then try to stop us. Otherwise, just move a little to one side—now," Filippo told him coldly.

Filippo's right hand was inside the pocket of his jacket as he spoke. Slowly, he pulled out a .38-caliber Smith & Wesson revolver and pointed it at the sailor's pelvis. The huge sailor took a closer look at Filippo and the gun pointed at his pelvis. Pietro was playing with a nasty-looking knife. The sailor looked at Filippo and then at Pietro. The other two brothers were leaning casually against a wharf post. Giovanni was scratching the inside of his jacket. The sailor turned red with anger, but he got the message that it might be better not to push these four too far at the moment. He knew there would certainly be bloodshed if he did, and it would most certainly be his.

If these four imbeciles think they have just won the war, they will be in one hellhole of shit before the trip is over, he mused.

He moved slowly aside and let them pass past him, just as the captain and another sailor appeared on deck.

"I told you not to let anyone through, you fuckin' dumb ox!" the captain roared at the sailor.

"It wasn't his fault, Capitano," Filippo told him. He had the gun out of the captain's sight. "We told him we did not want to be left behind. And he thought it wise to listen. We are not after any trouble, sir, but we do not want to be left behind either. If we are on board, all will be well, sir. Would you be so kind as to show us our rooms?"

"You four fuckin' arseholes just turn around and get off my damn ship until I damn well tell you when you can get on board, if at all," the infuriated captain bellowed at Filippo and his friends. The captain turned and motioned to a group of sailors who were now watching. "Throw these ignorant imbeciles off the boat."

The four brothers were all on board now, and Filippo was not far from the captain. He stepped towards the captain, showing him the .38-caliber Smith & Wesson revolver, and then held it towards the captain's chest. "Great things, these American shooters. They hold six bullets, and they shoot the six before you can move a step." Cudoni gave the captain a cold stare. "Remember, my friend, we paid our way and don't want any trouble." He emphasized the *we* as he spoke, and his hand indicated the four of them. Pietro was also holding a revolver in his hand.

The captain's face had turned a nasty blue. No one had ever told him who could or could not come aboard, and he was determined not to appear a fool of in front of his men. "You think you can shoot all of us, you dumb idiot?" he snarled.

Filippo Cudoni grimaced as he shook his head. "I don't need to. Just you and your two stupid men here. I bet the other sailors will be happy to see you go."

A number of other people and some sailors had started to gather around. The other sailors had grouped together but stayed where they were as Filippo spoke. It was obvious they would do as the captain ordered, but they did not appear to be in a hurry to help the captain now. The captain realized that if he was not careful, he could be—or rather would be—the one being shot.

"Get back to work, you lazy layabouts!" the captain shouted to his sailors. "I will talk to you four later, my dear friends," he snarled through clenched teeth, pointing to Filippo and the other three men. "Tonetto, show these men to cabin 26 and get back to bloody work."

Filippo knew that he had made two enemies. The first was the burly sailor, who would have no hesitation in throwing him over-board once out at sea if the opportunity arose, and the second was the captain. He was more concerned about the captain; he knew that the captain would be a ruthless killer if the opportunity arose.

It was only an hour before the ship left, but there was no doubt some people had been told to board even later. Some ten more people came aboard before it left. Room 26 had four bunks and one tiny table in it. There was barely enough room to fit the suitcases and bags that they carried. The room was located above the steam engines and alongside the chimney stack.

The captain had certainly done them no favors. In fact, they knew the little room would be a hellhole in normal weather and absolutely impossible to live in in hot weather.

Filippo had made sure they carried some water and extra food— such as dried bread, cheese, and cured salami—in their bags. He had learned from Batiste Raso on the first voyage that it paid to carry some supplies. Filippo warned his brothers and Pietro to be on full alert during the trip. He stressed to them that they should never wan-der around the ship alone. They should stay at least in pairs.

The trip to Marseilles took five days. A heavy downpour of rain and hail on the third night broke the heat and monotonous sound of the engine room in their small cabin. During the day, the four men made sure they stayed together but still kept an eye on their lug-gage. After one outing on the third day, when they returned to their cabin, they were sure someone had been in their room. The four had taken most of their belongings with them, so the intruders had found nothing. They knew the break-in served as a warning to be careful. The captain would get even.

The small ship anchored in Marseilles for two days. Filippo, Pietro, Giovanni, and Peppino all went ashore the first day. They knew that the ship would not leave before the next day.

Filippo took them to see the Milano family, and they had dinner there that evening. Filippo introduced his brothers and Pietro to the Milano family. His brothers could see why Antonio had fallen in love with Marcella, who asked why Antonio was not with them. Filippo told her what had happened to Antonio and said it would be at least another twelve months before he would be returning to America.

Filippo purchased some flagons of fine red French wine and two large containers of fresh water to carry aboard with them.

They slept on board that night. The next day, they stayed close to the *Alexandria*. The crew of the ship spent most of the day unloading and loading new cargo and supplies. It seemed to Filippo that most of the crew was of Sicilian origin, along with some of Napolitano origin, and they appeared nervous and shifty as they loaded some of the cargo.

That night, the brothers again slept on board, not trusting the captain to sneak off during the night. The ship left the next day, and Filippo was sure that two people he had seen on board during the trip from Naples were not on board when it left.

It was another three days to the Strait of Gibraltar. This ship was a bit faster than the *Fiore* had been on Filippo's first trip to America, but it would still take about eighteen days from Gibraltar to New York. The ship sailed a more southerly course than the one Filippo and his brothers had sailed on the first time, and it avoided the colder autumn weather farther north.

It was during the middle of the first night in the open ocean that huge trouble found one of the four men. It was a fairly calm and warm night for this time of year, and one of the men needed to answer a call of nature. Rather than wake any of the others, he decided to relieve himself over the side of the ship. His door was only two paces from the side of the ship.

He cautiously peered out of the door to make sure no one was nearby. He stepped to the side of the ship, and after doing what he had come to do, he silently stepped back towards the cabin. He was reaching for the door handle when a smooth, wet hessian rope dropped over his head and onto his shoulders.

Instantly, the rope tightened around Filippo Cudoni's neck, and someone above yanked him upwards. He felt the rope draw tight around his neck, then the rope was pulled higher; his feet came off the deck's floor as he tried to yell for help but could only muster a strangled yelp as the rope got even tighter around his neck.

Filippo Cudoni knew instantly he would need to cut the rope around his neck in the next second, or he would quickly choke to death as it was now too late to call for help. He grabbed the rope in his left hand to take some of the weight from his neck while his right hand reached for the knife he had stuck in the top of his trousers. As he pulled the knife out of his trousers, the person or persons stringing him from above gave a mighty jerk on the rope. The knife in Filippo Cudoni's hand clattered to the deck floor as he grabbed the rope from around his neck in both hands and tried to take his body weight from around his neck.

The noose got tighter as he struggled desperately to free himself. He realized he was fighting a losing battle unless he was able to remove the noose around his neck. He tried to reach above the slip knot with one hand but one hand was not enough to support his weight.

The American dream flashed through his mind. He thought of Rosina, but all that, was now becoming a violent, deadly, and hazy illusion as he struggled to remove the rope around his neck. Despite his struggles the noose around his neck tightened even more.

As the noose got tighter his feet dangled violently in the crisp air. His face started turning red as the air stopped reaching his lungs. "Die, you Americano piece of shit" were the last words Cudoni deciphered as he tried desperately to yell for help. He heard the strangled gargle in his voice and knew the end was near

www.ingramcontent.com/pod-product-compliance
Lightning Source LLC
LaVergne TN
LVHW021651060526
838200LV00050B/2297